Tom Wood is a full-time writer born in Burton-on-Trent who now lives in London. After a stint as freelance editor and film-maker, he completed his first novel, *The Hunter*, which was an instant bestseller and introduced readers to a genuine antihero, Victor, an assassin with a purely logical view on life and whose morals are deeply questionable. Like Victor, Tom is passionate about physical sport, being both a huge boxing fan and practising Krav Maga martial arts, which has seen him sustain a number of injuries. He has not, however, ever killed anyone.

He is also the author of the psychological thriller *A Knock at the Door*, writing as T. W. Ellis.

UNLUCKY
FOR SOME

TOM WOOD

SPHERE

SPHERE

First published in Great Britain in 2025 by Sphere

1 3 5 7 9 10 8 6 4 2

Copyright © Tom Hinshelwood 2025

The moral right of the author has been asserted.

*All characters and events in this publication, other than those
clearly in the public domain, are fictitious and any resemblance
to real persons, living or dead, is purely coincidental.*

A CIP catalogue record for this book
is available from the British Library.

Hardback ISBN 978-1-4087-2344-9
Trade paperback ISBN 978-1-4087-2345-6

Typeset in Sabon by M Rules
Printed and bound in Great Britain by Clays Ltd, Elcograf S.p.A.

Papers used by Sphere are from well-managed forests
and other responsible sources.

MIX
Paper | Supporting
responsible forestry
FSC® C104740

Sphere
An imprint of
Little, Brown Book Group
Carmelite House
50 Victoria Embankment
London EC4Y 0DZ

The authorised representative
in the EEA is
Hachette Ireland
8 Castlecourt Centre
Dublin 15, D15 XTP3, Ireland
(email: info@hbgi.ie)

An Hachette UK Company
www.hachette.co.uk

www.littlebrown.co.uk

For Bodo

ONE

Few of Victor's contracts were ever easy to fulfil – no surprise given the size of his fee – and yet some were next to impossible. Gustavus Håkansson was the twenty-five-year-old heir to Malmö's largest organised crime family. He lived with his father in the family home, a fortified mansion hidden behind high walls in the city's wealthiest district. Advanced motion detectors, thermal imaging cameras and digitised locks on reinforced doors made the property almost impregnable even without the armed guards patrolling all hours of the day and night.

Victor's client had assured him each member of the security team had been handpicked by the patriarch, Jorund Håkansson, for both their impeccable military service records and their unwavering loyalty. Although not an army, there were twenty-four personnel in total in the organisation's employ. Accounting for twelve-hour shifts, four days on and four days off, six were awake and operational at any time. When they were not guarding the family home, they were accompanying Jorund Håkansson and his only child wherever they went.

And when they did venture out from behind those walls, they did so in a state-of-the-art armoured limousine.

So used to planning the execution of his contracts with a surgeon's precision, Victor knew this particular job's success would come down to improvisation. He would need to exploit an unpredictable gap in the family's defences should one arise.

Or engineer one himself, of course.

Malmö unfolded around Victor as another piece of the puzzle he had to solve. The city had the charm of old Europe with a sheen of modernity that gave it a facelift of youthfulness. Pedestrian walkways wound through cobblestone squares, cafés spilled out onto pavements, and the air carried the mingling scents of fresh bread, sea salt and diesel fumes. Everything seemed pleasant on the surface.

Victor had no interest in the pleasantries. Cities were organisms, alive and breathing, their arteries filled with patterns of movement and sound, rhythms that only revealed themselves to those who knew how to watch. This was what he understood best: how cities worked, how they lived, and how to move through them without leaving a trace.

He crossed Gustav Adolfs Torg, his eyes scanning the old cemetery ahead while his mind catalogued details. Families gathered around food carts, couples strolled hand in hand, and cyclists moved in predictable streams along designated paths. It was a weekday, early afternoon. The city was awake but not fully alive. It would change as evening settled in, shedding its calm veneer for something faster, more chaotic.

Victor walked at a measured pace – not too fast, not too slow. Blending in required balance. Too much purpose suggested he had to be somewhere. Too little encouraged attention.

He changed direction, crossed a square and turned down a narrower street towards Hansa, the upscale shopping mall where the crowds were thicker and the sound of footsteps and conversations echoed from the polished marble floors. The bright displays of designer shops and electronics retailers framed the mall's main concourse. Victor stopped at a kiosk, purchasing two cheap phones and prepaid SIM cards. Burners. Disposable and untraceable if discarded before they became a problem.

He doubled back to help identify shadows before he headed to Malmö City Library, blending into the quiet hum of tourists, students and office workers taking their lunch breaks in the modern, glass-walled space. The library's open atrium and high ceilings made it impossible for anyone to linger unnoticed. Too many sightlines, too many angles – a place where someone watching him would have to remain exposed.

He walked past the self-checkout stations, heading for a row of public-use computers along the eastern windows. He took a seat near the far end, setting down the shopping bag containing the burner phones. He unboxed one, peeled off the sticker covering the screen, and powered it on. A cheap, disposable Android, running the bare minimum of apps. He was convinced certain manufacturers designed stripped-down handsets to cater for criminals. Although the primary market for such devices had to be dealers selling drugs as opposed to professional killers.

He inserted the SIM card, connected to the library's public Wi-Fi, and logged in to a secured messaging platform – an obscure encrypted service routed through layers of an-onymized traffic.

His client was already online.

The username was 'Eriksson21' – one of many aliases for his anonymous client.

Victor typed the first message.

I've arrived. I'm beginning preparations.

Eriksson21: *Understood. Do you have a timeframe?*

The job will take a while, Victor typed. *The mansion is not viable and there are no other options right now.*

What about when he leaves?

The coastal road would work as a strike point but the limousine is a tank. It would need an RPG, thousands of rounds of armour-piercing ammunition. You hired me, not a whole team. I need to know where he's going to be before he's en route.

I can't give you a schedule but I have two possible oppor-tunities for you.

One opportunity could be good enough but two were much better.

Go on.

The target will be attending the opening of an art gallery. His father will not be present. He's sick and will be receiving medical treatment at the hospital that day.

Victor asked, *Their security detail?*

Will be split between them.

Victor leaned back. This was good.

Jorund Håkansson was the primary reason the heir was so well guarded. With him absent, security would still be tight, but their structure would be weaker. They were used to operating as a team of six, not three.

When is the gallery opening?

Eriksson21: *A week's time.*

The time limit was an issue, but a minor one. Already in Malmö, already deciphering the city, he could make it work.

Gallery details?

Eriksson21: *Small, private exhibition in Stora Nygatan. Limited guest list.*

Victor pictured the area. Stora Nygatan – the old town. Narrow streets, some the armoured limousine would not be able to navigate. But limited chances of a decent sniping line.

What kind of guest list?

Eriksson21: *Investors. Snobs. No direct ties to his father's organisation. This is purely the target's endeavour. A passion project.*

Intel on security procedures?

Eriksson21: *Venue will be swept before the heir arrives. There will be a metal detector at the entrance.*

Not ideal.

Surveillance?

Eriksson21: *None. The gallery will have CCTV eventually when it's open to the public but it won't be in place at the ceremony.*

Victor sat in silence for a moment, watching the cursor blink. He ran through the variables.

Time limit? Unavoidable. Father's absence? Advantageous. Security? Manageable. Exit strategy? Still undefined. The main drawback was the public setting that meant witnesses.

Tell me about the second opportunity.

Eriksson21: *The target and his father will be attending mass this coming Sunday at St Petri's church.*

Victor thought. Even less time to prepare, and travelling together meant the full security detail, but St Petri's was a huge building with plenty of open space around. That might mean a chance of a long-range kill. Fewer risks. No witnesses.

Eriksson21: *Will either of these work for you?*
We shall see.

Victor logged out, removed the SIM card, snapped it in half, and left the burner phone behind in a rubbish bin while he strolled through the cold Malmö afternoon.

In a coffee shop, he sat with a black Americano and unboxed the second of the phones. The scent of freshly ground coffee mingled with the hum of conversations. He inserted the SIM and powered up the device, thumbed in the number his broker had provided, and waited as the line connected.

'What can I do you for?' A male voice answered with the rough cadence of a Scottish accent – Aberdeen, maybe.

'I believe you have a care package for me.'

'That depends on who you are.'

'You may call me Roman,' Victor said. 'Who might you be?'

'You talk like you were born in another time and place altogether.'

'I assure you; I wish I had been.'

The man said, 'I'm Scragg.'

'A pleasure to make your acquaintance,' Victor said. 'How do we do this?'

'I'll text you the address closer to the time.'

'What time?' Victor asked.

'Midnight.'

'How evocative.'

Scragg said, 'It's the time that works for me. Take it or leave it.'

'I'll take it,' Victor replied. 'Did Lambert tell you about me?'

'Not a thing,' Scragg said. 'None of my business.'

'Then please know I'm a nice guy,' Victor told him. 'I'm polite, I'm punctual. I'll treat you with nothing but respect.'

'Is this an exchange or are you asking me on a date?'

'I'll jump through whatever hoops you need me to for you to feel safe about this.'

'If you want the care package, you follow my rules,' Scragg said.

'Exactly,' Victor agreed. 'I have to do what you say.'

'I'm not sure what you're trying to tell me.'

'I'm a nice guy,' Victor told him again. 'But it's a choice to be one. Don't put me in a position where I no longer have that choice.'

A pause. Then Scragg said, 'I'll see you at midnight, Mr Nice Guy. And, just for your benefit, I'll make doubly sure to be on my best behaviour, don't worry.'

'I never worry,' Victor replied. 'Because rest assured I am always on my best behaviour.'

TWO

The address provided by Scragg led Victor to a weather-beaten apartment complex in a rougher district of the city. As he passed it by, cold wind found its way beneath his collar, sliding down his spine. The sky above was starless. Streetlights cast pale halos across damp asphalt. Traffic signals cycled through green, amber and red, their reflections shimmering in the wet gutters. Passing cars added to the fractured nightscape, some headlights harsh and white, others tinged yellow.

As the traffic thinned, a relative peace settled over the streets. Some cities enlivened after dark; others slumbered. Malmö hovered somewhere in between, as though it resisted sleep long past the hour it should have closed its eyes.

In a nearby doorway, a young man leaned against the frame, taking slow drags from a cigarette. Inside the kebab shop behind him, two Middle Eastern men in aprons and hats slumped on the counter, eyes glazed with boredom. The hum of fluorescent lights mixed with the sizzle of frying oil.

Further along, an unseen voice caught Victor's attention before he turned the corner. The measured cadence suggested neither drunken rambling nor conversation with another person. When Victor rounded the bend, he found a man walking, dictating into his phone with the deliberate clarity one might use with a child. The man's footsteps echoed as he passed into the distance.

Approaching a major intersection, the flow of traffic and pedestrians increased. To Victor's left stood a modern building with commercial spaces on the ground floor and apartments above. Neon signs in Japanese script marked a sushi bar still serving patrons spilling from nearby bars. The air carried the sound of laughter and clinking glasses. A worker emerged from a side alley, pushing a trolley stacked with flattened cardboard boxes. His expression suggested a man for whom hope had long since become a stranger.

Victor looped back towards the address. The white door mentioned in Scragg's subsequent message stood at the rear of the apartment building, beside a ramp leading down to a sealed underground garage. A freestanding metal fence, covered in grime and graffiti, blocked vehicle access to the garage, rust streaking its vertical bars. The ground beneath Victor's feet was cracked asphalt, worn thin from years of neglect.

Fifteen minutes before midnight, Victor knocked four times on the white door.

The sound echoed with a metallic rattle – a security door.

When no one answered, he knocked again.

After a second minute of waiting, he tested the handle and found the door unlocked.

So much for security.

Inside, a narrow corridor extended ahead, lit dimly by flickering fluorescent strips. Dampness clung to the air. Pipes ran along the walls and ceiling, their surfaces stained and chipped. Water dripped somewhere in the distance.

Music echoed from deeper within the building.

Victor moved towards the sound.

As the music swelled into a chaotic assault of drums, guitars and screamed lyrics, Victor picked up other sounds beneath the cacophony – cheers, shouts and the rhythmic stomping of feet.

At the end of the hallway, a heavy drape hung from the ceiling, acting as a makeshift door. Victor pulled it aside with his left hand, revealing a cavernous space that had once been a part of the underground garage. Now, the area pulsed with the raw energy of a crowd gathered around a makeshift fighting ring outlined by a low stack of tyres.

Concert speakers on metal stands blasted music loud enough to rattle Victor's ribs. The vocals were less singing than guttural screams, the lyrics lost to distortion and echo. Flickering halogen lights overhead provided intermittent illumination, with several portable spotlights aimed at the centre of the ring, where two men traded blows with brutal efficiency.

A bouncer stood just beyond the draped doorway, his focus on the fight rather than his post. Victor had stepped several paces inside before the man even noticed him. When he did, he barked something in Swedish that was lost to the noise and thick accent, and Victor couldn't read his lips in the uneven light.

'I'm here to see Scragg,' Victor shouted above the din.

The bouncer scowled, his response unintelligible. His

body language, however, needed no translation. He wanted the stranger out.

Victor repeated himself, slower this time, exaggerating each word while the vocalist shrieked about consequence and bad decisions – advice the bouncer seemed ready to follow as he stepped forward to eject Victor by force.

Big guy. Wide and strong.

Amateur stance.

The shove came fast but clumsy, a stiff right palm aimed at Victor's chest.

Stepping into it, Victor intercepted the wrist in a pincer grip – index finger over the knuckles, thumb pressed against the bone beneath – and twisted clockwise. The bouncer's elbow locked straight, forcing his entire body to bend with it to relieve the pressure. His knees buckled as he struggled to stay upright.

Victor resisted the urge to break the arm. Instead, he wrenched the bouncer closer and his face into a heel-palm strike that connected with the bridge of his nose. The cartilage crunched beneath the impact, blood gushing from the nostrils.

The bouncer dropped with a grunt, half-conscious and gasping.

The music's sheer volume ensured no one else heard the altercation.

Victor threaded through the crowd, his gaze sweeping the space as he searched for Scragg. He had no physical description – only the knowledge that the man had been in the military alongside Victor's broker, Marcus Lambert. A former paratrooper now fixer capable of sourcing black-market firearms wouldn't be young. Likely in his forties or fifties.

That narrowed the possibilities, ruling out the majority of the spectators.

None of the onlookers had their phones out – either a rule of the venue or enforced through less-than-polite methods.

The fight itself was raw and unrefined – neither boxing nor mixed martial arts, but a no-frills brawl. Both men were stripped to the waist, one in faded jeans, the other in black jogging bottoms. Neither wore gloves, and their swollen knuckles bore the evidence of repeated impact. Occasionally, one would throw a clumsy kick or knee strike, though the concrete floor discouraged grappling or takedowns. A bad fall could shatter bones as easily as fists broke faces.

One fighter was younger, pale and Swedish, with a lean but undertrained physique. His movements were quick but imprecise. The older man – maybe fifty, slower but more ex-perienced – had the advantage of timing and endurance. His salt-and-pepper facial hair and shoulder-length dark hair clung to his face in sweat-slicked strands. Pakistani, Victor decided. The harsh spotlights distorted fine details, but Victor guessed late forties. His left arm bore an aged tattoo: the winged emblem of the British Parachute Regiment.

Scragg.

The man's gaze flicked towards Victor, easy enough to pick out since he was the only spectator not cheering, not dressed in denim or sportswear, and not drinking from a can of beer or energy drink.

Blocking a rapid series of punches, Scragg twisted his head to shout above the crowd, '*You're early.*'

Then, seizing the moment, he stepped inside his opponent's guard and drove a left hook into the younger man's chin.

UNLUCKY FOR SOME

A spray of sweat and blood glistened in the glare of the spotlights as Scragg's punch sent his opponent spiralling down for the count to the thunderous roar of the crowd.

THREE

While two different men from the crowd stripped to the waist and kicked off their shoes, the unconscious fighter was revived with the help of a bucket of cold water. Scragg led Victor towards a distant corner of the parking garage, away from the ring and spectators. Here, a rough cluster of mismatched furniture surrounded an electric heater, an old three-seater sofa, armchairs with torn upholstery and a couple of folding deck chairs. A scratched dining table stood nearby, cluttered with bottles of water, energy drinks, beers and a large canvas shoulder bag.

Scragg grabbed a dirty towel from the back of a chair and wiped sweat from his torso, arms and face. He pushed back his damp hair with both hands, revealing a high forehead and a pronounced widow's peak. A cut on his left brow glistened with petroleum jelly.

Twisting open a bottle of beer, he drank half in one go, then lowered it with a long, growling belch.

'You want one?' he asked, holding the bottle towards Victor.

He shook his head. 'I'm good.'

'You look like you can fight,' the Scotsman said, rubbing the dark red blotch on his ribs from repeated body shots. 'Do you?'

'Not if I can help it.'

'But you can, though, right?'

'Why do you say that?'

'A fighter knows another fighter,' Scragg replied. 'How much do you weigh?'

'Eighty-five kilos by this time of day.'

Scragg frowned. 'How much is that in proper weight?'

'One hundred and eighty-seven pounds.'

'I said proper weight, not Yankee digits. Stones, lad.'

'Just stones? Or should I measure it in pebbles too?'

Scragg chuckled. 'Funny man.'

'I'd be a light heavyweight in the ring or a middleweight in an octagon.'

'Aye, that's more like it.' Scragg gestured to the canvas bag. 'Here's your care package. As promised.'

'Everything in there?'

'See for yourself.'

He unzipped the canvas bag and stepped aside, giving Victor room to inspect the contents. Victor noticed Scragg's eyes tracking him, assessing. Not surprising. It wasn't just curiosity – it was instinct, ingrained from too many situations where misjudging a man could get you killed.

'You're not like Lambert's usual lads,' Scragg observed.

'I'd be surprised if I were. You're no typical Norseman either.'

Scragg laughed, his expression one of mock offence. 'What

are you talking about? I'm one of those famous Kashmiri Scottish Vikings. You weren't taught about us in school?'

'I must have cut class that day.'

'Where are you from?'

Victor ignored the question, checking the items inside the bag: a magnetic card cloner, burner phones, motion-activated cameras, and two handguns with suppressors, empty magazines and a box of nine-millimetre ammunition.

'Couldn't get that fecking Fabric Nation thingy,' Scragg said.

'Fabriqué Nationale Five-seveN.'

'Aye, that one. Like rocking-horse shite on the black market. You've got a pair of Taurus G2Cs instead. Best I could do. Suppressors. Bullets for days.'

'I'd prefer if you didn't swear,' Victor said.

Scragg grinned. 'Aren't we precious? Whatever you want, Princess. Still didn't say where you're from, I notice.'

'Nothing gets by you.'

The rifle Scragg had acquired was, as requested, a Sako TRG 22 A1. Its sleek, modular chassis was finished in matte black, designed for both urban operations and long-range precision. Weighing just over five kilograms unloaded, it balanced comfortably in his hands – light enough for rapid deployment yet heavy enough to absorb recoil and maintain accuracy. The rifle's overall length once assembled was just under 1.2 metres with the suppressor attached, striking a perfect midpoint between manoeuvrability and ballistic performance.

'Better,' Victor said.

Scragg smirked in a self-congratulatory way. He liked to impress. 'What are you planning to do with all that gear?'

Victor zipped up the large canvas bag and looked Scragg

in the eye. 'Did our mutual acquaintance fail to mention that I'm a very private person?'

'Aye, he told me in no uncertain terms to keep my trap shut and ask you sod all.'

Victor gave Scragg a questioning look.

'But he forgot that A, I'm a nosy bastard, and B, if someone tells me not to do something then I'm sure as shite going to do it.'

'Language,' Victor said again.

Scragg chuckled and offered a shrug of apology before draining the rest of his beer. 'We done?'

'We're done.'

A hand was held out to Victor, who looked down at it.

Scragg waited a moment and let his hand fall back to his side. 'Friendly, aren't you? Still, I could use a man like you.'

'You don't even know what kind of a man I am.'

'Oh, I can take a guess, Princess.'

'I'm already working and I don't moonlight.'

'You don't know what I'm offering yet. I know this city like I know my family jewels. You're an outsider here. Whatever your job is – or should I say *whoever* your job is – I guarantee I can help make your life a whole lot easier.'

Victor thought for a moment. If he decided to fulfil the contract at the art gallery, a public setting, that meant witnesses. Which meant he would benefit from a fast exfiltration from Malmö before the police could get a sketch of his face drawn or before the Håkansson organisation could retaliate. With a limited timeframe in which to prepare, he could only do so much on his own.

He asked, 'Can you acquire a new identity for me within five days?'

'Please, I could do it by the morning if I really tried.'

'What if I wanted to leave the city without anyone seeing me leave?'

'Have you seen the size of the port here? I work with the woman who runs it. I can get you on a cargo ship as a stowaway with no border checks, no questions, and no one will be any the wiser until you're halfway to Belize.'

'In which case, what do you need me for?'

FOUR

The air inside the cold storage warehouse bit at Victor's skin and seeped through his clothes. There was no escaping it. Condensation dripped from steel beams that criss-crossed the ceiling, faint plinks echoing in the cavernous space. Rows of frost-rimed shelves loomed in the shadows, their skeletal frames casting jagged lines of black against the pale light from overhead fluorescents.

'Why is it still kept at this temperature when it's no longer being used?'

Beyond the immediate clearing where they stood, the warehouse had many narrow aisles lined with metal racks slick with ice, stacked with frost-covered crates long forgotten or abandoned. The cold made sound carry in odd ways – footsteps seemed to echo from multiple directions, and the murmur of refrigeration units vibrated through the steel walls. The air smelled metallic, mixed with a lingering sharpness of chemicals once used to preserve perishable goods.

Scragg answered, 'Because it's a front for storing contraband. And it would look odd to the authorities if it was listed as still in operation but the power bill was zero.'

'It's yours?'

'Oh, aye, Princess. I have a huge cold-storage facility in my portfolio just knocking around doing nothing, waiting until I have a deal to make. Give over.'

The floor beneath their feet was a patchwork of concrete and gridded drainage panels, slick with moisture and scattered patches of frost that crunched with each step. Pools of melted ice gathered near the drains, reflecting the pale overhead lights in distorted, shimmering patches. A few crates had been left in haphazard piles against the walls – some splintered and broken, others intact but coated in a thin layer of frost. Rows of shrink-wrapping machines stood dormant at the ends of conveyor belts. The rumble of pipes expanding and contracting in the cold added a low, irregular bass note to the stillness, as if the warehouse itself was breathing beneath its steel skin.

'Then who owns it?' Victor asked.

'What's with the interrogation?'

Nearby, and talking among themselves, were three Danes Scragg had brought along. All big guys and yet not all of their heft was efficient. Still, they looked as though they could handle themselves better than the bouncer. Not professionals by any stretch of the imagination. The biggest had silver hair and a face so tanned that at a distance Victor might have mistaken him for a Sicilian. They didn't seem to have any hierarchy, although he did most of the talking. The other two were younger: a blond with a sharply defined face that was a stark contrast to the third man whose nose had been broken so many times it was almost flat against his cheeks.

Despite the break in protocol, Victor kept his hands deep in his coat pockets. When the time came, he would take them out, which was better than having his fingers ready, yet frozen, at all times.

His gaze swept across the entrances and exits, weighing distances and cover points. 'If you're such good friends with this Järnberg guy, why am I here?'

'Because even good friends aren't stupid enough to stand around with a bag full of cash in the middle of the night without backup.' Scragg grinned, teeth white against the blue tinge of his dark lips. 'That's my world, like it or not.'

'Then what are your friends for?' Victor asked, referring to the three Danes.

'Pure numbers,' Scragg replied. 'I'm a one-man band and we've had a spot of bother in this fair city with criminals too lazy to do their deals taking to robbing us more hard-working entrepreneurs. The Danes are scary enough to put off any such thieves who might think I'm an easy target. But that's the extent of their usefulness. Hence why I wanted you by my side for this. The Danes look the part but they're not players like you and me, Princess.'

'I think it's time we retire that nickname.'

Scragg grinned.

The rumble of an engine echoed through the space, dulled by the walls and the constant noise of the refrigeration system, and yet unmistakably a large, diesel-powered vehicle. Victor pictured a van or truck parked outside the rolling doors. The engine died, followed by the sound of multiple doors opening and closing. Victor shifted his stance, resetting his shoulders as his focus sharpened. He removed his hands from his pockets as he watched the shadows near the entrance until one of the roller doors buzzed into life and eight figures stood in silhouette against the night.

When the door had lifted, one man stepped in first, a clear stride ahead of the others.

Broad-shouldered and barrel-chested, he had a mess of curly hair and a dense, ruddy beard. His leather jacket strained against his bulk, especially that of a monstrous belly.

'That's Järnberg,' Scragg said. 'He's sensitive about his weight so try not to draw attention to it.'

Behind him, the other seven moved into the half-light – one wiry and long-limbed with a pale, drawn face, his hoodie loose over jeans where the outline of a concealed pistol disrupted the fabric's natural fall. Another man, thick around the waist, with a permanent sneer, carried himself with the heavy-footed gait of someone used to breaking down doors. He held a steel container the size of a toolbox in his left fist. The third, tall and lean with hunched shoulders, adjusted his thigh-length jacket in a way that told Victor he carried a submachine gun or similar-sized weapon. The fourth one followed a little behind the others. Young. Twitchy. The fifth, Somalian, stood out as the only non-white Swede. The sixth and seventh looked like a couple: a man and a woman, both with facial tattoos and piercings, walking side by side.

'Scragg,' Järnberg said, spreading his arms in a gesture of welcome. His voice carried, echoing in the cold air. 'A pleasure to see you looking so well.'

'Likewise.' Scragg stepped forward, clasping hands with the man in a firm shake. Then, gaze dropping to Järnberg's belly, he added, 'You're looking good . . . trim. I take it you're still robbing blind those who can't count fast enough?'

Järnberg laughed, a deep sound that rolled through the warehouse. 'And, naturally, you haven't stopped trying to talk your way out of paying full price?'

'What's with the platoon?' Scragg asked, gaze passing over the crew of seven behind Järnberg. 'Don't tell me you think I'm going to try anything funny?'

'You? Not at all. But you know about the gang robbing people like you and me?'

'Aye, I do. Hence my own backup.'

'Well, I've already lost one shipment to them. I'm not risking losing another.'

Victor watched as they exchanged a few more pleasantries, but his attention stayed on Järnberg's entourage. Their eyes flicked towards the duffel bag at Scragg's feet and back to Victor. The twitchy one's fingers tapped against his thigh in an unconscious rhythm. The thickset man, the one with the metal case, let his gaze linger on Scragg's bag longer than the others. He licked his lips in what might've been anticipation or trepidation. The couple and the wiry one moved to either flank, and Victor adjusted his position so he could see all seven at the same time. The tall, lean man sneered Victor's way, unimpressed with whatever he saw in him. He detected no evidence of stress hormones affecting them – young, twitchy one aside – so there was no pre-planned course of action suggesting violence was coming.

Still, Scragg hadn't brought Victor along for his good looks and charm.

The Danes were stiffer, and if Victor hadn't already had Scragg's description of them to go with his own assessment, he might have thought they were going to be a problem. But it was just nerves. As Scragg had said: they looked the part but that was it.

'Let's get to it, then,' Järnberg said, stepping back. 'I can already feel my big, beautiful balls trying to retract up into my pelvis.'

'Wouldn't want that.' Scragg crouched, unzipped the duffel, and lifted a heavy metal case onto a nearby crate. With a click, he opened it, revealing neatly stacked banknotes.

Järnberg gestured, and the thickset guy stepped forward. He placed the steel case on the crate beside Scragg's duffel and unlatched it. Inside, sealed plastic vials held a dense, dark powder.

'One kilo of the finest osmium powder you'll find outside a government lab,' Järnberg said.

Scragg had explained to Victor that osmium was one of the rarest and heaviest elements on Earth. Harder than steel, with a melting point high enough to shrug off all but the most intense heat, it strengthened alloys for aerospace, coated surgical implants and gave electrical contacts their longevity.

As such it was more valuable than gold.

Which made a whole kilogram of osmium well worth killing over.

FIVE

Järnberg said, 'Tell me, since when has a man like you been interested in rare-earth metals?'

'"A man like me"?' Scragg asked. 'Sounds suspiciously close to an insult. Although, since the osmium is not actually for me I can't pretend to be offended. This powder is for the fair lady Leila Farahani.'

'You've moved up in the world,' Järnberg said with something like respect.

'Aye, that's the plan. I want to start making deals in a suit and tie, not with the snot freezing in my nostrils.' He picked up a vial, rolling it between thumb and forefinger. 'Feels right. As heavy as the only lass not dancing at a disco.'

'Do I need to count the money?' Järnberg asked.

'If you want to be here all night and turn those beautiful baby-makers of yours into snowballs, be my guest.'

Järnberg chuckled and reached for the duffel bag. 'Always good to do business.'

'Hold your horses,' Scragg said before Järnberg could scoop up the bag. 'I need to test it first.'

Inside a side pocket of the duffel bag was a small black case that Scragg unzipped. As he did, Victor noted the way Järnberg's crew shifted their weight, shoulders tightening, eyes darting between Scragg and Järnberg. Only the tall, lean man kept his gaze on Victor.

Järnberg sighed. 'You're wasting your time and it's too cold to spend even another minute in here.'

'Won't take a sec,' Scragg said.

He opened up the case kit with deliberate care and laid it flat on the crate. Inside, neatly arranged glass vials and precision tools gleamed beneath the overhead lights. His gloved hands moved with practised ease as he selected a small silver spatula and a heat-resistant glass dish. The cold air made the glass fog as he placed it on the crate. He unscrewed one of the osmium vials and tapped a tiny amount of powder into the dish, the dense granules falling with a faint, granular hiss.

He leaned backwards as he did to create as much distance between himself and the osmium. It could oxidise into osmium tetroxide, a toxic compound as harmful to the lungs as chlorine gas.

Victor watched the gang's subtle reactions – tightened jaws, fingers flexing at their sides – as Scragg selected a second vial from his testing kit, this one filled with a clear reagent fluid. The viscous fluid swirled inside the glass. Scragg uncapped it, holding the dropper above the powder, his hand steady despite the cold.

The first drop fell, landing with a faint sizzle as the powder absorbed it. A thin wisp of vapour snaked upwards, its faint, acrid tang cutting through the air. Scragg added a second drop, then a third, eyes narrowing as he leaned closer.

Scragg's brow furrowed, but he kept his expression neutral as he set down the dropper and reached for a glass stirring rod. With slow, deliberate movements, he stirred the mixture.

Then he set down the rod and straightened, exhaling a breath that ghosted white in the air.

'We have a wee problem.'

Järnberg's smile hadn't dropped, but the humour behind it faded. 'What's wrong?'

Scragg stared at the dish. 'Oh, nothing's wrong at all except for the fact that this isn't osmium.'

'Impossible,' Järnberg said.

'Quite literally possible. That powder in there should be shimmering like an oil slick by now with so much reagent and me stirring it. Instead, it's as dark as the ring around my bathtub.'

'Your test is wrong,' Järnberg said. 'Maybe your reagent's bad. The cold might've ruined it.'

'These compounds are stable to minus twenty. Don't try that line on me, lad. I'll have you know I got a B– in Chemistry.'

Frosted air curled from Järnberg's mouth. His beard was flecked with white.

Scragg said, 'That powder in there is tungsten, guaranteed. Heavy and looks the part to the uninformed.'

'That's only your opinion,' Järnberg said. 'I brought you the goods you asked for at a fair price. As far as I'm concerned, the deal is done.' He sighed. 'I would not have gone to the trouble of securing this powder if I had known you were going to try such theatrics to force down the already fair price.'

The air thickened with tension. Victor's eyes flicked between the gang members – the squaring of shoulders, the shuffling of feet. The lack of blinking.

The Danes were showing even more signs of unease because even with Victor alongside them it was still almost two-to-one.

'I don't want it even for free,' Scragg said, incredulous, almost laughing. Then, his tone became serious again. 'Please tell me you didn't know it was counterfeit.'

Järnberg said nothing.

Scragg said, 'What do you think would happen to me if I took fake osmium to Leila Farahani? She'd turn me inside out, that's what.'

Järnberg's lips stayed closed.

In the silence, Victor saw the subtle shift of elbows, and the tell-tale tightening of fingers near concealed weapons.

Victor moved before they did.

His pistol cleared his coat, the suppressed barrel aimed dead centre on Järnberg as his crew were reacting in jagged bursts of motion as they went for their own weapons.

The wiry man's fingers had closed around the grip of his pistol, half-drawn before Victor's move froze him mid-action. The thickset guy had already started to clear leather, the muzzle of his handgun just breaching the edge of his jacket. The tall, lean man clutched the handle of a slinged SMG, the stock emerging from under his long coat.

'Don't,' Victor told them all.

One word, flat and final.

The young, twitchy one, the Somalian, and the couple had either not been quick enough or had failed to read the signs because their hands were nowhere near their weapons. Likewise, the Danes were lagging behind proceedings – assuming they were even armed.

The gazes of Järnberg's crew were all locked on Victor, their breath fogging in the cold air as muscles tensed beneath coats and sweat pricked at brows despite the chill. His aim was unwavering, his expression emotionless as he weighed the fate of every person in the room with the pressure he was holding steady on the trigger.

Nobody moved. Nobody blinked.

Scragg was staring at Järnberg. 'I think we're all about three seconds away from making a very bad decision,' he said. 'Let's not.'

The thickset man shifted his weight from foot to foot, eyes flicking between Järnberg and Victor. His breath fogged in faster clouds than the others.

Järnberg's eyes never left Victor's but he was speaking to Scragg. 'Tell your man to put his gun away.'

'Does he really look like he would listen to little old me? I'm not his mammy.'

'If he shoots me,' Järnberg continued, 'my people will kill you all.'

The tall, lean man, one hand on the grip of the SMG, used his free hand to draw a finger across his throat as he stared Victor's way.

Victor raised an eyebrow.

Although his focus was on Järnberg's crew, he could see in his peripheral vision that the Danes were panicking. They weren't players, Scragg had stressed.

Järnberg saw it too.

Still eyeing Scragg but speaking in Danish, he told them,

'You don't need to be here for this. If you go now, no one is going to stop you.'

'We barely know him,' the silver-haired Dane said to Järnberg, but the justification was to himself, Victor knew.

'Then don't die for him.'

They exchanged glances with one another and hurried away, circling as far from Järnberg and his crew as possible.

'*Cowards*,' Scragg called after them.

Järnberg said, 'Now instruct your man to put his weapon away.'

'That's not happening,' Victor told him.

The thickset man's fingers flexed hard on the grip of his half-drawn pistol, a faint tremor running through his hand as stress hormones made his heart rate soar and impeded his fine motor skills.

Järnberg, calm with a gun pointing at him, was growing frustrated. 'It doesn't have to be like this.'

'Then walk away,' Scragg suggested. 'You take your powder and I take my money and we put all this down to an unfortunate misunderstanding. Which is a polite way of saying I know you tried to rip me off but I'm willing to overlook it to avoid a bloodbath.'

'Last chance.'

'For who? For you? My guy will turn your head into a canoe if you so much as clear your throat too loudly. Take a look at him, will you? He's got stone-cold psycho killer stamped all over his face. There's nothing he wants more than to watch your blood turn to red ice.'

Järnberg gritted his teeth, his jaw muscles flexing. He knew his hand was weak because he would be the first to die if he tried to play it.

'Do the smart thing and walk away so no one shoots anyone,' Scragg told him. 'Easy peasy.'

It should have been easy, as Scragg said, but sweat was tracing down the temple of the thickset guy. His gaze was fixed on Victor's gun with wide, unblinking eyes. The man could hear every word spoken between Scragg and Järnberg and yet he was no longer listening. The expression on the man's face was the kind of terror that was incapable of comprehending reason. It was pure instinct. No thought. No logic. Life and death distilled down to a binary choice. One Victor knew was accelerating at speed towards an inevitable conclusion.

Kill or be killed.

The thickset guy's fingers twitched.

Victor shot him.

SIX

The shot – muffled by the suppressor but sharp and echoing through the large space – punched through the forehead of the thickset man. His gun clattered to the concrete as he staggered forward and pitched over, gasping for a breath of air that never reached his lungs.

Seven enemies including Järnberg, two with hands already on weapons.

Far too many and far too spread out to shoot them all before bullets came back his way, so Victor dived behind a nearby stack of frost-covered pallets, scrambling to harder and harder cover of shelving units and crates as planks splintered and shards of wood went flying.

He returned fire, darting out of cover, catching glimpses of the gang scattering – the tall one with the SMG breaking left behind one of the vertical H-shaped steel support beams rising to the ceiling; the twitchy young guy darting between shelves; Scragg crashing into Järnberg before the man could draw his gun, the force of their collision sending both sprawling onto the slick floor.

Muzzle flashes bloomed in the dim light as the SMG fired blindly towards Victor's cover, forcing him to duck back.

Sparks flew as bullets struck shelves and support beams, and ricocheted at sharp, unpredictable angles.

Victor saw the wiry man crouched low behind a stretch of conveyor-belt apparatus, his pistol clutched tight, aiming with quick, jerky movements that betrayed adrenalin more than skill.

A near miss sent him flailing into cover.

Victor leaned out from behind some crates, letting off rounds in quick double-taps at whomever he could see before leaning back to avoid the inevitable return fire. He saw the Somalian dashing between shelving and support beams – moving too fast to risk a shot. One shot clipped the twitchy guy's shoulder, spinning him sideways with a cry before he vanished behind a crate of his own.

They were no coordinated force, otherwise they would already have flanked Victor, but their lack of professionalism had sent them scattering in fear in different directions and rewarded them with a significant advantage in positioning.

However, they preferred to remain stationary, reluctant to abandon cover once they were behind it.

Victor never stayed still, sliding between crates and darting between support beams to avoid being pinned down and to deny firing lines. The fewer enemies targeting him at once, the better he could pick his shots. The tall man was the biggest threat with the SMG, but he was also lean enough to hide his whole person behind the H-beam he refused to leave.

Reloading, Victor realised the Somalian had appeared to his right, having circled around to flank him. A smart move, but the man kept moving as he squeezed the trigger, the resulting bullets hitting anything except their intended target.

Victor had no window in which to return fire because the tall, lean guy with the SMG had edged out of cover enough to spray rounds Victor's way.

Bullets shattered overhead lighting, raining down sparks as the shooter let off a long burst of automatic fire that he could not control.

Glass shards pattered the concrete as Victor ran to another position – shooting blind in the Somalian's direction to discourage pursuit – and sliding behind the shrink-wrapping station at the end of a conveyor belt.

The air thickened with smoke and the acrid bite of gunpowder by the time the SMG was empty.

Victor, having waited for the inevitable lull, snapped out of cover to send a bullet that grazed the arm of the tall man before he could hide himself behind the steel beam again. He yelled in pain and for the others to get closer to protect him.

None of them did as requested.

Victor swivelled his head back and forth, aware the two with the facial tattoos and piercings had yet to show themselves. In a perfect world they would have fled like the Danes but nothing about the current situation was perfect from Victor's point of view. He imagined them keeping low, acting with consideration and stealth unlike the others, waiting for the best opportunity to strike when Victor's back was turned.

He tracked the rhythm of gunfire, noting the staccato bursts and the pauses as each man reloaded with the clatter of spent magazines hitting concrete or the faint metallic click of new ones slamming into place.

He shifted behind another stack of pallets, shoes skimming across the slick floor with his measured speed. A burst of gunfire ripped through the air where he'd just been, bullets shattering wood. Victor dropped low, ducking behind steel drums as splinters lodged in his coat.

He waited – one breath, two – then darted out from the side of the drums. A shot clacked from his pistol, precise and swift, punching through the shoulder of the tall man behind the support beam. The first graze had only hurt him but this one counted.

Victor sprinted behind a rusting forklift truck, using its frost-slick solidity as an impenetrable shield. Bullets clanged and sparked against its steel shell as the gang fired as one. Timing again – he counted their rounds, how long it took each to reload, waiting for his moment. Another burst tore into the floor beside him, concrete fragmenting and water splashing onto him but he didn't break cover. He waited, ready.

His seeming passivity made them more confident, braver.

The wiry guy shifted position at last, leaving the conveyor belt as he gained the confidence to try approaching Victor's right side. He leaned out from behind the forklift truck just enough to bait him, a flash of movement that drew gunfire. The next time, Victor leaned out the same way again, inviting another volley of shots that pinged off the engine truck. On the third move, when the man anticipated the same angle, Victor ducked out from the opposite side.

His shot echoed, loud and final, catching the wiry

guy clean in the face, dropping him straight down to the floor.

To a professional like Victor, the sight of a sudden, gruesome death garnered no reaction, but amateurs had a habit of freezing in shock and horror, maybe even grief.

Victor exploited that, shooting the twitchy young guy whose mouth hung open as he stared wide-eyed at his wiry associate on the floor.

The impacts staggered the young guy sideways, his weapon clattering across the wet floor before he clutched his neck in a futile attempt to dam the arterial spray as he sank beside a stack of splintered crates.

Victor's focus returned to the Somalian, who had learned from his previous reckless charge that haste and accuracy did not mix. He was now taking cover behind a stack of crates, his pistol aimed towards the end of the forklift Victor had last fired from, not realising that Victor could see him as he peered through the gap separating the load backrest from the mast that lifted the forks.

The gap was too narrow to take a shot through, however, so Victor waited for the rhythm of the man's breathing to break – for the clouds of exhaled vapour to change their rhythm – for the tell that would give Victor the edge.

When the clouds formed faster as the waiting became too much to bear and told Victor the Somalian's skyrocketing heart rate meant his aim would be awful, Victor hopped straight up and fired three times through the empty space of the truck's cab.

Blood bloomed across the Somalian's coat before he collided with a shelving unit, knocking metal containers clattering as his handgun remained tight in his grip. He snapped it up to return fire, not understanding the futility of doing so until Victor shot him twice more to ensure he reconsidered the situation.

With his magazine empty, Victor loaded in a fresh one.

Which was the exact moment the two with tattoos and piercings had been waiting for to launch their attack.

SEVEN

A pincer movement.

Flanking at the same time – and yet not on the same axis so no danger to one another – the man appeared to Victor's two o'clock and the woman from his six. They were slick and coordinated, but amateurs. If they had been professionals, he would be dead.

Instead, they had waited too long to catch Victor off-guard. Now, he had only three enemies to pay attention to, not seven.

As such, he glimpsed the tattooed man first – seeing him emerge from the concealment of shelves stacked with boxes – and dropped low behind the forklift truck to finish slamming in the fresh magazine before the man could open fire.

Ducking, Victor swivelled to check his flanks and saw the tattooed woman making her move, emerging from behind the same shrink-wrap station he had hidden behind moments beforehand. She was smart to have been following his path. She had some talent.

He opened fire as she did.

Between them were several rows of metal shelving units. Some with boxes and crates, most empty. Still, enough irregularity of cover to deny any clear lines of fire.

She had been trying to sneak closer, and so it surprised her to find him looking straight at her; as a result her first shots had little accuracy. Some clanged into the forklift. Others sailed through the open space of the cab.

His were better, but she was a moving target, and closer to the shelves – they gave her more cover than they gave him in return.

He saw holes plug into plastic boxes and spark off the metal frames of the shelving units.

One might have clipped her on the side of the head but he couldn't hang around to find out. He knew the tattooed man would be moving fast to take advantage of this moment.

Victor dropped to the cold, wet concrete, cutting off the woman's line of fire, and rolled out from behind the forklift truck.

The tattooed man was caught out in the open, mid-dash, expecting to circle the rusting vehicle and execute Victor while he was facing the other way. It almost worked too. As he rolled out and saw the enemy's approach, they had less than two metres separating them.

Victor's gun was low to the ground so he shot out the tattooed man's shins first, then his knees, the space between impacts growing as Victor's aim accelerated upwards – more to the thighs, then liver, chest, and face, only ceasing firing when the spinal column was hit and no nerve signals could reach the pistol-holding hand to shoot back at point-blank range.

Mag empty once more, Victor jumped to his feet and sprinted as the tattooed woman let out a keening wail.

A couple then, as he had suspected.

Automatic fire came his way from the tall man, having abandoned the H-beam in favour of a cluster of barrels on which he could rest his SMG to compensate for his wounded shoulder.

Victor slid behind the same conveyor belt the wiry guy had been so unwilling to leave earlier in the exchange. The man lay spreadeagled on the floor, his blood expanding in a wide pool as the wet concrete thinned and spread it further.

Victor had no further magazines for the Taurus – Scragg had only been able to supply three – so he glanced around for the wiry guy's pistol. It wasn't next to the corpse. Victor hadn't seen it fall but it could not have landed far away. He pictured it on the floor, having slid beneath a pallet or shelving unit nearby.

No time to search for it.

Two remaining – assuming Järnberg was still wrestling with Scragg. In all the commotion, Victor had lost sight of that struggle and could not hear them either with all the other noise.

'*I'm going to murder you,*' the tattooed woman screamed.

Via his incredible powers of deduction, Victor had already figured out this had always been her intent and so he felt it was a redundant statement. Still, seeing as he had no firearm with which to murder her first, she had a decent chance of predicting the future.

A quick scan of the immediate area told him that no one else had died nearby. The closest gun was the SMG used by the tall, lean guy who was still alive, if wounded.

Instinctual behaviour was hard to change. Unlearning was always more difficult than learning, in Victor's experience. The tall, lean guy had stayed behind the H-beam as though he was magnetised to it, only switching position when the bullet in his shoulder meant he could no longer aim and shoot the SMG with any kind of effectiveness. Now he was behind a number of barrels he could rest that weapon upon and therefore overcome his injury, he wouldn't leave it until he was forced out.

Both enemies would have seen where Victor had darted to, but only she would be closing the distance. She would not follow his path this time and risk him looking her way. She was smart enough to play the long game, to circle all the way around the periphery of the space, unseen and unheard, to come at him from the other side, knowing the tall guy's SMG was pinning Victor in place. If he rose past the protection of the conveyor belt, a hail of rounds would come his way.

Together, they made a perfect team – one trapping him in place, the other preparing to strike from behind. A superb tactic, but given they weren't communicating, an accidental one. Still, the end result was the same.

Victor's gaze flicked over the nearby terrain – the slick concrete, the forklift truck, and the silent conveyor belts that ran through the centre of the room like arteries through a body. The conveyors themselves offered limited cover, but the machines attached to them – the rollers, metal housings, packaging units, the rolls of plastic sheeting – created pockets of blind spots along with the shelving units alongside them. That was his only advantage.

The tall man's SMG fired a short burst, shredding the air

over where Victor had been crouching. The shots sparked off metal, punching holes through plastic-wrapped boxes.

Not panic fire, but close. The tension, the silence, was too much for an amateur to bear. Doing something, even if that something achieved nothing, was better than the creeping feeling of dread that resulted from inaction. Fight or flight was always the more favourable option than the midpoint between the two: paralysis.

Victor stayed low, crawling alongside the conveyor belt's metal frame. An adjacent line of stacked barrels provided concealment enough for him to rise a little without the tall guy seeing him.

Victor's gaze locked onto a pallet partially wrapped in plastic film. Gripping a loose tail of plastic, he pulled it taut and wove it across the path between one of the steel legs holding up the conveyor belt and the adjacent shelving units. A low snare – simple, quick and effective. Nowhere near invisible and yet it might just be missed by someone so focused on revenge.

He then rolled low beneath the conveyor belt, sliding through the narrow gap where the rollers fed plastic wrap onto pallets. Cold metal grazed his shoulders as he pressed through the confined space.

He waited.

He heard her first, as expected. However light her footsteps, his breathing was quieter. She moved well, a balanced gait. Once more, he recognised her talent.

He saw her as she made her play. Expecting to find him pinned down and vulnerable behind the conveyor belt, she exploded into the narrow corridor of space, either knowing the inarguable fact that action was always faster than reaction or just acting on instinct. She was too good to be wasted in an outfit like Järnberg's when she had what it took to be a professional.

Victor felt bad that he had to end such a promising career before it had even begun.

Almost felt bad, at least.

EIGHT

The downside to her explosive speed was she had no chance to see the snare of plastic wrap waiting in her path.

The tattooed woman caught it hard with her lead shin, the sudden reduction in speed sending her flying forwards in a chaotic flailing of limbs that tossed her pistol sailing away into the distance.

Victor rolled out from underneath the conveyor belt behind her.

He rose to a half-crouch as she was recovering her balance – unaware of his location and his impending attack – showing an athleticism and gracefulness that was as rare as her other talents.

Her sudden acceleration from slow and quiet tactician to floundering without warning had deadly consequences.

The tall, lean guy, desperate for an end to the perpetual agony of inaction, opened fire as soon as a shape on the far side of the conveyor belt entered his view.

For a second, she danced on the spot to the rhythm of the bullets' impacts.

As she pirouetted and fell – her head swivelling in Victor's direction – her eyes found his long enough to witness his nod of respect before she crashed to the floor, gasping and crying for the few seconds of life she had left.

Her gun having clattered to the floor far away, Victor tore off a stretch of plastic wrap.

Now he no longer had to protect his flank, Victor moved low and fast, weaving out from the conveyor belts and between metal shelving units and crates, circling wide as the tattooed woman had done moments before.

Back behind the forklift truck, he saw the lean tall guy had remained in place, his SMG braced on the barrel still, his aim and focus locked on the conveyor belt Victor had left behind. Although now the tall man's head was rotating back and forth as his eyes searched the space with increasing desperation.

Wrapping the strip of plastic around both fists, Victor twisted and tightened it to a thin cord of about thirty centimetres between his hands. He circled around the gunman and closed the distance.

The tall, lean guy shifted, sensing something – far too late.

Victor surged forward, looping the taut strip of plastic around the man's throat and pulling tight. The SMG went off, spraying rounds at the walls, then the ceiling, as Victor wrenched the man closer as he dragged him down to the floor, pinning the tall guy's head against his chest to intensify the pressure and convert the wire of plastic wrap from noose to garotte.

Victor hooked his ankles between the tall man's knees to lock him in place.

The SMG clicked empty and clattered on the concrete as Victor's hands became slick.

With one arm already wounded, the tall man had only a single hand free with which to fight back, but instead of attacking, those fingers tried fruitlessly to dig out the wire of plastic already buried in flesh.

The man jerked and writhed, pinned in place, his heels kicking out and scraping against the wet floor.

Pulling hard – first with one hand and then the other – over and over again, in rapid succession, Victor sawed deeper through the thin layers of skin and fat, muscle and, finally, arteries.

Either side of the oesophagus, the carotids ruptured as one, the sudden release of pressure painting Victor's vision red and transforming the tall, lean guy's thrashing into one, final juddering spasm.

NINE

Pinching and swiping the blood from his eyes, Victor approached the only other sounds that were not his breathing or his footsteps.

Unhindered by the gunfight going on around them, Scragg and Järnberg were wrestling on the floor. Both men had red faces, laboured breathing, and had rolled around so much that there was not a stitch of clothing or strand of hair not dampened by the wet concrete.

Järnberg was by far the bigger and younger man, and no slouch in hand-to-hand combat, but Scragg had the superior skills.

That they had been fighting the entire time was a testament to the evenness of the duel.

As Victor scavenged spare nine-millimetre rounds from the guns of his dead enemies and fed them into an empty Taurus magazine, he wondered what the outcome was going to be – whether the stronger but heavier man would tire quicker and give Scragg the edge he needed to finish the matter, or if the Kashmiri Scottish Viking's age would steal his stamina first and doom him despite his skills.

With a grunt of effort, Scragg rolled onto his back with Järnberg on top of him but on his back too, fighting off Scragg's attempts to choke him out with a combination of sheer size and strength, and the stinging punches and elbows he hammered into Scragg's ribs.

However tired Järnberg had become, the thuds of impact told Victor the man had lost none of his power.

Scragg's face contorted more and more with the pain of every strike. He had made a mistake going for the choke because Järnberg's weight was now compressing his ribs and preventing Scragg from getting the air he needed.

However even the struggle had been until now, it was only going to end one way, Victor saw as he finished loading his gun and stopped nearby.

'*Feel free to just bloody stand there watching,*' Scragg growled at him. 'Don't be such a shite, help me the hell out.'

'Only if you promise to stop swearing and blaspheming.'

Scragg yelled, '*Swear to fecking Christ.*'

Victor put a bullet into Järnberg's heart.

The big man stiffened and then shuddered as Scragg let out a cry of panic. '*You've bloody shot me.*'

'I shot at an angle,' Victor explained. 'No way the bullet would go diagonal through a man that dense and out the other side.'

As Järnberg wheezed his last breath, Scragg wriggled out from beneath him and Victor offered a hand to pull Scragg to his feet. Who took a few steps as his gaze then swept the scene – the many bodies, the spent casings glinting on the concrete, the blood spatters, and the faint wisps of smoke rising from bullet-riddled crates.

His gaze locked onto Victor.

'*What were you thinking?*' Scragg barked, stepping forward, fists clenched at his sides. 'I was talking them down. Järnberg was listening. It was almost over and you go and—'

'That's a strange way to thank me for saving your life,' Victor replied, calm as he tucked the pistol away beneath his coat.

Scragg's shoulders tensed. 'Did I tell you to kill everyone? Did I? Because I don't remember discussing that plan beforehand. I was handling it. What's wrong with you?'

'You brought me along for a reason,' Victor said. 'And I did the job you asked of me.'

Scragg held his stare for a long moment, breath misting between them in angry bursts.

'You're alive and they're not,' Victor said. 'So why are you so upset?'

Scragg fumbled in his coat pocket for cigarettes and a lighter, fingers stiff from the cold and adrenalin. His shoulders were tight, movements jerky with the post-battle spike still coursing through his veins. Victor recognised the signs – the jittery tension that came after the violence, the body clinging to the fight even when the danger had passed. Scragg's hand trembled as he set a cigarette between his lips and lit it.

'This has really screwed me over. I'm in trouble now.'

'With Leila Farahani?'

'I gave assurances,' Scragg muttered as he exhaled smoke.

'Who is she?'

'One of the top players in the city. She doesn't get her

hands dirty – that's where you and I come in – but she's partnered up with a man who painted these fair streets red in his day before he turned *civilised*, Jorund Håkansson.'

'The name rings a bell,' Victor admitted but said nothing further. Then, wondering if he had partaken in a job on behalf of the father of his target, he asked, 'Was the osmium ultimately for him?'

'I got the impression from Farahani that it was destined to go overseas, so no.' Scragg grunted. 'Not that any of that matters now. I always knew Järnberg was a shite but not that much of a shite.'

'Language,' Victor reminded him.

Scragg looked him up and down, taking in the veil of arterial blood that coloured Victor red from head to foot.

'Do you realise you look like a massive fecking tampon?'

'There's no need to be so crude.'

Scragg laughed, incredulous. '"Crude", he says, after massacring eight people he didn't need to. I feel like your priorities are kind of messed up, Princess. Next time, we do things my way, okay?'

'You weren't going to walk in here without backup when you had a bag full of cash because that's your world,' Victor reminded him, then: 'If you shoot second in a gunfight, you die first. That's my world.'

TEN

The mansion stood on the edge of Malmö's wealthiest district, a looming testament to power and permanence. On the cliffs just north of the city, its high stone walls and wrought-iron gates protecting a legacy that had taken decades to build. Behind those walls, the house itself was a monument to strength – every line of its architecture, every carefully chosen detail in its interior, designed to project dominance without ostentation. The windows gleamed under the afternoon sunlight, their reflections lost in the expanse of manicured lawns and curated hedges.

Jorund Håkansson sat at the head of the dining table, his presence as solid and immovable as the mansion itself. His suit, charcoal grey and immaculately tailored, fit him as well as a plate harness worn by a knight of old. It was his third new suit in as many months. He refused to wear clothes that were too big for his ever-narrowing frame. Looking at his hands, he noted his pale skin looked almost translucent in the flickering light, the veins standing out like faded ink on parchment.

Across from him, Tobias Malmgren, Deputy Mayor of Malmö, leaned back in his chair, one leg crossed over the other. His suit was impeccable – stone brown, with just a hint of sheen. He held his drink with the casual ease of a man accustomed to getting what he wanted, though his eyes betrayed the restlessness beneath his polished exterior.

After taking a sip, he said, 'The way I see it, we have a real opportunity here. Not just to continue as we are, but to expand. Clean energy is the future, they keep saying. And nothing moves faster than a lie people want to believe. The market's hungry. For lithium, cobalt, all the rare earths they need to keep up their green revolution. The problem is, the legitimate supply is wrapped in red tape. Ethical sourcing, sustainability – impossible burdens for companies that need volume yesterday. That's where our existing logistics framework comes in.'

Håkansson's primary business was in counterfeit industrial equipment shipped in from offshore factories – China, the Balkans, sometimes India. Substandard turbine blades, engine components, control systems – anything that could be produced cheaper and passed off as the real thing. Håkansson made deals that were too good to be true happen, moving the shipments to buyers across Europe who were more concerned with price than integrity.

On paper, the parts met the standards. The materials were listed as tested, the compliance documents forged with meticulous attention to detail. No company wanted to slow down production by verifying the paperwork. And if they did, Malmgren had already ensured the inspectors had been taken care of. As Deputy Mayor, he handled the legal structure, setting up shell companies, filtering payments through holding firms that made it impossible to track them back to the source.

Malmgren continued: 'We bring in the material, no questions asked. From places where no one's worried about permits or worker protections. The Congo, Myanmar, wherever the earth gives up what we need. It moves through intermediaries, crosses enough borders that by the time it reaches the port, it's clean. A harmless shipment, just another link in the supply chain.'

Håkansson's fingers drummed once against the table. 'And once it's in?'

'Then it's a matter of placing it where it needs to go,' Malmgren said, stretching one hand out, palm up, as if presenting something obvious. 'Manufacturers, suppliers, refineries – they're all eager to buy, so long as the paperwork's in order. And, thanks to my office, it always is.'

In between them, and to Håkansson's left was Leila Farahani, sitting not like she belonged there, but like the seat had been waiting for her long before the meeting was arranged. She was poised, composed; the kind of woman who knew the weight of silence and let others rush to fill it. Dark eyes, unreadable, framed by the sleek precision of her jet-black hair, not a strand out of place. She never fidgeted, never gave anything away for free. A woman who built empires without raising her voice, who understood that control wasn't about being the loudest in the room – it was about making others want to hear her speak.

Farahani's lips curled, the ghost of a smirk. 'And this equipment you want moving alongside it? It's not enough to supply the raw materials, you want to flood the market with your own product too?'

Malmgren gave a small shrug. 'Our government loves green initiatives. The EU loves green initiatives. You sell them an efficient solar panel, an EV battery, they'll write the cheque before they even look at the specs. That's where our second revenue stream comes in – substandard, low-cost equipment. Panels that degrade twice as fast, turbines that break under real-world conditions, batteries with a fraction of the promised capacity.'

He leaned back, satisfied. 'But because they meet the most basic compliance standards, they still qualify for subsidies. And investment firms eat them up, because they look good on paper. As long as the right agencies rubber-stamp the projects, no one questions whether they work as advertised.'

Farahani swirled her drink, eyes sharp beneath her re-laxed posture. 'And you can ensure they do?'

Malmgren smiled. 'My office ensures that the right companies get the right certifications. Once the investments roll in, we take our share of the subsidies, and everyone walks away happy. Naturally, you ensure the materials reach land.'

The port was Farahani's domain, and without it, nothing in Håkansson's business moved. A single delay, a simple customs flag, and the entire supply chain ground to a halt. The crates arrived at her docks in standard shipping containers, cleared by customs officials who knew better than to scrutinise too closely. The labels were real. The packaging was legitimate. No one suspected that the industrial parts inside would fail years before they should, that entire systems were being built on components that wouldn't survive long enough to justify their price tags.

Legitimacy wasn't about what people saw – it was about what they assumed. And when a shipment looked right, when the documentation was clean, no one looked any further.

'And I suppose it's me who has to scour these third-world hellholes and cozy up to warlords and dictators to make it all happen?'

The fourth person at the table did not do subtlety. Where Farahani wielded silence like a weapon, Nikola Petrović filled space with sound, with movement, with the gleam of too much gold on his wrists, his fingers. His suit was a little too sharp, a little too tailored, the kind of wealth that demanded to be noticed. He liked the sound of his own voice, liked the way people listened when he spoke – not because they respected him, but because he didn't leave room for anything else. He talked as a man who believed that volume and confidence could outpace competence.

Malmgren said, 'No one else at this table has your unique charm.'

Petrović laughed and even Håkansson showed a small smile.

Whatever the product, Farahani ensured the shipments passed through the port without issue. Malmgren controlled the paper trail, making it look like those shipments were legitimate, signed off, accounted for and processed. Petrović sourced the products and ensured the shipments arrived in Malmö without interruption. Håkansson made the deals with companies and governments all over Europe and ensured they received their orders.

A closed loop. Each of the three people Håkansson had brought together played an essential role in the operation. It was a perfect system he had built. He had made his money in the traditional way – drugs, prostitution, extortion – and had invested that money into a far more profitable enterprise. Now, it was so efficient, so effortless, there was little for him to actually do to keep it running any more.

There was only one problem, and it was an enormous problem that he was powerless to solve.

Jorund Håkansson was dying.

ELEVEN

Victor walked along the opposite side of the narrow street, hands outside of the pockets of his dark coat despite the chill, gaze drifting along the façade of the building that would house the new gallery. Stora Nygatan was a tight corridor of cobblestones, old-world charm layered with modern commerce. Rows of thin windows reflected the afternoon, and beneath the building's second-floor window, a deep red awning jutted out over the pavement – a perfect shield for anyone stepping from an armoured limousine.

The building itself was a renovated slice of the city's history, once a printworks that had produced high-end fashion catalogues before going bankrupt three years earlier and standing empty between then and now. The brickwork had been cleaned, the windows refitted with modern glass that still matched the century-old frames rejuvenated with new paint.

The adjacent street-level shopfronts – an upscale watch

boutique and a minimalist Scandinavian furniture show-room – framed the entrance: an ornate double door of dark-stained wood with brass handles polished to a mir-ror finish. The plaque above it read GALLERI CELANDER, named after its fictional founder – Victor had already con-firmed the name was a fabrication.

The client had supplied more details since their last con-versation. Victor knew the opening ceremony, the party, would be held on the third floor of the building.

He imagined the armoured limousine would glide up the street, slow and deliberate, tyres murmuring over the cobble-stones before coming to a stop outside. The target, Gustavus Håkansson, would step out within the awning's cover. Even if Victor could somehow secure an elevated position in the surrounding buildings – most of which were narrow apart-ments above retail units – any angle would be compromised by the awning's coverage and the limousine's reinforced glass. A sniper shot wasn't impossible, but the odds of a clean kill without being spotted or intercepted were tiny and not worth the risk.

Victor continued on his way, walking to the head of the block, then turned into a side street that ran parallel behind the row of buildings that housed the gallery. This service lane was one way, narrower still, designed for deliveries and waste collection only. Pale concrete walls, loading bays and steel fire doors.

The gallery's rear door was propped open, revealing a glimpse of the interior: stacks of crates, protective sheeting and workers moving in and out despite the hour – some carrying wrapped paintings or unpacking sculptures from wooden crates.

On the night of the event, caterers and staff would likely use the same entrance, which might offer an opportunity for entry.

Parked beside the loading bay was a large moving van with a boxy cargo area high enough to stand inside without stooping. The side of the van was emblazoned with a faded logo depicting a stylised lion's head within a circle, its mane rendered in jagged lines of red and gold. Beneath the logo, the slogan in Swedish translated to 'Moving with Pride'. The cargo door stood open, revealing more crates secured by straps against the van's interior walls. A man in overalls stood nearby, taking a drag from a cigarette as he waited for another load.

No one so much as glanced Victor's way more than once as he strolled along the service lane. He could be anyone and everyone was busy.

The height of the van was notable – parked against the building's rear, it offered a natural platform halfway to the second floor. Not high enough to access the opening ceremony on the third floor, but enough to reach the second-floor windows if needed. From there, ascending to the third floor would depend on the interior layout.

Victor headed back out of the service lane and paused at the corner, leaning against the wall as if checking his phone. Instead, he rotated his head to see the gallery's rear entrance from the corner of his eye then back to sweep the junction to the service lane and environs. Timing and traffic flow would determine his approach – getting inside would be easy enough if he moved during a delivery or shift change. Exiting, however, would be harder. The narrowness of the streets and the nearby intersections meant any pursuit would be hard to shake if he had not managed to complete the contract without alerting the security detail.

Victor's gaze shifted to the left, along the perpendicular street that curved towards a small public square. Beyond that lay a maze of older streets, alleys and back courtyards – hard to navigate, but easy to disappear into if he knew the layout. He made a mental note to explore those routes later.

Satisfied, he stepped away from the wall and continued walking. He didn't look back as he turned the corner and blended into the afternoon foot traffic of an adjacent main thoroughfare. The gallery was not an impossible challenge, but it had many distinct disadvantages no amount of planning could mitigate.

Victor always had a plan, but he was also used to improvising.

One way or another, Gustavus Håkansson was a dead man.

TWELVE

The dining room walls were lined with dark, polished wood, broken only by carefully positioned modern art pieces that hinted at wealth and taste rather than screaming it. A large antique chandelier hung above the long dining table, its crystals catching the soft light and casting muted patterns across the silver and porcelain laid out beneath and illuminating a room designed to impress without intimidating. Floor-to-ceiling windows revealed the garden beyond, the outlines of trees haloed by the sunlight. Not a single leaf moved in the cold Malmö afternoon.

Nikola Petrović made a low sound of amusement. 'And when they realise their wind farms don't produce enough energy to keep a lightbulb on?'

Tobias Malmgren spread his hands. 'By then, we'll be selling them the next big innovation. Carbon capture, hydrogen storage – whatever buzzword gets them excited. They'll throw more money at the problem, and we'll be the ones holding the solutions.'

Petrović let out a dry chuckle. 'If nothing else, it sounds like fun. I'm in.'

Leila Farahani nodded her agreement. 'I agree that we either innovate or we get replaced. And I'm not ready to retire anytime soon.'

All eyes turned to Jorund Håkansson. They were all partners, but it was still his operation. Until he died, he was in charge. If he declined, there would be no expansion.

He said, 'I believe this will be good for everyone. And especially my son. Gustavus will be more invested in leading an entirely new direction for the business. It will feel more like his own to be there from the beginning.'

Farahani set her glass down with deliberate care. 'If Gustavus is to take over your involvement, that means some things will need to be restructured. Simply to reflect his naivety. We cannot let the success of our endeavours, current or future, rely on his inexperience.'

Håkansson waved a hand. 'We keep things as they are. He will be ready. He will do what I do now. Any inexperience will be overcome by youthful energy. Besides, we don't reinvent the wheel. My people move the product that Nikola sources, your docks let it in, Malmgren keeps the books neat. That's the way it works now. That's how it will work with my son in charge.'

Malmgren, Farahani and Petrović exchanged glances but said nothing.

They needed no words, however, because Håkansson could not only see their doubt, he could feel it too. It saturated the air and yet he would not yield to it.

His son would rule.

Outside, the city hummed on, oblivious.

Before Håkansson could continue, the door to the dining room opened without a knock. No hesitation. Just the solid weight of oak swinging inward with a controlled authority that mirrored the man who held it open. Håkansson looked up, unsurprised.

Magnar Kaale filled the doorway, broad shoulders straining the seams of his tailored suit. Not tailored for vanity – tailored because nothing off the rack could contain him. Six foot six and two hundred and eighty pounds, he was built with the density of a man whose strength had been carved through purpose, not aesthetics. His suit was black, of course. Always black. Pressed without a wrinkle, though it did little to soften the sense that he'd be more at home in tactical gear with a rifle in his hands.

'Police Director Wallin is here,' Kaale said, his voice as deep as the North Sea.

Håkansson held his gaze a moment longer, then nodded. 'I'll receive her in the study.'

Kaale inclined his head, just a fraction, then stepped back into the hall. The air seemed to expand with his departure, as if the space had been holding its breath. Håkansson allowed himself the briefest flicker of satisfaction. A man like Kaale was worth ten of anyone else. Knowing that after Håkansson had died, Kaale would still be here to protect Gustavus gave the old man much comfort.

'Please forgive my terrible manners,' he said to Malmgren, Petrović and Farahani. 'I'm afraid I have to cut our luncheon short. If Director Wallin has come all the way here to see me I imagine I will be a while. Feel free to have dessert without me.'

His business partners exchanged more glances and he

imagined they would have much to discuss while enjoying the delightful rainbow sorbet his chef had prepared.

'We have a serious situation you need to be aware of,' Wallin said as soon as Håkansson had stepped into the study and closed the door. 'A professional assassin has recently arrived in Malmö.'

THIRTEEN

Victor stood at the edge of Själbodgatan, a narrow, cobble-stone street on the south side of St Petri's church. The imposing fourteenth-century Gothic edifice loomed over the surrounding buildings, its red-brick façade weathered by centuries yet everlasting. The church's architecture, reminiscent of the Marienkirche in Lübeck, bore testament to Malmö's historical ties to the Hanseatic League.

Surrounding the church, the medieval street layout remained largely intact. Narrow cobblestone streets like Själbodgatan and Östergatan were lined with historic buildings that had witnessed the city's evolution. Victor noted the pedestrianised zones around the church, with limited vehicular access directly to its entrances. However, Själbodgatan allowed for vehicle drop-offs, making it the probable choice for Gustavus's arrival. Especially given the church's nearby side entrance that was framed by intricate brickwork archways. Above, flying buttresses had graceful arches that supported the nave and added to the structure's overall grandeur.

Victor's gaze shifted from the church to the buildings opposite the southern entrance. Directly across the single-lane street stood a modern office building. None of its windows appeared to open – sealed units designed for energy efficiency. The roof was the only possible vantage point, but Victor dismissed the idea. The distance was too short, the angle too steep. From that height, the limousine's roof would obscure most of Gustavus's body as he stepped out, leaving only a fleeting moment when his head and shoulders might be visible.

Even if Victor timed the shot to perfection, proximity increased the risk of being spotted. A competent security detail would sweep the area as they approached, would emerge first and check such an obvious danger spot, and any civilian glancing upwards might catch sight of a figure on the roofline as he set up to shoot. It wasn't worth the risk. The shot would need to be rushed as a result and a hurrying sniper was a contradiction in terms.

Victor moved his attention to Kyrkogatan, the street continuing where Själbodgatan left off, running east from the far side of the pedestrianised area that spanned the church's eastern side. As Kyrkogatan stretched out, its buildings' staggered fronts created potential observation points that viewed the church's southern flank on a parallel plane.

About one hundred metres down, he saw a building whose façade protruded out further than the nearer building, creating a narrow rooftop area with a parapet. Standing in front of the church's side entrance, Victor had a perfect view of the parapet. Not even a lamp post would intrude on the line of sight of any shot taken from that position.

From there, he could monitor the approach without

the steep angle issues posed by the building opposite. The increased distance also provided a broader field of view, allowing for better assessment of the security detail's movements and a much earlier indication of the limousine's arrival. The risk of being seen, both by the guards and any passing civilians, was also vastly reduced.

However, the horizontal tracking required for a shot from this angle introduced its own set of challenges, demanding precise timing and calculation. The competent security detail would do their best to make it even harder.

Stepping inside the church, Victor smelled centuries-old stone and beeswax. The towering Gothic columns rose high into shadows that the afternoon sunlight couldn't quite reach, their worn surfaces lined with the scars of history.

The tourists who trickled through the church paid him no attention, their gazes fixed upwards at the vaulted ceilings or downwards at their phones as they followed digital guides. St Petri's was known for its sheer size, the largest church in Malmö. The heavy walls and medieval architecture had stood against war, fire and time itself. Now, it was just another stop on the sightseeing circuit – more backdrop than sacred space.

For Victor, it was something else: a sanctuary of anonymity. A place to disappear in plain sight. More than that, it was a place that connected him to a past he did everything possible to forget. When he had been taught the necessity of leaving his old life behind, one habit had been impossible to shake.

Every year without fail, he gave confession.

He moved towards the main aisle, his eyes adjusting to the dim light filtering through the stained-glass windows. They told fragmented stories in muted reds and blues, fractured images of saints and angels that seemed almost indifferent to the people below.

In places like this, history felt heavier. The walls seemed to hold it, their stones soaked with the weight of countless prayers, secrets and regrets. Malmö had changed over the centuries – first a trading hub for the Hanseatic League, later an industrial city, now a modern blend of cultures and contradictions. But the church had remained, its stones un-touched by time's compromises.

It remined him of how the past never quite disappeared, no matter how deep it was buried.

Memory is distraction, he had been taught. *Distraction will get you killed.*

A woman lit a candle near the front of the chapel, her head bowed in silent prayer. Victor watched her for a moment, not out of curiosity but as part of his constant calculation of the space. She was in her mid-thirties, dressed in muted colours, her posture rigid. Her hands trembled as she struck the match, the flame catching on the wick with a soft flare of light.

Grief, Victor thought. Not recent but still raw enough to cause the small shake in her hands. He didn't linger on the thought – it was an impolite intrusion to her privacy – but it was a detail that stuck with him nonetheless.

The priest stood near the main entrance, speaking quietly with a young couple. His robes were simple, black with a small silver cross around his neck. He glanced up as Victor passed, offering a polite nod.

Victor returned the gesture; his expression was neutral but the weight of judgement upon him was crushing.

He stepped out into the pale sunlight, the sudden brightness forcing his eyes to adjust. The square outside the church was lively, filled with market stalls selling everything from fresh produce to handmade crafts. The smell of roasting chestnuts mingled with the salty breeze from the nearby harbour. Musicians played on the corner, their instruments blending into a pleasant hum that filled the air.

Victor crossed the square, his pace steady but unhurried. He noted the positions of the CCTV cameras mounted on nearby buildings, their lenses sweeping back and forth in slow, mechanical arcs. The crowd moved around him, fluid and unthinking, each person caught in their own small world.

He turned towards the street that led back to the rented apartment that served as his safe house, his mind already shifting towards the next phase of his preparations.

The church or the gallery?

A difficult rifle shot, or the inevitable presence of witnesses combined with the unpredictability of an enclosed environment?

Neither was perfect, but strike points had an annoying habit of never making it easy for him.

FOURTEEN

Elise Wallin waited in Håkansson's study, sitting in an armchair as though it was her throne, the cut of her navy uniform crisp enough to slice through air, her gold rank insignia gleaming beneath the overhead lights. Police director for the Malmö region was a title that carried weight. She oversaw every officer, every station, every operation. When orders came from her desk, they echoed across the city. Courts, politicians, corporate magnates – all paid attention when Wallin spoke. Some listened out of duty. Others, like Håkansson, out of necessity.

He took in the details as she rose from the armchair. Tall, a dense build. Her greying hair, pinned in place with precision, as if chaos itself wouldn't dare touch her. Eyes grey-blue, clear, cold. She could scan a room with a glance that could strip lies to the bone. Her gaze settled on Håkansson without an ounce of warmth. If he listened to her out of necessity, her words were only offered for profit.

Her reputation preceded her. Decades in law enforcement.

A career forged through dismantling criminal networks and pulling political strings with equal finesse. Not just a cop – a strategist. She'd risen faster than most, her ascent fuelled by a blend of intelligence, ruthlessness and timing. It wasn't just what she knew. It was who she knew. The right politicians, the right businessmen. She had a knack for turning allies into stepping stones without leaving footprints behind. And yet, despite the uniform and the polished veneer of law and order, Håkansson could see the cracks. The compromises that added up in a pile so high it would cause it to topple one day. Favours exchanged in the shadows where badges and law books never reached could never be withdrawn.

He chuckled. 'An assassin has come to Malmö? How incredibly amusing. Has no one told them they're wasting their time?'

He smiled and shook his head as he paced the study, a room of dark wood and muted elegance. Oak panelling lined the walls, its grain rich and deep, aged to a warmth that seemed to absorb the light from the brass-shaded lamps. Built-in shelves framed the room, heavy with leather-bound volumes with spines embossed in gold, titles worn soft from decades of use. Between them hung paintings in gilded frames – landscapes of Sweden's northern fjords and snow-heavy forests. Above the fireplace, carved from black marble veined with white, a stag's head gazed down with glass eyes that seemed to watch everything.

'Whoever hired the hitman must be the only person in the city who does not know the truth by now,' he said as he poured himself a drink from a crystal decanter. 'That my pancreas has taken upon itself to murder me.'

The decanter stood on the desk at the room's heart,

a broad, imposing slab of mahogany, its surface unclut-
tered save for a crystal tumbler of aquavit, a fountain pen
resting beside a leather-bound ledger, and a brass lamp
with a green glass shade that pooled warm light across
the polished wood. Behind it stood a high-backed chair
upholstered in oxblood leather, its worn arms smoothed
from years of use.

'If they want to spare me the pain and indignity of wither-
ing away, then let them. It will be amusing to me to imagine
their faces when they find out they went to so much trouble
to achieve something that a few rogue cells will do for free.'

Tall windows with heavy velvet drapes overlooked the
gardens.

He took a sip of the spirit, swallowed.

'You are not the intended victim,' Wallin said.

His crystal tumbler shattered on the flooring.

He would have collapsed to his knees had he not thrust
out a hand to grab hold of the desk.

All he could say was, '*Why?*'

'That we do not know, but, as you say, people know of
your ... situation. There's no need to cut off the head of the
snake when that snake won't be around for long.'

'Never,' he said. 'Never in all my days on this Earth,
through the innumerable inhumanities I have inflicted, have
I ever harmed someone's child.'

'Times change,' she said. 'And, last I checked, Gustavus is
an adult.'

'He's my child. Gustavus will forever be my child.'

'I understand the depths of your feeling so I—'

'You are incapable of understanding the love I have for
my son.'

'Nevertheless, I knew this news would be hard to endure. Which is why I'm delivering it to you in person.'

'Why?' he demanded.

'I don't have those answers,' she answered, 'but I know it is a single killer who has been hired for the job. A man of exceptional talents who is already here in Malmö.'

'Find him. Stop him.'

'If only it were that easy I would not have needed to bother you.'

'Then your gifts are invisible,' he said. 'Unless you know who sent him? Which of those envious bastards is it? I will personally murder every single human being they love for this and I will make them watch me do it.'

'Sadly, the one who wants Gustavus dead remains unknown. The killer is getting ready to strike if our interpretation of the communications is to be believed.'

'So? I'm waiting.'

'He does not know that we know he's coming.'

'I'm still waiting.'

'You want to know who sent him? Who wants your son dead and why? He will tell you given . . . the right persuasion.'

Håkansson said, 'Unless you have a means of contacting him, this discussion is pointless.'

'I would not be here now if I didn't have something to give you.'

'Then I'm a child on Christmas morning and you are yet to fill the stockings.'

She told him her plan and he almost smiled.

'Perfect,' he replied. 'Let this killer come to us.'

FIFTEEN

The city moved around him, alive and unaware of the monster that stalked its streets. The rhythms were starting to make sense now – the city's patterns revealing themselves piece by piece. Soon, he would know it as well as he knew himself. Every street, every alley, every escape route. Malmö would become another tool in his arsenal, just like all the other cities before it.

Victor surveyed the block of buildings bordered by Kyrkogatan and Kampsgatan, evaluating how to reach his chosen vantage point overlooking St Petri's southern entrance. The neighbourhood featured a mix of historic and modern structures, housing various establishments but no residential properties, he saw. Residential buildings might offer access to the roof and would have little to no security as well as predictable patterns from the inhabitants.

On Kyrkogatan, he noted a wine bar known for its extensive selection of Italian wines and a modest, if carefully curated, beer assortment. The establishment's façade suggested a traditional structure, likely with limited roof access. There could be fire escapes to the rear of the buildings but there were no alleyways that were not blocked off with secure doors facing the street where witnesses could watch him picking the locks.

At the opposite side of the block from the church was the town hall that stretched the block's entire length. Almost certainly multiple routes to the roof, and yet the security, the cameras, would be extensive.

Which left several office buildings.

Modern office buildings often had restricted access, with security systems in place to prevent unauthorised entry. Not only at the main entrance lobby. A top-floor office with roof access in a building of multiple firms could very well have additional security of its own.

A building housing several offices would be better for his purposes, he decided. Less chance of standing out in a building of multiple isolated ecosystems than in one homogenous biome.

Three such buildings met that criteria.

Victor began by checking each building's online directory – noting the identity of each firm and researching where in the building they were located. Of those that occupied each of the buildings' top floors, he investigated their individual websites and online footprints until he found which business had the fewest number of employees.

A law firm with a senior lawyer, a paralegal, and a receptionist/researcher was almost perfect. Only three employees meant no security and behavioural patterns he could learn at speed.

Over the next few days, he gathered intel. The lawyer, Erik

Malmquist, finished work at the same time each evening, leaving his colleagues to lock up, before taking a predictable route towards the parking garage two blocks away. On Friday evening, his routine changed, meeting an acquaintance at the nearby wine bar for a single glass of Tuscan red before heading to his car. He didn't notice Victor's presence, nor when Victor checked the pockets of his coat to find out in which he kept the keys to his office and the swipe card attached to the keyring.

When Malmquist left, Victor followed, moving through the sparse foot traffic unnoticed. Timing was everything – Malmquist paused to check his phone, unaware of the slight brush of Victor's shoulder as he passed.

Should Malmquist notice the keys' absence, which was far from guaranteed, he would likely deduce he'd left them at the office and his employees could let him in to retrieve them come Monday morning.

Victor's chosen safe house was located a distance from the church that was close enough to be practical while maintaining tactical safety. He preferred tourist-heavy areas in which to blend in, forgoing the many neighbourhoods where Malmö's ethnic and immigrant communities were heaviest. A short-stay rented apartment in a small residential block was often the best choice for such safe houses and this one was no exception.

After performing countersurveillance to ensure he was not followed, he circled the area. When he found no evidence of threats, he entered the apartment.

Gun out, he swept the rooms one by one.

He checked his go-bag had not been tampered with and the other weapons were where he had left them.

UNLUCKY FOR SOME

The rifle, recently cleaned and oiled, had already been ze-roed for the distance in the forested hills far north of the city. It would remain in its case until Victor was ready to use it.

He performed an exercise routine tailored for strength, balance, mobility and flexibility, manipulating his body weight to provide resistance and only ending it when every muscle ached, every joint was loose, and a sheen of sweat covered every centimetre of his skin.

Tomorrow, Saturday, he would rest and lie low.

Sunday morning, he would go to work.

SIXTEEN

The conservatory was located along the southern side of the mansion, a long room enclosed by floor-to-ceiling glass panels framed in wrought iron painted matte black. Beyond the glass, the frost-laced gardens sprawled beneath a pale winter sky. Bare branches of pruned trees reached towards the horizon, their skeletal forms casting faint shadows across the white lawns. Low hedges, still green despite the season, lined stone pathways that wound towards the distant greenhouse and reflecting pool now crusted with ice.

A rectangular dining table of dark oak stood near the centre of the room, its surface arranged with the understated elegance that marked Håkansson's household. Three white linen placemats were set out with silver cutlery and crystal glasses polished to a flawless shine. A silver coffee service gleamed beside a platter of gravadlax, thin slices of cured salmon arranged in overlapping rows, their orange-pink flesh bright against the white porcelain plate. Small bowls of mustard-dill sauce, soured cream and pickled cucumbers sat nearby, alongside dark rye bread sliced thin. To one side, a wicker basket lined with white cloth held kanelbullar – cinnamon buns still warm enough to scent the air with spice – alongside golden-brown saffron buns shaped into coils. A glass pitcher of blood orange juice, its colour rich and deep, caught the light beside a smaller carafe of cream.

'Your palm is clammy,' Freja told him. 'It's really warm. Like, an inferno.'

Gustavus had told Dad all about her with such expectations last week. He had been excited to finally reveal he was seeing someone, someone special.

Now, he was nervous because he wanted everything to go perfectly. Dad would love her, that was a given. But he wanted her to love Dad just as much.

That was the sticky part.

Dad was an acquired taste.

Freja was on her phone because she was always on her phone. It was her career. Her social media profiles said she was a 'model, adventurer, traveller and child of Jesus'. She had over a million followers on one of those profiles alone. She was a goddess by any standard of beauty. Enhanced, yes, bust and buttocks, and yet she had yet to have a facelift or any major facial surgery. The nose job did not count, of course, because it was so common, and her lips had been filled, her upper cheeks filled, her lower cheeks contoured, her brows raised, her chin shaved, and everywhere even a hint of line or crease had appeared, the skin had been promptly injected and paralysed.

Gustavus considered all of this to be self-improvement. As did she, as did their generation. No different from working out or wearing nice clothes. If you weren't born beautiful, you could still make yourself beautiful. It just took some work. And putting in the work for something was worth far more than something someone was handed for free.

He was sure Dad would have to agree. He never shut up about being a self-made man.

'I just wish he understood your work,' Gustavus said. 'He's too old-fashioned. He couldn't get his head around it when I told him. I just know he'll want to talk to you about it.'

'Sorry to keep you both waiting.'

Jorund Håkansson entered the conservatory, his posture straight as ever, shoulders squared but narrow beneath a new navy suit with faint pinstripes that hugged his frame with precise tailoring. A silk tie, deep burgundy to match the leather chairs, knotted tightly at his collar. Polished black leather shoes tapped against the marble as he approached the table, his attire chosen not just for church, but for the reputation that accompanied his name.

They rose, and Freja stepped forward to hug but stopped herself when Håkansson took his seat.

She exchanged glances with Gustavus and they lowered themselves back down.

The first ten minutes went well enough, he thought. Serving and eating, chatting about the dishes. Exclamations of delight at the deliciousness of it all. Freja was as charming as he knew she would be and even Dad seemed to smile now and again.

'So, Freja,' Håkansson then stated as he wiped his mouth. 'My son tells me you *represent* brands. Is that correct?'

'That's right. I'm an influencer.'

'The brands you work with – whom you *influence* for – how much does one of these brands pay you for a promotion?'

Gustavus shifted in his seat, and yet Freja did not flinch.

'There are many brands, they all pay differently.'

'Give me an example.'

'I can't think of one off the top of my head.'

'This one,' Håkansson said, opening up his phone and pointing to her most recent post. 'Dated yesterday. A lipstick. How much did they pay you for this? You can't have forgotten already.'

'I don't think that's ethical.'

'If I guess, will you tell me if I'm right?'

Gustavus said, 'Why does it matter what they pay her? You're being extremely rude right now.'

'It matters because her bag costs more than three thousand and I dare not guess how much that dress costs, or how much those shoes are sold for.' To Freja, he said, 'I can see that you flew to Dubai only a few days ago and made sure to show yourself drinking champagne in business class. And yet I see no sponsorship for the trip, no posts while you were there. Therefore, no brand paid for it. That trip must have cost thousands upon thousands.'

Finally, she gave up trying to pretend she was not offended.

'Why do you care so much what I'm paid? Do you think I'm a gold digger? Look at my clothes, look at my bag. Like you said: I'm doing fine all by myself. Oh, and, as I'm sure Gustavus has already told you, we were dating for over three months before he told me who he really was, who his family are . . . and what they do for a living.'

Gustavus stood. 'I've had enough of this. Come on, Freja, we're leav—'

'YOU WILL SIT DOWN AND BE SILENT UNTIL I'M FINISHED,' Håkansson screamed, gaze still on Freja.

A shy toddler again, Gustavus fell back into his seat.

Håkansson stood and approached her. 'You cannot afford to fly business class. You do not have the funds to stay in five-star resorts in the Middle East. At least, not paid for by ... influencing. Am I wrong? Please tell me if anything I have said is incorrect but know you will have to use more than just words to convince me of my errors. Because the world has changed a lot since I was your age and yet some things are the same as they have always been.' He stepped closer. 'I know exactly how you pay for your lifestyle. Or, I should say I know who pays for it. Because you're not flying yourself to Dubai, are you? You are being flown out. I would very much like to say that someone is flying you out but the reality is that it's not a singular benefactor, is it? Since I'm a gentleman, I will not ask how many men have flown you to the UAE or elsewhere to spend time with them, but you will stop lying to my son about what your profession actually is. If you won't tell him, I will, only I shall tell him in what I imagine will be more *direct* language than that which you would prefer to use yourself.'

Gustavus, eyes growing wider and face redder, alternated his attention between Freja and his father.

'Why are you doing this to me?' she asked. 'What have I ever done to you? I love your son.'

'*That* is what you have done and it is enough,' he answered. 'You love him. But you do not deserve him. I have one son and I will not have a prostitute for a daughter-in-law.'

'I'm done here,' she said, rising. 'Gustavus, we're leaving. Your father will enjoy the church service alone today.'

'Before you go, perhaps you could tell him where you're going tomorrow night?'

'He knows I'm going to Paris. Why does that ... ?'

She didn't finish the question. He saw that she understood. Gustavus, however, was perplexed. Slow to understand.

'You're quick,' Håkansson told her. 'Naturally, I have all of the messages, arrangements, and explicit photographs to show my son if necessary but I think neither of us wants that.'

Silence.

A long silence.

Håkansson's gaze was locked on Freja but he could see Gustavus too, whose own eyes had ceased darting back and forth between his girlfriend and his father and were now only directed at Freja.

'You ... paid in full,' she said, disbelief replacing her rage, no longer feeling the need to pretend because the pretence was over. 'For a week.'

'Twenty-five thousand dollars is a small price to confirm my suspicions. Of course, an employee posed as your next ... *acquaintance*. Feel free to fly to Paris regardless. Enjoy first class. Enjoy the suite. It's booked in your name, after all. Consider the trip a parting gift.' He paused. 'Just don't forget to take lots of selfies.'

She left the conservatory without a word. Håkansson said nothing further to her as she collected her bag and walked out without so much as looking the way of Gustavus, who watched her the entire time, begging in silence for her to turn around, to deny his father's accusations and ask him to accompany her.

Even when it had been murdered, love was slow to die.

SEVENTEEN

At weekends, the office building had only a skeleton staff. One receptionist was seated behind a counter in the lobby large enough for three. The polished marble of the floors and walls reflected the faint morning light filtering through large windows that looked out into a quiet morning. The turnstiles stood silent and inactive, awaiting a swipe. Victor moved with purpose, not ignoring the receptionist but not making enough eye contact to warrant her interest, the lawyer's swipe card pressed for a second against the reader. A soft beep, and the turnstile unlocked. He stepped through without hesitation, his footsteps echoing in the near-empty space.

He avoided lifts the majority of the time, understanding they could be a death trap for a man of his profession. However, he knew the receptionist was paying him attention because there was little else for her to do and so he did not want to register himself deeper into her memory by opting for the stairs that so few people chose to use.

The lift carried him upwards, numbers ticking by in muted succession. On the top floor, the fifth, the hallway smelled of cleaning products and office-grade carpet. Victor used the keys to unlock the law firm's glass door, slipping inside. The interior was minimalist – grey walls, white desks, neatly arranged folders. But his focus was beyond the office itself. A maintenance corridor at the rear led to the roof access door, secured with a simple mechanical lock.

Seconds later, the lock clicked open by way of a tension rod and a smooth, thin pick.

One flight of stairs took him the rest of the way to the roof. Stepping outside, a nearby cluster of modern air conditioning units hummed. The building, characteristic of Malmö's architectural blend, featured a gently sloping roof covered in weathered terracotta tiles, their reddish hue muted by years of exposure to the Scandinavian climate. The dull metallic surfaces of the air conditioning units contrasting sharply with the traditional aesthetics of the roof. These units, elevated on sturdy metal frames, were connected by a network of insulated ducts snaking across the rooftop, secured with rust-resistant brackets. Near the units, a maintenance hatch, ajar, suggested recent servicing.

Peering over the edge, Victor observed the narrow street below, its cobblestone surface glistening from a recent drizzle. Directly opposite stood St Petri's church, its Gothic spire piercing the overcast sky. The church's façade, adorned with intricate stone carvings, bore the marks of centuries, each detail telling a story of its own. In the distance, the Turning Torso skyscraper twisted upwards against the horizon.

He headed across the rooftop, navigating the changes in elevation and obstacles as he passed from one building to the next. There were no gaps between roofs so he could move with speed, staying low to reduce his profile against the sky. He veered around one roof topped with chimneys of varying heights, constructed from aged brick, some exuding faint wisps of smoke, indicating active fireplaces below. Gutters lined with damp leaves hinted at the recent change from autumn to winter, while patches of moss clung between tiles, thriving in the cool, moist environment.

When he reached the rooftop with his chosen vantage point, he ducked even lower before dropping down from the neighbouring roof. There was about a metre's difference in height. Here the flat rooftop's perimeter was lined with a low parapet. Shorter than he had envisioned when looking up from below, it nevertheless provided a modest barrier and enough of a degree of concealment to meet his requirements.

The church's southern entrance was visible across the narrow streets, perfectly framed by the building's protruding parapet.

The distance was ideal.

The angle, clear.

The horizontal movement of the target was an issue, but solvable.

He could make it. He knew he could.

The question was whether the security detail would let him.

EIGHTEEN

The limousine emerged from the mansion's private drive-way, its polished obsidian exterior reflecting faint streaks of pale winter light as it rolled onto the snow-dusted street. A Mercedes-Maybach S 680 Guard 4MATIC, unmistakable in both presence and price. Beneath its elegant contours and signature chrome grille lay layers of reinforced steel and ballistic glass designed to withstand both high-calibre gunfire and explosive blasts – luxury armoured to the teeth.

The vehicle's modifications were seamless, betraying nothing to the casual observer. Only the slight thickening of the window frames hinted at the ballistic glass – certified to VR10 standards, capable of stopping armour-piercing rounds fired from military-grade rifles. Each window measured over two inches thick, the multi-layer polycarbonate coating designed to prevent spall, ensuring that even if struck, fragments wouldn't penetrate the cabin. The reinforced doors, weighing nearly triple that of a standard model, were sealed with electromagnetic locks capable of withstanding forced entry.

Beneath the chassis, additional steel plating protected the undercarriage from grenade blasts and mines, while run-flat tyres, armoured with Kevlar, allowed the limousine to maintain speed and control even if punctured. The suspension and braking systems had been reengineered to handle the added weight – nearly five tons fully loaded – without compromising agility.

This level of protection did not come cheap. The base model alone cost upwards of €500,000, but with custom armouring and security upgrades, the final price easily exceeded €1.5 million – money well spent for a man whose wealth made him envied and his son now hunted.

That son, sitting next to Håkansson, was silent.

Gustavus sat stiff-backed at the table, his hands resting in his lap as if unsure whether to clench or relax. His jaw worked against words unsaid, tension tight in his shoulders despite the stillness of his posture.

Wallin called to update Håkansson, although she had found out little. Still, he appreciated being kept in the loop even when there was no progress.

'I've been looking into the recent activities of Malmgren, Farahani and Petrović, but nothing stands out as suspicious.'

'It is one of them, I know. And they will have been careful,' he replied. 'They understand what I will do to them should they be discovered.'

'Have you told Gustavus?'

'No,' he said, glancing over at his sullen heir. 'That would only create unnecessary aggravation. Everything carries on as normal for appearances' sake lest we reveal to our *competitor* that we know their plans.'

'With increased security, I trust?'

'Naturally.'

'How are the German specialists I recommended working out?'

'They are ... creative,' he answered. 'And cunning in a way I could never contemplate myself. But when the time comes my own people will handle it.'

'Is that wise?'

'I trust your judgement, of course, and the Germans have an impeccable résumé, but when it comes to such an important task –' again, he looked at Gustavus, '– I need to know in my bones that those involved are beyond loyal to me.' She went to speak and he cut her off. 'If it makes you feel better, one of the Germans, Lukas Draeger, will oversee the operation.'

'Your call,' she said. 'I'll update later.'

After he had slipped his phone away, he said to his son, 'Do not mope. Do not be a brat.'

The insult worked. 'Why? Why did you do that to Freja, to me?'

His face was still flushed with rejection, with betrayal, with anger.

'I don't have the luxury of time any more, Gustavus. Not to watch you waste it on pretty distractions. You need a wife, not a girlfriend. Someone who can carry this family's future. That's the most important deal you'll ever make. More important than any business contract. You won't be paid in dividends or market shares – you'll be paid in children.'

'I love Freja.'

Twisting in his seat, Håkansson slapped him.

Hard.

A whole palm against his cheek, leaving it bright red.

Gustavus, shocked into silence, had no words again.

'My son, I'm sorry. I love you so much that I have to do what's best for your future even if that means hurting you now. And I have no time left to risk you not learning from me while I'm still here. I will not leave you behind if I think you're not ready and yet I cannot stay a second longer than I'm allowed.

'Dad . . .'

'You must marry. You must have children. You must have a son so you can leave him the kingdom I left you. You must have a legacy. Our name must live on. Your wonderful mother died too young before she could gift me more children. Thus, you are my only son,' he said, cradling Gustavus's cheeks in both palms. 'You are more precious to me than any wealth, any power. Without you, I would be nothing. I built all of this because of you. I built it for you. All my own father gave me were bruises. Look how tall you are. Look how much taller you are than I am. A son should be taller than his father and yet you are a giant compared to me. Why? Because for the first eighteen years of my life there was not a pinch of fat on my belly.' He gripped his flank. 'I could rest each individual finger in the crook between my ribs. I had no spare calories with which to grow. Every morsel of food I ate was used to keep me alive. You were chubby as a boy, I know, and you did not like it one bit. I force-fed you, didn't I? I made sure your growing body had calories to spare because I wanted you to grow tall even if you were unhappy you could not run as fast as your friends. But now, you dwarf them all. When you walk into a room, you command attention without even needing to open your mouth. I never had that. I had to yell just to be noticed. I made you

who you are today, this prince of men, and I made a kingdom for you to inherit. While you played with toys, I was
creating a throne that you would one day sit upon. That day
has come sooner than I expected, but you were bred to rule.
Today you are prince and tomorrow you will be a king and
then ...? Emperor?'

Gustavus shook his head, embarrassed. 'You're being
ridiculous.'

'There will be no limit to that which you can achieve but
you must promise me one thing. Just one. That is all I ask
of you. Promise me you will pick a wife who will be a good
mother, who will have strong children. Someone robust and
practical, and loving. Wide hips. She must be unselfish. She
cannot be self-possessed. She must want to raise her children
herself and put aside any career ambitions or superfluous
needs. That is what I did so that you stand here now before
me, tall and strong and worthy. An heir is no good if that
heir is weak, unworthy. Have a mistress if your lust cannot
be content with such a wife. Have many mistresses. But you
choose the right wife, the right mother. You love her and
only her.'

'Okay, okay. Jesus ... I'll pick a wife with big hips if it'll
make you happy.'

'It will make *you* happy. A life without legacy is merely
existence. Do you know how you get out of bed on those
cold, dark mornings when you didn't sleep, when you're sick
and exhausted and only want to roll back over and sleep
more? Purpose. That's the ultimate motivator. And there is
no greater purpose than legacy. Without children, without
an heir, this life will eat you alive and leave you broken and
alone. I never once rolled back over on those dark mornings.

I leaped out of bed every single time. I couldn't wait to get working for your future. My son, you will never know the depths of depravity I sank to to build this kingdom for you. I carved up my soul one piece at a time to ensure yours would remain pure. I regret nothing. I'm proud of every crime I committed and every unspeakable horror I inflicted upon anyone who stood in the way of your ascension. Had you not been born I would still be selling drugs on street corners or I would be long dead and unclaimed. Now I'm facing the end and living with the pain of a slow death, I am not unhappy. I can endure it for you. I would endure anything for you.'

'I don't know if I can do it ... I'm not you ... I don't have that same ... I just ... Look, I'm me, okay? Only me. I don't know how—'

'And you think I did when I was your age? That I had all the answers? I knew less than you. I knew nothing. Nothing. But I didn't let that stop me. God ... what I could have done if I had started at the top of the ladder like you instead of the bottom. There wasn't even a ladder back then. I had to chop down trees and saw wood and hammer nails before there was in fact a ladder for me to be at the bottom of. Did that stop me? Did it? But now, here you stand, the prince ... the king in waiting. You don't tell me that you can't do it. I did it. You will do it. If you don't think yourself worthy, think again. If you don't feel ready, you must pretend. Listen to me: my business partners must believe you are ready even if you are not.'

From the passenger seat, Kaale said, 'We're almost there.'

Ahead, St Petri's church, and destiny, waited.

NINETEEN

The .308 Winchester calibre of the Sako TRG 22 A1 offered proven stopping power with manageable recoil, making it ideal for both short and medium-range targets. The free-floating barrel, engineered from cold-hammer-forged steel, ensured sub-MOA accuracy, essential for a clean, single-shot kill. Victor's fingers traced the Picatinny rail along the top of the receiver, where the Schmidt & Bender PM II scope was locked into place with sturdy mounts. Its 5-25x56 magnification provided crystal-clear optics, capable of identifying a target's facial features even from several hundred metres away.

Every detail of the TRG 22 A1 spoke to its purpose: a rifle built not just for accuracy, but for reliability in the harshest conditions. As always, the weapon was more than a tool – it was an extension of his skill and intent, a means to shape the outcome of any confrontation with a single, precise trigger pull.

Victor kept the rifle low behind the parapet and out of sight as much as he could, but he still needed to practise. He needed the muscle memory. There would be only a tiny window of time in which to set the weapon up once the security detail had exited their vehicles and checked overlooking rooftops. How quickly and smoothly he could get the rifle into position was as important as the shot itself. Even half a second gained in the setup would make the subsequent shot significantly more viable.

He adjusted his grip on the rifle, settling into position along the rooftop's parapet. The cold stone pressed against his chest as he scanned the church's southern entrance through the scope. From this distance – a hundred metres – the shot should have been straightforward, but the horizontal movement added a layer of complexity.

He tracked the imaginary path Gustavus would take, picturing the man's stride: brisk but measured, surrounded by a moving wall of security. A clean shot would require precise timing, and timing meant calculations.

Distance: a hundred metres.

Bullet velocity: eight hundred metres per second.

Flight time – Victor's mind made the calculation – 0.125 seconds.

It didn't sound like much – an eighth of a second – but at a brisk pace of around 1.4 metres per second, Gustavus would cover about seventeen centimetres in that brief instant.

The wind blowing into Victor was a light breeze. Four or five miles an hour. Not enough to slow the bullet at such a short distance.

Hiding the rifle behind the parapet once more, Victor considered the firing techniques available. Tracking the target as he moved would be ideal – sweeping the crosshairs with Gustavus's pace to maintain alignment until the instant of the shot. But at this angle, with security flanking the target, tracking risked hesitation. The alternative: an ambush shot. Hold the crosshairs a fraction ahead of Gustavus's path, wait for the instant he stepped into alignment, and fire.

Faster. Cleaner.

Victor adjusted the scope, aligning the crosshairs not with where Gustavus's head would be, but just beyond – compensating for the forward motion that would carry the target into the bullet's path.

As the limousine glided towards St Petri's church, boxed in by two identical black SUVs carrying security personnel, Victor kept low, only the top half of his head above the parapet. His eyes tracked the vehicle's approach, noting the precise alignment of the security convoy. Every angle covered. Every potential firing lane minimised.

Pedestrians were passing and worshippers were filing into the church as the first SUV slowed to a stop and then idled along the kerb, lights still on, security personnel inside while the limousine stopped behind it. Victor was surprised the security detail in the lead SUV weren't out already, especially since the rear SUV had stopped and its occupants were spilling out.

Then, as the pedestrians on the pavement alongside the lead SUV walked by, Victor saw his plan was falling apart.

The SUV pulled up and onto the pavement, executing a ninety-degree turn to form a wall perpendicular to the limousine.

Not only did it offer a significant degree of protection due to its bodywork, it formed a huge barrier to Victor's line of sight.

He had been told the security personnel were good, but this was an elite tactic.

The guys inside were out in seconds, four of them joining the four from the rear SUV, making eight and not the six he had been told to expect, and taking up their positions with expert efficiency. The passenger in the limousine – a giant of a man in a black suit – opened the back door facing the church and was out and surrounded by the security personnel in a classic, and perfectly executed, diamond formation.

It was done so well that, combined with the SUV blocking the majority of the view, Victor couldn't even be sure whether it was father or son they were protecting until Gustavus was halfway to the entrance.

Victor snapped up the rifle, setting it in position.

His finger hovered near the trigger, pulse steady. There'd be no second shot. If the first missed – even by a centimetre – the target would be shielded and the security team would have him out of there before Victor had even worked the bolt action and shifted his aim.

He adjusted his aim for Gustavus's height, set the reticle for where he was going to be—

And it was too late.

He was already inside the church.

TWENTY

The only way to understand a city was to walk through it, Victor had found long ago. A vehicle – whether a taxi, tram, or bus – created a barrier, a filter between him and the city. Any large urban area was more than its roads, its intersections, its traffic lights. A city was its citizens. Without people, it was little else but a collection of buildings.

Victor spent the entire day walking. Some of this time he strolled along the canals and cobbled streets of Gamla Staden, Malmö's old town. He meandered through Södergatan, Malmö's pedestrianised thoroughfare, letting the flow of shoppers and tourists guide him. In such dense crowds, it was impossible to monitor everyone. Far too many individuals to analyse and evaluate even a fraction of them. But the reverse was also true – conventional shadows would find it hard to keep him in sight without risking exposure. They would have to get close, and in doing so, they would give him opportunities to spot them.

Tour buses with large windows rumbled past, ferrying

tourists through the city's highlights. A guided walking tour paused near Stortorget, where the guide gestured towards the bronze statue of King Karl X Gustav atop his horse. Victor kept moving. He wasn't here for history lessons, and blending into a crowd was easiest when he moved at its pace.

He stopped at a coffee shop with a view of the square. It wasn't busy – three customers inside, all seated at separate tables, none of them paying attention to anything beyond their phones or laptops. He ordered an espresso and took a seat by the window, positioning himself so he could watch the street while remaining partially obscured by a column.

After finishing his espresso, he walked towards the harbour, the air colder now as the sun dipped lower. The streets grew quieter and the scent of the sea became stronger. Cargo cranes loomed in the distance, their skeletal frames outlined against the darkening sky. A ferry horn sounded from somewhere beyond the docks, a deep, mournful note that seemed to hang in the air.

The harbour was more exposed than the city centre, but it offered its own advantages. Fewer eyes, fewer distractions. Victor walked along the waterfront, his footsteps blending with the sound of water lapping against the stone pier. He paused near a bench, watching as a container ship eased into port, its massive hull dwarfing the smaller fishing vessels nearby.

Victor stayed for a few minutes, then turned back towards the city. He adjusted his pace, matching the flow of pedestrians as they headed home for the evening. Streetlamps cast pools of golden light on the wet pavement as the night pressed in thick and cold, the air sharp with frost and the faint tang of exhaust fumes refusing to dissipate. A siren wailed somewhere across the city, its sound thin and distant against the low hum of traffic echoing through the industrial district. Streetlights flickered against the wet pavement, reflecting in shallow puddles that caught the glow like shards of glass.

Convinced he had not been shadowed, he met Scragg at the arranged time.

The Kashmiri Scottish Viking was walking a stocky bull terrier with a reddish-brown coat that blended into silver at her snout.

'This is Luna,' he announced. 'I'm looking after her for my friend Angela but she's such a sweetheart I may have to steal her for myself.' Luna wagged her tail and rushed to Victor for a fuss. 'Oh, she likes you,' Scragg grunted as handed over an envelope. 'Your new passport and documents.'

Victor took them, slipped them into a pocket of his own. 'Did you square things with Leila Farahani?'

'I'm touched you remember,' he answered. 'Well, she hates my guts now but at least they're still inside my belly. I'll take that as a win.'

'Good philosophy. The potential quiet exit from the city we talked about last week, is that still on offer?'

Scragg scrubbed at his facial hair. 'That's not quite as simple as it was when I made the offer.'

'Because Farahani controls the port and you're no longer allowed to exploit that,' Victor deduced.

'Aye, pretty much. However, a deal's a deal. I'll find a way to make it work around her even if it means I'll be out of pocket.'

'Uncommonly kind,' Victor said, not expecting such generosity from a criminal he had not long known.

'I know, that's me to a fault. You tell me when you want to scarper and I'll have a place for you on a ship leaving that day.'

'Thursday night,' Victor told him. 'Friday morning if you can't do that.'

'I'll check the departure timetables and let you know where and when I'll collect you for the drop-off. But these things are set in stone, Princess. You miss the pickup by one second and the ship will leave without you.'

'Understood,' Victor said.

He gave Luna one last stroke before stepping back and turning around, the soles of his shoes crunching on the thin layer of frost as he left the faraway wail of sirens behind and disappeared into the shadows.

TWENTY-ONE

Victor stood at the mouth of the service lane that ran behind the gallery, the night air heavy with the scent of rain and the rumble of traffic. The narrow passage stretched between tall buildings, shadows clinging to the corners where streetlights failed to reach. Across from him, the moving van still sat parked near the gallery's loading bay, its back doors halfway open, revealing crates marked with shipping labels from international art hubs. But now another vehicle had joined it – a white catering van, its rear doors wide open, interior lights casting a warm glow onto the asphalt.

He watched as a young caterer in a black uniform emerged from the van, balancing a platter covered with a pristine white cloth. The man adjusted his grip, glanced at his watch, then stepped through the propped-open service door leading into the gallery. The clink of dishes and muted laughter drifted out into the cool night air.

Victor needed no further invitation.

Moving with careful haste, he crossed the space and

approached the catering van. Inside, trays of champagne flutes and neatly arranged canapés gleamed beneath their coverings. His eyes scanned the assortment before he selected a platter similar to the one the caterer had carried. He adjusted his grip, ensuring the draped cloth concealed his hand, then turned towards the gallery's back entrance. His tailored black suit, simple yet refined, would pass as catering staff at a glance – details mattered, and Victor had planned for them.

He eschewed black whenever he could, and yet sometimes it was the best, and only, choice.

Inside, the hallway smelled of fresh paint and cleaned stone floors. Recessed lights along the ceiling threw muted pools of amber that barely touched the corners. Victor moved past stacked crates bearing shipping labels from Paris, London and New York, noting the murmur of ventilation systems and the clink of glasses from the main gallery.

A staircase led up to the first floor, second, then third floor where the chatter of guests mingled with the subtle strains of classical music. He paused at the top, scanning the corridor beyond. A catering station stood against one wall from which catering staff moved with efficient grace, carrying trays of glasses and hors d'oeuvres towards the main gallery. No one spared him more than a glance.

Timing was everything.

Blending into the flow of motion, Victor became one with the rhythm of the evening, each step taking him closer to the hum of conversation and the pleasant harpsichord music filtering through the air. He set the tray of canapés down before he continued into the gallery proper.

There, spotlights hung from the vaulted ceiling, illuminating abstract sculptures and contemporary paintings mounted on stark white walls. The stone floor gleamed under the soft lighting, broken only by the subtle shimmer of glass partitions that separated different sections of the exhibit.

Victor drifted through the crowd with the ease of a man who belonged. Guests milled in small clusters, glasses of champagne in hand as they discussed brushwork, symbolism, and the inflated prices of modern art. A large canvas dominated the nearest wall – a swirl of crimson and black that suggested both violence and desire. Victor let his gaze linger on it long enough to appear engaged before moving on.

Beyond the main gallery, a roped-off area occupied the far end of the room. Low lighting cast deep shadows across the space, broken only by the soft glow of spotlights illuminating select pieces of art.

Within the shadows, a figure stood near a marble pedestal, posture poised yet relaxed. Gustavus Håkansson. Even in silhouette, his height, his dignified stance and his slicked hair were recognisable.

The velvet ropes that separated the area from the rest of the gallery added to the air of exclusivity. Two security guys flanked the entrance, eyes scanning the crowd with the detached focus of men accustomed to long hours and predictable threats. However high their competence, this gig failed to challenge their skills and so they had become bored.

Victor let his gaze drift past Gustavus Håkansson without lingering, committing the angles and distances to memory.

His path took him towards the opposite side of the gallery, where a series of smaller rooms displayed more intimate works. Here, the lighting shifted – warmer, more inviting, with soft golden pools highlighting impressionist landscapes and minimalist sculptures.

The air buzzed with low conversations and the clink of glasses. Men in tailored suits and women in elegant gowns clustered in small groups, their laughter rising in polished crescendos that hinted at both privilege and performance.

He caught fragments of conversations as he passed – a couple debating the symbolism of a stark monochrome painting, their voices light yet quietly competitive. 'It's about isolation in modern society,' the woman insisted, her fingers trailing the stem of her champagne flute. Her companion tilted his head, lips curling with the suggestion of a smirk. 'Or maybe it's just a study in minimalism. Not everything needs to be profound.'

Nearby, a trio of art collectors discussed market trends, their eyes appraising each piece with the detached calculation of investors. 'Abstracts are holding strong this quarter,' one said, adjusting the cuff of his silk shirt. 'But the real money's in mixed-media installations. They're hitting record auction prices in London and New York.'

In another corner, two younger guests stood before a canvas of earth tones in blotches and spatters, their conversation tinged with the unguarded enthusiasm of those still discovering the art world. 'It's pure contradiction ... chaos, but beautiful,' the woman murmured, leaning closer as if a change in distance might reveal hidden meaning.

Her companion, a man with tousled hair and a shirt unbuttoned to show off his waxed sternum, nodded as if he understood. 'Yeah, it's absolutely the most beautiful thing I've ever seen and yet at the same time it's utter shit.'

His reconnaissance complete, Victor had seen enough.

The night was still young, but the moment was drawing closer.

TWENTY-TWO

Victor sipped champagne, ignored by the crowd. One of them and yet unembraced. None looked at him twice, no one smiled his way, no one asked him for the time. He was invisible to the other guests, who deemed him not worth their time. He was playing a role in contradiction to the one played by everyone else who was trying to be noticed, to appear important, to impress, to belong.

And yet his instincts were pulling at him, whispering in the back of his mind.

Something was off. He took another small sip of the champagne – decent quality, overpriced. His gaze drifted over the room, observing in the same way as the other guests who peered over the shoulders of the person they were talking to in the hopes of finding someone more important.

His threat radar, humming continuously, began to ping.

He realised there were one too many men standing too straight, moving with too much control. Broad-shouldered, square-jawed types in tailored suits, their heads on a subtle but constant swivel. A few women, too, just as composed, just as aware. A pattern emerging in a place where patterns shouldn't.

Maybe it was the world, he reasoned. The Håkansson family moved in illicit circles. Who knew how many others who moved in that same world were present now? Such guests would have security. Not obstacles to his goal and yet they could not be ignored. He had no wish to execute his target and find himself facing multiple threats from people against whom he had no conflict beyond circumstance.

He turned his attention to a nearby sculpture. Modern, an abstract mass of twisting metal, possibly meant to resemble a human form. Or a tree. Or nothing. He sipped his champagne, let his expression settle into mild curiosity, blending in with the others who stared at it, murmuring their half-baked interpretations.

'Does it speak to you?' a voice said beside him.

The woman who stopped alongside him had a flute of champagne in one hand and an easy, confident smile. Her dress was deep blue and clung to her figure, the kind that hinted at wealth without needing to be obvious. Her hair was cut into a sleek bob, dark brown, framing sharp, intelligent eyes. She was wearing subtle make-up, just enough to enhance but not enough to distract. Everything about her was controlled. Effortless. And yet, when Victor's gaze swept over her, there was something else. A restrained energy. Something beneath the surface.

Victor gave the sculpture a glance. 'If it is, it's speaking in a language I don't understand.'

She laughed, taking a sip of her drink. 'That's a shame. I was hoping you'd be able to explain it to me.'

'I could,' he said. 'But I'd be making it up.'

She studied him, just a little too long to be innocent. Then turned her attention back to the sculpture, as if giving him space to breathe. It was well played. He let the silence linger for a few seconds.

'You're not from here,' she said, still looking at the sculpture.

'Neither are you.'

Her accent had the edges of Australian English, softened by years of travel that had smoothed away its rougher consonants. It wasn't the voice of a tourist here for a gallery opening. Too composed, too measured. Not stiff, but controlled. He wondered what had brought her to Malmö. Business, most likely. But what kind of business brought someone like her to this place, tonight? The wrong question to ask aloud, of course. Even casual curiosity could plant a memory, and Victor's goal was to leave none.

She asked, 'Passing through?'

'Something like that.'

She nodded, letting his non-answer settle. 'I'm Saskia Olver.'

Victor hesitated for the briefest moment before offering his own name. 'Anthony Mitchel.'

A waiter passed by with a tray of hors d'oeuvres. Olver reached out at the same time Victor did, their hands brushing as they went for the same smoked salmon canapé. She hesitated for a split second, an almost imperceptible beat before she withdrew.

'You first,' she said.

Victor took the canapé and offered her a nod of acknowledgement before biting into it.

She watched him chew, amused. 'Fine art or fine food?'

Victor swallowed. 'I find canvas a little ... *chewy.*'

She smiled.

They discussed the art, the atmosphere, the champagne. Her responses were quick, light, but never careless. Still, he couldn't help noting the faint tension beneath her polished surface. Not nerves, but readiness. He recognised the type because he was the same. The thought lingered, an echo of instinct rather than conscious suspicion. It didn't matter. Soon, he would be gone, and this woman would be just another face among the crowd.

'Well, Anthony,' she said, shifting her glass to her other hand. 'If you ever figure out what the sculpture is supposed to mean, let me know.'

'I'll do that.'

She gave him a final, telling glance before stepping away, blending back into the crowd. Victor watched her go for a fraction of a second longer than necessary. Then he turned back to the sculpture, pretending to study it in case she decided to throw him another look.

He listened to the hum of conversation and the soft clink of champagne glasses. The air buzzed with anticipation, conversations punctuated by polite laughter and the occasional glance towards the stage, where a microphone stood waiting. The lights shifted, brightening to draw attention to a woman who stepped onto the low platform at the far end of the main room.

The curator, in a black dress with impeccable lines, her silver hair pinned into a sleek chignon that emphasised the sharp angles of her cheekbones.

'Ladies and gentlemen,' she began, her voice carrying

through the gallery with practised warmth. 'Thank you all for joining us this evening. It is both an honour and a pleasure to host such a distinguished group of guests. As many of you know, tonight's event is in support of the arts community, and as part of our fundraising efforts, we'll be holding a raffle shortly. Each of you received a ticket upon arrival – so now would be the perfect time to freshen your glasses and prepare. We'll be drawing the winning number in just a few minutes.'

Victor's gaze remained fixed on her, expression unreadable. He hadn't been given a raffle ticket because he had not used the front door – another detail that marked him as an outsider should anyone care to notice. Not ideal. But then, he didn't plan on lingering that long.

As the curator lowered the microphone, she scanned the crowd with a brief, sincere smile. Her gaze shifted towards the roped-off area at the far end of the gallery. The lighting remained low, but Victor caught the subtle movement of her hand – five fingers spread wide in a silent gesture.

Her lips moved without sound, but Victor read them clearly: *Five minutes.*

In the shadows beyond the velvet rope, Gustavus Håkansson shifted. The dim lighting obscured his expression, leaving only the outline of his suit visible as he inclined his head in acknowledgement. Then he turned, disappearing through a side door that blended seamlessly with the gallery walls.

Victor's pulse remained steady as he slipped his champagne flute onto a passing tray. He moved with the flow of guests, each step deliberate as he angled towards the corridor that led to the service area. He knew the gallery's layout by now – the hallway beyond that side door connected directly to the corridor he'd entered through earlier. A clear route, if timed right.

Victor headed back the way he had come, leaving the buzz of the exhibit behind as he moved past the catering station. The hum of refrigeration units and the clatter of dishes faded beneath the steady rhythm of his footsteps. Shadows folded around him as he approached the corridor that led to the back rooms.

Five minutes.

More than enough time to make the kill.

TWENTY-THREE

Victor made his way through the gallery's back hallway, the sound of conversation quietening as he moved further from the main exhibit. Two doors waited ahead. One stood open, revealing a small storeroom – bare shelves, stacked crates, a dusting of packing foam scattered near the floor. Empty. Which meant Gustavus was in the other room. Unlike the older wooden doors throughout the gallery, this door was pristine, steel-grey, its frame as new as the door itself. An oddity. No time to consider why.

He listened. Nothing. No footsteps. No voices talking. Maybe Gustavus was messaging a girlfriend or taking a quick hit of cocaine.

Either way, the target was alone.

His security detail elsewhere.

Victor eased the handle down, slow and steady, the click of the latch masked beneath distant laughter from the main hall. The door opened without resistance.

Dark inside. Only a single desk lamp provided illumination

besides a little ambient city light spilling in from a tall window overlooking the service lane at the back of the building. Stacked paintings wrapped in canvas leaned against the walls. Sculptures swathed in bubble wrap stood among crates marked with shipping labels. Open boxes spilled foam and plastic packaging across the floor, a tableau of half-unpacked wealth.

Gustavus stood near the far end of the room, back to Victor, his head angled downward, shoulders hunched, hands unseen and in front of him as though holding a phone. The height, the physique matched the photographs and description Victor had studied beforehand and had glimpsed outside the cathedral. The same build, the same haircut.

No hesitation. No words.

Victor drew his pistol.

The suppressor coughed three times in rapid succession.

Two shots. Centre mass.

A third to the back of the head.

And yet Gustavus did not fall.

He didn't even flinch.

Victor's pulse quickened – a rarity in such moments – though his breathing remained steady. Surprise was almost alien to him at this point in his career.

He never missed a shot at such short range, let alone all three.

His entire existence was predicated on controlling the uncontrollable. Predicting the unpredictable. And yet here it was – a moment that hadn't factored into any calculation.

His eyes refocused on the space between them, the glimmer of refracted light revealing the truth.

At the midpoint of the room stood a wall of cracked glass – invisible until now. Not the spider-webbed cracks of ordinary glass, but smooth impact patterns – a series of circular fractures radiating from the bullet strikes, the glass absorbing the force without giving way. The cracks were delicate white blossoms, every petal sharp and crystalline. Each shot had left a shallow indentation surrounded by fine, snowflake-like lines, stark against the transparency of the glass.

The *armoured* glass.

Victor adjusted his aim without thought, finger tightening against the trigger.

He fired again. Two more shots.

Then three.

Each round hammered the same point on the glass. Each shot blossomed into those white, circular fractures – petals of broken force – but the glass held. No give. No weakness. Ceiling to floor. Wall to wall. An impenetrable barrier with only a faint seam and a steel hinge on the far left, he saw now. And the lock – thick, reinforced, and deliberately placed out of reach. Victor took one look and knew the truth: he wasn't getting through it.

Gustavus turned at last.

Even through the distortion of the cracked glass, Victor saw the mask of calm settle over the man's face, eyes hidden in the gloom.

It wasn't Gustavus, just a man who looked a little like him. Same build. Same haircut. From a distance, in the dark, an easy deception.

The realisation was swift. Inarguable.

A switch thrown inside Victor's mind from confusion to certainty. This wasn't a coincidence. This was engineered.

UNLUCKY FOR SOME

He should have seen it coming.
Planned to perfection.
Victor had walked headfirst into a trap.

TWENTY-FOUR

The body double raised his hands. Slow. Deliberate. Until now in shadow, Victor saw what he had been holding in them. Not a phone.

A gas mask.

He slipped it on with unhurried precision.

A hiss echoed through the room.

Victor's gaze snapped upward. An air vent embedded in the ceiling, flush with the surface, hidden until it activated.

White gas poured out in a dense plume, curling downward in thick coils. Odourless.

Rapid.

Already thinning the air.

Victor pivoted towards the door without hesitation. His hand wrenched the handle. Twisted. Yanked. The mechanism didn't budge. Locked. An automatic seal triggered the moment the latch clicked shut behind him.

The new door. The new frame.

Trappings of the trap.

He braced his stance and drove his heel into the door next to the handle.

No give.

He raised his pistol. Fired into the lock. Sparks flew from the impact. Metal dented but didn't break. The reinforced steel absorbed the shot with ease.

Another kick. Harder.

Boot slamming into the door. Nothing.

Gas swirled around his knees, rising fast. His throat burned. Breath caught, ragged. His eyes stung as the chemicals seeped in.

Moments left.

Victor pulled his collar over his mouth, inhaled. Held it. Counted. He had seconds before the gas would cloud his mind, slow his muscles. Mere seconds more before unconsciousness or immobilisation or whatever might occur.

No hesitation.

He spun, gaze sweeping the scattered crates, sculptures, and packing materials. Plastic bags, foam, bubble wrap – junk until it wasn't.

There.

Victor snatched a plastic bag from a pile of packaging, tore it open with one sharp pull. Rough edges scraped against his fingers as he yanked duct tape from a supply cart. Tape stuck to his hands as he wrapped the bag over his head. Pulled it tight. Secured it around his neck with rapid, precise loops. The tape clung to his skin, biting into his collar. The plastic clung to his face. Maybe three breaths' worth of air inside the void.

His world began to blur behind condensation and white haze.

The gas thickened fast, spreading through the space in

opaque white clouds. Less dense than the air itself, it spread out with ease, stealing more visibility with each passing second until Victor could barely discern the outlines of crates and bubble-wrapped sculptures a few feet away. Beyond that, the world dissolved into shifting fog. The body double was gone from view – blurred, then vanished. Only the sound of movement from behind the armoured glass hinted that anyone was there at all.

The trap wasn't complete. Whoever wanted him unconscious or dead wasn't just going to leave him prostrate. They were waiting for the gas to do its job before entering to collect or kill him.

Victor had one shot. No time. No second chances.

He dropped low to the floor and braced himself for the next move.

Lying flat against the floorboards, face tight within the plastic bag, the air pressed against his face, saturated with the condensation, fogging the plastic until shadows smeared and shapes twisted into unrecognisable blurs. His eyes stung more with every blink, water spilling from them each time. The bag bought him extra seconds – no more. The gas seeped through, slow but relentless. Every heartbeat ate into his window of action.

The door would open any moment.

He aimed the pistol towards the entrance. No time to reload. He had burned through that when finding and fixing the bag over his head. No time for second chances.

They would arrive fast.

But they would be expecting him to be immobilised.

Victor took one of the three breaths and waited. The next move had to be perfect – or he wouldn't make it out at all.

Another breath. The plastic bag fogged more, vision closing in. His chest burned. His eyes stung.

The faintest creak of hinges before—

Footsteps rushed in. Heavy footfalls on floorboards. Multiple persons invisible through the fog of gas and haze of condensation.

Victor fired.

TWENTY-FIVE

The suppressed handgun clacked twice. A body hit the ground. Hard. He glimpsed shapes through the fog – dark silhouettes charging forward, coming closer, sweeping, searching.

Too many. Too fast.

His instincts flashed back to the main gallery – the physiques too solid, the postures too still. Not guests. Not the security of other criminals. Mercenaries. Assassins. Bodyguards. It did not matter.

He should have known. Too late now.

'*Where is he?*' one barked.

Another inhalation.

The gas worked fast – too fast. Even shallow breaths had pulled the poison into his lungs, seeping past the makeshift seal of the plastic bag. His head swam. Noises dulled.

He fired again. Twice. Heard another collapse. But more shapes rushed closer. Shouts broke through the hiss of gas – sharp orders and curses.

'*Stop him.*'

'*Don't kill him. Take him alive.*'

The last breath.

Victor's pulse pounded in his skull. He didn't have enough rounds in the magazine for blind shots into the fog. Every bullet had to count. But the gas would overpower him long before he could aim with any accuracy. If they rushed him at once, he wouldn't get off enough shots to stop them all. Hesitation meant capture. Slowing down meant collapse. Either way, the numbers were against him.

He couldn't fight through them. Couldn't shoot his way out. The door would have sealed itself again – impossible to break.

No way out.

The words beat through his head as if the gas itself whispered them.

Then he remembered the removal van outside.

A slogan half-glimpsed when he entered.

MOVING WITH PRIDE.

Victor acted before the thought could fully form.

He pushed to his feet, every muscle firing on adrenalin and instinct. Spun towards the window. The pistol barked – blind shots – his last remaining rounds punched through regular glass, splitting the pane with jagged cracks. The night air answered with shards and cold wind.

He ran.

The attackers closed in. Someone shouted. Another fired. But they weren't trying to kill. They needed him alive. That hesitation was his chance.

Victor barrelled through the blurs – elbows and shoulders driving into ribs, the empty handgun catching a jaw.

A man staggered back with a shout. Another lunged to grab him. Victor twisted, slammed the butt of his pistol into the side of the attacker's head, and kept moving.

Gunshots barked behind him. Not his own.

He reached the broken window. No time to gauge the distance. Impossible to do so with the gas impeding his brain.

Victor leaped.

He tucked in his chin, hands shielding the back of his head, elbows angled forward to break through any remaining glass. Air and broken shards crashed against him as the night exploded into motion.

He fell.

TWENTY-SIX

Impact.

Metal slammed against his ribs as he landed hard on the roof of the moving van. A fall of almost two storeys. The shock knocked the breath from his lungs, ripping through his chest like fire.

He rolled as he landed to disperse the energy, momentum carrying him towards the edge.

Victor hit the pavement in another lateral roll. Pain detonated through his side, white-hot and sharp, stealing the air from his lungs. His knees buckled as he staggered upright, the world tilting sideways as dizziness washed over him.

Plastic tore from his face as he gasped in air – cold, clean and beautiful.

He was home free.

And yet the pain of the fall endured, flaring beneath his ribs, deep and raw, the kind that slowed thought as well as limbs. A signal that something was wrong. Maybe a cracked rib. Maybe a shard of broken windowpane lodged in his flesh. But his fingers found no jagged edges, only warmth.

Wetness.

Blood soaked through his shirt, warm and slick against his palm. His breath hitched as confusion sharpened the edge of his pain.

Victor's mind scrambled to explain the injury, but adrenalin and gas blurred the details. With no shard of glass to explain the blood, it didn't make sense. The pain was too localised, too deep. He located the tear in his shirt – small, neat, precise.

Then he understood.

A gunshot wound.

Stress hormones surged through him – sharp, electric, clearing the haze of pain with a surge of raw survival instinct. He let them. He needed their help to resist the shock.

A bullet to his left side was better than the right, at least. It would have torn through his liver otherwise. Left side meant he had a chance. But there was no time to check if the bullet had passed through or lodged inside. The priority was distance.

He had to move.

Now.

Voices echoed from the shattered window above – shouts muffled by gas masks, urgent and close. The broken window framed shifting shadows, masked figures pushing through the cloud of white gas that poured into the night.

Victor turned away, each step pulling at the wound. The pain hit with every jolt of motion, piercing enough to steal his breath, but he pushed forward, burying it with the inescapable logic that pain was only a signal and he would fail to escape if he let it control him.

He heard the pulse inside his head, drowning out everything except the uneven slap of his shoes against the cobblestones. Running wasn't possible. His legs refused to cooperate, his body protecting the injury as best it could.

Gunshots cracked behind him – blind shots fired from inside the cloud of gas, chasing echoes into the night. Another shout. Orders barked in clipped voices. Too many to count. He didn't look back.

He moved faster, shoulder brushing rough brick as he pressed close to buildings alongside the gallery, using the acute angle as cover. His hands trembled from the incoming shock and exertion, blood smearing across his shirt, but he kept going. The pain would get worse. Every step he took made the wound worse. If he didn't get out now, none of that would matter.

Ahead, the service lane opened towards the street. The city lights blurred into the haze of his peripheral vision. He stumbled once, catching himself against the wall, pain again flaring hot enough to darken his vision. He pushed through it. He couldn't stop.

Because at any moment his enemies would be coming.

And he was bleeding fast. The blood loss would slow him further – how long until the weakness set in so deep that he could never recover from it? Fifteen minutes? Ten?

He pictured them spilling out of the gallery's rear exit by now.

Speed wouldn't save him here because he had none.

He had to lose them – disappear before the blood loss took away his legs. South-west led to the safe house, but he could not risk leading them in that direction. He needed to head north-east. Gain ground in the opposite direction, pull them astray long enough so he could double back without pursuit.

He had to rely on his wits now. His athleticism was an option reserved to the man he had been minutes before. Not this version.

Weak.

Slow.

He already had escape routes planned, although he had expected to be unimpeded. He had to improvise now, taking every new corner that opened up to cut down lines of sight. If they saw him, they would catch him.

Each breath was a torture.

Every footstep sent a fresh jolt of agony pulsating from his side, drowning out everything but the thought of gaining enough distance in which to vanish.

He stuck to the shadows, sliding along the brick walls, every movement calculated and yet too slow. His footsteps softened as he moved from cobblestone to damp pavement. The street ahead branched into a tangle of alleys and narrow lanes.

Victor resisted looking back under any circumstances, knowing such moves would give him away, each step a test of will against the wound in his side. His blood left occasional droplets against the pavement – a trail he had no time to cover, but they might not see it in the darkness.

The warmth of blood soaking into his shirt was a constant reminder of time slipping away. His breathing slowed as he forced himself to move with deliberate care.

No sudden sounds. No footsteps that would echo into the night.

Ahead, neon lights flashed against wet pavement. Bass-heavy music pulsed through the air, blending with ever-louder drunken laughter.

Victor pushed on towards the noise, towards the inevitable crowds enjoying the city's nightlife.

Lose them here, then double back towards the safe house. He just had to stay ahead long enough to blend in and disappear before the blood loss took him down for good.

He had to let the night swallow him whole.

TWENTY-SEVEN

People spilled from bars and clubs – clusters of friends leaning on one another, couples locked together, groups swaying
to music only they could hear. The air smelled of alcohol,
sweat and the mingling of many perfumes and colognes.

Victor kept his head down, moving through the crowd
with quick, deliberate steps, fighting the urge to collapse
with each jolt of self-serviced agony. He adjusted his gait,
trying to mask the limping shuffle as best he could. A pair
of laughing women stumbled past him, one almost colliding
into his shoulder, their obliviousness a perfect shield.

Behind him, shadows filtered into the neon haze.

His pursuers spread out along the edges of the crowd –
dark shapes of impending doom, eyes scanning the shifting
chaos. They moved with purpose, slower than they wanted
to, their presence restrained by the crowd's density. Running
would draw too much attention. Weapons even more.

They fanned out, breaking into smaller groups, sweeping
the area with more efficiency.

Victor slid between a group of men arguing over cab fare, using them as cover to pivot towards a side alley. His vision narrowed – fatigue gnawing at the edges of his adrenalin rush.

But he couldn't stop now.

He needed distance and yet he had lost the little lead he'd had. The business of the nightlife district bought him precious moments. If he could vanish before they tightened the net, he might just make it.

Bright lights faded into shadow, replaced by the buzz of a struggling streetlamp. He smelled grilled meat, fried dough and the tang of soy and spice. At the far end of the alley, rows of food stalls stood with their awnings sagging from age and rain, while vendors called out their offerings to revellers and tourists.

He passed a stall displaying hand-painted pottery, rows of delicate bowls and vases balanced precariously atop narrow shelves. His shoulder clipped the edge of a display as he passed, sending ceramics crashing to the ground. A vendor shouted in frustration as shards scattered across the pavement, the sudden noise cutting through the low murmur of the market.

Victor didn't stop. The commotion drew attention but still bought him seconds – enough to blur his trail as his pursuers paused at the alley's entrance. He slipped past a stall where skewers of meat smoked over an open grill, the air thick with grease and heat.

At the market's far edge, fluorescent lights marked the entrance to an underground rail station.

Concrete steps descended, promising tunnels and crowds – cover, if he could reach them. Victor's steps faltered as dizziness surged, but he forced himself forward. The pain in his side was rising. The adrenalin that had dulled it was beginning to fade and the willpower he was using to supplement the hormonal painkiller could only do so much when he had to focus on avoiding his pursuers.

The sound of hurrying footsteps against pavement echoed behind him, closer than before.

No more mistakes. No more noise.

Victor crossed the final stretch of pavement and disappeared down the stairs, vanishing into the depths of the city's underground labyrinth.

Moments later, he lowered himself onto a bench along one of the platforms, agony flaring beneath his ribs as his blood-soaked shirt clung to his side. His breath came shallow, controlled, though each inhalation sent fresh pulses of heat through his chest. Ever more sweat glistened on his brow. He kept his head down, gaze away from anyone who might see his distress and offer their help.

Swedes were nice people.

Niceness here would get him killed.

The platform stretched ahead – quiet at this hour between the end of the working day and far from the end of a fun evening. A nearby man scrolled through his phone, oblivious. A couple murmured to each other near the edge, waiting for the next train. A woman adjusted her shopping bag, glancing at the display overhead.

The rumble of trains echoed through the station, accompanied by the occasional drip of water from unseen pipes. Posters for concerts and local events peeled at the edges, their colours faded and smudged with city grime.

A billboard advertised private health insurance.

Too late for that, Victor thought.

Vibrations trembled through the concrete floor – distant trains moving somewhere deeper within the tunnels. The tracks expanded into darkness, their steel rails glinting where the light touched them before vanishing into the void. Along the far wall, a digital schedule flickered with the arrival times of the next trains.

He scanned the platform, aware now of how cool the air felt against his face.

He tried not to clench his jaw as the pain intensified. His strong masseter muscles would pop out in hard relief under the stark lights above.

More and more people filled up the platform as the time to departure grew closer.

The display told him he had one more minute to endure.

Just one more minute and he had escaped.

He would return to his safe house to patch himself up and hurry to meet Scragg at the rendezvous.

He had failed to complete his contract, had walked into a trap in the process, and none of that mattered right now.

He would meet Scragg, board the cargo ship and he was gone.

When he was far away from here he could start working out what had gone so wrong.

Somewhere nearby, the mechanical groan of a train slowing into a nearby platform reverberated through the tunnels, a reminder that escape was close – but not without risk.

Victor's gaze focused on the far end of the platform where shadows appeared in the stairwell.

Moving with haste.

They were coming.

TWENTY-EIGHT

Not chasing – searching, he realised. Checking every corridor, every platform. They'd anticipated this move. The station entrance was an obvious possibility they could not ignore. He had been predictable and yet there had been no other choice.

If they saw him now, there'd be nowhere to run. The next train would only trap him in a steel carriage with no escape.

Victor stood, putting his back towards the approaching silhouettes before they could lock in on him. He veered towards a nearby corridor branching off the main platform, footsteps controlled despite the urgency.

The rumble of an approaching train loudened behind him, masking the echo of footsteps and the shuffle of searchers moving closer.

They hadn't seen him yet because he heard no shouts for people to get out of the way and no running footfalls either.

But they were close.

Navigating his way back through the station, Victor

emerged via a different exit, the rush of night air biting against his sweat-dampened skin. The city sounds seemed louder for some reason – the honk of car horns, the hum of traffic mixed with laughter carried on the breeze.

Across the street, beyond the halo of a flickering street-lamp, a fairground sprawled across the park. Bright lights of many colours spun and flashed against the night – reds, yellows and electric blues streaking across the dark shapes of trees.

Those lights beckoned him.

He crossed the street, each step now dragged against the ground, every jolt through his wounded side also sending waves of nausea all the way through his body and into his head. The warmth of his blood-soaked shirt was almost a pleasant embrace against the chill he felt more and more with every passing second.

The mechanical groan of carnival rides clashed with the high-pitched screams and laughter of unseen men and women and even a few children up late, their shrill joy an eerie contrast to the piston that was Victor's pulse. As he neared, the greasy scent of fried dough and roasted nuts were thick enough to cling to his tongue, now so dry it stuck to the roof of his mouth.

Inside the park's boundaries, to his right, a rusted barrel burned with orange firelight, casting dancing shadows on the grass. The hunched forms of homeless men huddled close to the flames, coats wrapped tight against the evening air. One of them in a long coat glanced up as Victor passed, eyes dulled and weary. The man's gaze lingered with curiosity but without alarm, as if sensing a familiar, and yet wholly different, kind of desperation.

Victor paused to catch his breath, shoulders tight, jaw clenched against the agony burning beneath his skin.

He glanced over his shoulder.

Figures rushed out of the station. Intense faces. Searching eyes.

They were good.

Anticipating his every move. Or the gunshot wound was dulling his edge.

Either way, this wasn't working.

Outside of the light of streetlamps, they couldn't see him. Yet. But, like him, they would see the fairground and be drawn towards it. They would catch up to him before he reached the safety of its crowds.

Fleeing was hopeless.

He needed to hide. The fairground was close, thirty seconds away, and that was twenty seconds too far.

Instead, Victor limped towards the circle of homeless men gathered around the burning barrel, each step a physical effort that almost broke him.

No one spoke as he approached – some ignored him, eyes fixed on the fire, while others glanced up with suspicion or muted confusion.

'Mind if I ... join ... you?' Victor asked, voice rough with pain and exhaustion.

No one answered.

No one told him to leave.

As welcoming an invite as he needed. He stepped into the circle, finding a gap between two men bundled in layers of worn coats and threadbare scarves.

Mimicking their postures, he extended his palms towards the fire, letting the heat seep into his chilled fingers. Flames cracked and snapped inside the barrel, the smoke rising in thin ribbons that blurred the colourful glow of the fairground beyond.

The warmth of the fire sank through his skin in an embrace he never wanted to leave.

He stood with his back to the rest of the park, shoulders relaxed as he strained to hear footsteps behind him – the crunch of shoes on grass, the rustle of approaching bodies. Sweat clung cold against his skin despite the fire's heat.

The air felt tight, expectant.

They had to be here by now.

Maybe they were standing behind him, weapons drawn. Maybe they'd charge him to the ground, pinning his arms before he could react. Not that reacting would make a single iota of difference in his weakened state.

Maybe this was the moment they dragged him into a waiting van, out of sight and sound of the world. Never to return.

There was no way to know. No move Victor could make.

It was rare to feel so vulnerable.

A new experience to know there was nothing more he could do to stay alive.

He pictured being bundled to the ground with no strength to fight back except to bite. Maybe tearing off the end of a nose, spitting it back to distract and horrify as he went for a gun.

Kill one or more before they took him.

Die fighting.

A fool's hope only because any bite would lack the force to split cartilage, any disarm attempt would be weak and clumsy.

Victor, a fighter until the very end, had no fight left in him.

A cough broke the silence beside him. The man who'd glanced up before – the one in the long coat who recognised Victor's desperation – grunted, 'They've gone.'

Victor's gaze snapped to the man's face. No surprise there – just a faint glimmer of understanding. He didn't know Victor's enemies, didn't know the stakes, but he recognised the weight of hopelessness when he saw it because he knew it well himself.

Victor nodded once – solidarity exchanged without words.

Little by little, he turned his head, muscles tightening in anticipation of movement behind him and yet anticipation was all they had to offer.

Nothing.

The grass stretched empty beneath the colourful glow of the fairground. The silhouettes of trees swayed against the haze. Somewhere beyond the flashing rides and laughter, distant shapes moved – his pursuers swept past him and into the chaos.

Victor exhaled, forcing air past the tightness in his chest. His fingers curled against the fire's heat as his gaze once more found the man with dulled eyes. 'How much ... for ... your coat?'

TWENTY-NINE

She swirled the champagne in her glass, watching the delicate bubbles spiral up towards the rim. The curator had just finished her speech, prompting polite applause and the faint murmur of anticipation for the upcoming raffle. Around her, guests adjusted their posture, fingers grazing the edges of raffle tickets as they exchanged casual predictions of winning.

And then the men began to leave.

It wasn't a slow trickle of guests excusing themselves. It was purposeful – rehearsed movements breaking the rhythm of idle mingling. Suits brushing past one another with clipped steps, eyes locked straight ahead. She noted the way they moved – not with the hesitant pace of someone leaving a dull event, but with the determination of men heading towards something preordained.

Something serious. Perhaps dangerous.

She took a slow sip of champagne as they disappeared through side doors and rear hallways, their absence leaving a curious void in the atmosphere. The gallery's ambience had shifted – still polished on the surface, but with an undercurrent of tension that most guests, absorbed in their conversations and glasses, hadn't yet noticed.

Then came the sound. Muted, but unmistakable.

Gunshots.

Her ears caught the sharp cracks even above the hum of music and murmurs of conversation. Guests paused mid-sentence, exchanging puzzled glances. Some dismissed the sounds as something innocuous – a champagne bottle breaking, perhaps. Others stiffened, their expressions tightening with uncertainty.

More shots. Louder this time.

Panic rippled through the room. Conversations fractured into startled gasps and hurried whispers. Someone dropped a glass, the shatter ringing through the air like an exclamation mark. Guests clutched coats and purses, eyes darting towards exits.

Through the doorway, she glimpsed movement. The same men who had vanished earlier now returned – some crossing the gallery without a glance, others rushing past the open doorway towards the side street at the back of the building. The flash of their dark suits caught the light as they moved with the same practised urgency, their expressions carved from stone.

She watched them with curiosity, her pulse steady despite the rising tension around her.

Guests began to cluster near the main exit as the curator reappeared, her professional calm now strained beneath a taut smile. 'Ladies and gentlemen, I'm afraid there's been an incident. We must ask everyone to leave the gallery for the evening. Thank you for your understanding.'

With panic already setting in, the guests needed no further encouragement to hurry to the exit.

Saskia Olver finished the last sip of champagne, placed the glass on a nearby tray, and stepped into the cool night air.

She walked away from the gallery, her heels clicking against the pavement, her mind already turning over the night's curious events – and the questions they left behind.

She made her way to where a large SUV was parked a couple of streets away. A black people carrier with tinted windows, it sat in the shadows, unremarkable yet deliberate in its presence.

Without hesitation, she opened the rear door and climbed inside.

Four pairs of eyes turned towards her, expectant and sharp. The dim interior lights illuminated their faces – men and women whose postures balanced anticipation with restrained curiosity.

None of them spoke, waiting for her to break the silence.

Olver adjusted her coat, brushing non-existent dust from the fabric as she leaned back against the seat, eyes reflecting the glow of nearby streetlights as they met the expectant gazes locked on her.

She told them, 'I think someone just tried to kill Gustavus Håkansson.'

THIRTY

Victor stumbled through the door of his safe house, his pulse sluggish from blood loss, every step heavier than the last. The click of the lock sliding into place echoed in the silence as he pressed his shoulders against the door, head tilted back, breath shallow. Pain dulled the edges of his thoughts, but instinct carried him forward.

His hand clutched a shopping bag stuffed with medical supplies bought from a pharmacy nearby. There were several in walking distance still open so he had chosen the largest for the sake of anonymity, his awkward gait and pale, sweaty face less notable in a busier environment. The long, dirty coat hid any signs of his injury and the blood that had seeped through his shirt, jacket and trousers. He already had a first aid kit among his provisions, of course, but he knew it would not be enough to handle an injury this severe.

He moved through the apartment with care, each step a calculation against collapsing where he stood. The bathroom light flickered and shadows clung to the corners of the small room as Victor removed the coat, the jacket, and then unbuttoned his blood-soaked shirt, peeling it away, revealing the neat hole beneath his ribs.

The bullet sat just below Victor's left costal margin, having penetrated the external oblique muscle and grazing the underlying internal oblique. The round had passed through the soft tissue with enough force to tear muscle fibres but had slowed fast due to its subsonic velocity, lodging roughly five centimetres beneath the surface. The entry wound was clean – small, round, and dark with coagulating blood – but the internal damage was more complex.

Blood leaked from severed branches of the intercostal arteries, which supply the muscles between the ribs. Though none of the larger vessels – like the internal thoracic artery – had been struck, the smaller vessels' persistent bleeding had already led to notable blood loss. Victor estimated he'd lost roughly five hundred millilitres since being shot – enough to weaken him, but not yet life-threatening. The pain radiated through his thoracic region with every breath, the damaged muscle tissue pulling against the intact fascia.

Had the bullet struck the spleen or perforated the stomach, his condition would have been critical. Its trajectory suggested a shallow angle, possibly due to the shot's origin or his own movement when hit. With no exit wound, the projectile's presence would continue to irritate surrounding tissue, causing localised inflammation and increasing the risk of hematoma.

With the depth of the bullet estimated at five centimetres, Victor judged that it sat close to the costal cartilage, likely resting near the lateral edge of the rectus abdominis. The absence of haemoptysis – coughing up blood – suggested his lungs remained intact, though the proximity of the round to the pleural cavity meant even a slight shift in trajectory could have punctured the lung, resulting in a pneumothorax. Despite the pain and blood loss, his body was holding together. The key now was stopping the bleeding and preventing infection.

He considered his options.

He could try to remove the bullet himself. If successful, the localised inflammation would not worsen and the healing process could begin in earnest. Then, a few days holed up here until the wound had healed enough for him to travel. However, it was a huge risk operating on himself without a sterile environment and the proper tools. He could make things worse. He could damage more arteries in the process. He could cause an infection.

Not worth it.

He could not afford to remain in the city for a few days given that by now the police would surely be looking for him alongside his other enemies. Enemies good enough to have trapped him once already.

He needed proper medical assistance to remove the bullet and for that he needed to get out of Malmö.

To make his rendezvous with Scragg, he would only be able to do a rush job. A quick clean of the wound and then bandage it up. Good enough to make it to the cargo ship and leave the city, but then what?

Two weeks on the open ocean with a bullet in his side.

A death sentence.

Scragg, and Victor's arranged exfil from Malmö, would have to wait.

He needed to patch himself up, rest for the night, then find a doctor to remove the bullet, clean and dress the wound and give him a course of antibiotics to ensure no infection.

A few more days in the city would be a huge risk, of course, and yet a lesser risk than a fortnight drifting injured on the Atlantic.

The first aid kit waited packed into his go-bag – a compact, meticulously stocked case that had seen too much use. Victor placed it beside the sink, forcing his breath steady as he laid out antiseptic, sutures and gauze pads with methodical precision.

The sting of antiseptic burned sharp and deep as he cleaned the wound of blood and debris from his clothing.

His hands remained steady as he threaded the needle, the practised rhythm of each stitch pulling flesh together with precise tension. The pain built with every pull, sweat dripping from his brow as muscles clenched and spasmed. The bathroom walls seemed to close in as dizziness threatened to drag him down, but Victor gritted his teeth and continued.

Minutes passed in silence, broken only by ragged breathing and the faint hiss of his exhalation as he secured the last suture. A pressure dressing wrapped tight against his ribs, sealing the wound and staunching the blood flow. The adhesive clung to sweat-damp skin as he secured the final strip.

Victor leaned against the sink, palms pressed flat against cold porcelain, breath shallow but steady. His reflection in the mirror was a hollow-eyed figure, pale with exhaustion but alive.

The worst was done.

For now.

Pushing away from the sink, he moved to the bed with his last reserves of strength. The mattress creaked beneath his weight as he collapsed onto his back, the ceiling swimming as his pulse throbbed in his ears. Each breath tugged at the fresh stitches, but the pain was more muted now – overshadowed by sheer exhaustion.

As the stress hormones left his blood, thoughts began to piece themselves together, fragments of the night falling into place. The trap. The glass. The gas. His mind replayed each moment in sharp flashes, questions forming even as fatigue dragged him towards sleep.

He recalled the moving van and the workers unloading the heavy panes of glass on the trolley. He had watched them ferry in the pieces of the trap and yet had been oblivious to his peril.

He needed rest.

Forty-eight hours at least – long enough for the body's natural clotting and tissue repair processes to take hold. Moving too soon risked internal haemorrhaging and shock. It was a gamble either way. Staying put meant risking discovery. Maybe his attackers would be combing the city, eyes on every railway station and checkpoint, searching alleys and abandoned buildings.

But out there, injured and slow, he'd be easier to catch.

Here, in the safe house, he had supplies. Shelter. Enough food and water to see him through the next few days. The walls were thick, the blinds heavy and drawn. It wasn't perfect – no place ever was – but it was the lesser of two evils.

He'd wait. Let his body gather strength. Then, when the bleeding slowed and his muscles could bear weight without screaming in protest, he'd move. Find a surgeon who could remove the bullet properly, away from prying eyes. After that, reach out to Scragg and arrange another cargo ship out of here.

But until then, the only way forward was to stop.

To endure.

THIRTY-ONE

The bullet impact marks in the armoured glass had a certain beauty to them, Jorund Håkansson thought. More pleasing by far than the bodies of two of his security personnel lying splayed on the floor. Cold air blew in from outside via the shattered window but could do nothing to reduce the temperature of his fury.

Resting his palms on the glass wall, he set his forehead against it too.

'Someone explain to me what went wrong,' Jorund Håkansson growled, his voice low and edged with contempt. 'Gas. Armoured glass. An unbreakable door.' Håkansson's hand slammed the glass wall. 'And still, he got away.'

He turned around.

By the door, Magnar Kaale stood as a statue carved from dependability – tall, broad-shouldered, his eyes cold and watchful, betraying nothing. His face belonged to a different time – sharp-boned and angular, the kind of features carved from hard winters and harder work. In that other time, he would have been first to leap off the longship, axe in both hands.

Kaale had not been involved in the fiasco.

Unlike Håkansson's security personnel, unlike the body double.

Lukas Draeger waited with a presence defined by a quiet confidence earned through years of experience. His large, lean, muscular frame spoke of a lifetime spent honing his body for combat, and though he wore civilian clothes now – clothes from Gustavus's own wardrobe – the efficiency of his movements betrayed that military past. His short-cropped blond hair and sharp facial features bore just enough similarity to Gustavus Håkansson that, with the right tailoring and dim lighting, he could pass for the younger man at a glance.

Draeger had built his reputation as a close-quarters battle specialist within the Kommando Spezialkräfte – the KSK – Germany's elite special forces unit. Years of high-risk missions had made him an expert in both lethal takedowns and protective detail, a combination that, along with Wallin's recommendations, had convinced Jorund Håkansson that Draeger was the right man to safeguard his son by trapping the assassin. This was Håkansson's first time working with Draeger, though the crime boss had long relied on outside talent to fill the gaps where his own organisation fell short. While Håkansson commanded significant resources and influence, his network was built on power and control rather than paramilitary strength. His men were skilled at protecting him and his assets, but when precision and tactical expertise were required, outside specialists like Draeger became essential.

'My plan was solid,' the German said. 'The glass, the gas – all of it worked as intended. We lured him exactly where we wanted him. The problem –' he said in a careful tone, '– was the capture team. I feel the need to remind you that my advice was to use the other members of my operation. Like me, they are KSK-trained operatives with experience in close-quarters takedowns. But you insisted on using your own personnel. Loyalty over expertise comes with such costs.'

Håkansson's hands curled into fists. Fury burned beneath his skin, but he kept his expression cold. He knew Draeger was right. Loyalty had its limits. Yet admitting fault in front of subordinates was a weakness he couldn't afford.

The air in the gallery's back room shifted with the arrival of Police Director Wallin.

'We're mobilising every resource available to track down the assassin,' she said without preamble. 'All CCTV footage is being reviewed and a sketch is currently being composed from witness descriptions. My officers are monitoring transportation hubs. Hospitals are being watched – if he's wounded, we'll find him.'

'And if they find him, I trust they won't try to arrest him.'

'Of course not,' Wallin replied. 'If he's spotted, we'll alert you immediately so your people can handle the situation.'

From the corner of the room, Draeger stepped forward. 'Mr Håkansson, this won't be over until we finish what we started. I recommend again you bring in the rest of my team. I can lead the operation personally.'

Håkansson studied him, weighing the man's confidence against the night's failure.

His own men had fallen short, but Draeger's KSK

operatives had the skills and discretion he needed. 'How soon can they get here?'

'By tomorrow,' Draeger replied. 'If the money's right.'

Before Håkansson could respond, Wallin edged closer. 'There might be a better option. We can still use this situation to our advantage.'

Håkansson's gaze hardened. 'How?'

'We spread the word that Gustavus is dead,' she said. 'Publicly, the assassination was successful. It buys us time to hunt down the assassin without scrutiny – and protects your son from any further attempts on his life. Plus, whoever ordered the hit may reveal themselves, thinking they've won and you are without an heir.'

Draeger's brow furrowed, considering the tactical implications.

Kaale remained motionless, his gaze never leaving Håkansson.

Who said, 'Gustavus will not like the idea of being cooped up in the mansion.'

'But he will be safe,' Wallin countered. 'Behind your walls, guarded by your security, he is untouchable. No one but us will know he is there.'

'The boy needs to learn patience, so maybe this can be his lesson. Okay, we shall make them believe Gustavus is dead,' he said. 'And while they celebrate, we'll finish this.'

'There's only one problem with the plan,' she said. 'If we want people to believe Gustavus is dead, it needs to be convincing. Irrefutable.'

Silence followed, heavy and expectant. Håkansson's gaze sharpened, absorbing the unspoken implication beneath her words.

Draeger stepped forward. 'My team can be here by morning. I know how this assassin thinks. I've seen him in action. With my people, we can track him down and capture him. No more mistakes.'

Håkansson didn't respond. His focus remained fixed on Wallin's words, the weight of them sinking deeper with each passing second.

'It needs to be irrefutable,' he repeated, voice low and deliberate.

He moved until he was standing in front of Kaale. Close enough that no one else could see that, without a word, his loyal bodyguard reached into his coat and withdrew a .45 calibre pistol, handing it over with effortless discretion.

Draeger kept talking, his voice rising as he sensed the change in the room's atmosphere. 'Mr Håkansson, with the right resources, we can—'

The shot silenced him.

A single, sharp crack that echoed against the walls and rumbled out through the broken window.

Draeger's head snapped back, the bullet having passed through the front of his skull and exited out the back of it and then into the night beyond the broken window.

He collapsed straight down to the floor.

Håkansson kept the pistol aimed and his expression calm as he surveyed the body at his feet.

Kaale stood motionless beside him, eyes unreadable, as Wallin inclined her head – a silent acknowledgement of the necessity that had just played out.

She said, 'You identify the body as Gustavus, who – unbeknownst to you – took a last-minute holiday. When the threat has been neutralised, he returns from his trip, and your grief and failing health explains away the misidentification. All that remains is ensuring this deception is—'

'Now,' Håkansson interrupted, emptying the magazine into the corpse so nothing remained of Draeger's face, 'it's irrefutable.'

THIRTY-TWO

Victor's sleep came in fragments, torn apart by pain and nausea. When exhaustion dragged him under, twisted dreams chased him – shuddering images of glass shattering, gas swirling and faceless figures closing in. He woke every few minutes. Each time the agony spiked beneath his ribs, it wrenched him back to consciousness. Sweat slicked his skin, soaking the sheets beneath him until the fabric clung cold and wet against his back.

The room smelled of blood and stale air, thick enough that he could taste copper at the back of his throat.

When he woke to see the grey light of morning slipping through the window blinds, his body felt leaden, muscles aching with the weight of fatigue. Blood soaked through the sheets, dark and stark against the pale fabric.

He peeled back the blanket and stared down at the stain spreading beneath him, the wound at his side leaking where the stitches had torn open during the night.

Stronger pain flared as he touched a hand against his ribs, skin clammy beneath his fingertips.

Heat burned beneath the surface of his skin, radiating outwards despite the freezing cold that made him shiver and shake worse than any winter he had ever known.

The bleeding was insignificant compared to the reason for the uncontrollable shivering that took over his entire body.

He had a fever because the wound was infected.

Victor pushed himself upright, dizziness swaying through his head that reminded him of the thunderous punches of an Israeli beast who had beaten him half to death.

The sheets, soaked with sweat and blood, stuck and tangled around his legs as he swept them over the side of the bed.

His hands trembled as he braced them against his knees, the fever ensuring that no part of his body could remain still.

The pain of rising almost made him fall back down again.

The leaking wound required new stitches and yet blood loss was the least of his concerns. When the infection found its way into his blood, he would die of sepsis before the sun went down.

Victor's breath came in shallow gasps as he steadied himself against the kitchen counter, sweat as cold as iced water soaking every millimetre of his skin.

There was no time to wait.

He had no antibiotics with which to kill the fever, so he had no choice but to let his body fight it. But to do that, he had to remove the source of the infection.

The bullet had to come out – now.

He moved the kitchen table to one side to free up space on the floor.

He took a freestanding mirror from the bathroom, placing it on a chair and angling the mirror towards the floor. Then he pulled open drawers and cabinets with hands he struggled to control, searching for the tools he would need to supplement those he already had from the first aid kit. On a tray he laid out antiseptic wipes, gauze pads, surgical tape, a needle and thread for sutures, and a small bottle of isopropyl alcohol. A pair of scissors and medical gloves followed, though the latter were thin and already bloodstained from suturing the wound last night. From the kitchen, he added a sharp paring knife, clean dish towels and a roll of paper towels to keep the area clean and soak up blood, a wooden spoon and a lighter.

Finally, a pair of tweezers.

Fighting through the pain and nausea, he placed the tray on the floor and lowered himself down beside it, lying on his back.

The cool tiling sent a shockwave of shivers through his entire being that made him feel so cold he almost passed out.

Victor poured isopropyl alcohol over the tweezers, the paring knife and the needle, watching the liquid pool in a stainless-steel bowl he'd taken from the drying rack. The harsh scent burned his nose as he swirled the tools inside, ensuring every surface was drenched. He clicked the lighter to life, passing the flame beneath the tip of the knife and tweezers for added sterilisation.

He tore open a packet of antiseptic wipes, scrubbing the skin around the wound until the sharp sting cut through the fog of fever. Blood had dried along his ribs, dark and sticky, but fresh warmth seeped out still. The hole itself was swollen and raw, angry red against his pallid flesh. The fever had already begun to tighten its grip – if he hesitated any longer, the infection would sap what little strength he had left.

Victor's pulse made for a deafening bass in his ears as he positioned the handle of the wooden spoon between his teeth. His fingers curled around the paring knife's grip.

He stared at his reflection in the mirror on the nearby chair – half dead, hollow eyed, yet unflinching.

There was no other way.

This had to be done.

THIRTY-THREE

In the mirror, Victor stared at the wound's swollen edges and the darkened flesh surrounding the bullet's entry point. He bit down hard on the handle of the wooden spoon, the rough grain pressing against his teeth. The faint taste of old wood filled his mouth as he braced himself.

He had found nothing suitable to stretch and open the bullet hole wide enough for him to insert tweezers and remove the bullet.

Which meant he needed to widen the hole himself.

The paring knife's blade gleamed in the morning light sneaking in between the blinds.

The blade was sharp, of that he was grateful. And yet it was nowhere near sharp enough for the duties for which it had not been designed.

The first cut failed to break the skin.

He tried again, his left forefinger and thumb either side of the wound to stretch the skin taut.

He sawed more than he sliced.

Blood bloomed and a jagged, searing burn sent shock-waves of agony through his body. Victor grunted around the spoon, breath hissing through his nose as he forced the blade deeper, parting flesh with slow, deliberate precision.

Underneath the skin, the miniscule layer of subcutaneous fat yielded with sickening ease, pale tissue parting with the pressure of the blade.

Each millimetre dragged fire through the nerves below his skin.

Sweat poured down his face, pooling on the kitchen tiles under his head.

He angled the knife, slicing through the fascia with short, controlled back-and-forth sawing motions, every movement deliberate despite the tremor in his fingers. The muscle below resisted the blade – dense, fibrous. Honed from years of physical perfectionism. There had been no steak knives in the kitchen drawers otherwise he would have swapped to one for this task.

Sawing through skin, fat, and fascia posed little problem – it didn't matter if those cuts were messy.

Now, threaded with the muscle he had to saw through, were veins, arteries. One wrong cut and . . .

He concentrated.

Reminded himself of the mantra that had served so well for so long. Pain was only a message. A signal from the body to the brain.

A message, however loud, could be ignored.

And yet now that message was a booming thunderclap that could burst eardrums.

There was no ignoring it.

Maybe the fever or the exhaustion or the horror of

sawing a blade deeper into his own flesh meant even his self-discipline, the iron will forged through years of training and survival, was no longer sufficient.

Logic had failed. Reason offered no refuge.

His body trembled with the shock of blood loss and torn flesh, nerves ablaze with signals too intense to compartmentalise. Yet he knew that surrendering to the pain meant death.

There was only one option: escape.

Not through movement, but through memory.

Victor forced his mind to shift, wrenching his focus from the searing agony beneath his ribs to the distant corridors of his past – the places he had locked away, recollections buried beneath layers of purpose and control. Each memory was a door he had sealed with deliberate force, knowing what lay beyond.

Yet now, those same memories offered a refuge from the pain consuming his present.

He let the first door crack open.

The air changed around him.

No longer cool tiles beneath his back but cold stone beneath his knees. Not his laboured breathing and his pulse in his ears.

Instead, a voice – sharp, authoritative – echoed through the space.

'If you become no one,' she had told him while laying out playing cards on the floor. 'You will feel as no one.'

His heart rate slowed as the weight of the present faded, replaced by the shadows of a time when pain had been both a lesson and a consequence. The memory wrapped around him, harsh yet grounding, pulling his awareness further from the agony that threatened to consume him.

'I don't care.'

'Today you don't care,' she said. 'Tomorrow you will go insane without a sense of identity.'

He looked at the three jacks in his hand. 'Why do we play so many games of cards?'

'Because you need to be patient and you need to read other people and not be read in return.'

'I thought I just had to put a bullet in a target's head.'

'Every dead killer you encounter in the future will have thought the same.'

Victor's mind elsewhere, he tried again, sawing the paring knife's blade through the muscle with a hand that only trembled a little.

Blood welled up to fill the hole and spill outwards.

He swapped out the two other cards and drew two more. He kept his face even as he saw the fourth jack.

'Didn't you once tell me I had to become nobody?'

'You need to be a nobody, forgettable, unremarkable. But you cannot be "no one" because you will always be you, even leaving your old life behind. You need to know who you are, even though you'll be the only one who will.'

He dropped the knife with a clatter and snatched a folded towel, pressing it hard against the wound. Pressure sent fresh misery rippling through his side, and the wooden spoon creaked between his clenched teeth.

He forced himself to take slow, shallow breaths, counting each inhalation against the pulse of pain that threatened to drag him under. The room swayed around him, fever and blood loss seeping into the edges of his vision as shadows waiting to steal away the daylight.

'You are young,' she said to him. 'You will get it one day.

But, until then, you only need do as I tell you. Pick a name. Choose who you will become. The first name that pops into your head is the person you are from this point forward.'

His lips parted.

'No, don't tell me,' she barked. 'That name is for you and you alone. That name is now you, the "you" you are now sitting before me and the "you" you will always be from this moment onwards. Any name you had before now belonged to someone else. If you survive for any length of time in this life then you will have dozens, if not hundreds, of identities. You will refer to yourself by thousands of names, have thousands of different people call you those names, think of you as those names, believe you are those people. If you're not careful, you too will start believing you are these people. Then, when you need to take off that mask and be you once more, that "you" will be diluted and that will be when you're killed. And yet, if through all those identities, all that acting and pretending, you have the name you choose for yourself kept locked in your head at all times, when the mask comes off the you behind it shall be terrifying.'

When the worst of the bleeding slowed, Victor set the towel aside, hands slick with sweat and blood as he picked up the tweezers.

He stared hard into the mirror, eyes searching through the torn muscle for the dull gleam of the bullet lodged deep within.

Nothing but blood and yet he knew it was there, sunken beneath the bright red pool.

His jaw clenched tighter, the wooden spoon cracking beneath the strain of his teeth. Splinters bit into his gums, the taste of wood not unpleasant as he lowered the tip of the tweezers into the hole he had widened.

Deeper they went, two centimetres inside his body, three.

His hand shook, jerked.

The tips of the tweezers scratched against rib, a sensation that rattled through him as pure horror.

But he ignored it because—

He went all-in. She did the same and laid down her cards: a full house of kings and threes.

There.

In the mirror, he glimpsed gleaming steel in the blood.

Metal met metal with a faint click.

Victor inhaled and reduced the pressure of his grip on the tweezers so the tips spread.

With tiny motions he moved them back and forth until he found the edges of the bullet.

He lowered the tweezers deeper and clamped them around it. The pressure sent a fresh searing dagger through his side, bright and blinding, but he didn't stop.

Every millimetre he withdrew the tweezers he hoped for death to end the suffering.

Sweat poured into his eyes as his fingers trembled with the effort to hold the tweezers steady.

The wooden spoon cracked.

Splinters stabbed into his gums, sharp enough to draw blood, but he bit down harder, refusing to let go.

His vision swam with black spots. His hands shook. But he kept pulling.

He smiled and showed the four jacks.

Four centimetres, three, two—

And then—

Victor's grip faltered.

His sweat-slicked fingers clamped tighter around the tweezers, but the smooth, blood-coated bullet slipped free of the metal arms with a sudden release of pressure that sent it springing backward – deeper into torn muscle and raw nerve endings.

A white-hot bolt of torture ignited beneath his ribs, sharper than any pain that had come before.

The world contracted into a pinpoint of fire, nerves screaming as they were ripped out from his flesh one by one.

The black spots swimming in his vision burst and spread, each pulse of pain dragging him deeper into the dark. The edges of the mirror blurred.

His reflection faded into shadow.

And then, there was nothing.

THIRTY-FOUR

The bright lights from the café's windows cast muted shadows across the table where the six Fugitive Recovery Agents drank coffee and smoothies, and ate muffins and sandwiches. Each member of the team was no stranger to danger, subterfuge and high-stakes assignments. They were sometimes referred to as Private Rendition Specialists, but the spectre of the War on Terror had never gone away and 'rendition' was a dirty word in many parts of the world.

Besides, Saskia Olver preferred simpler terminology.

She was a bounty hunter.

Former Australian Intelligence with a long career in covert missions and human intelligence, Olver had been cut loose after a scandal involving an unauthorised black-site operation in South East Asia. Rather than fade away, she pivoted into private contracting. Now, she led a group who specialised in tracking, capturing and extraditing fugitives who believed they could evade justice by crossing a border. Her team worked for the highest bidders – often governments, corporations, or intelligence agencies, amalgamations of all three, or private clients.

A few years ago, Lukas Draeger – whose latest gig was pretending to be Gustavus Håkansson – had been hired as a private contractor for a high-profile security detail in Central Africa, protecting a corporate magnate with ties to international oil interests. What started as a routine protection assignment in a volatile region spiralled into a much darker situation. Draeger, operating outside the bounds of any official military or intelligence framework, had been tasked with securing a meeting between his client and a group of local government officials – officials with suspected links to arms trafficking and organised crime.

The meeting took place in a warehouse full of military-grade weapons stored in secret. Draegar, seeing an opportunity, later raided the cache and sold the weaponry to arms dealers in a neighbouring country. In doing so, he ensured that the weapons found their way to the black market, where they were subsequently used to fuel violence against civilian populations.

Thousands died in the resulting conflict, and Draeger's involvement was eventually uncovered. Interpol issued a Red Notice for his arrest, charging him with complicity in war crimes, trafficking weapons and aiding a foreign government's destabilising actions. The initiating party – those who wanted Draeger to face justice, and who had petitioned Interpol – was a coalition, stitched together by necessity rather than loyalty. Governments had their reasons – Draeger had sold classified information, brokered deals with criminals, leaked intelligence that cost lives. But they were not the ones who put up the real money. That came from corporations, from men in suits who didn't carry guns but who could make phone calls that were just as lethal. Draeger had stolen from them too. Not just money, but power, leverage, the kind of secrets that shifted economies and unseated executives.

The bounty on his head was pushing seven figures. More than enough for Olver's team to share and be well paid for a few weeks' work.

They had tracked Draeger to Malmö but had not a clue what he was doing until they had observed him entering the mansion of Jorund Håkansson. Utilising a combination of parabolic microphones, spyware, remote mics and cameras, they had learned his job in the city was to pose as Gustavus Håkansson.

Again, Olver had been in the dark as to why until last night at the gallery opening.

Throughout the day, local news had reported that Gustavus Håkansson had been killed.

'That's it then,' Ezra Greer said, his voice growling with frustration. 'We've wasted all our time. Draeger is dead, so we're left with nothing.'

Greer was a former US Ranger and her expert in direct action, urban warfare and close-quarters combat. His dark eyes were sharp and always moving. While Olver masterminded the strategies, Greer ensured they were executed. Grey haired and grey bearded, he had more experience than Olver had years on this Earth.

Next to Greer was Celeste Perrot. Former GIGN, Perrot's reputation as a sniper was legendary. After a failed counterterrorism mission that led to civilian casualties, she left her unit and found a new home in private contracting. She operated in the team almost entirely as backup. They extradited targets, not killed them. Still, it was easier to make the capture knowing Perrot was peering down her scope. Her cool, composed demeanour made her the perfect counterbalance to Greer's aggression.

Perrot, in her rustic French accent, asked, 'And now we're done we just walk away?'

Greer leaned back, arms crossed, his expression dark. 'We've burned resources on this. The time, the effort. All for what? A corpse.'

Olver's lips barely moved as she spoke, but her voice carried an air of calm certainty. 'That's not the whole story. There's still a chance of a payday.'

Daria Novak's eyes flicked to her phone, keeping one ear on the conversation, but her mind seemed elsewhere. 'How? We were hired to bring him in alive. There's nothing left now but a body. No life, no bounty. We're all in the red now. I really needed this payday.'

Novak was their tech and recon specialist. Former Russian Military Intelligence, Novak could infiltrate any system, track mobile devices and manipulate electronic security with a few keystrokes. She was the unseen eye of the team, always watching, always listening, ensuring their tracks were covered while they pursued their targets.

'Draeger was playing the part of Gustavus Håkansson,' Olver began. 'But why? A body double, obviously. One hired just before it's been announced Gustavus is dead? Please, that's no coincidence. Something's going on, something that Old Man Håkansson put a lot of effort and money into. We know Draeger charged a pretty penny.'

Greer grunted. 'I haven't slept enough to decipher your riddles.'

Olver smiled. 'Remember: every reaction needs an action. Therefore a body double for Gustavus was needed because Daddy found out there would be an *action* against him.'

There was a long pause.

Draganović spoke first, his voice blunt. 'Draeger was bait to lure the assassin into a trap.'

Marko Draganović was the team's heavy hitter. Ex-Special Police from Croatia, Draganović was raw, aggressive and effective. He wasn't subtle, but he got results. When the plan required brute force, Draganović was the one to break down the door, clear the room and get the job done.

Therefore, Olver was a little surprised that he had worked it out first.

'Not that I knew it at the time,' she said, 'but I met the shooter at the opening.'

She enjoyed the accidental, yet satisfying, synchronicity of everyone's head rotating towards her at the same time.

'He didn't say much, but he looked … off. Something about him didn't feel right. I couldn't quite place it, but my instincts told me he was more than just a guest. Now, I've worked it out. He didn't ask a single question. Not about me, not about my dress. Nothing. I didn't do it either, naturally, and yet I was blind to the fact he was working from the very same playbook.'

Draganović furrowed his brow. 'Why does any of this matter now? You mentioned the chance of another payday and I'm not seeing it.'

Emil Syed had not spoken so far, his sharp eyes scanning the room with quiet intensity, but his eyelids were heavy. Once an officer in Egyptian Intelligence, Syed was a pure tracker – a master of forensics, footprint analysis and behavioural analysis. He was the reason why the team never lost a trail, the reason they always knew where their target would go next. His uncanny ability to predict movements made him invaluable when a target was elusive.

Olver gestured for Syed to explain.

'I was in the side street behind the art gallery last night,' Syed said to his teammates. 'I saw the guy throw himself out of a window, land on a moving van, and roll off onto the cobblestones. He was so focused on escaping the Håkansson security guys behind him, he wasn't looking for someone already ahead of him.'

'A lot of good that does us,' Draganović hissed. 'He could be anywhere by now.'

Olver laughed. 'Oh, Marko, you sweet summer child.' She turned her head to look out of the window and across the street to where a row of town houses lay. Most had been converted into apartments long ago. 'Third floor. He's been there all night, hasn't he, Emil?'

Syed yawned.

'Before you ask,' she continued, 'no, we don't know who he is and we don't know if there are any international warrants on him that we can cash in. But a man like that has a chequered past just doing his job. Someone out there will pay good money for him, I'm sure. Except that isn't necessary. Lest we forget, Jorund Håkansson went to a lot of trouble to lure him into a trap that failed. Imagine how pleased, and *generous*, he will be when we knock on his door to deliver the assassin wrapped in a bow.'

THIRTY-FIVE

Scragg had been busy all morning, handling a few clients, making some arrangements and dodging the occasional trouble that seemed to follow him like a shadow. There were always people looking for a fixer, someone who could get things done without asking too many questions, and plenty of those looking for that fixer didn't want to be best friends. But now, with a bit of a break, he needed to fill his stomach. And when it came to food, Scragg didn't mess around. He wanted something that reminded him of home, something with substance.

He'd found the truck parked by the harbour – one of those shabby vehicles that looked like hygiene was a theory seldom put into practice – run by an older guy who probably didn't know the first thing about Kashmiri cuisine, but the kebabs were a damn sight better than anything else in the city.

He bought a skewer of lamb, fragrant and smoky, wrapped in naan with a scoop of raita on the side. It was all he needed – spiced just right, with a bit of heat but nothing that'd scorch the insides of his mouth.

Scragg found a bench by Malmö Castle, the sprawling parkland around the old fortress providing the kind of quiet he could appreciate. The sound of the nearby fountain kept things peaceful, the occasional bird call added a little bit of life to the air, and people passed by in their own worlds, too busy to pay any mind to a man like Scragg sitting alone with his food.

He had many things to do, many deals to organise, many relationships to maintain, but above all that he needed to find a way to get back into the good books of Leila Farahani.

Her ladyship was not best pleased Scragg had failed to provide the osmium he had promised and had made it clear in no uncertain terms that she would never deal with him again.

Still, at least he was alive thanks to that trigger-happy psychopath he knew only as Roman.

And for that, Scragg could forgive him for the no-show last night.

Scragg settled onto the bench, his legs spread out comfortably as he dug into the kebab. His hands were soon messy with the sauce, but it didn't bother him. Eating wasn't about being delicate. He took a big bite, savouring the lamb, his mind drifting a little. Things had been quiet for a few hours now, which always made him feel like he was due for some madness.

Which happened right on cue.

At first, Scragg didn't look at the man who flopped down onto the bench beside him.

Instead, he kept eating, one hand on the food, the other swiping some of the sauce from his chin.

But that ... that stench.

It was like someone had managed to distil the worst of a gym locker room and added something even fouler to the mix. Something dirty. Meaty. Bloody.

He frowned, feeling his appetite start to wane.

'You know, lad, you might want to feck off and treat those around you to that little slice of civilisation we like to call the humble shower.'

He didn't bother looking at the guy. Just kept chewing, hoping the bloke would get the *hint* and move on.

No sale.

'I canny be the first to tell you that you stink like a dead rat that's been blocking up a sewage pipe ... for a week.'

But the man didn't get up. In fact, the man seemed to lean a little closer, his presence seeping into Scragg's personal space.

He had to do a double take.

The man – who was still staring straight ahead, not acknowledging Scragg – looked like hell. His face was a frightening mask. Pale, feverish. His cheeks were hollowed out like someone who hadn't seen a decent meal in days. His eyes had that dead, sunken look, as if he'd been dragged through some kind of nightmare. He looked as though he'd just crawled out of a grave, still clinging to whatever life was left in him.

Scragg squinted for a moment, staring at the guy and not quite believing this was the same person who had saved his life when that bastard Järnberg turned on him.

The trigger-happy psychopath himself.

Roman.

'Bloody hell, what happened to you?' he said, his voice

losing a bit of its usual roughness, though it still held a lot of disbelief. 'At least now I know why you changed your mind about our cargo cruise. You know, it's been a long time since I've been stood up like that, Princess.'

Roman's voice came out weak, a rasping whisper. 'I've been shot. I need a doctor. One who can come to me, who can keep quiet.'

Roman was in bad shape, his whole body sagging under the weight of his injury. His skin was clammy, his eyes bloodshot. He wasn't just tired, he was *sick*, and not in a normal way.

'I can do that,' Scragg said, wiping his fingers on his trousers. 'But you look like you need that fast. And fast ain't cheap. You want quick? That's going to cost you a pretty penny, Princess. You look like you're dying already, so unless you've got deep pockets, you're not gonna last long if I have to start pulling strings.'

Roman, though still ghostly pale, managed a rasping laugh, though it sounded like it hurt him to do so. 'Money's no object. Just get me help. I need someone to take a bullet out of me. Someone who's got the tools, the experience. Antibiotics. Local anaesthetic. Someone who can … fix me, and fast.'

Scragg sighed, running a hand over his beard. He wasn't sure if this was something he wanted to get mixed up in, but there was something about the weakness in the man's voice that made him stop.

'All right,' Scragg muttered, 'I'll see what I can do. But like I said, Princess, fast costs a fortune. You got the cash to back that up, or are you just blowing smoke?'

Roman's gaze never left Scragg's as he nodded. 'I have the money. Just get it done.'

Appetite ruined, Scragg tossed away the last of his kebab before wiping his hands on his jacket. He wasn't sure how this was going to go down, but one thing was certain: it was going to get messy, and it was going to cost him a lot more than a kebab.

'Can you make it to my car?' he asked Roman. 'Or do you need me to carry your scrawny arse?'

THIRTY-SIX

The basement smelled of old rust and mildew, a toxic blend of stale air and forgotten machinery. Concrete walls, cracked and chipped, lined the space, and overhead, a couple of bare fluorescent lights hung bowed and skewed. Their flickering light cast an unsteady, harsh glow, making the shadows dance across the dirty grey floor. The tiles there were cold and uneven, some cracked and others missing, leaving a jagged pattern of smoothness and coarseness.

Victor was sitting slumped on a filthy deckchair that was present in the room for some reason he would never know. His fever was burning him alive, his vision swimming in a riptide and his body seizing with every passing second as he became unable to command it to move.

Without intervention, death was certain at this point, he knew.

His shivering was a relentless whole-body vibration impossible to stop.

'Bish bash bosh,' Scragg muttered, trying not to grimace

as he looked at him. 'You'll be right as rain by the morning or your money back.'

The Kashmiri Scottish Viking was perched on the countertop, arms crossed, looking at the woman he had brought along to fix Victor. A British national, she had a kind, pretty face and huge, bright eyes. Her movements, though – nervous and twitchy – spoke volumes about how unsure she was of the situation. She wore an oversized medical jacket and her hands were trembling as she checked through the small kit laid out before her.

'Of course,' he continued, 'if you want your money back it'll mean you're not right as rain so that will mean you're dead. In which case, I'll make sure you have a lovely send-off. Violinists and such. Tulips, whatever. The eulogy will be heart-wrenching. I'll tell the mourners the story of how you came to look like a massive fecking tampon.'

Victor glanced over at Scragg, who gave him a little wink, a crooked smile tugging at his lips.

'I'm pulling your leg,' Scragg said, leaning back with his arms folded. 'Christal is the best in the business, Princess. She works magic. She'll have you patched up in no time.'

On an old trolley near Christal, a black surgical bag lay open, its contents neatly arranged on a battered, chipped metal tray. The surgical instruments gleamed in the light, their cold steel almost out of place in the dim, grimy basement. There were scalpels with razor-sharp edges, neatly arranged forceps and long, thin tongs for gripping. A needle lay next to a small vial of local anaesthetic, the tiny bottle catching the light in a way that made it look far more fragile than it should have been. IV fluids hung in a plastic bag on a stand she had brought along.

Christal barely looked up as she continued setting up her tools. 'That's not true,' she said under her breath, almost an apology. Her voice was soft, reassuring despite her nervousness. 'Mr Scragg is being far too kind.'

Victor stared at her for a moment, trying to control the focus of his eyes that had no consistency. 'You've done this kind of thing before?'

His words were slurred from the exhaustion and the fever.

She hesitated, biting her lip as she looked over at him. 'No,' she said, as she adjusted a syringe. 'This is my first private gig like this ... like *really* private.' She avoided looking at him, the anxious energy radiating off her in a way he understood and she did not.

'I understand,' he wheezed. 'I'm ... grateful.' He wiped his forehead with the back of his hand, the sweat sticking to his skin. 'But I need to know ... discretion is part of the deal. This can't ... leave this room.'

Scragg let out a short, loud laugh and slouched back in his chair. 'Discretion?' He shook his head. 'That's the least of your worries right now, Princess. Maybe prioritise the big shite. Focus on staying alive, eh?'

Christal looked at Victor, her expression more serious now. 'Don't worry,' she said, a softness in her tone. 'None of this will go further. If anyone found out ... I'd lose my licence. I ... I can't afford that.'

Victor nodded, trying to steady his breath, but the pain from his wound and the fever pounding in his head were making it difficult. He managed to find enough focus to ask, 'Have you ... removed many bullets before?'

The question made her laugh, though it was more a release of tension than anything to do with humour. 'Oh no, not exactly.' She wiped her forehead with her sleeve, still jittery. 'That's not really . . . part of what I see at my practice.' She gave a sheepish smile. 'But I have removed plenty of rocks – rocks that get stuck in stomachs or intestines. I don't think this will be much different.'

Victor blinked, confusion marring his fevered face. He was too weak to be shocked, but it didn't stop him from raising an eyebrow. 'You're . . . a vet?'

Christal nodded, still fiddling with the tools in front of her, her face flushing with embarrassment. 'Well, I mean, not . . . *just* a vet.' She chuckled, nervous, her hands trembling again. 'I'm a surgeon. But, yes. I mostly deal with farm animals these days . . . horses, cows, things like that.'

Victor gave Scragg a look.

Who let out another laugh from the side. 'Beggars can't be choosers, Princess,' he said with a wink. 'She could be a fecking tree surgeon and she'd still be your best shot at avoiding slipping off your mortal coil.'

Christal's eyes flicked up to meet Victor's own, and she smiled, the unease still present but now tinged with a little more determination.

'I won't let you down,' she said.

As Christal began to prepare the anaesthetic and other supplies, the air in the room felt heavy, thick with the urgency of the situation. Victor was never comfortable trusting his fate to someone else and yet he had no choice.

Scragg moved in without a word, his hands firm but gentle as he helped Victor up. Who was shaking with pain, fever, and exhaustion, unable to stand on his own. Scragg had the strength to make up for the lack of Victor's own. He guided Victor's weight towards the old metal table at the centre of the room. It was cold, unforgiving, the surface slick and hard beneath Victor's skin as Scragg eased him onto it.

Victor's vision swam, growing fuzzy around the edges.

Christal was already by the trolley, pulling on a pair of latex gloves that snapped sharply against her wrists as she tightened them. She guided it towards the table with a quiet hiss of the wheels on the cracked floor, and the sound seemed to echo louder than anything else in the room. Victor's eyes flitted to her, watching as she set out her instruments, trying to steady herself. The sterile tools glittered in the dim light, cold and impersonal.

And then he felt it – Christal's touch, cool and methodical, as she leaned over him.

The needle pricked into his wound, the stinging sensation of the local anaesthetic seeping into his skin. It was a welcome relief to feel a different type of pain. She swabbed his skin with disinfectant, the alcohol burn sharp and biting.

Scragg stood by his side, his face a mix of sympathy and gruff determination. 'You've got this, laddie,' he said, his voice low and steady. 'It's gonna be okay.'

Christal's hands were sure now, steady as she held up the scalpel, the blade catching the flickering light overhead. It gleamed under the harsh, stuttering illumination, and for a split second, Victor thought it looked almost beautiful – something out of a dream. But then the reality hit him – the cold pressure of her fingers against his flesh, the blade hovering just above his skin, ready to cut.

He felt the faintest shift in her hands, the first touch of the scalpel against his skin. The pressure was subtle at first, then deeper, as the blade pressed into the wound.

'*Fecking hell*,' Scragg muttered.

Victor turned his head to the side just in time to see Scragg – his face twisted in disgust – look away.

'I can't watch this.' Scragg groaned. 'I've not long had my lunch.'

Victor did not need any effort for his mind to drift away from the moment and he found himself back on that cold stone floor.

'*I was lucky,*' *he had said, smiling as he eyed his four jacks.*

'*There's no such thing as luck,*' *she told him.*

Not an opinion. Fact.

Always afterwards, he would believe it.

THIRTY-SEVEN

The entrance hall of Håkansson's mansion loomed with cold elegance. Stone arches framed the space, their smooth marble glinting in the low light. High above, antique chandeliers hung from the vaulted ceiling, casting a golden glow that pooled on the polished floor.

Jorund Håkansson stood near the grand staircase, a glass of whisky resting in his hand as he watched the five figures approach. Their presence was palpable – a shift in the air that carried the weight of purpose. Magnar Kaale, ever watchful, stood near his master, his shoulders squared as his eyes tracked the figures nearing.

Leading them was Erik Stahler. Håkansson knew the man's reputation well. A former KSK captain, Stahler had led Germany's elite special forces in some of the most dangerous operations across the globe. His record was one of success through precision and calculated risk, though the scars beneath his tailored coat told a different story. There was something particular about the way he moved, as if every step had been planned before it was taken. His gaze, a pale blue that seemed to miss nothing, locked on to Håkansson with unwavering focus.

Behind him walked three other members of the team. One, broad and heavy, with a frame designed for brute force. Another moved with a predator's grace, silent and careful. The smallest, the only woman, was quiet and deliberate, with a gaze that seemed to weigh Håkansson against an invisible ledger. The fifth held back behind the others as a watchful sentinel.

Håkansson inclined his head, a gesture of greeting that stopped short of warmth. He said nothing because Stahler and his team were not here for small talk.

'Tell us what happened to Lukas.' Stahler's voice was calm, but there was steel beneath the words. A restrained anger. Muted grief. Quiet disbelief.

Håkansson motioned towards the hall beyond. 'Come. Let's sit down in the study—'

'No,' Stahler cut him off, his tone final. 'This won't take long. What happened to him? How did our friend die?'

'Very well,' he said. 'I trusted Draeger's judgement, but ...' He let the pause linger. 'The assassin was highly skilled. Draeger was overconfident. He didn't think it was necessary to include the rest of you in the takedown. He was content to rely on my men. I followed his lead.'

'Overconfident?' the brute stepped forward, so much tension in every fibre of his frame that Kaale shifted a little closer. 'Lukas was careful. He wouldn't have underestimated anyone without reason.'

'Careful isn't the same as invincible,' Håkansson replied, meeting the stare with measured calm. 'I trusted his

181

judgement, as did you. Maybe it was a money issue. Did he need the entire fee for himself to pay off debts?'

Stahler scoffed. 'Nothing like that. And even if so, Lukas would never put payment over a plan.'

'He had trouble in Africa a while back,' Håkansson reminded them. 'An Interpol Red Notice.'

Stahler had no choice but to offer a nod of acknowledgement. 'Whatever his other problems, strategic errors were not one of them.'

'I understand,' Håkansson replied. 'I have my friends in the police force doing everything they can to locate the assassin. When they track him down, you can find out first-hand what happened.'

For a moment, no one moved. Then Stahler inclined his head. 'Whatever you learn, we need to know it.'

'Rest assured, you will be the first to know when we find the assassin.'

'No.' Stahler's gaze held Håkansson's. 'You will tell us before you find him.'

Silence closed in around them as a held breath. Kaale straightened, his stance adjusting to the change in the room's atmosphere.

Håkansson nodded once. 'Very well.'

Without another word, Stahler turned and led his team towards the door. Their footsteps echoed through the hall until the heavy doors swung shut behind them.

'They know I'm not telling them everything.'

Magnar Kaale stepped forward from the shadows. 'I got that impression too. And I imagine they will be hunting him in conjunction.'

'If they find the assassin before we do they're not simply

going to shoot him, are they? They're going to question him. That would be bad for us.'

'Why would they believe him over you?'

'Because they already don't believe me.'

'Maybe Director Wallin can hinder them.'

'That will only strengthen their suspicions. We need to find this killer first and finish it. On our own. Did you reach out to your Russian friends?'

'Associates,' Kaale corrected. 'And yes, they were most helpful. They've recommended a gifted hunter of men who can be on the next flight should you still believe more outside assistance is prudent.'

'Wallin can only do so much for us. However sweet her promises are, knowing my time is short, she will choose her badge over my donations if she's pushed into a corner with this. When it comes to my legacy, when it comes to my son, that is nowhere near good enough. Have your Russian associates instruct their man to head straight to Malmö. Press that haste and secrecy are paramount. Money is no object.'

'Consider it done.'

As Kaale began to walk away, Håkansson asked, 'Before you go, what is the name of this hunter?'

'Funny thing,' Kaale replied. 'He has no Christian name as far as they tell me. But the Russians have a curious epithet for him.'

'Go on.'

'How much do you know about Greek mythology?'

THIRTY-EIGHT

Victor swam upwards through a sea of unconsciousness, head clearing the surface to suck in the air of reality once more.

The world around him seeped in as fragments of sound first: muted echoes against tile, a cough. His breath sounded shallow in his ears, every inhalation stirring the ache in his chest. The air carried a metallic tang, laced with the faint antiseptic bite of alcohol and iodine. Beneath it all lingered the stale scent of old concrete and rust.

His eyes flickered open, vision blurred and shifting as though the world had been smeared across glass. Shadows danced above him – harsh overhead lights softened by fatigue. The ceiling's cracked tiles and metal beams shifting into focus.

Something tugged at his arm.

Victor shifted his gaze downwards, blinking through the haze until the translucent line of an IV drip took shape. A bag of clear fluid hung nearby, the slow drip of liquid marking the seconds in a steady rhythm. The faint stretch of tape against his skin anchored the cannula in place.

Awareness crept back into his limbs. His fingers flexed, sluggish but obedient.

The fever that had burned through him was gone, leaving only a dull fatigue in its place. With a slow, controlled breath, Victor lifted a hand to his side. His fingertips brushed against gauze – clean, tight and expertly layered over the wound. Beneath the dressing, only a little heat radiated from the closed skin, and the sharp constant pain had dulled to a manageable throb.

Relief unfurled within him. The bullet was gone. The infection that had gnawed at his body had retreated.

He swallowed, tasting the bitter dryness of his throat, and let his eyes drift closed for a moment. There was still work to do – still danger waiting beyond these walls – but for now, in this moment, he was alive. And that was enough.

'You're awake, finally.'

The words came from the shadows beyond the pool of yellow light. Victor turned his head, vision sharpening enough to make out Scragg slouched in the chair against the far wall. His posture was relaxed but heavy with the weight of long hours. The faint rasp in his voice hinted at fatigue.

'How long . . . ?' Victor's throat felt tight, the words rough against his tongue.

'Eleven hours,' Scragg replied, stretching his shoulders with a wince. 'You've been out cold since she started to slice and dice you.'

Victor shifted, testing the stiffness in his side as he sat up. Pain flared, but the fevered weakness was gone. The ache in his muscles felt clean, the kind that promised healing rather than decay. His gaze flicked to Scragg. 'You've been here the whole time?'

He shook his head. 'Me and Christal took turns. Didn't want you choking on your own breath or something.'

Victor managed a half smile, the corners of his mouth pulling tight against dry skin. 'Thank you. Both of you.'

Scragg waved the words away with a casual flick of his hand. 'Don't get sentimental. It's all part of the service.' His grin tugged wider, eyes glinting with mischief. 'Besides, you've not seen my hourly rate yet, Princess.'

Despite himself, Victor chuckled, the sound rough but genuine. The pull in his side was sharp but worth it for the small moment of genuine mirth.

He shifted, testing the limits of his newfound strength. 'Where's Christal?'

'Getting a wee spot of dinner,' Scragg replied. 'Figured she earned it after digging around in your guts. I'll go fetch her now that you're awake.'

Once Scragg had disappeared down the corridor, Victor took a few deep breaths. Bracing his hands against the edge of the metal table, he pushed himself forward, lowering his feet to the cold tile floor. The chill shot through his bare soles. His legs, though stiff, held firm beneath him as he stood.

No stumble. No wobble.

The absence of that debilitating fragility was almost more profound than the relief from pain. His body, honed for strength, speed and endurance, had felt like a cage of dead weight since the injury. To stand now – to feel the return of balance, muscle and control – was transformative.

A tremor ran through his limbs, not from weakness, but

from the joy of movement. He drew another breath, deeper this time, savouring the stretch of his lungs. He was not whole, not yet, but the core of who he was – the strength that defined his trade – was no longer out of reach.

He took his first unassisted step and now understood the smile of pure elation a baby made when they did the same.

A creak of the doorway broke the silence.

Victor turned as Christal stepped into the room, chewing the remains of whatever she had been eating.

'You're looking good. Better than I expected, honestly.'

'Thanks to you,' Victor replied.

'It's not all down to me, you know. You did a good job cleaning and suturing the wound yourself. If you hadn't, it would've been too late by the time I got involved.'

Victor opened his mouth to respond, but she raised a hand to cut him off. 'And before you say anything about the infection – that's not on you. Wounds like this can get infected even in a hospital setting. Anything that goes inside the body brings bacteria, debris, bits of clothing, dirt – you name it. Infections happen even when everything's done by the book.'

'How bad was it?'

'The bullet might've hit some nerves and caused you a lot of pain, but it missed anything vital. Now that the wound's closed and clean, you'll have to deal with the discomfort, but at least the worst is over.'

Victor inclined his head in acknowledgement, though the tension in his shoulders didn't quite ease.

'Still,' Christal added with a pointed look, 'you need to rest. Be careful with unnecessary movement. No heavy lifting, no sudden twists. And travelling is not an option, at least for now.'

'That's out of the question. I need to travel. And quickly.'

Christal's eyes hardened with a mix of concern and frustration. 'Then it's not over,' she said. 'Standing up and sitting down on trains or planes for long periods is going to cause the damaged muscles to seize up. Internally, it's only pressure and coagulation that's stopping you from bleeding to death right now. Your body needs time to repair those blood vessels. Even if the wound doesn't open on the outside, it can reopen on the inside – and that's even worse.'

Victor held her gaze, but her next words struck home.

'You've already lost a lot of blood. I couldn't get more, and I didn't know your blood type anyway. At this point, even a small loss could cause serious damage.'

The door creaked open, and Scragg stepped back into the room, his gaze flicking between Victor and Christal. Catching the tension in the air, he raised an eyebrow. 'Don't tell me you're thinking of running off already,' he said, shaking his head. 'You'd be crazy to go through all that again. You've got a safe spot here. This chemical plant has been disused and abandoned for decades. No one knows you're here except me and Christal. Lie low, get some rest. A few days will make all the difference.'

Victor remained silent. Every instinct urged him to keep moving, to stay ahead of the inevitable danger closing in. He had walked into a trap. He had been set up. The client was the most obvious candidate for an enemy, and if they wanted him enough to go through all that effort, they wouldn't stop. Especially knowing he was injured.

Yet Christal's warning echoed in his mind. The risk of re-opening the wound – inside or out – was too great to ignore. Staying meant vulnerability, but leaving meant gambling with his life. Right now, resting here in this facility was his best shot at survival.

He nodded and they both smiled.

Whoever was hunting him would just have to wait.

THIRTY-NINE

The night clung to the exterior of the abandoned structure as a second skin – cold, silent and waiting. Rain had come and gone, leaving the air dense with the scent of wet concrete and rust. The skeletal framework of the plant loomed against the moonlit sky. Pools of stagnant water gleamed beneath shattered windows, their surfaces rippling at the brush of unseen currents. Graffiti scrawled across corroded storage tanks hinted at years of trespassers. Broken fences sagged along the perimeter, barbed wire twisted and tangled beneath the harsh orange glow of distant industrial floodlights.

Saskia Olver crouched behind the ruined shell of a loading truck, binoculars pressed to her eyes as she scanned the main building. Through the lenses, she tracked the faint glow of light beyond dirt-streaked windows, marking the layout in her mind. She adjusted her focus, picking out a faint silhouette behind a ground-level window.

Behind her, Ezra Greer adjusted the suppressor on his carbine with slow, deliberate motions. His gaze flicked towards her, but he said nothing. Years of working together meant they didn't need to waste words.

To Olver's right, Celeste Perrot lay prone atop a weather-stained shipping container, her rifle resting on its bipod. Her breathing came slow and even, her finger poised beside the trigger guard.

Marko Draganović paced a few metres behind them, shoulders rolling with pent-up energy. The Croatian moved with the tension of a hungry beast waiting for the cage door to open. His gaze kept drifting towards the building as if willing the target to step outside to be charged down.

They had tracked the assassin for over a day, maintaining a careful distance as they observed his movements. Injured and slow-moving, he had been easy to follow when he left the safe house, his pace betraying the extent of his pain. Their surveillance led them to a meeting with a local fixer – identified through background checks as a Scottish man named Scragg. The fixer then transported the target to this disused chemical plant, where a woman – Christal McCalla – later confirmed to be a veterinarian, had been waiting – presumably to treat the injuries that slowed him.

Since that moment, the team had maintained their vigil. Hours of patient observation, studying every exit and tracking every sign of movement within the facility.

Yet Olver's team had not moved.

Rushing a building blind, with civilians who could interfere or escalate the situation, was not their style. Success came from control – knowing the layout, the number of occupants and their routines before striking. Their patience was what made them effective. They waited not out of hesitation, but because they understood the value of time.

The longer they watched, the more predictable the target became. Eventually, either the civilians would leave, or the target would step outside – and when that moment came, they would be ready.

There was no need to step into the unknown when he would come to them.

'He's still inside,' Daria Novak said, updating from near the perimeter fence. Her voice was low, the faint blue glow from the tablet illuminating the angles of her face. Earlier, the thermal drone feed had revealed heat signatures within the building through the gaps in the roof – three figures, one moving more sluggishly than the others. But not since they had disappeared under more solid roofing.

'Quiet,' Emil Syed added, crouching beside Novak. He was listening with a parabolic microphone, trying to hear what the drone could not see. 'I can hear footsteps, but not from inside. There's a civilian on the nearby pavement.'

An industrial area, there were factories and warehouses surrounding the disused chemical facility. Civilians passed by now and again. As long as the team kept low and whispered, there was no danger of discovery.

'We should make a move now they've patched him up,' Draganović muttered. His breath fogged the air as he exhaled through gritted teeth. 'But before he recovers. We've waited long enough.'

'Patience wins the fight,' Greer countered, his voice calm but edged. 'This man's dangerous. No need to rush in with two civilians inside to complicate things—'

'One of whom is a veterinarian,' Draganović interrupted. 'I don't mind that kind of complication. Besides, they could be leverage. Maybe he will give himself up without a fight if he thinks they're in danger.'

Olver lowered her binoculars, eyes sweeping the team. 'They're not in danger, that's the point. We're here for him alone and we leave them be. No one gets hurt. No one ever gets hurt.'

Draganović said, 'If we wait too long, we lose the advantage. He'll heal, regroup and vanish.'

'And if we charge in, we could walk into a kill box,' Greer replied, locking eyes with him.

'Don't tell me a badass like you is scared to go in there.'

'Of course I'm scared. Only idiots are never afraid. It's fear that gives you your edge. I didn't get through Fallujah in one piece without being terrified. Tell me what courage has got you through?'

Before Draganović could answer, movement on the screen caught Novak's eye. 'Someone's leaving. Coming this way.'

Olver raised her binoculars.

'Target in sight?' Perrot asked through the comms.

'Hold.'

A figure stepped into the open air – broad yet lean – the fixer named Scragg. They had learned a lot about the man, his businesses, his habits, since observing the assassin meeting with him the previous day. A criminal, and former paratrooper, there was a good chance he could prove to be a problem.

Scragg's breath ghosted white as he lit a cigarette, the orange flare illuminating his face before he cupped his hand around the ember.

Draganović took a half-step forward, ready.

'This is our shot,' Greer whispered. 'We deal with Scragg

now, quiet and easy, and then either someone comes to check on him and we deal with them, or we move in and catch the injured hitman with his pants down. I'm not sure we will get a better chance.'

'Agreed,' Olver said after a moment's consideration. 'We move in.'

Draganović was the first to slip through the gap in the fence, boots far from silent on wet gravel. Perrot shifted position, tracking Scragg through her scope as she adjusted for the distance. Syed and Novak followed the Croatian's lead, their approach measured and precise.

Greer fell into step beside Olver as they moved in.

Scragg wouldn't know what had hit him.

FORTY

Scragg breathed out smoke into the cold night air, watching the ember of his cigarette flare and fade. The overgrown yard expanded around him – knee-high weeds poking through cracked concrete, rusted machinery leaning against sagging chain-link fences.

Somehow, Roman had survived the surgery.

The stone-cold psychopath didn't die easy, that was for sure.

The Kashmiri Scottish Viking couldn't help but smile.

A faint scuff against gravel shattered his mirth.

Instinct gripped him – sharp and sudden.

The rational part of his mind whispered that it was just the wind, maybe a rat moving through the weeds. But something deeper, older – his Para instincts that had seen him through Helmand – stirred in his gut. Trouble was coming.

Scragg pivoted fast, cigarette clamped between his teeth.

Shadows spilled from the dark – figures moving with purpose and precision. Black tactical gear, sleek and stripped of insignia, clung to lean, athletic frames. Not a uniform, but close. Balaclavas covered their faces. A variety of weapons held steady. Pistols and SMGs. One carbine.

'Fecking hell,' Scragg said as they neared. 'Don't you think you're taking this paintball lark a bit seriously?'

None of them reacted.

One figure stepped forward – a big guy with shoulders that could fill a doorframe. His carbine never wavered. When he spoke, his accent marked him as American. 'Where's the man you brought in here?'

Scragg took another drag, exhaled slow. 'I think you have me mistaken for someone else.'

'Don't waste our time,' another said.

To Scragg's right, a shorter man with a stocky frame shifted his grip on a compact submachine gun – Eastern European, judging by the hard consonants. Scragg's ear was not good enough to pin the accent down further.

There were two women, one of whom stepped closer, lowering her pistol and speaking in a softer tone. An Australian.

'We know he's in there, we know he's wounded. We know you met a veterinarian here to fix him up. Don't make this difficult. If you talk to us, if you cooperate, you don't get hurt and neither does he.'

Scragg rolled his shoulders, the cigarette burning low. 'Oh, you mean my mate Stavros? You just missed him, I'm afraid. Once we stapled him up he didn't fancy hanging around for tea and biscuits.'

The American said, 'Then why are you still here?'

'I like this place,' he answered. 'I stayed behind to enjoy the ambience. Place has a certain charm – bit of nostalgia. It's private. Perfect place for a marathon session of the five-finger shuffle.' He grimaced and rolled his hand around. 'That's why I stepped out for a ciggie. Got a *bastard* of a wrist cramp.'

The Eastern European's laugh came rough and sudden.

The American stepped closer, carbine aimed square at Scragg's chest. 'Last chance.'

'Fine,' Scragg said, sucking on the cigarette, the embers burning bright and hot, 'He's over by the—'

He spat the cigarette into the American's face.

As the big guy grunted and flinched backwards, Scragg lunged sideways, shoulder slamming into the stocky man's chest. The SMG went wide as Scragg knocked him down, snatching at the weapon.

Hands grasped at him as he tried to angle the gun to track the flailing American. Scragg twisted and elbowed, trying to break free as an arm snaked around his throat.

The Australian woman, calm and composed, pointed her suppressed pistol at his face, 'Don't make me.'

Scragg let his body go loose. 'You win.'

His compliance worked and the hands grabbing his limbs also loosened.

He snapped up the SMG.

FORTY-ONE

The muffled crack of a suppressed gunshot reached Victor's ears – a sharp, unmistakable sound even through the thick concrete walls. His mind registered it without hesitation, as familiar as his own heartbeat.

Outside. Close.

Scragg had stepped out for a cigarette a couple of minutes before.

Too much of a coincidence.

No time to think. No time to wonder if Scragg was dead, wounded, or still standing. No time to question who had fired the shot. Victor's body moved before his mind finished processing.

'Where are my things? Where's my gun?'

'I don't know … Scragg must've …' Christal blinked, startled. 'What was that? Where's Scragg?'

His hand closed around Christal's wrist, firm but not rough.

'We need to move. Now,' he said. 'No time to discuss it. Trust me.'

Confusion flashed across her face, but she didn't resist as Victor pulled her out of the room and through the doorway to the corridor leading deeper into the plant.

'Which way out?' he asked. 'But not the way Scragg went.'

She pointed to their left.

Victor moved with light steps, conscious of every breath, every heartbeat. His side ached with each stride, muscles stiff and slow to respond. Speed still wasn't an option. He could only move at a walking pace and that took every ounce of energy he had.

Christal's breathing was even faster now, audible in the still air. Her eyes were wide and her shoulders tensed with fear and uncertainty as the corridor opened out into an industrial mixing room of hulking steel vats, their corroded surfaces flaking under pale moonlight filtering through broken skylights.

Shadows pooled in the corners where pipes tangled overhead. The air was thick, holding the bitter scent of old chemicals, faint but clinging to the back of the throat. Rusted catwalks and suspended chains hung motionless above.

The quiet crunch of footsteps echoing somewhere beyond the vats – soft, deliberate – made Victor stop.

More steps. Closer.

He guided Christal to a cluster of overturned machinery – an old assembly station with rusted conveyors frozen mid-motion. Then he gestured for her to hide behind a low control panel, its corroded metal frame almost invisible in shadow.

She opened her mouth as if to ask something but stopped, swallowing the question.

Her fingers gripped the edge of the panel tightly enough that her knuckles paled. She crouched lower, hands braced against the cold steel as she tried to slow her breathing. It took him longer to lower himself, teeth gritted as he went first to one knee and then the other.

More footsteps.

A professional's gait.

Victor's eyes searched the darkness for a weapon. With his strength still lacking, he wanted something sharp he could drive into a throat, but saw nothing suitable.

If whoever was coming checked behind this section of machinery, there was nothing he could do about it.

He had no weapon. He had no speed. He had no ability to fight.

The footsteps grew quieter, the professional continuing their search elsewhere.

When he could no longer hear them at all, he gestured to Christal to rise. She did, then helped Victor do the same, his hands gripping her arms and then shoulders to compensate for the weakness of his core.

Victor moved as fast as his injury would let him, guiding Christal out of the mixing room and through another narrow corridor. His breath came short and controlled, but every hurried step sent a jolt of discomfort through his side.

The air around them cracked apart with the sharp, suppressed bark of gunfire.

Metal screamed as bullets bit into pipes above.

Steam burst from a ruptured valve, pressurised water vapour locked inside for decades hissing as it filled the corridor with thick clouds.

The clang of ricochets echoed off the walls, and Victor yanked Christal sideways as shards of metal rained against the floor.

Victor glanced back – through the haze of steam, a single dark figure emerged at the corridor's far end.

The silhouette moved with purpose, weapon raised, closing the distance with steady steps.

Victor hauled Christal through the nearest open doorway, shoving her against the wall as he pressed his shoulder against the frame.

Her fingers trembled against the sleeve of his jacket. 'Who are they?'

'Doesn't matter. Focus on getting out,' Victor said, his voice low but unyielding. 'Your car – where is it parked?'

'By the machinery yard. The same spot where Scragg parked his car when we arrived.'

Victor nodded. Despite the fog of fever and half-consciousness that had dulled his memory earlier, the image came clear – the sprawling yard beyond the plant's outer wall, where rusted machinery stood like the bones of a forgotten age.

'Good. Get to the car and wait.'

'But—'

'No arguments,' Victor cut her off. 'I can't move fast enough. If you stay with me, I can't fight them and keep you safe. This is your only chance. Our only chance. Go.'

Christal's lips parted, her eyes bright with fear and hesitation. 'I—'

'When you get there, don't get in the car. Stay low. Hide somewhere you can see the car and the path leading to it. Wait three minutes – no longer. Check your watch the moment you arrive. If you don't see me after three minutes, I'm not coming. Get in the car and leave. Do you understand?'

Her mouth opened to protest.

'Go.' Victor's gaze locked on hers, unwavering. 'You helped me, now let me help you.'

Christal stared for a moment longer, her chest rising and falling with shallow breaths. Then she turned and ran, her footsteps fading into the shadows beyond the doorway.

In the corridor outside, the dark figure was approaching, steady and relentless.

Armed.

Victor let out a slow exhalation, pleading with his body to be strong again, to let him move with speed. The only answer it gave him was pain.

That pain could wait.

Survival could not.

FORTY-TWO

Victor hobbled forward, each quick step a deliberate trade-off with the fire gnawing at his side. The space extended ahead as the ribs of a steel beast – towering vats rising towards the ceiling, their corroded surfaces streaked with decades of grime. Catwalks criss-crossed overhead, their rusted frames casting jagged shadows down below.

The floor beneath Victor's shoes was a patchwork of cracked concrete and twisted metal debris – old tools, sections of pipe and shattered glass scattered across the ground. Puddles of stagnant water reflected glimmers of pale moonlight, their surfaces rippling with each distant vibration from the building's ageing infrastructure.

Once more, he would have preferred a weapon that was sharp, something he could use to pierce flesh with his limited strength. Once more, the environment denied him.

With no other choice, he lifted a length of rusted pipe from the floor.

The simple action was agonisingly difficult and ate precious seconds he did not have to spare.

Knowing his pursuer would be entering the space any moment, Victor hid himself, pressing a palm for support against the cold steel of a nearby vat, feeling the pulse of pain in his side as he controlled his breathing.

In this environment – a labyrinth of rusted machinery and broken catwalks – he could face an enemy with a weapon and emerge triumphant, exploiting the terrain, the shadows. But he needed his speed to do so, he needed to duck fast and riser faster. He needed his athleticism to act at the right moment, to slide or roll, or just to set his foot down in a slow, controlled manner to hide his footsteps.

He could do none of that here, now.

He had outfought many enemies because he could outthink them and outmanoeuvre them. He could still do the former but he could no longer back up those thoughts with action.

A professional in pursuit would not be reckless, he knew.

They would not choose the quickest, most obvious path of pursuit even when they had a lame quarry.

There were three main corridors of space: the central, most open one Christal had run down. Then one to the room's right when entering from the adjoining hallway, and one to the left.

He pictured this enemy as they entered the space, sweeping through the doorway

First, aiming to the left since a right-handed gunman – he had glimpsed that at least as they emerged through the shadows – found it easier and quicker to do so, then clearing right. Then, instinct and training would make them veer to the left.

Victor shuffled around the vat, heading towards that corridor. Moving out beyond the vat to a rusted hunk of machinery impossible to identify, pipes protruding from it and snaking around it and up and over the nearby corridor of space to then disappear into the darkness.

A professional always had to balance speed with caution.

A slow, methodical approach would not work here in normal circumstances because that would mean losing a fleeing quarry.

However, this professional knew Victor could not flee.

Listening hard, he waited.

Footsteps.

Again, a professional's gait, slow and controlled. Each footfall measured and patient.

Victor pictured the black-clad figure with their weapon held high and hugged close. A compact submachine gun, it had too short a profile to protrude ahead of them and give them away when they passed his corner.

Not that it would have helped.

If he attacked that weapon, he could not wrench or manipulate it out of their hands and he had no strength to bat it away even with the pipe.

He listened, trying to deduce the proximity of those footsteps with sound alone.

Seven metres away? Five?

He moved, slow and controlled, positioning himself at the edge of a hulk of machinery. His breathing slowed. Focused.

His fingers tightened around the pipe as the footsteps neared.

Only one chance.

Once he committed to the attack, it had to work.

He had to stun or disable his pursuer with a single blow because any counterattack by them would be impossible for him to defend against.

He adjusted his grip on the rusted pipe clutched in his hand as he pictured the enemy's approach. The pain in Victor's side pulsed in sync with his heartbeat, but he forced it aside, retelling himself it was only a message. He already knew he was injured.

The reminder served no purpose.

A shadow edged along the floor, creeping out from around the corner of the machinery.

Victor swung the pipe.

But at the machinery itself, making an almighty *clang* as loud as a gunshot.

Such a sudden, violent noise so close would rattle even the steeliest of nerves, would trigger survival instincts almost impossible to ignore.

That was all Victor needed.

An instance in which his enemy felt under threat, in danger, to flip the mental switch to change his demeanour from predator to prey.

Victor lunged as fast as his injury let him, emerging around the corner, pipe in mid-swing,

A figure, black-clad and holding a compact SMG, a mask over his face hiding his features but not his eyes full of surprise and alarm.

Not knowing how tall his target would be, Victor's swing was low to ensure his one chance to strike his enemy did not sail over his head.

It collided with the man's lead shoulder, the left, the impact jarring both the black-clad figure and Victor alike, whose breath caught in his chest as pain locked his muscles iron taut.

The gunman grunted and staggered to the side, colliding with the machinery.

Before he could recover, Victor forced the pain away and swung the pipe again, this time able to aim and cracking the gunman on the skull above the ear.

He dropped straight down to the floor.

Discarding the pipe, Victor retrieved the SMG from where it lay next to the dead or unconscious gunman.

Already suffering from making the attacks with the pipe, bending down was agonising.

But for a gun, he considered that a fair trade.

FORTY-THREE

Saskia Olver threaded through the network of machinery with her pistol raised, breath steady despite the adrenalin tightening her chest. The air smelled of rust and oil, tinged with the bitter residue of old chemicals. Beside her, Ezra Greer moved with practised ease, footsteps swift and precise, his superior combat experience reassuring her by his presence alone.

The echo of suppressed gunshots had destroyed any semblance of her calm professionalism moments before, and they advanced towards the sound, fearing the worst.

A groan led them to Emil Syed slumped against the base of a rusted machine, his head lolled to the side, blood matting his dark hair where the pipe had struck him. He had taken off his balaclava to compress it against the wound.

'*Emil*,' Olver gasped, crouching beside him.

His eyes fluttered open, conscious but dazed.

'He blindsided me,' Syed mumbled, wincing. 'Didn't see him until—'

'Don't talk,' Olver said, assessing the wound. 'We need to get you out of here.' She glanced towards Greer. 'Help me get him on his feet.'

'I messed up,' Syed groaned. 'I shot over their heads to scare them, but it didn't work. I gave myself away. I'm sorry.'

'Shh,' Olver told him. 'It's okay, it's not your fault.'

Greer gestured. 'He can't have got far. He'll be right there.'

'I don't care,' she snapped back at him. 'No payday is worth this. No one gets hurt, remember? That's what we used to say. We don't take risks. We all retire someday, play golf and checkers in the sunshine. That was the plan. It *is* the plan.'

Greer pointed at Syed. 'And we also said that we would look after one another. We would back each other up no matter what.'

She pulled off her mask so he could see the plea in her face. 'Don't,' she said. 'I'm begging you. Let this go. Let him go. We head back to the safe house, back to the studio, and we plan our next move. We stay calm. We keep our heads.'

Still pointing at Syed, he said, 'You want that piece of shit to get away with that?'

'Who says he will? But not here, not like this. When have we ever rushed in before? That's not our style. That's not who we are. Why? Because it doesn't work. It didn't work here. I shouldn't have given the go-ahead.' She paused. 'And, we have other options now, don't forget.'

'Fine.' Greer let out a growling sigh as he reached down to lift Syed up and over his shoulder. 'Whatever you say.'

'It's not over,' she reminded him. 'Not by a long way.'

FORTY-FOUR

He had not noticed when the rain had started but now it streamed across the car's windscreen in thin rivulets swept away by squelching wipers, blurring the city beyond into streaks of gold and red. Headlights from passing cars flared before vanishing into the night. Each drop of rain that struck the roof seemed to echo, hollow and thin, as though the world outside had retreated just beyond reach.

Victor watched the buildings pass, his gaze steady but distant. Each window, each alley, each silhouette was noted and discarded, quantified by instinct more than thought.

The passenger seat was an unexpected indulgence, the back support a welcome comfort that gave his core a break and in doing so dulled the agony in his side.

He saw how Christal gripped the wheel, her arms rigid. He saw how tonight would be one of the most defining experiences of her entire life. Up there with her future wedding day, with having children. She would never forget hiding in the dark, running from gunfire. Every moment from this point onwards would be different for her now. If she slept at all, when she woke in the morning the world would never be the same again. One day in the future she would tell her grandchildren about tonight and it would be so outlandish to them that they would laugh and maybe worry she was losing her mind.

To Victor, once he was out of Malmö, he would not think of it again. The experience, the successes and failures of it, would all be lessons learned. He would modify his protocols and his skills would incrementally improve through the adaptations he had been forced to make, but ultimately it was just another day at the office for him.

She asked, 'Who were they?'

'I don't know.'

'What's happened to Scragg?'

Victor glanced sideways, the faint scent of her shampoo lingering in the air. 'It was a single shot. Maybe to the head. Or it was only a warning. They could have captured him. They might have let him go.'

'Maybe we should call the police,' she suggested, darting looks at him. 'Anonymously, I mean. Tell them we heard gunshots. They might be able to—'

'No,' Victor said. 'He's either dead or he's not. In both cases, there's nothing the police can do about it and there's nothing I can do either.'

It was a difficult thing to admit. He was not used to having no options, and when there had been none for him to exploit in the past, he engineered his own. Here, he was no more capable than a civilian.

Less so, even.

A civilian could always simply run from danger should it come to it.

'How's your side?'

'It doesn't hurt at all.'

She smiled at the lie. 'What are you going to do now?'

'I don't know.'

If Scragg was still alive, the cargo ship exfil could still be on the table. Otherwise, he had the new legend with which to travel. A huge risk now when his sketch would have been distributed far and wide and his enemies have had time to regroup.

'What about ...?' She trailed off, thought hard before continuing. 'I won't tell anyone. I really won't. I promise. I've helped Scragg before and I've not told a soul. You can trust me. I swear I wouldn't—'

'I'm not going to hurt you,' Victor told her.

He saw the rigidity in her arms increase and realised it was not only the stress and fear of what happened causing it, she was afraid of what might happen next.

Of what he might do.

He glanced down to see the SMG in the footwell between his knees, realised he had kept his right hand on the stock the entire time.

He removed the hand, resting it on his thigh instead.

'That's not my style,' he continued. 'I'm a very bad person, Christal. I won't pretend otherwise. The worst human being you'll ever meet, guaranteed. But you saved my life and I'll never forget that. As soon as I can, I'll send more money.'

'And I'll send it back,' she said.

He glanced at her and saw the seriousness in her face.

Victor thought for a moment, and said, 'Fine, but before

we part ways, I'll give you a means of contacting me should you ever need help. Hopefully, you'll never see me again but if in a year from now or in ten years' time you're in trouble, if you need the kind of aid no one else can provide, contact me.'

'I don't know what to say to that.'

'You don't need to say anything,' he told her. 'Like I said: ideally today is the first and last time you ever see me, everything in your life henceforth works out for you and my offer is something you never need to seriously consider. Just know it stands. Like an insurance policy. If you ever contact me and I don't respond, it means I'm dead. Otherwise, whatever the problem, I'll be there in a heartbeat.'

'Thank you ... I guess.' She forced a smile. 'Maybe if I can ever afford to buy a house you can help me move. I'm guessing with all those muscles you can carry a lot of boxes. When you're healthy again, I mean.'

'With pleasure.'

'I can still help you, you know? You can stay with me – I can look after you until you're well enough to travel.'

Her words shocked him into silence.

It was perhaps as generous an offer as he had ever been given and yet it had been delivered as if it was no big deal.

Maybe to her, that was just what people did for those in need.

'No,' he said. 'No, thank you. You've done enough already and I've put you in too much danger as it is. I don't see a ring on your finger, but do you have a partner?'

'Nothing serious. Why ... ?'

'Not like that,' he assured. 'Children?'

'One day, I hope.'

213

'Then take a trip,' he said to her. 'Once we've parted ways, go home and get your passport. If you can pack a bag in less than five minutes, do it. Otherwise, you head straight back out. Go somewhere you've never been. Where have you never been before?'

'I ... I don't know. I've always wanted to go to Italy.'

'A great choice. The weather in Florence is uncommonly good for this time of year.'

'What do I tell work?'

'Family emergency, which is only half a lie. Because this is an emergency.'

'They're going to come after me?'

'They wanted Scragg or they wanted me. There's a good chance they know about you but a minuscule chance you are of interest to them. But in this business, you don't take that risk. A couple of weeks off will be enough. By then, whatever this is will be over one way or another.'

'Okay,' she said.

'Don't tell anyone where you're going. Not even your closest friends. Not your mother.'

'She'll worry.'

'Better than the alternative.'

Outside, fluorescent lights pooled across damp concrete, streaked with the glow of timetable screens at a tram hub. Shapes moved behind the glass, people hiding from the rain beneath the transparent roofs of the shelters.

'Drop me off here, please.'

Once the car had stopped, he asked for her phone and added in the details to a message board on the dark web where she could contact him if she ever had the need.

Then Victor tucked the SMG beneath his jacket before

struggling out from the car seat, saying a curt 'No,' when Christal unclasped her seat belt and reached for her door to rush around to aid him.

She had told him that travelling was out because sitting down would cause him to seize up and standing again carried the risk of reopening the wound. He hadn't doubted her, but he hadn't expected to find out just how right she had been so soon.

'Be careful,' she told him. 'You can stitch yourself back up if the wound reopens, I know. But you can't afford to lose more blood.'

The genuine worry in her voice made him uncomfortable. Was it the shame of his weakness voiced by another that he could not bear?

Or something else?

An inability to accept someone caring about him, maybe, because he knew in every fibre of his being he was so utterly undeserving of even the tiniest amount of anyone's concern.

He had been told so over and over again as a young boy and he had gone on to spend his entire adult life proving it to be true.

Vertical at last, he used one hand to brace himself against the bodywork, and told her once more, 'Leave the city. Two weeks. No less.'

'Take care of yourself.'

He nodded, heaved the door shut and shuffled towards the nearest tram stop. His jacket was not long and keeping the SMG hidden beneath it and tucked in place with his elbow made his movements even more awkward.

He watched her pull away and the headlights of her car shrink and fade into the distance. A quick check of the timetable told him what trams he would need to return to his safe house.

He needed his go-bag, he needed more medical supplies, and he needed to rest.

Given the trap at the gallery and the attack at the chemical plant, it was a risk, he knew.

But, once again, Victor had no other options.

FORTY-FIVE

The door swung inward without a sound. No creak, no resistance, just an absence where once there had been a barrier. Victor had already stepped inside before the thought registered, the weight of habit carrying him forward. The apartment was as empty as when he had left it.

Or it should have been.

The bed remained untouched, the chairs undisturbed, the kitchen unused. But the air was wrong. A stillness hung over the space, the kind that preceded a storm.

He stepped to the side, easing the door closed behind him.

He shifted his weight, listening. The faintest impression of breath, the quiet patience of someone waiting.

Victor's eyes flicked to the drapes – a little open. Not how he'd left them.

A blade of light from the city outside cut across the room, landing on the small dining table. A mobile phone lay there, placed where it would be seen, face down.

All rooms had blind spots. This apartment was no

different. Victor didn't need to look to know someone was standing there right now.

That they hadn't killed him already disturbed him as much as the fact that they had found him.

He turned, tempted to snap the SMG up from under his coat and yet at the same time understanding with utter certainty that any such move would prove fatal.

From the shadows outside of the ambient light, a figure emerged.

Controlled, deliberate, moving without haste.

Just a slow step forward, bringing his face into the low half-light, expression unreadable. The eyes – always those eyes – calm, empty of anything resembling humanity.

No reaction.

No tension.

No emotion.

The first time they had crossed paths, it had been in Marseille, on opposing sides but neither of them working directly against the other.

A few words exchanged. An understanding that they would meet again and that reunion might end in violence.

Only it had not because they had ended up working for the same client. When that client had been murdered, each man had suspected the other to be the murderer and again the expectation had been violence would follow.

Instead, when the culprit had been identified, they had worked together.

A partnership. As brief as it was effective.

Victor had never worked alongside such a deadly ally.

He had hoped that would be the last time he ever had to look into the eyes of the killer the Russian mafia named after the mythological figure who ferried the souls of the dead across the River Styx.

The Boatman.

Six feet, maybe an inch over. Lean, but not thin – dense, built for efficiency rather than mass. The kind of frame that could be mistaken for average, until he moved. That was what Victor had witnessed in Moscow when they were allied. The sudden, brutal acceleration, the way he covered distance with illusive swiftness. His strength was in timing, not raw force.

He had no gun in hand and still Victor kept the SMG under the coat.

The Boatman's reaction times and the speed with which he could draw a weapon or reload a magazine were phenomenal.

He had no distinguishing features. Just the bland neutrality of a man who had somehow erased himself from existence without altering his physicality. The same empty calm as always. His hair was cut short, practical but not military, the first specks of grey showing at the edges. He was older than Victor, but not by much.

Victor had to ask, 'How did you find me?'

The Boatman answered, 'Easily.'

Victor said, 'I take it you didn't square things with the Bratva's new leadership?'

'We agreed it was time to move on. I heard they hired a team of Slovakians to hunt you down.'

'Not just the Slovakians,' Victor said. 'So you're freelance now?'

'Like you.'

'Small world.'

The Boatman's eyes maintained a focused, unchanging hold on Victor, who had never once seen uncertainty in them. Not in Marseilles when they had seen each other for the first time and recognised what they saw, not in London when they had measured their options, not in Moscow when they had been forced to trust one another.

Absolute calm. Not arrogance.

Certainty.

Victor had spent enough time deciphering the Boatman – watching, cataloguing, assessing his posture, his balance, his presence. He had broken him down physically, mapped his movements, studied his timing, his control. The moment he decided to act, he did.

But what Victor couldn't understand – what he had never been able to read – was what went on behind the eyes.

Because there was nothing there.

Victor watched the Boatman now, standing there with the same quiet stillness, and tried to picture what the man saw when he looked back.

Was he assessing? Calculating? Did he see Victor as a variable in some ongoing equation? Or was there just blank space?

Victor had encountered men who viewed him as a threat. He had encountered men who viewed him as an equal. But he didn't think the Boatman viewed him at all.

Not as a man. Not as a rival.

Just as an entity that existed in the space between action and inaction. A moving organism. A temporary consideration. Not an adversary to be beaten – just an obstacle to be navigated.

Victor shifted, keeping his breathing smooth, his

movements deliberate. His pulse didn't spike, his muscles didn't tighten, but his mind sharpened – an instinctive preparation for what might come next.

The Boatman stood with unnatural stillness. Not stiff, not rigid, but perfectly centred. His posture lacked the nervous energy of lesser men, those who feigned relaxation to hide tension. He didn't square his shoulders in a false display of dominance. He didn't try to make himself smaller to deceive. He stood balanced, weight evenly distributed, as if ready to move in any direction at any time.

His hands were motionless at his sides, fingers loose, natural. No tension. No sign of a prepared attack. Which didn't mean anything. Victor had seen him kill from that exact stance before.

'What are you doing here?' Victor asked him.

The Boatman glanced at the dining table, at the phone left like a marker.

Victor looked back at him. 'For me?'

A nod.

Victor stepped towards the table and turned the phone over, pressed the button. The screen lit up.

A face. His face.

Victor's expression tightened. 'You're here to kill me.'

The Boatman's voice was even as he answered, 'Yes.'

FORTY-SIX

'Although not yet,' the Boatman added.

Victor had been in difficult situations before. He had been outgunned, outnumbered, trapped in places where survival required something beyond skill, beyond experience – pure adaptation, the ability to think and act faster than should be possible.

But this was something else.

Victor had already considered the Boatman a dangerous opponent, a formidable enemy. He had seen him work. Not just the lethality, but the efficiency. A man who never rushed, never hesitated, never wasted movement or breath. The kind of threat that wasn't merely skilled but inevitable.

That alone would have been enough to put him at a disadvantage.

Most of Victor's enemies had not understood him.

They had made mistakes, miscalculations. They had un-derestimated him or failed to see beyond the surface. Even the best had been blind to the way he thought, the way he operated. That ignorance had been his greatest advantage.

The Boatman did not have that weakness.

Because in the same way Victor had watched the Boatman – had studied his movements, his efficiency, had catalogued every habit and instinct – the Boatman had done the same to him.

He had witnessed Victor in action. Had analysed him. Had learned.

And that wasn't even the worst of it.

Victor was injured.

Not just recovering. Still far from recovered. His body had limits now – ones he couldn't ignore, ones that would betray him at the wrong moment. The dull ache in his side, the stiffness in his ribs, the hesitation when he moved in case he moved too fast.

If the Boatman attacked him now, it would be as close to a hopeless situation as Victor had ever been in.

'How did you find me?' Victor asked again.

'You know how,' the Boatman told him.

And Victor did, he realised. The gallery was the strike point so the Boatman knew Victor would want his safe house to be a certain distance away. Close enough to be practical but far enough to be tactical. No nearer than one kilometre and no further than two. A circle one kilometre wide. An area of almost nine-and-a-half square kilometres. An impossibly large amount of city to search.

Or was it?

In his escape from the trap, he had headed north-east because his destination was to the south-west. He would never head straight there and risk leading his enemies to his safe house, especially while injured. The Boatman would know that. From a 360-degree ring around the gallery to 45 degrees, or just over one kilometre square.

Still, about eighty city blocks in Malmö. Far too many for one man to search even with weeks to do so.

But when many of those city blocks were predominantly populated by Malmö's many non-white ethnic citizens, they could be discounted. In such neighbourhoods, Victor would stand out, not blend in.

He would, however, disappear in the tourist-heavy areas.

Twenty city blocks was more manageable if the quarry was a civilian and not a professional in hiding.

The Boatman was as good a hunter as Victor had ever known but Victor was no easy prey.

'I'm injured,' he said, thinking out loud. 'You knew I wouldn't use a hospital and yet I would need medical supplies.'

'Six pharmacies in walking distance.'

'You couldn't investigate them all so fast,' Victor said.

'Three were still open that night. You went to the largest one, the busiest, thinking there was less chance of you being noticed.'

'I was trying to hide from the police, the crime family's people, whoever set the trap.'

'You don't need to make excuses,' the Boatman told him. 'Besides, your logic was faultless. You succeeded.'

'And yet here you are.'

'You couldn't have known the game was rigged,' the Boatman said.

No boast. No ego.

A statement of empirical evidence.

The Boatman said, 'My client loves his son more than anything in the world. My client's time in this world is limited. He won't leave it while his heir is in danger. That's why you walked into a trap. My client is not interested in you, he is only interested in who sent you. If you tell me, I don't have to make you.'

'It was all done anonymously, so I have no idea.'

'I believe you.'

'Did you know it was me when you took the contract?'

The Boatman answered, 'No.'

'Would you have still taken it had you known?'

The Boatman answered, 'Yes.'

'Not personal, right? Just business.'

'No different than when you agreed to kill Gustavus Håkansson.'

'But you told me "not yet",' Victor said. 'What are you waiting for?'

'The game is rigged when I'm sitting across from you, but I don't cheat.'

Victor said, 'You're giving me a head start.'

'When we parted ways we were still on the same side. I knew if you saw me on the street here in Malmö you would hesitate because of that. That's unfair.'

'I didn't know you took sportsmanship into consideration.'

'Sportsmanship, no. Civility, yes. Whether right now or in a few days' time, your place on my ferry is assured. But just because I'm going to kill you doesn't mean we can't still be courteous to one another.'

Victor almost smiled. He had said similar to many foes who could never quite understand that there need not be hard feelings involved in such matters.

'I appreciate that,' he admitted.

'You're welcome,' the Boatman said, and though his expression had not changed and the intonation of his voice remained even, there was the barest hint of emotion, as though he wanted to express regret.

Victor had seen the Boatman display emotion once before.

London. A mortuary, cold and silent. Their employer – dead on a metal slab, skin waxen under the fluorescent lights. The man had been more than just an employer. He had been loyal, in a way few men in this world were. He had respected Victor, and Victor had returned it in kind. It wasn't friendship. It wasn't attachment. But it had been something rare – an understanding between two men who had seen each other clearly and without judgement.

To Victor's surprise, the Boatman had reached out and laid a hand in tenderness on the dead man's chest.

Now, standing here, watching him, Victor realised he had been wrong.

The Boatman hadn't felt grief.

Like a child repeating pleasantries not out of understanding, but because they had been taught to, the Boatman had touched the body because that was what men did when they lost someone important. He had performed emotion, because that was what was expected.

Which meant the hint of regret in his voice was a lie because the Boatman felt none.

Except that made no difference.

To him, expressing it was the same as feeling it.

Victor asked, 'How long do I have?'

The Boatman retrieved his phone and moved towards the door.

UNLUCKY FOR SOME

No theatrics, no parting shot meant to rattle his prey.
Just calm, methodical inevitability.
The Boatman said, 'I'll take a walk around the block.'

FORTY-SEVEN

Victor was moving before the door finished closing behind the Boatman.

The go-bag was already packed, sitting beneath the bed. Inside were clothes, medical supplies, cash, burner phones, some high-calorie snacks. He took out the second Taurus G2C, suppressor attached, and the two spare magazines. He added the SMG he'd taken at the disused chemical plant.

He had no time to change or clean up himself or the safe house. The latter wasn't sterilised at all. His blood, his DNA, was everywhere. He had been careful before being wounded, wearing his silicone barrier to prevent fingerprints, wiping down surfaces when needed, but he could do nothing about all the evidence he was leaving behind now. He still had the lease for almost three months. Maybe he could come back. Maybe hire cleaners who would not ask questions. Decisions for another day.

He had to survive the Boatman first.

A walk around the block wasn't long.

He slung the go-bag over his shoulder and moved to the window, pressing himself just out of view before peering into the street below. The night air hung heavy, the pavement slick with earlier rain. A tram rumbled past, headlights sweeping the empty road. No movement. No figures waiting in the dark.

It meant nothing.

The Boatman had said he would give Victor a head start. But the Boatman wasn't like other men. He didn't lie, only the truth didn't matter to him because nothing did. He could be waiting outside the front door right now, standing in the shadows, gun already drawn. Or he could be at the rear exit, predicting that Victor wouldn't risk the street.

He had to assume both were compromised.

He turned, scanning the room one last time before heading for the door. Not the front. Not the back.

He needed another way out.

The hallway was empty. The silence unbearable. Townhouses, and those converted into apartments, varied in design – some old, some modern, some hybrids of both. This one had a rooftop access hatch. He had checked on his first day here but never thought he would need to use it.

Now, he had no choice.

The stairwell door groaned as he pushed it open, every noise a signpost to his death. He climbed, breathing controlled but tight, every step sending a dull throb through his ribs. The discomfort was manageable. Not debilitating, but there, waiting for him to make a mistake so it could make him pay.

The hatch above was locked.

Victor set down his bag, braced his stance and drove his

shoulder up into the wood. A flare of pain darkened his vision. He gritted his teeth and hit it again. Once. Twice. The lock snapped.

Retrieving his bag, he pushed the hatch open and climbed through, the cold night air rushing over his face.

The rooftop was flat, lined with HVAC units, old brick chimneys and ventilation shafts. Beyond the edge, another building stood five feet away. Another townhouse separated by an alleyway.

He stepped to the ledge. The gap was possible. Just.

Before today, it would be so little challenge he would cross it without breaking stride. But now, with the wound?

Victor exhaled, tensed his legs and jumped.

For a second, he was weightless.

His vision tunnelled, the pain forgotten. Then his feet hit the rooftop, his right leg buckling from the impact. He staggered to maintain his balance, agony exploding through his side. If he fell, he would pass out, the wound maybe reopening.

Three staggered steps.

Five.

He slowed, steadied himself.

Stopped.

He checked the wound. It hadn't reopened, Christal's excellent suturing keeping it closed even when he pushed the boundaries of what it could tolerate.

Victor forced his body forward, moving to where a fire escape led down to the alleyway. He climbed over the railing, slow and controlled, keeping his weight balanced, trying not to give his injury any more excuses to punish him.

The ladder to the alley was retractable. He jerked it free,

slid it down, and descended at a pace so slow he was sure the Boatman would be waiting for him at the bottom.

No sign of his hunter.

Maybe he had kept his word and was performing his circuit of the block.

Maybe the Boatman was baiting him into a trap.

The alley joined another that bisected the block and ran between the fences of back yards. The go-bag was slung over Victor's left shoulder so he took the branch of the alleyway that headed right, pausing at the mouth, listening for footsteps. He heard none and peeked out into a wide street, tram lines running parallel to the road. A tram was still visible, just ahead, stopping at an intersection. A taxi sat at the kerb nearby, the driver leaning against the hood, smoking. Options, finally.

Victor didn't hesitate.

The tram was too slow. If the Boatman was looking for him, he would check the public routes first. But a taxi? Immediate, unpredictable.

Victor crossed the street, stepping into the back seat of the taxi as the driver stubbed out his cigarette.

'Where to?' the driver asked in English, figuring him for a foreigner.

Victor glanced at the road ahead, making a choice in less than a second.

'Kroksbäcksparken,' he said back in Swedish.

The driver nodded and pulled into traffic.

Victor kept his breathing calm, his body rigid against the pain. He watched the reflections in the window, scanning the streets for anything out of place.

Nothing. No sign of the Boatman.

But that didn't mean anything.

Victor didn't relax. Not yet.

Kroksbäcksparken was one of Malmö's largest neighbourhoods, a sprawling mix of residential and commercial buildings and open spaces. It gave him options. He could disappear into the streets, change direction, reassess his next move.

The taxi pulled to a stop near a recreational ground. Victor paid in cash, stepped out, and headed towards the tree line.

He had escaped.

For now. He knew he could not outrun his pursuer, not with the wound still healing, so he would have to hide instead.

The Boatman hadn't followed. He had said he would give Victor a head start but the head start was over.

The game rigged against him had now begun.

FORTY-EIGHT

The water stretched out in all directions, an endless slate-grey sheet under a sky thick with low, unmoving cloud. The sea was calm beneath the pleasure craft's slow drift. It was a sleek yacht, a little over twenty-five metres in length with five cabins. Given Nikola Petrović had no wife and no children, it seemed a waste to Jorund Håkansson. Still, the Serbian liked to entertain both business acquaintances and young women, so the extra space would come in handy. Håkansson sat at the aft deck, the curve of the seating wrapping around a polished wooden table, his coat heavy across his shoulders.

Petrović sat opposite him, his back straight, hands resting on his thighs. He was the most at ease, or at least he played it the best. He enjoyed the sea and the outdoors. He was forever going on hunting trips in Sweden and across the world.

To his right, Tobias Malmgren sat with the posture of a man who had spent too much of his life in conference rooms and government offices. His suit was dark, uncreased, the cut a shade too conservative for the occasion. The kind of man who never quite adjusted to the setting, always carrying a little stiffness in his shoulders, an unconscious need to appear in control.

Leila Farahani was the only one not playing the same game. She was leaning back in her seat, gaze on the water, her expression distant but never unguarded. She was dressed in a red blazer, clean lines and understated wealth, her hair pinned back. Not quite relaxed, but not rigid either. Just waiting. Watching.

The table had been set with the kind of casual indulgence that suited Petrović's style – a bottle of vodka already opened, beads of condensation running down the glass, a bowl of cut lemon beside it. Small plates of cold meats, olives, and dark bread. No one had touched anything yet. Not until the conversation moved past the part where appetites were performative.

Petrović lifted his glass, turning it in his hand so the light caught the curve of the crystal. 'To Gustavus,' he said, voice smooth, warm, the weight of the moment pressed into every syllable. 'A tragedy. A loss for all of us.' His gaze never left Håkansson. 'Jorund, I want you to know – when I heard the news, I cried until all the moisture had left my body. If there is anything I can do – anything at all – you only need ask.' But Petrović didn't stop there. He spread his hands, a gesture of openness, of camaraderie. 'And let it not be said that we do not honour those who came before us. My next venture – whatever it may be – will bear his name. A dedication. A tribute to all he stood for. Perhaps my next yacht.' He glanced towards the wheelhouse, his expression thoughtful, as though the idea had only just occurred to him. 'Yes. That would be fitting. Gustavus. A name that carries weight.

Strength.' He turned back to Håkansson, his expression carefully measured. 'It would be an honour.'

Tobias Malmgren leaned forward, folding his hands together on the table. 'Jorund, I won't pretend to know what you're feeling but my own children are everything to me and I would do everything for them. If there is anything I can do, anything at all, do not hesitate. From one father to another.'

The politician's move was obvious, of course. Håkansson had expected Malmgren would play that card. He knew he wasn't Petrović. He wasn't a businessman, a man of wealth, a player in the world of physical commodities. Malmgren's power was in legislation, in back-room deals, in making problems disappear through influence rather than force. He had no subtlety.

Leila Farahani finally spoke. 'Gustavus will have justice, I know it.'

'All my remaining days left on this Earth will be dedicated to exactly that,' Håkansson told her, told them. 'Wallin is doing everything she can and I have an outside consultant looking into it at the same time.'

Petrović asked, 'Who is this consultant exactly?'

'He is known as the Boatman. Until recently, he worked for the head of the Russian mafia as his chief enforcer ... and executioner.'

Petrović, Malmgren and Farahani exchanged glances.

Håkansson wasn't interested in what they said outright – he was watching for what they weren't saying. Their posture, their reactions, the way they chose their words. Each of them knew why they had been invited onto Petrović's pleasure craft. Gustavus was gone, which meant the inevitable discussion of what came next. Håkansson wasn't dead yet, but they were already dividing his kingdom.

It was Malmgren who began such proceedings. 'With everything that's happened, I think we can all agree that stability is the priority.' His hands were still folded on the table, expression neutral. 'This business has functioned so well because we each play our part, but that balance has always been maintained under your leadership, Jorund.' A small pause. 'If that's no longer going to be the case, we need to ensure continuity.'

Petrović drank vodka. 'The way I see it, the supply chain is broken into three parts. Acquisition, logistics and distribution. You manage the imports, Leila. You control the flow in and out of the port.' He gestured at Malmgren. 'You ensure the paperwork is clean. The funding, the permits, the subsidies. I make sure the goods arrive in the first place so it makes sense that I can also ensure they get where they need to go after they arrive.'

Håkansson remained silent, watching. They were circling each other, testing boundaries, each trying to carve out the most profitable piece of the empire for themselves.

Farahani's expression didn't change. 'What you're suggesting is a restructuring.'

Malmgren cut in before Petrović could respond. 'We don't need restructuring, we need streamlining. The more hands involved, the thinner the margins. If the operation is too fragmented, it creates vulnerabilities. The more vulnerabilities, the more oversight needed. We all know what happens when the wrong people start asking the wrong questions. That's what I do, and I can do even more.'

Farahani said, 'I've been the one keeping that side of the

operation secure. I've ensured that every shipment, every clearance, every document passes through without issue. That system exists because I've made it exist. And after you, Jorund, there needs to be a clear handover. One that doesn't destabilise what's already been built.'

Petrović laughed. 'Let me guess. You're the most qualified to handle that, aren't you?'

Farahani didn't look at him. 'I am the one who has been handling it.'

Håkansson exhaled slowly, finally speaking. 'I'm glad to see you're all thinking.' He glanced towards the water, where a Scorpion Serket 88 speedboat bobbed against the hull – another of Petrović's toys. 'But the one thing none of you have considered is that it doesn't matter who loses out if this thing we've built falls apart.' He turned his gaze back to them, settling first on Petrović, then Malmgren, then Farahani. 'It only matters who wins if it doesn't.' He leaned forward, letting his gaze pass over each of them in turn. 'When my son was taken from me, it was not just a personal loss. It was an attack. Gustavus was my heir. The continuation of everything I built. His death is not just something to grieve. It is something to be avenged.' No one spoke. No one moved. 'I will find the man who pulled the trigger. I will find who sent him. And when I do, I will repay the debt in full.'

He let that linger, his tone quiet, resolute.

He turned his gaze towards the water for a moment, watching the slow, steady movement of the waves. When he spoke again, his voice had shifted – colder now, more deliberate.

'So I ask myself,' he said, 'who benefits?'

Across the table, Petrović shifted, reaching for his glass, taking his time before lifting it to his lips. Malmgren remained perfectly still. Farahani said nothing at all.

'And the answer always leads me back to the same place.' His eyes scanned them again, taking in every flicker of movement, every shift in posture. 'To this table.'

Petrović's lips parted, but no words materialised. Malmgren's expression hardened, his hands coming apart at last. Farahani remained still, unreadable.

'One of you is guilty.'

Petrović's eyes flicked towards Malmgren, then towards Farahani. She didn't look at him, her gaze still locked onto Håkansson, her expression unchanging. Malmgren scoffed, shaking his head, but there was tension in his face now.

Håkansson sat back, pleased.

They were doubting each other now.

He let the moment linger, the paranoia settling into their bones. The guilty one would make a mistake.

'And I will find out who.' A pause. 'And when I do, one of you will receive a visit from the Boatman.'

The water outside lapped against the hull, the sound slow and steady. The yacht rocked with the shift of the tide.

The silence after Håkansson's words sat heavy between them. A stillness on the surface, but underneath, the current had shifted.

He had just planted a depth charge in the middle of them, and now he waited to see who tried to swim clear first.

FORTY-NINE

Director Wallin's heels crunched over fragments of glass and debris scattered across the concrete floor. The air inside hung heavy with the acrid aftertaste of gunpowder, mingling with the metallic bite of rust and oil that clung to the machines. Dim beams of moonlight sparkled through broken skylights, casting irregular patterns of light and shadow across rusted industrial equipment from the skeletal remains of catwalks above.

She used the light from her torch to illuminate a bloodied pipe and nearby spatter.

'The responding officers found this but no sign of any bodies.'

'And the killer?' Magnar Kaale asked, his voice low and yet still booming.

Her gaze flicked towards the distant corridor leading deeper into the plant. 'No sign of him. Except ...'

She led Kaale to another room, in which, near the centre of the space, was a makeshift operating table – an old metal workbench – surrounded by discarded medical supplies. Blood had soaked into the rough canvas beneath the table, drying to a dark, iron-smelling stain.

'Seems he found someone to patch him up.'

'And then what happened? You said your men responded to reports of gunshots.'

'That's right. We had a patrol car close by. Sheer luck. Officers responded within minutes – faster than I would've preferred.' She paused, brushing a stray lock of hair from her eyes as she turned to face Kaale. 'Thankfully, I was able to intervene and delay procedures until you and your *friend* arrived, but we don't have long. Forensics will be here within the hour.'

Together, they made their way outside and into the chill night.

'He gives me the creeps,' she told him.

Given Kaale was twice the Boatman's size, it surprised him to admit, 'Me too.'

'Who is he?'

'He is no friend of mine but an outside consultant here to assist Mr Håkansson,' Kaale explained. 'Given the need for speed and discretion, it was decided that more assistance could be of benefit. Especially since Lukas Draeger's German friends are less than satisfied with the explanation they were given.'

The Boatman moved with slow, deliberate steps, searching the weed-ridden ground near to where the chain-link fence surrounded the plant.

He stopped next to a patch of flattened grass to crouch low, fingers brushing the earth. The grass had been crushed – the blades still green and pliable, not yet dried from exposure.

'Someone was kneeling here for a long time.'

'Who?' Wallin asked, approaching.

He rose and turned on the spot, facing the building's main entrance. 'A lookout.' He expanded his search, gaze downwards. 'Lookouts,' he corrected. 'At least three or four.'

He noted footprints in the dirt. Followed them. Each step over gravel and broken concrete was precise, deliberate.

'When they moved, they did not go in a straight line,' he said, following a path that took him from one piece of cover to the next. 'They split up to circle someone.'

Kaale and Wallin exchanged looks.

The Boatman stopped just outside the entrance to the building. He pointed and they walked over.

They watched as he picked up a cigarette from near the edge of a broken concrete slab, long and wet. He held it between thumb and forefinger, and studied the paper and filter, noting its ash was not scattered and clung to the end. It had still been warm when the rain began falling.

'Recent,' the Boatman said. 'Someone was here smoking when the others moved in. Only managed a few inhalations before they were interrupted.'

He rose again and continued his search, gaze downwards at the weeds, at the asphalt.

'There,' he said.

Kaale's torch reflected from the brass casing of an expended shell gleaming in a patch of disturbed gravel.

'Just one,' he noted. 'Nine-millimetre. Handgun or submachine gun. No blood anywhere out here so it never hit its target or was never meant to.'

His gaze shifted towards the nearby walls, eyes sharp as they scanned the chipped concrete. A small impact mark caught his attention, low on the far wall. He approached, fingertips tracing the rough indentation. The bullet had struck at an angle, leaving a shallow gouge with fragments of lead and copper embedded in the surface.

'Too low for a deliberate shot. This happened during a struggle,' he said, straightening. 'Someone fired mid-fight. And only one shot – it ended quickly. They overpowered the smoker but they didn't hurt him or her.'

He turned around on the spot, gaze still searching. He took a few steps and then stopped, and Kaale saw he had found shallow marks in the dirt – parallel lines.

'They took the smoker,' he said, following the marks step by step. 'Dragged them this way. Two of them did it, one at each arm. Their footprints flank the drag marks.'

The trail led to the perimeter fence where a section of chain-link had been cut through and bent back, forming a narrow gap. The Boatman ducked through and emerged on the pavement of the industrial street beyond. Sodium streetlights buzzed overhead, casting pools of orange light across the empty road and weathered concrete buildings opposite.

Wallin followed but Kaale stayed on his side of the fence. The hole was far too small for a man of his dimensions to squeeze through without shredding his clothes.

His height was such that he could still see what the Boatman was doing. The man scanned the pavement until his eyes caught tyre tracks where rubber had pressed clean the damp asphalt. The tread patterns indicated a heavier vehicle – an SUV or van – based on the width and depth of the marks. The lines arced away from the kerb, their origin clear.

'They loaded whoever they captured into a vehicle here.'

Kaale followed his gaze and caught the gleam of a security camera mounted on the opposite side, angled to cover the area near the parked vehicle.

'Get access to that footage,' the Boatman said to Wallin. 'It will show the vehicle.'

Kaale asked, 'Was it the assassin they took?'

The Boatman looked down at the tyre tracks, silent for a moment. Then he shook his head with a certainty that Kaale could not decipher.

'Someone who helped him.'

'How can you be so sure?'

The Boatman offered no explanation and yet Wallin felt the certainty of the man's silence.

He scanned the tyre marks once more before straightening.

'Whoever they are, they found the assassin once. They might know how to do so again.'

'It'll take time to get the footage from the CCTV,' Wallin explained. 'Longer still to identify who owns or rented the vehicle. If it's stolen or was acquired with forged papers, we have nothing.'

'Not nothing,' the Boatman said, producing a mobile phone. 'This was inside the building near to where the pipe and blood were found. Someone was hit, fell. It slipped from a pocket or pouch. When they heard the sirens nearing, they fled without realising they had lost it.'

'You shouldn't have taken that,' Wallin said. To Kaale, she said, 'I'll have it examined but again it'll take time to bypass the security to see who it belongs to. Even then, it might not reveal much that can help us in the time window we have. If it's just a burner, then it could give us nothing at all.'

She reached out a hand to take it from the Boatman and then realised he had no intention of giving it to her.

He backtracked through the gap in the fence and headed to where his car was parked. A Volvo XC60. Black. A common vehicle in Sweden, as anonymous and forgettable an appearance as the Boatman himself.

They followed, watching as he opened up the boot.

'What is he doing?' Wallin asked.

Kaale shrugged his huge shoulders. 'I wish I knew.'

FIFTY

Inside the boot, a matte black laptop with reinforced casing sat secured to a custom frame – rugged. Built for fieldwork. The Boatman powered it on, the modified BIOS booting into a stripped-down OS designed for speed and security, no unnecessary software to prevent digital traces.

Plugging the phone into a specialised data cable, he launched a brute-force tool embedded in his forensic suite – software capable of cycling through thousands of passcodes per minute.

As the program initialised, he considered the risks. Full-disc encryption was standard in most modern phones. Too many failed attempts could wipe the data as a preventative measure. The software would simulate manual input, but success was a gamble. The algorithm churned through combinations – four-digit, six-digit, moving progressively into more complex patterns. The phone's screen blinked with each failed attempt. A timer in the corner of the laptop screen tracked progress, seconds slipping past with mechanical inevitability.

Then the phone's screen went black.

The system had locked down. Too many attempts, and the device had triggered a security measure that wiped its internal storage. No messages, no logs, no GPS history.

Nothing.

There was no sense of disappointment, no frustration. It was part of the process.

He disconnected the phone and laid it on the boot's rubber mat.

Kaale and Wallin watched from nearby.

From a compact case beside the laptop, he unfolded a precision toolkit – thin-handled screwdrivers, plastic spudgers, tweezers and a suction cup designed to separate modern smartphone screens without cracking the glass. The device was sealed with adhesive meant to withstand tampering, but he had handled worse. Heating the edges with a portable heat gun, he waited until the glue softened, then pried the back cover loose with practised care.

The phone's internals were compact – battery, motherboard, and beneath a protective shield, the SIM card slot. Using fine-tipped tweezers, he slid the SIM card free and inserted it into a reader the size of a thumb drive, plugging it into his laptop.

His fingers danced across the keyboard, launching a forensic analysis suite used by law enforcement to extract data from mobile devices. The software scanned the SIM card's storage, pulling residual metadata from its internal memory. Even with deleted call logs, the SIM retained vital information since mobile networks required it to store identifiers and connection history. The system accessed the International Mobile Subscriber Identity that gave the SIM a unique identity within cellular networks, and the MSISDN – the phone number associated with the SIM.

By extracting the Location Area Code and Cell ID from each record, the software triangulated approximate locations of recent connections.

The Boatman focused on the most recent entries – locations where the phone had connected to nearby towers. Each entry marked a point in space and time, plotting a loose trail of the phone's recent movements.

He cross-referenced the coordinates with maps of Malmö available online, noting clusters near the chemical plant and further out towards the city's industrial outskirts. No use to him. He already knew they had been here. He wanted to know where else they had been. He ignored all the entries except the ones with the greatest frequency – where the phone had been the most and for the longest duration.

A single entry appeared hundreds of times over the past several days.

In particular, aside from tonight when it had been at the chemical plant, it registered at the same tower during each preceding night.

In an urban environment, towers were set a few hundred metres apart to ensure there was enough signal strength for a high volume of simultaneous users. That tower covered a dense cluster of residential buildings near the waterfront in the Västra Hamnen region – far too many options to search door by door. However, the SIM had been registered at a nearby tower six hundred metres away several times before being registered at the primary tower again between fifteen minutes and half an hour later.

Frequent, short trips. Regular intervals.

Supply runs.

The long wheelbase of the SUV or truck suggested more people than the three or four sets of tracks he had found. He pictured a team of five or six adults. Each required two to three thousand calories a day. Over the course of almost a week that was a lot of food. The number of trips told him that where they were staying did not have the capacity to store enough provisions in one go. No large house, then. A small apartment or non-residential property would be their safe house.

The frequency of a tower registering a SIM depended on many factors. When not in use, that could be every five to fifteen minutes. In use, it was every few seconds to maintain a stable connection.

Patterns emerged through the data – three distinct trips over the past week, each moving from the coverage of the first tower into the second. Each journey began within the first tower's range, travelling away from the waterfront district and into the boundary of the second tower. Then a return journey matched the first.

He focused on the intervals. Each trip showed a consistent travel time between the towers, averaging just under seventy seconds. The shortest took sixty-five seconds, the longest seventy-two, with one seventy-second journey marked by pings every five seconds as the phone crossed the boundary. Unlike idle pings spaced minutes apart, these sequences were tighter – indicative of the phone being in active use. An important call. Information to be shared that could not wait.

Urban speeds ranged between thirty and forty kilometres per hour – eight to eleven metres per second. At seventy seconds, that placed the total distance travelled between 560 and 770 metres.

He analysed the entries, calculating timings and distances while studying the map of Malmö. The first tower covered an area of dense residential housing and waterfront businesses. That area connected to the rest of the city by two main arterial roads, one of which was flanked by more residential properties. The other, however, had larger commercial properties along it. Those buildings included a DIY superstore, a gym, a discount clothing outlet and a supermarket. The latter would be perfect for a supply run catering for five to six adults.

With the supermarket located approximately three hundred metres into the second tower's coverage, the remaining distance within the first tower's range narrowed the search to a corridor of 260 to 470 linear metres.

A search area of less than half a square kilometre.

The Boatman shut down the laptop and closed the boot.

He climbed behind the wheel.

'What are you doing?' Kaale asked him.

The Boatman said, 'I've found them.'

FIFTY-ONE

Victor moved through Malmö's late-night streets with the slow, measured pace of a man who belonged nowhere. The homeless guy's coat hung loose around his frame, its thick wool damp with the city's cold humidity. The city pulsed beyond the edges of his vision – cars rolling past in slow rumbles, pedestrians wrapped in scarves and conversation, the throb of bass from bars still open to those who could afford warmth and indulgence.

The wound in his side was a constant presence, a heat beneath the layers of skin, gauze and clothing. The pain had settled into something manageable, provided he kept his pace slow and light. He had no illusions – it was a temporary reprieve. A balance that wouldn't hold for ever. The stitches might hold, but the rest of him was wearing thin. He needed rest.

He passed beneath flickering streetlamps, through the glow of signage and the glare of headlights. Victor walked without hurry. Without purpose. That was the trick. People with nowhere to be didn't draw attention.

As much as he wanted to stop and rest, he had to first ensure the Boatman could not track him to his ultimate destination. No point resting to let the wound heal if his hunter gave him a more permanent injury.

An hour on his feet was all Victor could endure, however.

The park loomed ahead, its entrance swallowed by a row of skeletal trees. Their bare branches twisted against the night sky. The fairground lights had dimmed, the last remnants of neon flickering against the glass of an empty bus shelter. Rides that had spun and whirled hours earlier now stood motionless, skeletal frames silhouetted against the glow of Malmö's skyline. The laughter and shrieks that had filled the night replaced by the rustling wind through branches.

Victor saw them before they saw him, of course. The same group, more or less.

Shapes hunched near the barrel's warmth, wrapped in layers of salvaged fabric, their faces half-lit by the shifting glow of flames. Others had retired for the night to their sleeping bags or makeshift shelters. The ones still awake didn't react to his approach. That was part of the understanding here. No questions. No introductions.

Victor stopped a few feet from the fire, the heat reaching out in tentative waves. He stood there for a moment, adjusting to the rhythm of the space. The shuffle of fabric, the occasional cough, the way no one quite met each other's eyes. The unspoken agreement of the forgotten: you keep to yourself, and you get left alone.

One of the men shifted, turning, his face catching the firelight. Victor recognised him from before – the one with the dulled eyes who had given away his coat, the slow movements of a man who had spent too many years surviving rather than living. He had replaced the coat with a sleeping bag that was wrapped around him. He didn't speak, just met Victor's gaze for a brief moment before looking away again.

That was enough.

Victor lowered himself to the ground next to a hedgerow to use it as a little cover against the elements, easing down with deliberate care, mindful of the pull in his side. The earth was cold beneath him, the damp seeping through the fabric of the coat.

The fire popped, embers swirling up into the night, their glow flickering before vanishing into the dark.

Time passed in the slow way it did in places like this. The city moved on without them, distant and indifferent. Somewhere in the streets beyond the park, people lived their lives. They laughed in bars, waited at tram stops, checked their phones beneath the glow of café lights.

Here, none of that mattered.

A few men spoke in low murmurs, words exchanged with the rhythm of people who had long since abandoned the need for urgency. Stories were told not because they were expected to be heard, but because silence meant more time in which to think and no one here wanted to think any more than necessary.

Victor listened without listening. Let the words wash over him, let the fire's warmth work its way into his skin. His body ached, a slow, steady throb that settled into his bones.

The wound in his side pulsed with each heartbeat, but lying down, resting at last, he could ignore it.

The man who had given up his coat approached and took a seat on the ground next to Victor.

The man's skin was thin over sharp cheekbones, his beard patchy, scruff peppered with grey. His nose was crooked, broken more than once. Beneath the bulk of his layers – a thick hoodie under the sleeping bag – his frame was lean, wiry in a way that suggested he had spent most of his life fighting for whatever scraps he could hold on to.

He held out a plastic bottle filled with something brown and sharp-smelling.

Victor shook his head.

The guy shrugged, took a long pull, then wiped his mouth with the back of his hand. His fingers were rough, cracked from cold and exposure.

'You're back,' he said, voice rasping with years of cheap liquor and cheaper cigarettes. 'What's your name?'

'I don't have one.'

He nodded. 'Me neither, but call me Rikard anyway.'

For a while, they just sat there, watching the flames flicker inside the rusted barrel. The others nearby continued conversations that had no real beginning or end, just words passed between them to fill the void that should have been filled with life.

Rikard took another sip from his bottle and smacked his lips. 'I see it all the time. Lot of us down here are running from something. Debt, bad choices, people who want us dead. Some of us just don't like the world up there.' He gestured vaguely towards the city skyline. 'But you ... you ain't one of us.'

Victor let the words go unanswered.

Rikard chuckled, tapping a cigarette from a battered pack and lighting it with a cheap plastic lighter.

'You got money,' Rikard said, exhaling smoke through his nose. 'Maybe not in your pockets right now, but you ain't starving. You're hiding, not surviving.'

Victor glanced towards the fire. 'Maybe.'

'Definitely.' Rikard took another drag. 'Difference is, we don't get to leave. But you ... you're just passing through.'

Victor didn't argue.

Rikard rubbed at his stubbled chin. 'So what's it like? The world you're from. The one with clean suits and places to be.'

Victor thought about it. About the hotel rooms, the airports, the cities that blurred together. The jobs. The violence. The meticulous, calculated efficiency of his life.

'It beats working for a living,' he said.

Rikard exhaled, his amusement fading. 'I used to be a trucker. Long-haul. Across Europe. Drove through every border you can think of. Knew the best rest stops, the best places to get a decent meal on the road. Thought I had it all figured out.'

Victor waited.

Rikard rolled the cigarette between his fingers. 'One night, I get stopped. Sweden–Norway border. Customs guys pull me over, tell me there's a tip-off, want to check the cargo.' He took another pull from the bottle. 'Turns out the company I'd been driving for? They weren't just moving auto parts.' Rikard stared at the fire. 'Three years in prison. Lost my licence. Lost my wife, my kids. Came out with nothing. Couldn't get work. Fell into drinking. The usual story.'

Rikard took another sip, then held out the bottle again.

This time, Victor took it.

The liquid burned his throat, sharp and biting. He swallowed once, then passed it back.

They sat there for a while, silent.

Rikard flicked the cigarette butt into the fire. 'You can crash here as long as you need to. Anyone comes asking about you, we'll keep you hidden.'

The night pushed on. The fire burned low. One by one, the figures around him faded into sleep, their bodies curled beneath layers of scavenged fabric, their breathing slow and steady.

Victor didn't sleep. Not yet.

He let his head rest on the cold earth, eyes half-lidded, watching the way the smoke curled against the night sky. He listened to the wind in the trees, the hum of the city beyond the park's borders.

Somewhere out there, the Boatman was looking for him.

Somewhere out there, others were too.

For now, this was enough. He had to rest. He had to heal.

For now, all he could do was wait.

FIFTY-TWO

The Boatman arrived at the supermarket, parking in the almost empty stretch of asphalt before it. He looked around for a large SUV or van in case they were making a late-night supply run, but he saw nothing suitable. Leaving again, he drove along the arterial road connecting to Västra Hamnen. It was mostly straight, with limited intersections, letting the vehicle maintain a steady speed. Side streets branching off the main road were too narrow and slow for the consistent timing he observed. He stuck to precisely thirty-five kilometres per hour.

So late at night, the roads were clear. There were no pedestrians. Buildings were dark.

He drove through the narrowed corridor he had already determined was only a few city blocks wide, all leading towards the waterfront. Restaurants, bars, small apartment blocks. The safe house had to be within this stretch – close enough for quick supply runs, yet far enough from the main roads to avoid unwanted attention.

Repeated connections near the waterfront indicated that the safe house was close to the road, where the tower's signal would be clearest. Buildings deeper within the neighbourhood or behind dense structures would have weaker signals, causing the phone to switch towers more often.

He eliminated the bars and restaurants – too exposed, too much foot traffic, and would have enough refrigeration space to negate the need for multiple supply runs. Modern residential complexes with extensive surveillance were also ruled out. These professionals would have chosen a building with limited security measures, fewer occupants, and easy access to the main road for quick getaways. That left only a handful of older apartment blocks within the search radius.

An apartment in such a block would be consistent with the multiple supply runs necessary to keep the team fed.

The soft rush of waves against the shoreline drifted through the cool night air. Overhead, faint halos of streetlights reflected off the glass façades of modern residential complexes, their sleek lines and minimalist designs standing in stark contrast to the older, more utilitarian buildings closer to the main road.

To his left, Dania Park stretched along the waterfront – open grassy spaces broken by clusters of sculpted stone and paved walkways that snaked along the shoreline. Sparse trees stood motionless in the still air, their branches casting faint shadows beneath the sodium glow of streetlights. Beyond the park, the dark water of the strait shimmered beneath the distant lights of passing ships.

Closer to the main road, the architecture shifted – sleek, glass-fronted apartments rose above narrow streets, their balconies offering views of the water and city skyline. Many of these buildings were part of the Bo01 residential area, a sustainable development known for its energy-efficient construction and contemporary design. Vertical gardens clung to sections of the façades, their green leaves stark against the steel and glass.

Further inland, older apartment blocks with brick exteriors and fewer windows broke the pattern of glass and steel. Their weathered surfaces and narrow alleyways offered more seclusion – less visible from the street and harder to monitor with surveillance cameras. Small courtyards lay hidden between these buildings, accessible only through gated entrances or narrow passageways. A few ground-floor units had drawn curtains and dim lighting filtering through the cracks, while upper floors remained dark and silent.

At the midpoint of his search radius, he stopped his Volvo. Across the street, a row of parked cars stood in front of a three-storey building that had residential properties above a row of commercial shopfronts facing the street. An alleyway along one of the building's sides offered access to the rear. Security cameras protecting the businesses did not cover the alley, he noticed.

The windows were all dark at this time of night.

The team had captured someone associated with the hired killer whose name the Boatman did not know. The team wouldn't have simply returned and gone to sleep as though nothing had happened. The adrenalin of a mission lingered long after its completion, keeping minds sharp and bodies restless. Even if some had gone to sleep, at least one of them would remain awake – watching, waiting, ensuring their captive didn't escape, or perhaps all were awake, interrogating him.

The properties of the ground floor consisted of a dry cleaner's, an off-licence and a Korean takeaway. None of them were open, of course. Neither was the yoga studio, its white-washed windows a sign it had long since closed.

On foot, the Boatman circled around the back of the building to where there was a designated parking area for residents and a separate area of space for the commercial properties.

Parked there was a large seven-seater Peugeot 5008 SUV. It was directly behind the rear entrance to the yoga studio.

From a small, frosted window, warm light spilled out.

FIFTY-THREE

The yoga studio had two separate studios so two classes could be run at the same time: a beginner and an advanced class. The business had failed regardless. Each space had three white walls and a mirrored far wall reflecting the soft overhead lighting that could be adjusted with a dimmer switch. Saskia Olver and her team used one of them for sleeping and so it was outfitted with cots and sleeping bags, while the other was for planning and day-to-day activities such as meals and downtime. Chairs and other furniture had been brought in here from the reception area and the small offices at the rear of the establishment. There were two entrances into each studio: one that led to the reception and offices, the other that connected directly with the changing rooms.

The yoga studio only had a small kitchenette with a tiny refrigerator so frequent trips to a nearby supermarket were essential for fresh food.

Scragg was sitting at the centre of the second studio space, bound to a sleek, minimalist chair, his hands secured behind his back with cable ties. Over his eyes, a black blindfold obscured his vision, and ear plugs muffled the world around him, ensuring he heard nothing of the conversation happening mere feet away.

Across from him stood Olver, her posture poised but tense, arms crossed as her sharp gaze drilled into him. Ezra Greer was sitting on his haunches, scratching at the back of his head. Celeste Perrot leaned against one of the desks they had brought in, her fingers tapping a slow, thoughtful rhythm against the veneered surface. Marko Draganović paced near the mirrored wall. Emil Syed was asleep in one of the other chairs, his head bandaged and his bloodstream full of opioids to ease his pain. Daria Novak lay atop the other desk, yawning.

'This is pointless,' Draganović muttered, rubbing his palms together. His movements were restless, a man wound too tight. 'We've got nothing. No leads, no location. We're wasting time.'

'We have him,' Perrot countered, her voice calm, deliberate. 'He knows where the assassin is.'

'And he's not talking,' Draganović snapped.

Greer whispered, 'We're professionals, not kidnappers. This isn't what we do.'

'We do what we have to,' Olver said, her tone cold but controlled. 'We've invested too much to walk away with nothing. I think we can all agree on that.'

She stepped forward, pulling up Scragg's blindfold and tugging out the earplugs. 'Tell us where he is. We're offering you a way out. No more threats, no need for any pain. You help us, and we'll split the money with you. Håkansson's willing to pay a lot – far more than the assassin ever paid you, I'm sure. This could be the biggest payday of your life.'

Scragg considered her words for a moment before his lips curved into a faint, humourless smile. 'Money,' he said, his voice rough but steady. 'That's what it always comes down to, doesn't it? People like you think everyone's got a price. The man you're after – he saved my life a few nights ago. A job went wrong. I paid him to stand around and look menacing. When it all went south and he did far more than he got in return, he didn't ask for a raise or tell me it wasn't what he signed up for. Just stepped in and pulled me out of a situation I wasn't walking away from on my own. You think I'm going to turn around and sell him out because you're flashing some cash?' His eyes hardened, the humour fading from his expression. 'It's not about morals – it's about knowing who's got your back when no one else has. That's worth more than *any* money you can possibly offer.'

Silence settled over the room, thick and heavy. Olver's gaze didn't waver, but her expression tightened. Draganović muttered a curse under his breath, pacing again with even more energy. Greer stood and growled with frustration. Shaking his head and flexing his fingers.

Perrot pushed off the desk, her eyes narrowing as she stepped closer to Scragg, but Olver held up a hand.

Scragg said, 'So either put a bullet through my skull or let me go. Either way, we're done here.'

Greer took a short step forward, and punched him in the face.

The force rocked Scragg back in the chair, the impact reverberating through the room with a dull thud.

Scragg winced and grunted.

Then his gaze met Greer's and he said, 'You punch like an Englishman,' before spitting out a streak of foamy blood onto the pristine hardwood floor.

Greer's nostrils flared, his fists clenching at his sides, but Olver stepped between them.

'Enough,' Olver said, her voice low and firm. 'Take him to one of the offices. Lock him up.'

She reset the blindfold and the earplugs.

Greer yanked Scragg from the chair, and pushed him through the doorway and down the hallway, and then through a doorway into a small space filled with moving boxes.

Without ceremony, Greer shoved Scragg to the floor.

'Sleep tight,' Greer muttered before he delivered a swift kick to Scragg's ribs, then another for good measure.

He slammed the door shut, and locked it with a heavy click.

His footsteps echoed down the hall as he returned to the others, leaving Scragg alone in the dark.

It had been a long time since they had failed to collect on a bounty, even longer since they had made so many mistakes.

Deciding it was time to cut their losses and go home before anything else could go wrong, Greer stepped back into the studio, the creak of the hardwood floor beneath his feet sounding louder in the unnatural stillness.

Something was wrong.

His gaze flicked to Novak first. Moments ago, she had been lying on one of the tables, yawning and looking like she would fall asleep at any moment. Now she was standing up, wide awake with no hint of fatigue.

Draganović had been restless – pacing the floor in tight, frustrated strides, hands flexing and clenching, shoulders rolling with barely restrained tension. Now, he stood so still that he looked frozen mid-motion, as if someone had hit pause and left him suspended in place.

Perrot, who had leaned against the desk with her usual air of sharp-edged control, stood straighter now. Her shoulders were squared, her chin lowered, eyes locked forward with the unwavering focus of someone assessing a threat. One hand still rested on the edge of the desk, but her other hovered near the holster at her hip – close, but not drawn.

Olver stood near the centre of the room, feet shoulder-width apart, her weight balanced as if bracing for sudden movement. Her gaze was fixed on something – or someone – across the room, her breath slow and steady despite the tension etched into the lines of her shoulders.

Greer's pulse quickened as his eyes followed their line of sight.

They were all looking in the same direction.

Then Greer saw him.

A man stood near the far wall, in the doorway to the changing rooms, motionless against the dark as if he had been formed from the shadows.

The cut of his dark coat was precise, uncreased, yet it did nothing to soften the danger wrapped around him. He stood with his hands at his sides – empty, relaxed, but there was no mistaking the lethal intent beneath that stillness. His gaze moved across the room with deliberate slowness as if memorising every detail, every breath, with a machine's certainty.

Greer's muscles tensed even as his mind scrambled to process the man's presence.

How had he got inside? How had none of them noticed until now?

The American's hand fell to his thigh where his pistol was holstered but he hesitated.

Something told him that would be a bad idea.

Besides, nothing had actually happened.

Then Olver spoke, her voice low, steady, but taut as a wire pulled to breaking point. 'Who the hell are you? And what do you want?'

The intruder's eyes were dark and fathomless. When he spoke, his voice was smooth and deliberate and yet monotone – someone who spoke only when it mattered.

'You may call me the Boatman.'

The air seemed to grow cold around them all, the name echoing through the room as both warning and prophecy. His voice was calm and quiet and yet it carried the full weight of inevitability.

'And I am here as the sum of all your failures.'

FIFTY-FOUR

Greer felt the hairs on the back of his neck rise. The air seemed heavier now, as if the room itself held its breath. The Boatman took a few steps forward, slow and deliberate, his pace steady.

'And what I want,' he continued, 'is to trade.'

Olver glanced to the other members of her team, as if reassuring herself. Her breath came faster now, not quite a gasp but edged with the tension locked inside her chest.

'What do you mean, trade?' she asked.

The Boatman's gaze didn't waver. 'You successfully tracked the assassin who targeted Gustavus Håkansson. You captured his associate. Tell me everything you know about the assassin.'

'We – we don't know where he is,' she said, the words tumbling out with more force than control. 'We've tried. Scragg won't talk. Threats, bribes – none of it works. He's locked up right now. We found the assassin by chance. At the gallery.' She explained their mission to capture Lukas

Draeger, their speciality in extraditing international fugitives. How Syed had tracked the assassin to his safe house and how they had then shadowed him the next day. She went through every detail of what they had observed and heard when the assassin had spoken with Scragg before they had gone to the disused chemical plant. She recounted their failed capture attempt. 'Given we lost out on the bounty for Draeger we figured the assassin might earn us a consolation prize.'

The Boatman stood motionless, as though her explanation was a puzzle piece sliding into place. His eyes, cold and impassive, did not change.

'Where is the associate of the assassin now?'

She answered, 'Tied up in a back room. One of the offices.'

'Has he seen your faces?'

'Some of us, yes. He's blind and deaf right now, however.'

'What else can you tell me about the assassin?'

'We don't have more,' Olver added, her voice thinner now, as if the air had grown scarce. 'We can't give you what we don't know.'

'You said we were trading,' Draganović interrupted. 'What are you offering exactly? What are we getting in return?'

The Boatman's unblinking eyes remained on Olver. 'She understands what you get in return.'

Draganović glanced at her, confusion creasing his face. 'What's he talking about?'

The Boatman ignored him, asking Olver, 'Do you think it's a good deal?'

Olver's face paled, her lips pressing together before she gave a small, hesitant nod. 'Yes.'

The Boatman's voice cut through the air again, monotone

and deliberate. 'You mentioned the assassin stood up Scragg. What does that mean?'

Olver swallowed, her gaze flicking towards Perrot before returning to the Boatman. 'It was before they went to the chemical plant. They were talking on a bench and Scragg joked it had been a long time since someone had stood him up. We were listening with a parabolic microphone but didn't catch every detail. There was something about a cargo cruise.'

The Boatman was silent for a moment. 'What do you know about Scragg?'

Greer shifted with unease, so much combat experience but out of his depth right now.

Olver answered. 'We know something about him. He's a fixer – works with people who need things done quietly. Connections, resources, transport. He knows how to make people disappear.'

'Does he have a cargo ship in his name?' the Boatman asked. 'Or in the name of any of his companies?'

'No,' Olver replied. 'Not as far as I know.'

'Does he have a unit at the port? Warehouse space. Offices. A Portakabin?'

'Yeah ... an office. Why?'

Greer watched as the Boatman's head began a slow rotation, his eyes sweeping across the room in an unhurried arc. The motion was deliberate, methodical – as though he was analysing something.

The Boatman's gaze passed over Perrot first – lingering just long enough for her shoulders to tense further, her fingers twitching near the holster at her side. Then Novak – her jaw clenching as if to mask the pulse that visibly beat at her temple. When the gaze fell upon Greer, it was like those eyes did something to the air between them that seemed to thin it into a sudden chill.

Greer tensed with the urge to move, to act, but something about the stillness of that stare pinned him in place.

The Boatman's head continued its slow turn until his eyes returned to Olver once more.

And then – the faintest shift of the Boatman's stance.

Not a step, not a movement towards any of them. But something in the room changed.

As if the countdown had begun.

Olver swallowed, her voice breaking the heavy silence. 'That's all we know. It really is, honestly. If we knew how to find the assassin, we would tell you. I swear it.'

The Boatman's gaze lingered on her for a heartbeat longer, unblinking. Then, with a tilt of his head, he replied, 'I believe you.'

Perrot asked him, 'Why do you call yourself the Boatman?'

'I don't. Others do.'

'Why do they?'

For a heartbeat, Greer's mind seemed to disconnect from reality, as though his eyes and ears had fallen out of sync.

The Boatman moved so fast that Greer's thoughts lagged behind, struggling to process what was happening.

The gun seemed to appear in the Boatman's hand – no flourish, no wasted motion – just the smooth, lightning fast extension of his arm as the first shot cracked through the air.

Olver's head snapped back, her eyes wide with shock that never had time to transform into fear. The bullet punched through her forehead, and her body crumpled before Greer's brain could comprehend the sound of the shot.

The Boatman didn't move his feet. Only his arm shifted, precise and mechanical, as if each motion had been programmed in advance.

The muzzle flashed again, the sharp report echoing through the room as Draganović collapsed against the mirror, leaving a smear of red against the glass as his body slid to the floor.

Perrot's mouth opened – just enough to inhale, to start a scream that never had time to form. Despite her hand being so close to her gun, the sudden escalation into violence had frozen it in place, useless.

The next shot silenced her before sound could escape her open mouth, her body folding sideways as her hand slipped from the edge of the desk.

Novak followed, trying to run, but only remained alive long enough to take a short, pointless step.

Syed, still unconscious, would never wake up again.

Time caught up with Greer in a single, shattering moment.

The sequence of sound and motion, the hollow thuds of bodies hitting the floor, the sharp tang of gunpowder in the air – two whole seconds.

The Boatman moved with a speed that defied comprehension – fluid, precise, lethal.

It was almost beautiful in its horrifying efficiency.

And when Greer's senses finally became thoughts that aligned with reality, his gun was then in his hand rising up fast, but too late.

Far too late.

FIFTY-FIVE

Scragg sat with his back against the cold wall of the small room, knees drawn close to his chest. His wrists burned where the cable ties bit into skin. The blindfold pressed too tight against his eyes, and the plugs in his ears muffled the world into distorted echoes. His breaths came slow and controlled. Panic burned oxygen. Waste nothing, he told himself.

Whoever they were, they hadn't broken anything yet. A few kicks, a couple of punches. Nothing designed to shatter him. Just enough to say, *We could.*

That was fine. He could wait. His ribs ached from the boots, but he'd taken worse.

This wasn't torture. Not yet.

Footsteps thudded outside the door that to Scragg were the faintest of taps. He did not hear the door creak open.

Hands grabbed him – rough, business-like.

Scragg twisted, testing their grip. Iron-strong fingers clamped onto his arms and hauled him upright.

He stumbled as they pushed him forward, legs clumsy without balance. The floor changed from thin carpet to something rougher – outdoors. The air hit his face, sharp with cold and fresh.

His pulse jumped.

Outside wasn't good.

Scragg jerked against their grip. 'Oi, where the hell are we going?'

No answer.

'Come on – there's no need to be so handsy. If you want to take me to dinner, just ask.'

Still nothing.

Someone shoved him forward. His knees buckled. He hit cold metal with a grunt. Hands shoved him into a confined space, feet first. The steel rim of the boot bit into his back as they forced him inside.

'*Take it easy.*'

The reply came fast – a pistol whipped across his temple. Pain burst through his skull. Stars flashed white behind the blindfold. Another blow struck his cheekbone, jarring his teeth. His head snapped sideways from the force. Before he could gasp a breath, another hit drove pain deep into his skull.

He felt the earplugs fall out. Maybe the rubber string attaching them to one another had caught on something.

'*Okay – okay.*' His voice slurred from the blood pooling in his mouth. 'I get it. I get—'

Another blow. Sharp, deliberate. Then nothing.

Silence, except for the pulse and pain thudding in his skull.

Breathless, shaking, Scragg lay sprawled against the boot's rough interior, heart hammering. The boot slammed shut.

Without the plugs muffling all sounds, a voice reached him – quiet with the boot closed between them but clear enough to twist his stomach.

'I don't care where. Just make sure he's never found.'

Darkness. Cramped metal walls. No air.

An engine rumbled to life. The floor vibrated beneath him.

Scragg tried to keep his breath steady – long, slow inhalations through his nose.

Stay calm. Don't waste air.

The vehicle picked up speed.

Scragg swallowed hard.

Now he was scared.

FIFTY-SIX

The park was its own world, a place that belonged to the city but was separate from it. It had rules, its own quiet hierarchy, its own invisible boundaries. And for now, Victor was part of it.

The homeless clustered in one corner, away from the better-lit paths, near skeletal trees and hedgerows that shielded them from view throughout the day. A small wooden pavilion stood nearby, a relic from when the city had invested in beautifying all parts of the park. As the homeless population grew and congregated near it, the pavilion had been left to the elements. Now it served as a makeshift shelter, a space to sleep when it rained or snowed.

During the day, the park was alive with movement. Runners passed by, their breath clouding in the morning air. Parents pushed strollers. Cyclists weaved through the paths. People came to eat their lunches on benches, a few to take smoke breaks from nearby offices.

At night, the park emptied now the fairground had gone.

The quietness was Victor's favourite part. Some days no one said a word to him and he said nothing to anyone in return.

Pure bliss if not for the pain, cold, hunger and relentless anticipation of the Boatman's bullet.

After spending his first night sleeping beneath the hedge, the others had allowed him to use the pavilion. The wood was always cold against his back, and the damp air defeated his meagre bedding. He had a refuse bag as his main blanket, the plastic an effective material at trapping in his body heat until he had foraged some cardboard boxes and flattened them for increased luxury.

The others left him alone for the most part. That was the way of it here. No one asked questions. No one offered comfort. They all had their own burdens. Here, sympathy had to be earned. Suffering had to stand tall far beyond the baseline for anyone to even notice.

Victor spent most of the daytime sitting near the fire, conserving energy, watching, listening, healing. The others moved through the hours with practised rhythms. Some begged, their faces etched with years of sun, wind and disappointment. But it was rare. Professional beggars were rampant here as they were all over Europe. Backed up by the criminal gangs that employed them, the genuine homeless were beaten if they *stole* the profits of the gangs. Most were forced to scavenge, picking through bins behind restaurants, waiting for the workers to toss out the day's leftovers. A few collected bottles, filling plastic bags with recyclables, exchanging them for coins at the depot.

Victor didn't beg and he didn't leave the park. He wouldn't risk being seen. He wouldn't put himself in front of strangers, wouldn't let them study his face, make eye contact, remember him.

Instead, he took only what was discarded.

It was slow going. A half-eaten sandwich in a bin near where the fairground had been. A takeaway container with a few scraps of rice and vegetables left on the path. A bottle with a quarter of its bright blue energy drink thrown into the bushes.

Hunger wasn't new to him, however. He had gone without food before, had trained his body to function on starvation rations. But this wasn't the same. This wasn't a controlled fast, a test of discipline for a mission. This was survival at its most stripped down when his healing body needed calories the most.

Already weakened from blood loss, from the effort spent evading pursuit, he needed an excess of food. But the act of searching, of reaching into bins and finding nothing, of swallowing food that had begun to sour, drained more from him than it gave.

Each day followed the same pattern.

Victor washed his wound in the park's public restrooms when he could, peeling back the bandages, replacing them when he found rags that seemed clean enough. The water was cold, the hand soap harsh, but it was better than infection.

He slept when the city slept. Breaking his protocols that instructed him to be awake all night and sleep in the morning. Not possible here. He needed to blend in with the others, sleep when they slept. Besides, if they caught him asleep when they were awake, they would steal his shoes and he could not blame them for that.

The police came through every so often, making their presence known, sometimes dispersing them, sometimes just watching. The homeless had ways of avoiding trouble – knowing where to move, when to scatter. Victor followed their lead.

By the third night, he felt the exhaustion settling deep.

Rikard noticed.

Victor had not eaten that day, his strength running on fumes, when Rikard dropped into the pavilion beside him and handed him a paper bag.

Rikard sucked on a straw emerging from a plastic cup, condensation beading along the surface.

'For you.'

Victor looked at the bag, then at Rikard.

The older man sighed. 'I didn't poison it. If I wanted you dead, I'd have just sold you out.' He gestured to the food. 'Eat, man. You look like you're about to drop.'

Victor opened the bag. A burger, still warm. Fries, greasy and limp. He took one, chewed. It tasted like salt and starch. It tasted like fuel.

Heaven.

He had to tell himself to take his time, to chew, to not eat it so fast as to make himself sick and waste the precious calories.

Rikard stretched his legs out. 'Used to be this lawyer, real sharp guy, used to sleep out here. Had a good job, family, everything. Then one day, just walked away. No drugs, no mental breaks, just … left. Nobody knows why. Couldn't go back, though. Whatever made him leave, he couldn't undo it.'

Victor kept eating.

Rikard gestured towards the others. 'That guy over there? Won't take his meds. Talks to people who aren't there. That woman? Used to be a nurse. Got hooked on painkillers after an accident. Now she shoots up when she can. That man? Ran from something. Won't say what.'

Victor finished the burger. Awful in every way and yet it tasted divine as the first solid food he had eaten in days.

Rikard tapped his cup against the wood of the pavilion, then offered it. 'Milkshake?'

Victor took it, drank. The cold, sweet thickness of it coated his throat, shocking after days of stale water and sour scraps.

Rikard nodded. 'Good, huh?'

'The best.'

Victor passed it back.

Rikard wiped his mouth, then looked at him, really looked at him. 'How long you planning on staying with us?'

He didn't answer but Rikard saw the truth.

For now, Victor was going nowhere.

FIFTY-SEVEN

The room was cold. Not the kind of cold that bit at the skin, but something deeper, heavier. It settled under the skin. It seeped deep into the lungs. The air smelled of antiseptic and worse, the kind of air that had been scrubbed too clean. The overhead fluorescents cast a pale, sterile glow on the room's metal surfaces, on the rows of compartments that lined the walls, making everything seem flat and lifeless.

Which was fitting, he thought.

Erik Stahler stood motionless, staring down at the body on the metal slab.

Draeger wasn't covered. Not any more. They had pulled back the sheet as soon as the mortician left them alone. The bribe had been easy enough. Money always bought silence in places like this.

The tag on the toe read Gustavus Håkansson.

His team stood beside Stahler, gazes locked onto what was left of their friend. He had been the first to pull the sheet back. Hadn't hesitated. Hadn't flinched. Now, though, his shoulders were rising and falling with slow, deliberate breaths. His nostrils flared.

No one had spoken since they entered the mortuary.

The only woman in his team, a former spy with the BND, held the autopsy report in her hands. She hadn't looked at the body. Not really. Just glanced before focusing on the paper, using it as a barrier. Her grip was white-knuckled, but her voice, when she finally spoke, was steady.

'Twelve rounds,' she said. The words were clinical, detached. 'All to the face.'

No one responded.

She exhaled, flipping the page. 'The rounds that were recovered were .45 calibre. Some fragmented, some intact. At least five rounds passed through entirely. The wounds suggest—'

Stahler's gaze stayed on Draeger's corpse. The bullets had done their job well. The features were gone. Obliterated. The bone and flesh that had once been Draeger's face were now unrecognisable. Just ruin.

Stahler had seen a lot of corpses. Had made a lot of corpses. But this – this was something else.

'This wasn't a hit,' he said finally. His voice sounded rough, even to his own ears. 'No professional does this, empties an entire magazine into one man's face. Two, maybe three to confirm the kill. This? This is—'

'Excessive,' she finished. 'And loud. None of these rounds were subsonic.'

Stahler frowned. 'So whoever did this didn't care about being quiet.'

'Or,' she said, flipping through the report again, 'they wanted to make sure no one could identify him.' She paused, then looked up, meeting Stahler's gaze. 'And it worked. We only know it's Draeger because he's one of us.'

Silence settled over them again.

Another of the team let out a slow breath, stepping away from the table, having seen enough. 'So what are we saying? That the assassin went berserk and just kept shooting?'

Her voice was quieter this time. 'Maybe the assassin shot him. Then someone else saw an opportunity.'

The words hung heavy in the air between them.

Stahler grunted. 'So Håkansson sees Draeger dead, realises no one will know who it is, and decides to use the body to fake his son's death?'

'Maybe,' she said. 'But we don't know for sure.'

Stahler stayed quiet, turning the facts over in his head. It didn't fit. None of it. The execution didn't match what they knew of the assassin. The volume of fire was unnecessary. The forensic details were messy. And yet Draeger was dead, and the only way to get answers was to find the one man who could give them.

Stahler said, 'Håkansson said nothing about the excessive number of shots. He did not say he saw an opportunity to fake his son's death.' The German straightened, rolling his shoulders. The anger had settled now. Hardened into something else. Something colder. 'All the bullets are the same, yes?'

She nodded. 'Every single one. Same calibre. Same markings. Fired from the same gun.'

'We have a new job in Morocco,' Stahler reminded his team. 'We start in three days so it means we need to leave here tomorrow to be ready.'

All gazes on him, waiting.

'That job is worth a lot of money to us all. Not only that, but its timely completion is invaluable to our reputation and our continued ability to earn a living.'

Still, they waited.

'I will not judge any of you who wishes to leave for Morocco,' Stahler continued. 'But I am going nowhere until this is done.'

He let his words settle for a moment, then reached forward and pulled the sheet back over Draeger's body.

No one spoke. No one left.

There was no conversation about what needed to be done.

Each member of the team was on the same page.

The Moroccan job, the money, their reputation, their future earning potential.

None of that mattered to them

The only thing that did, was vengeance.

FIFTY-EIGHT

The days had blended into a monotonous rhythm, each one marked by the slow healing of Victor's wound and the unspoken camaraderie with Rikard. The park had become more than a temporary sanctuary, its familiar sights and sounds offering a semblance of stability in an otherwise chaotic existence. As a man who had no home even when well, it was a surprise to have been welcomed into the home of so many.

Victor's side still ached – a persistent, dull throb that reminded him of his vulnerability. The scab had begun to peel at the edges, a sign of progress, though the tightness in his movements betrayed the lingering weakness. He had learned to mask the impediment, adjusting his posture to stand straight, his gait now steady enough to avoid unwanted attention.

Rikard sat on a bench, his weathered hands cradling a steaming cup of tea, the aroma mingling with the crisp morning air. Victor approached, the crunch of gravel underfoot announcing his presence.

Victor glanced into the distance, the city stirring to life beyond the park's borders. 'I'll be gone soon.'

'Figured as much. You're looking a lot better.'

Victor unclasped his watch.

It had a simple black leather strap and an unassuming white dial. He held it out to Rikard.

'It's more valuable than it looks. Take it to a reputable jeweller or pawn shop. Make sure they know you know it's a Jaeger-LeCoultre Polaris. Sell it and it'll keep you going for a long time, and I don't mean living in the park. You can rent a small place for a year with that watch.'

Wearing an expensive yet understated watch let Victor carry a portable asset that could be liquidated when necessary. It ensured he always had resources at his disposal, even across borders.

Rikard's eyes widened. 'Why give it to me?'

Victor stood, adjusting the coat he had been given. 'Because I can.'

The past week had taken its toll; he could feel the weight he had lost, his body leaner, muscles more defined and yet weaker. The enforced diet had depleted his glycogen stores, but he knew they would replenish fast once he resumed his usual regimen.

Rikard took the watch. He said nothing further.

Victor told him, 'Take care of yourself.'

As he left the park behind, the noise and movement of the wider city was a stark contrast to the relative peace of the last several days. In seconds, Victor blended into the crowd, just another face among many, his presence unremarkable despite his unshaven face, his dirty clothes. But beneath the surface, he remained vigilant, every sense attuned to the environment, ready for whatever lay ahead.

He walked into the first clothing shop he came across and felt many gazes on him. The stares came from both customers and staff – some subtle, others blatant. He didn't blame them. He looked like he belonged outside, not inside.

The coat was stiff with dried sweat and street grime. The jacket and shirt underneath still stained with his blood. His trousers were loose now, the evidence of weight lost over a week on starvation rations. The shoes had once been worn but functional – now they were just battered. He caught a glimpse of himself in a passing mirror.

A stranger looked back at him.

The shop wasn't high-end. Chain-brand, affordable. He picked out dark jeans, straight cut. A plain black T-shirt. A fitted navy sweater. A charcoal overcoat – something practical, warm but not bulky. Socks. Underwear. Everything off the rack, everything forgettable. He kept it simple, utilitarian. Clothes that would let him blend.

At the self-checkout, the machine beeped with every scan. No cashier to raise an eyebrow, no questions. He paid in cash, took the bags, and walked out.

In another shop, he grabbed a pack of wet wipes and a disposable razor from a nearby shelf, added them to a pile of toiletries.

The hotel he selected was a budget chain, one of the newer ones that had fully embraced automation. No receptionists, no front desk staff. Just a bank of touchscreen terminals near the entrance, glowing blue in the dim lighting. It was quiet. Anonymous. A place where no one would look for him.

Victor stepped up to one and tapped through the prompts. Standard room. Single night. Paid in cash. No ID required. The machine spat out a key card with a soft mechanical click, and he took it without hesitation.

The lift smelled of cheap cleaning products. He would have taken the stairs but he wasn't sure he had the energy to climb them.

The hallway was sterile, bland. His room was small but functional – a bed, a desk, a bathroom with a shower stall.

Victor locked the door behind him and exhaled.

He set the bags down and moved to the bathroom, twisting the sink's tap. Water rushed out, splashing against the ceramic. He cupped his hands beneath it, bringing it to his face, scrubbing away the film of dirt and sweat.

The water ran brown at first, swirling down the drain.

He never showered. Showers were dangerous. Impossible to hear what was going on outside the bathroom.

Instead, he stripped and used the wet wipes to scrub himself down in a methodical manner. The grime and dried blood came away in layers. He then shaved with a beard trimmer, and then with a razor in short, efficient strokes, rinsing the blade every few seconds. When he was done, he ran a hand over his face, feeling the smoothness beneath his fingertips for the first time since before beginning the contract. A beard was one of the most useful disguises and its removal changed his appearance in a fast, dramatic way. As did cutting his hair. He used scissors to reduce the length enough for the beard trimmer to do the rest. Not quite a skinhead – that kind of severe look drew attention – but so short it did not need combing and completed the transformation.

He changed into the new clothes. The fit was good – too loose to look good. The heft of the coat on his shoulders felt right.

His old clothes went into a plastic bag. He'd dispose of them later, far from here.

The burner phone he had bought along the way was cheap, preloaded with credit, the kind sold over the counter with no questions asked. He sat on the bed, powered it up. The start-up animation flickered briefly before fading to black. A basic handset. That was all he needed.

He inserted the SIM card, connected to a secured messaging platform and waited. A moment later, the messages came through.

1 New Message – Eriksson21

Your payment has been processed. Thank you for your service.

Victor stared at the screen.

His account balance had increased. The second half of the contract fee had been deposited. The job was marked as complete.

Except he hadn't completed it.

Gustavus Håkansson was still alive. His death had been faked, a body double standing in his place behind armoured glass. A trap to catch Victor, and yet the client had paid him in full.

Which meant they believed Gustavus had been killed that night.

Something didn't add up. Many things, in fact.

None of it mattered. Victor's priority was to get out of the city while he was still breathing. Everything else was a secondary consideration.

Victor stared at the screen for a long moment, then backed out of the message.

There was another one. From Scragg.

ha ha cant believe you left me just joking i know you were in a state christal says you both managed to get away lets grab a beer

Scragg was alive. Another surprise, and yet this one came with more relief, which Victor had not expected. He put it down to gratitude.

However, there were too many unknowns. What happened that night at the chemical plant? Who were the professionals? How did Scragg escape them? And why was he *this* casual about it?

If Scragg had been tortured or coerced, he might have talked. If he hadn't, he might still be able to get Victor out of the city undetected.

The job was over, but nothing felt finished. Victor still had to leave.

He sent a message in reply, pocketed the burner phone, grabbed his coat and stepped back into the city.

Malmö had been waiting for him to return.

Also waiting somewhere out there was the Boatman.

FIFTY-NINE

Victor chose the location with care. It had to be somewhere public, but not just *any* public place. A coffee shop was too enclosed – too little control. A bar was worse. Too many people lingering, too many unpredictable variables.

He needed a place that was enclosed but busy. Somewhere with limited but clear entrances and exits. Somewhere he could observe from a distance before committing to the meeting.

He chose a railway station.

A week since the gallery disaster, the police would have moved on in their priorities. Still, his threat radar was in full operation even if he looked little like the man they were looking for now he was clean shaven and his hair was just a few millimetres in length.

Not the platforms, where movement was too chaotic, where people surged in and out unpredictably. Instead, the main concourse where coffee kiosks and fast-food chains lined the walls, where travellers sat killing time before departures. The ceiling was high, the walls lined with security cameras. No vantage points for a sniper. If the Boatman was somehow here, he would need to be close to complete the kill.

Victor arrived an hour before the meeting time.

He moved through the station like a traveller with nowhere urgent to be. He bought a coffee he didn't drink. Sat on a bench with a newspaper he didn't read. He scanned the crowd, filtering out the obvious civilians. The ones who didn't move with intent. The ones whose body language was relaxed, whose attention was buried in their phones or in the weight of their own daily routines.

Then he watched for the others.

Anyone of the Boatman's dimensions were the primary focuses for his attention. Six feet or thereabouts. Lean build. Men who moved like they knew exactly where they were going, but not like they were in a rush to get there. People whose eyes moved too much, scanning rather than observing. People who stood too still, as if waiting but without checking a phone or a watch.

He saw no one who could be his hunter.

Still, he waited.

Twenty minutes before the meeting, he did another circuit, moving through the flow of foot traffic, doubling back, taking a different route, stopping, changing again. Watching. Looking for anyone who adjusted their pace to match his own. Anyone whose direction shifted when his did.

Nothing.

He circled back to the communal eating area.

The Kashmiri Scottish Viking was sitting on a bench near a sandwich kiosk, his legs crossed at the ankles, a half-eaten wrap in one hand, a cup of coffee in the other. He was, relaxed, so relaxed that Victor didn't buy it. The casual demeanour was real, but Scragg wasn't stupid.

Victor watched him for a full minute before approaching.

Scragg saw him coming, lifting his cup in a lazy salute.

'Figured you'd come early,' he said as Victor took the seat opposite. 'Didn't think you'd be watching me for ten minutes first.'

Victor didn't correct him. 'You're alive.'

'Nothing gets past you,' he said with a smirk, then, referencing the shave, the haircut: 'You look even more like a stone-cold psychopath than you did before.' He grunted. 'I like it. Maybe had you looked like this before we could have walked out of the cold-storage place without leaving a massacre behind.'

'I prefer people don't see the real me until it's too late.'

Scragg laughed.

Victor didn't smile. 'How did you escape?'

The older man shrugged. 'Same way as you, I suppose. Right place, right time. Or wrong place, wrong time, depending on how you look at it.'

Victor said, 'Tell me what happened and I'll decide.'

Scragg explained how he was captured by the team outside the disused chemical plant, how they had taken him away to the yoga studio that was their safe house, how they revealed they were bounty hunters who had been tracking Lukas Draeger, how Scragg was bundled into the boot of a car and heard someone say, 'Make sure he's never found.'

'And then what happened?' Victor asked.

'You best buckle up, Princess. It's quite the ride . . .'

*

Scragg lay twisted in the boot, his breath becoming more and more ragged in the suffocating dark. Each jolt of the vehicle slammed him against the cold metal sides, jarring bone and muscle alike. The air grew thicker with every shallow inhalation, stale and warm with the tang of exhaust gases.

The car swerved – rapid, sharp – tyres skimming slick asphalt, and Scragg was thrown around inside of the boot. Pain flared, biting and immediate, but terror dulled the edge. His heartbeat drummed faster with every bump in the road – a countdown he couldn't stop, measuring the seconds until ... what? A bullet? The cold shock of drowning?

The boot already felt like a coffin sealed shut.

Then the tyres screeched.

The sudden halt sent Scragg sliding again, his head colliding with unyielding metal. The engine's growl dropped to a low idle, and in the suffocating stillness, he strained to hear.

A rocking motion told him a door had opened and someone had climbed out.

He heard voices – loud, tense – barked orders into the night, but their meaning was lost in Scragg's panic.

He pressed against the boot's walls as if sheer will could break through steel. His shoulders shook with the effort to stay silent.

Gunshots.

Each one a physical blow that reverberated through the vehicle that Scragg felt in his bruised ribs as he flinched. Another shot – louder, closer – pierced the night with brutal finality, followed by the brittle shatter of glass raining onto asphalt.

Then nothing.

Scragg's pulse roared in his ears as he waited, counting heartbeats.

No footsteps. No voices.

Just the hum of distant traffic, distant lives that would never know he'd been there.

Nothing he could do but wait.

Scragg lay twisted and motionless. He strained to hear – anything to hint at what was happening – but heard nothing amid the ambient noise of the city.

Seconds felt like hours.

His shoulders ached from the awkward position, his wrists raw where the cable ties bit into flesh, his ribs burning from the earlier kicks, but it was the waiting that gnawed at him – the not-knowing.

Each heartbeat seemed to tick down to something inevitable, though he had no idea what.

Why had it gone quiet?

Then light burst into the boot, searing his eyes because the blindfold had come askew.

Scragg flinched, turtling tighter, expecting the worst.

Hands grabbed him and hauled him upwards.

As his eyes adjusted to the new light, he saw the red and blue strobe of a police car's lights painting the night in fractured pulses.

'Hold still,' a uniformed police officer ordered, gripping Scragg's shoulder to steady him as he dragged him from the boot. Asphalt bit into his knees as they lowered him beside the car.

The blindfold pulled off revealed the scene around him – two police cars parked at odd angles, their lights reflecting off shattered glass scattered across the road.

The vehicle he had been dragged out of had its driver's door open, and no driver was inside or nearby. The night echoed with the babble of police radios.

The officer knelt beside him, checking the cable ties around his wrists. 'We'll get you out of these. Can you walk?'

Scragg's voice cracked as he tried to speak. 'Where ... where am I?' His chest still heaved with ragged breaths, adrenalin coursing through him as a fire he could not control.

'You're safe now,' the officer said, cutting through the ties with a quick slice of a pocketknife.

Scragg stared at the broken glass, the open driver's door and boot, and the flashing lights, the last remnants of terror still clinging to the edges of his consciousness. He swallowed hard against the lump in his throat and forced himself to believe the officer's words.

'You're a lucky man,' the cop told Scragg.

'There's no such thing as luck,' Victor told him.

Scragg scoffed. 'Spoken like lucky feckers the world over.'

Victor raised an eyebrow.

Scragg leaned forward. 'What's your plan?'

Victor didn't answer right away. His gaze flicked across the immediate area, sweeping for anyone who didn't fit. The crowd was shifting – travellers hauling luggage, commuters on lunch breaks moving with impatient efficiency, families wrangling children – but nothing stood out. No one watching. No one waiting.

No Boatman.

Scragg watched him, waiting.

Finally, Victor spoke. 'Can you still get me out through the port?'

Scragg frowned. 'You're telling me it isn't the exquisite pleasure of my company that warranted this reunion? Princess, you have hurt me deep in my cold black soul.'

Victor remained silent.

Scragg rubbed the back of his neck. 'But yeah, it's still doable,' he said. 'Only it now comes with a price tag, I'm afraid to say.'

Victor kept his expression neutral. 'What price?'

Scragg pushed back his bench and stood. 'Come on.'

'Where are we going?'

'Where do you think?' The older man grinned, grabbed his coffee and took a slow sip before adding, 'We're going to see a man about a dog.'

Victor didn't like vague answers. He didn't like following anyone anywhere without knowing what was waiting at the other end. But Scragg was already walking, weaving through the crowd with a careless confidence that made him blend in without effort because the thought of imminent ambush was an alien concept to him.

'*Let's get a shift on, yeah?*' Scragg shouted loud enough for everyone in the communal eating area to look his way.

Trying not to frown, Victor stood and followed.

SIXTY

'Bastards,' Håkansson said as he walked with Police Director Elise Wallin back to where Magnar Kaale and the armoured limousine waited. Another meeting with Leila Farahani, Nikola Petrović and Tobias Malmgren had been concluded without conclusion. 'They cannot help themselves. They do not have the good manners to wait until I'm in the ground before they feast upon me.'

Wallin nodded. 'I fear this false glimpse into a very profitable future has whetted the appetites of Petrović, Farahani and Malmgren too much for them to accept a poorer one when the truth comes out.'

'I did not believe it would take this long. I thought we would know by now which of them is my enemy. Instead, I have ensured all of them will be the enemy to my son after I'm gone.'

She asked, 'How is Gustavus getting on?'

'He is a young man imprisoned in his own home. How do you think he is? Cut off from his friends, from everyone and everything, he is moody, sullen, angry, resentful. And worst of all, he's scared. The longer this continues, the more he thinks about assassins and bullets and death. He's in his prime. He should only be thinking about a glorious future. Every time I see him stare off into space or that he hasn't slept well it is a slap to my face. I am failing him as a father.'

'Has the Boatman not uncovered anything further about the assassin?'

'He knows that the killer intends to leave Malmö via the port using a local fixer named Scragg to get him on board a cargo ship or some such. Scragg is the man your officers rescued when you kindly agreed to the Boatman's request to have his car pulled over.'

She nodded to say that it had not been a big deal. 'So, this Scragg believes his escape was luck and presumably the arrangement he has with the assassin is unaffected.'

Now it was Håkansson's turn to nod. 'As such the Boatman has Scragg's office at the port under surveillance and will be ready to intercept when the assassin attempts to slip out of the city. Until that point, he remains hidden. So, tell me, why haven't your people made progress?'

'I have steered many resources to find him. All major public transportation hubs were being watched and hotels, guesthouses and private rental hosts were given sketches. But ... it's been a week. There's only so many resources I can now dedicate without our arrangement being dragged into the daylight. Other crimes have been committed since. More still will be committed. Whoever he is, he's been good at lying low or he's already gone.'

'It doesn't really matter at this point,' he said.

'I do not understand.'

'Each day I feel weaker,' Håkansson admitted. 'The stress, the worry of this is eating away at me as much as the cancer. My time is short already and now I fear this will finish me. It cannot. I *will* not leave this world while my son remains unsafe.' He looked back to the private club in which Farahani, Petrović and Malmgren continued their discussion. 'Until I know which one of them is guilty, they are all guilty.'

Wallin held his gaze, understanding.

She did not attempt to dissuade him. Instead, she asked, 'How?'

'The Boatman, naturally.'

'You risk war,' she said. 'Once it begins and the others realise, they will entrench. They will fight back. Once aligned against you, it's over.'

'Then it will happen swiftly, or all at once.'

'You haven't just decided this, have you?'

He shook his head. 'It has been a consideration that I have already discussed the practicalities of with the Boatman. He is ready whenever I give the word.'

'And he is … capable of such a feat?'

'He kept the entire Russian mafia playing from the same hymn sheet for decades.' Håkansson wavered, and, if not for the sudden, steadying hand of Kaale, would have fallen. 'I had hoped it would not come to this because everything I have built will crumble as a result. Gustavus will not inherit a kingdom as I had planned, but he will be alive and that will be enough.'

All Wallin could say was, 'When?'

'Soon.'

SIXTY-ONE

The Turning Torso twisted upward against the night sky as a helix of glass and steel. Its segmented design seemed to defy geometry, each cube offset from the one below in a spiral until reaching a pinnacle that leaned towards the sea. Victor regarded the structure without admiration. Like with music, anything constructed after 1900 was too modern, too cold for his tastes. Still, he wasn't here to critique architectural design.

Stepping out of the lift at the penthouse level, a tall man waited for them. He wore a royal blue suit, white shirt, and sky blue tie, his black hair slicked back and curling at the nape of his neck. He had a strong physique, but a fighter's build. Not the showy muscles of a bodyguard who needed to intimidate, this man had the shape of someone who expected to use it.

Scragg nodded to the man. 'Darius.'

He gave each man a pat down, which Scragg had warned about, so neither he nor Victor were armed.

Darius Mehran did not like him one bit, Victor saw, but he opened the doors to the penthouse and gestured for them to enter. He acknowledged Scragg with a glance and yet all of Mehran's attention was fixed on Victor, the unknown quantity.

The doors whispered open into a foyer of polished stone and smoked glass. The air smelled of saffron, a subtle hint of Leila Farahani's Iranian heritage woven into the sterile Scandinavian design.

Mehran led them through a corridor lined with stark sconces that threw warm, gold-tinted light against walls of pale limestone. The corridor opened into the main living space, and Victor paused, assessing. Floor-to-ceiling windows wrapped around the space, offering an uninterrupted panorama of Malmö's cityscape and the distant sweep of the Øresund Bridge.

Turkish rugs of deep crimson and indigo lay over pale oak floors. Low-slung sofas in rich emerald velvet faced each other around a brass and marble coffee table adorned with intricate Persian filigree. Along the inner walls, narrow alcoves displayed delicate Iznik ceramics and gilded calligraphy panels inscribed with classical Persian poetry.

Overhead, a contemporary chandelier of hammered brass discs cast soft, dappled shadows against the ceiling. To the right, a glass partition separated the living space from what Victor assumed was Leila Farahani's office – visible through the transparent wall were dark walnut shelves lined with leather-bound volumes and a brass globe atop a mahogany sideboard. The only painting in the room was a large canvas of swirling gold and cobalt blue, its abstract curves suggestive of calligraphic script.

Mehran gestured towards the seating area. 'Wait here.'

'I don't know if you noticed,' Scragg whispered. 'But he already fecking hates you, Princess.'

Victor raised an eyebrow. 'And yet I'm so incredibly loveable.'

His gaze returned to the cityscape beyond the glass, the headlights of cars threading along the Øresund Bridge like tiny sparks of movement. The elegance of the room did nothing to dull the awareness that, beneath its polished surface, this was still the domain of a criminal.

The click of footsteps announced Leila Farahani before she entered the room with the unhurried grace of someone accustomed to commanding attention without demanding it. She moved like silk over stone – fluid, deliberate, each step measured without appearing forced. Mehran followed, taking up position on the room's periphery.

In heels, Farahani stood only a few centimetres shorter than Victor, her figure slender but not fragile, poised with the elegance of someone who had earned her status. Her skin carried the warm tone of her Iranian heritage, smooth and unblemished beneath the soft amber glow of the room's lighting. Dark eyes, oval shaped and sharp with intelligence, regarded Victor with the calm confidence of a woman who saw more than she revealed.

Her gaze didn't challenge. It assessed. Weighed. Calculated.

Thick, raven-black hair, swept back from her face in a low chignon, revealed high cheekbones and the precise angles of a sculpted jawline. Gold earrings, shaped like stylised pomegranate flowers, caught the light as she moved. Her make-up was minimal – just enough to define her eyes and the full curve of her lips, painted a shade of deep plum that hinted at the boldness beneath her composed exterior.

She wore a midnight-blue silk blouse with a subtle sheen, its fit accentuating the delicate lines of her collarbones and the curve of her shoulders. The blouse was tucked into high-waisted ivory trousers that fell in crisp, straight lines to her ankles.

'Thank you for coming.' Her voice was smooth, low, and accented with the faintest trace of her Persian roots – a warmth that softened the precision of her English without diminishing its clarity.

'Our pleasure,' Scragg replied.

Victor didn't respond, studying her as she returned his gaze without a flicker of uncertainty. Her authority was quiet, rooted in control rather than force. This was a woman who commanded through expectation and consequence, not violence.

Power, distilled into poise.

She inclined her head, a gesture that was neither deference nor invitation, then moved past him to the seating area, the faintest scent of rose trailing in her wake. As she lowered herself onto the emerald velvet sofa, she gestured to the chair opposite with a slight motion of her hand.

'Please, sit.'

Scragg remained by the entrance, hands clasped in front of him.

Victor lowered himself into the chair opposite Farahani, leaning back just enough to signal composure without robbing himself of stability by moving his head too far away from his hips.

'I understand,' she began, her tone even and polite, 'that

Mr Scragg wishes to make use of my port without the inter-ference of customs officers or security inspections.'

'That's right,' Victor said.

'Unfortunately, he has ... lost his privileges in that regard.' Her attention slid towards Scragg, a flash of dis-approval passing through her otherwise placid gaze. 'And I have recently learned that he attempted to circumvent my authority by arranging a stowaway passage without my con-sent. Which is yet another black mark against his name.'

Victor asked, 'Then why am I here?'

A smile touched her lips, cool and yet not unkind. 'Straight to business. I appreciate that.' She leaned forward, elbows resting on her knees. 'The reason concerns a substance called osmium – one kilogram, to be precise. Mr Scragg was tasked with acquiring it, and in doing so, he made certain promises. I, in turn, promised that same osmium to a very powerful arms dealer named Vladimir Kasakov. Perhaps you've heard the name?'

Victor remained silent, but she read the flicker of recog-nition in his gaze that she would put down to Kasakov's reputation preceding him. She could not have known that Victor's path had crossed with the Ukrainian on more than one occasion.

'When Mr Scragg failed to deliver the osmium to me,' she continued, her tone cooling, 'I, too, failed to meet my obli-gation. As a result, Kasakov has severed ties and excluded me from his network. That ... is not a position I am accus-tomed to.'

Victor noted the slight pause, the restraint in her voice. This wasn't a woman prone to emotional displays, but the loss of influence had hurt her in ways beyond just financial.

'And now?' he asked.

Farahani's gaze didn't waver. 'Now that I have been excluded from Kasakov's network, he has found an alternative supplier. I have reason to believe that this supplier is in possession of the very osmium that should have come to me.' Her lips pressed together, more calculation than frustration. 'It appears that Järnberg, instead of delivering it to Scragg as promised, chose to sell the osmium at a higher price to another network. At the same time, he attempted to deceive me with a counterfeit substitute.'

Although his gaze was on Farahani, Victor made sure to pay equal attention to Mehran as well, who did not speak as he stood as a typical bodyguard.

Except he was not.

There was a considered deliberateness to him that most security personnel lacked. Not simply present, he was listening. Watching. His eyes, dark and sharp, did not focus on Victor and yet they absorbed everything.

While Victor was assessing him, Mehran was doing the exact same thing to him in return.

Farahani paused, weighing the next words before speaking them. 'I heard what happened to Järnberg and his crew. An avoidable, and yet well-deserved, incident.' Her eyes reflected nothing but pragmatic interest. 'If the individuals who now possess my osmium were to lose it while meeting a similar fate, it would simplify matters considerably. More importantly, it would restore my standing with Kasakov's network.'

Victor remained silent.

He preferred more directness when it came to his line of work but he understood that to most people it was more palatable to have fellow human beings murdered without using explicit terminology.

They regarded one another across the space between them, silence measured in breaths and intentions.

Farahani's smile was small and deliberate. 'And for the one who accomplishes this task, I offer safe passage out of Malmö.'

SIXTY-TWO

The kettle had begun to steam, a thin, curling whisper of heat rising towards the ceiling. Darius Mehran moved with quiet efficiency, setting out the glasses, dropping two cubes of sugar into one, leaving the other untouched. He worked without haste, though there was tension in his shoulders, she could see.

Leila Farahani sat near the window, the city stretching out beyond the glass. She had loosened her blouse at the collar, but otherwise, she was as composed as she had been in the meeting. She reached for the cigarette resting in the tray beside her, tapping off the ash, watching Mehran as he poured the tea into delicate, handle-less glasses.

'You don't like him.'

It was not a question.

Mehran lifted the kettle from the flame, setting it down. He let the silence sit between them for a moment, then exhaled through pursed lips. 'No.'

He brought the glasses over, setting one in front of her, the other beside his own seat. The deep amber liquid caught the low light, rich and strong. Chai shirin. He had added sugar to hers, the way she preferred it. His, he would drink bitter.

'You don't trust anyone.' Farahani took a sip, inhaling the steam. 'So this is no surprise.'

Mehran sat opposite her, forearms resting on the table. He let the tea cool. 'This is different. He is dangerous.'

Farahani tilted her head, watching him. 'They all are. Why is he different?'

'Because he saw me.'

'He saw you?' Farahani swirled her tea around, watching the ripples shift against the light. 'What did he see?'

Mehran's fingers clutched the hot glass. 'Most men see the suit. The gun. The fact that I stand at your shoulder and assume I am there to stop bullets and nothing else.'

Farahani smirked at him. 'Aren't you?'

Mehran frowned, the closest he would come to laughing. 'He saw what I am to you. What you are to me.'

'He knew what I was the moment he saw me.' He shook his head. 'Most men would look at me and see an obstacle. He looked at me and saw a variable.'

Farahani leaned back, studying him. 'You think he's going to be a problem?'

Mehran finally took a sip of his tea. 'I know he is.'

Between them, the smoke from her cigarette rose in a thin coil.

'Using him like this when Håkansson is tearing the city apart to find him ... that's the kind of risk you don't usually take.'

Farahani sipped her tea. 'All progress is a risk.'

Mehran set his glass down, leaning forward. 'You don't

need to do this. Håkansson won't be around for ever, and without Gustavus, his network will be yours for the taking. Why not just sit back and wait?'

'This is bigger than Håkansson.' Farahani smiled, but it was a small thing, private. She reached out, running a fingertip along the rim of her glass. 'He, like Malmgren, like Petrović ... they see Malmö. They see Sweden. They see *now*.' She tapped the glass. 'I see further. I see into the future. This city, these arrangements – all stepping stones, nothing more.'

Mehran studied her, unreadable. 'If anything goes wrong with this ... If Håkansson finds out then it's a war we can't win.'

She leaned forward. 'Retrieving the osmium reopens a door that I thought closed to me for ever. To Vladimir Kasakov. To his network. To the world beyond this city. That's worth the risk.'

'Please,' he said. 'Be careful.'

Farahani's expression softened. She reached out, her fingers brushing his wrist in a small, intimate gesture. 'I don't need to be.' She met his eyes. 'I have you.'

Mehran held her gaze for a long moment, then nodded once. 'Always.'

'Besides,' she added. 'You're forgetting our inbuilt contingency in case anything does go wrong.'

'Which is?'

'We have Gustavus's killer,' Farahani began. 'Imagine how pleased Håkansson will be if we decide to hand him over.'

SIXTY-THREE

In the affluent district of Limhamn, located on the south-western outskirts of Malmö, Deputy Mayor Tobias Malmgren resided in a contemporary villa that epitomised modern Scandinavian design. The exterior showcased clean lines, large floor-to-ceiling windows, and a façade combining white render with natural wood accents. Inside, the villa comprised five spacious bedrooms, an open-plan living area, a state-of-the-art kitchen and a private study.

The study – Malmgren's personal retreat – reflected his preference for order and efficiency. The room featured a sleek, minimalist aesthetic save for floating shelves lining the walls, holding a cluttered selection of books and a few personal mementos.

As Malmgren worked late into the evening, his mind oscillated between his official duties and his clandestine dealings. The following day promised a series of engagements: a meeting with the city council to discuss urban development projects, a luncheon with local business leaders to attract new investments, and a press conference addressing recent public concerns about infrastructure. These responsibilities required his full attention, yet his thoughts were ever focused on his association with Jorund Håkansson.

The partnership had been lucrative, intertwining political influence with business ventures that benefited both parties. However, recent events had introduced a myriad of problems that gave him the feeling that their carefully constructed empire was teetering on a precipice.

He leaned back in his chair, rubbing his temples. Balancing public service with private interests had always been a delicate act, but now the stakes were higher than ever. Håkansson was becoming unstable in his grief and the entire operation's future was in question.

It was well past midnight. He knew he should rest. Instead, he reached for his tablet, intending to review the latest reports once more, hoping to find some semblance of control in the data before him.

The power cut was an unexpected annoyance.

The whole house went black. Only the light from his tablet provided any illumination.

He could hear nothing from the nearby bedrooms. His wife, Linnea, and the children – Elin and Max – were asleep. Good.

Malmgren stood, using the torch on his phone to light the way downstairs. He headed towards the breaker box in the double garage.

His bare feet were near silent against the heated tiles as he moved through the kitchen and into the adjacent hallway, then into the garage that smelled of damp and oil. His Tesla sat in the centre, polished and untouched, beside his wife's Volvo. Shelving units lined the walls – tools he rarely used, ski equipment, a collection of old suitcases covered in dust.

Malmgren ran his fingers along the breaker panel, found the switches and flipped them back up. The power hummed back to life. Light flooded the space as the overhead bulbs flickered on.

He exhaled. Just a trip, nothing more.

Malmgren made his way back into his study, the residual tension from the power cut still prickling at his nerves. At first glance, nothing seemed out of place. The soft glow of the lamp cast long shadows across the minimalist furniture, the cool blue light of his monitor idle on the sleek desk.

But then his gaze moved to the chair behind the desk.

A man was sitting in the chair.

He was so unremarkable. That was Malmgren's first thought.

A plain face, short, neat hair, a build neither muscular nor slight. Dressed in dark, nondescript clothing that wouldn't stand out on a crowded street. If Malmgren had passed him earlier that day in the city, he wouldn't have looked twice.

But here, in his home, the presence of the man was profoundly wrong.

Then Malmgren noticed what was truly missing.

The man did not move.

He didn't shift in his seat, didn't tap a finger, didn't adjust his posture. There was no habitual twitch of expression, no flicker of emotion. The face was set – not blank, not passive, but *fixed*, as if his features had been locked into place.

The eyes were worse.

Cold, unblinking, they regarded Malmgren with the same

311

lifeless intensity as a surveillance camera, as if processing data rather than looking at him.

There was no hostility in them, no impatience, no curiosity.

Just quiet, cold inevitability.

When the man spoke, his mouth moved only as much as necessary. The words came in a low monotone, free of emphasis, free of intonation. A voice that was not interested in persuading or threatening – only in emotionless statements.

'Sit down.'

Malmgren had never met him before, but he knew this was the Boatman.

He knew because the man had that presence. That stillness. The kind that made his body register danger before his mind had even caught up.

'I should have known,' Malmgren said, keeping his voice even. 'The power cut.'

The Boatman nodded. 'Your security system is state of the art and yet it still needs electricity.'

Malmgren looked around, scanning the room, searching for a weapon, for anything.

The Boatman just watched him.

Malmgren exhaled. 'Why are you here?'

'You know why.'

The voice was flat and yet smooth.

'Jorund's lost his mind,' Malmgren said, voice cracking. 'I didn't do it. I would never ... I – Listen, why would I kill his son? I want business to continue unimpeded. He must know – he knows – I urged him to make Gustavus ready. Tell him, tell him he's wrong – just do that for me – I'm innocent.'

The Boatman said, 'I don't care.'

Malmgren scoffed. 'Of course not. You just follow orders.'

'It's not for me to decide who I take across the river.'

A shiver ran through Malmgren's body. He swallowed his fear. He kept his voice calm. 'You could let me go. I have money, you know? A lot. I can't spend it while in office so it's grown and grown over the years. You can have it all.'

The Boatman told him, 'When you are standing on the shoreline waiting for me, nothing can change that.'

'I'll call him,' Malmgren pleaded. 'I'll convince him. He's paranoid. He's not thinking straight.'

'Do you understand what paranoia is?'

Malmgren said nothing.

'It's pattern recognition in overdrive,' the Boatman continued. 'Jorund sees the pattern. But he is not paranoid. It doesn't matter if you are guilty or one of the others when you're all dead.'

Malmgren took a step back, eyeing the door. His breath was steady, but his hands had started to shake. 'If you're here to kill me, why haven't you done it yet?'

'Because suppressors aren't silent.'

Malmgren's blood ran cold.

'If I shoot you here, there's a better-than-average chance your wife or children will wake up. And if they wake up ...'

He let the sentence hang in the air, unfinished.

The fear Malmgren felt for himself was replaced by the pure horror he felt for his family.

'Instead, you're going to walk back downstairs to the garage,' the Boatman said. 'You're going to lock the door behind you. You're going to call the police and tell them you're about to kill yourself. Tell them where to find the spare key so they can get inside without disturbing your family.'

Malmgren swallowed. His mouth was dry.

The Boatman stood. 'I'm sure I don't have to tell you what happens if you change your mind when you're alone in that garage.'

'*I'm begging you.*'

'No,' the Boatman told him. 'You're trying to convince me that when I walk out of this room my pistol will remain holstered.'

Malmgren thought of his beautiful wife, his beautiful children.

He had worked so hard for so long for them, to give them everything they could ever need. The power, the wealth, meant nothing without them.

His life meant nothing compared to their lives.

He nodded as he exhaled. 'I'll do it.'

The Boatman didn't respond. He walked past him and out through the door without drawing his weapon.

Malmgren sat for a while.

When he stood, he moved like he was in a dream, his limbs detached from his mind. He crossed the room, poured himself a drink with shaking hands, downed it in one swallow. He thought about Linnea, asleep in the next room. He thought about Max's football game this weekend. He thought about Elin's birthday next month.

Then he poured himself another drink.

He let out a long breath.

He went downstairs.

He opened the garage door, stepped inside and locked it behind him.

Then he called the police.

And prepared the rope.

SIXTY-FOUR

Scragg steered the car off the narrow road and down a dirt lane lined with bare trees, their twisted limbs silhouetted against the dark sky. The crunch of tyres over loose stone seemed too loud in the still air as they approached the drop-off point Victor had decided upon.

The car came to a stop and the engine, and the lights, were killed before the wheels had ceased moving.

A few hours after the meeting with Leila Farahani, there had been no time to plan, no time to prepare. Just long enough to secure equipment and weapons.

'Good luck,' the Kashmiri Scottish Viking said.

'There's no such thing as luck,' Victor said.

Not opinion. Fact.

'I'll be here when you're done,' Scragg assured.

'If not, I'll hunt you down.'

'Oh, aye, Princess. I believe you will.'

Victor climbed out of the car – an act that was no longer a struggle – and collected his things from the boot.

He knew the route – had spent a whole fifteen minutes studying maps – and set off into the stretch of trees, and then circled the field beyond, heading towards the lights that filtered through the hedgerows on the other side.

Sprinting was still out of the question, but he could move with speed, accepting the discomfort in his side and glad it was no longer the kind of suffering that required every iota of will he had to beat.

The property's perimeter was marked by dense hedgerows, their branches woven together to create a barrier dense enough to discourage casual trespassers, the greenery blended into the surrounding landscape with deliberate subtlety. Behind the hedgerows, a stone wall ran parallel to the property line – simple, unadorned and tall enough to deter anyone without determination or purpose.

No motion sensors or visible cameras along the boundary – security here relied more on distance and design than technology.

It was a house, not a fortress.

Secure enough to keep out the curious and the careless, leaving only those who knew what they wanted. And how to take it.

His full mobility yet to return, it was slower to scale the wall than he was used to, and yet it felt good to overcome this small challenge that would have been no challenge beforehand.

He crouched down among the foliage inside the grounds, quiet and still.

Dressed all in black, he disappeared into the silhouette of the wall behind him. No lights illuminated this end of the property so far from the house itself, which sat deep within almost two hectares of land. The main building was a pale stone structure with steep gables and tall windows that reflected the grey light.

The building rose two storeys, its façade a blend of limestone and weathered brick. Large windows punctuated the ground floor, revealing a bright interior. A separate structure – smaller but no less refined – stood to the side, a guesthouse or staff quarters. Between them, a glass-walled orangery extended perpendicular from the main house, its interior illuminated by warm lighting that silhouetted the shapes of ornamental plants and expensive furnishings within.

Victor allowed himself a brief moment to wait. Fifty metres ahead, the property glowed, the windows that overlooked the grounds revealing flashes of modern luxury. The back garden stretched between him and the house – immaculate hedges, stone pathways and a large swimming pool with gently rippling water.

The dark storm clouds gathering overhead danced across the surface.

Victor reached into his pack and pulled out a pair of binoculars. HikMicro Raptors, compact and built for purpose – thermal imaging and night vision combined into a single tool. High-grade, anti-reflective lenses, the device powered on with a faint hum, its digital display activating.

With Scragg's resourcefulness and Farahani's connections, there had been few limitations to the equipment he could use.

He raised the Raptors to his eyes, the house coming into view in perfect clarity.

His magnified gaze pierced the tall windows of the main entertaining room. Inside, four men stood around a billiards table.

Victor adjusted the focus, his mind categorising every detail.

At the head of the table stood Antti Streng, tall and fat, his presence as blunt as his reputation. A Finnish chemical engineer, Streng was the man Farahani believed to be responsible for Järnberg reneging on the original deal. Streng was the one who would have the osmium on him – or close to him – at all times.

Next to him, Johan Nyström leaned on his cue. Calm. Polished. His suit tailored, his sharp features hiding a ruthless nature. Nyström was the logistics expert of this particular operation. He was also a career smuggler. Murderer when necessary.

On the far side of the table, Artur Volkov sipped whisky with practised detachment. Volkov's eyes carried the hard edges of a man who had survived long enough in the Russian underworld to make it an art form. He didn't play games unless he controlled the stakes. His connections had given them all access to Kasakov's representative.

Who was Luis Aranda.

A diplomat of criminals – negotiating deals, brokering alliances – Aranda wasn't on Victor's kill list.

Farahani had been explicit in her orders that he was to leave the Spaniard alive because Aranda was the conduit to Kasakov. Without him, there was no deal to be made and no way for Farahani to repair her relationship with the arms dealer.

He was the only one who seemed at ease; the other three men had stiff postures and serious faces. The deal mattered more to them than to Aranda.

Three targets, another man to be spared.

Victor memorised their positions, their interactions, the

unspoken hierarchy between them. Every detail mattered. Every pattern revealed something useful.

Three guards inside the house itself, he noted.

Two near the entrance to the entertaining room, compact submachine guns slung across their chests. Another patrolled the hallway beyond the room. Professional, steady movements, but their posture was relaxed. No one expected trouble.

Victor shifted his gaze to the exterior.

He tapped a button on the binoculars, switching to thermal mode. The view changed, the house's structure becoming a cool blueprint, interrupted by the warm outlines of human figures moving inside. Heat signatures pulsed in contrast to the colder surroundings.

Outside, the world was darker, shadows thicker, but the guards stood out in shades of orange-red against the cold blues of stone and foliage. The first sentry walked a predictable patrol near the pool, assault rifle slung across one shoulder, his pace slow and deliberate. After so many laps, he was bored.

Another stood at the far end of the garden, near the house, taking a drag from a cigarette. The glowing tip flared bright in the thermal display before fading. Victor noted his position and moved to the third one outside. Also close to the house, he seemed to be paying more attention. He might be new – trying to make a good first impression, maybe.

Aranda and his entourage would be leaving soon, according to Farahani.

The Spaniard liked to get to know with whom he was dealing before introducing them to Kasakov himself. Hence tonight. Hence the billiards.

When Aranda left, Victor would move, fast and silent.

Three targets to kill.

One kilogram of osmium to retrieve.

Until then, he stayed a part of the dark. Waiting, calculating. Determined.

Above, the storm clouds churned in the darkness.

The storm would be as relentless as it would be merciless. Just like him.

SIXTY-FIVE

Although Victor could see three guards in his field of view and three in the house, there were more. Streng, Nyström, Volkov and Aranda each had an entourage of their own. Leila Farahani could not provide accurate numbers, believing there would be a 'handful' per target. Pressing her, she expected that would be two or three. With nothing else to go on, Victor had no choice but to expect six to nine. With Aranda's included, that meant eight to twelve present.

Such excessive security had two purposes.

The first was protection against obvious external threats such as raids by the authorities and rival factions. They were doing a deal within Håkansson territory as well as having ripped off Farahani, so their paranoia was justified. Secondly, now Victor could see them interact with one another through his binoculars, he saw in their tense body language that they did not trust one another.

The guard circling the swimming pool had a high-end assault rifle. The two others out back had modern SMGs. He could see none of them were communicating and they were not coordinating their movements. They thought their presence was enough, and, typically, it was enough.

Numbers meant strength and that dissuaded most threats by default.

In the minds of the guards, of his targets, the threat posed by a lone professional was not even a consideration.

Victor was always grateful for such oversights.

He scanned the entertaining area again, the targets inside unaware of their situation. The game of billiards continued, conversation flowing despite the tension in the air. Time running out with every word, every casual gesture.

Victor remained part of the dark, his breath steady and controlled, waiting for the moment when shadows would become his weapon and silence his ally.

His thoughts ran through probabilities and variables, calculating multiple outcomes, readying himself for every unexpected interruption.

Here, tonight, there was no planning.

It was all improvisation.

Slipping the binoculars away now he had studied each of the guards out back and knowing there were no others nearby to interrupt, he took up one of his weapons from where it hung down his right flank, slung to his tactical harness.

Of the weapons available via Scragg and Farahani, Victor chose the Ruger American Rimfire Compact bolt-action rifle for this mission. Custom modifications had shortened this rifle's barrel, which, combined with its integrated high-efficiency suppressor, reduced both size and sound to an absolute minimum. The rifle's short profile ensured smooth handling, even in confined spaces. Combined with subsonic .22 LR ammunition, it enabled Victor to eliminate targets with almost no noise.

For a contract like this that required him to get close to his targets so he could retrieve Farahani's osmium, and wherein he did not have accurate numbers regarding security, he did not want to give himself away at any point.

The Ruger was so quiet he could shoot the three guards in the garden one by one and none of them would hear the others die.

When Aranda left, Victor would do just that.

Again, thanks to Farahani's connections, Scragg had been able to acquire a Brügger & Thomet APC9K submachine gun in case Victor was unable to complete the mission with the Ruger alone. And, as Victor's backup, Scragg had even managed to find him an FN Five-seveN.

Otherwise known as *'that fecking Fabric Nation thingy'*.

Keeping low, Victor hugged the perimeter until he was as close to the house as he wanted to be while remaining unseen to the guy patrolling around the swimming pool.

Settling into position on one knee, rifle up and ready, the wound in Victor's side caused him only a little discomfort, and, more importantly, it did not in any way restrict his movements.

Realising this, Victor almost smiled.

It was good to be back.

SIXTY-SIX

The entertaining area buzzed with conversation and the occasional thud of a cue striking a ball. Smoke lingered in the air, caught in the golden light from overhead fixtures. Tall windows reflected the four men standing around the table, their silhouettes framed by the darkness outside.

Artur Volkov leaned against the billiard table, swirling his whisky in slow circles. His gaze remained fixed on Nyström, who lined up his shot with theatrical care.

'I hope you're not planning to spend the rest of the night thinking about that shot,' Volkov said, his voice deep, amused. 'You'll bore our guest to death.'

Johan Nyström chuckled without looking up. 'Quiet, Artur. That's why logistics never suited you. You want everything fast and dirty. Patience wouldn't kill you.'

Luis Aranda, seated nearby in a leather armchair, watched the exchange. His tailored blazer hung open, his posture relaxed yet deliberate. He observed rather than participated.

They were trying to impress him, not the other way around, after all.

'That's enough,' Atti Streng said with a smile. 'Let's at least look like professionals before Luis here realises he's made a big mistake dealing with us.'

Smiles and chuckles from everyone.

'Too late for that,' Aranda whispered.

Nyström, still grinning, took his shot – and missed.

'What did you say about patience?' Volkov said, laughing.

Streng pulled another cigar from a pocket of his coat and rolled it between his fingers. He flicked his silver lighter, but no flame appeared. His lips tightened in irritation.

Aranda smirked. 'I trust you are better at refuelling your trucks.'

Streng smiled through the taunt, still flicking the lighter with mounting frustration.

'Here,' Aranda said, producing a gold-plated jet-flame lighter from his pocket. He held it out between two fingers, the gesture casual yet intentional. 'Try this.'

'Gracias.'

Streng took it and lit the cigar, his irritation fading as the flame caught. He took a long pull, filling his mouth with delicious smoke before blowing it out as a long, thin plume.

'I will never understand how you can possibly enjoy that,' Volkov said with a grimace. 'Even the scent is poisonous.'

Cigar between his teeth, Streng called him a peasant.

Before Aranda could ask for the gold lighter back, his phone blared with a ringtone reserved for a single individual in his contact list.

'I have to take this,' he said, and left the room to speak with Vladimir Kasakov himself.

With Aranda gone, the three business partners chatted among themselves, hoping they had given the Spaniard a good impression. They were nervous and excited in equal measure. This deal could lead to profits the likes of which they had never known before.

When Aranda returned he said, 'We're done here.'

Streng asked, 'Everything okay?'

A nod. 'Other business requires my attention but I've informed Mr Kasakov that he can deal with you without concern if that's what he decides.'

Streng smiled. Volkov nodded. Nyström missed another shot.

'I can't speak for him,' Aranda continued, 'but now I've confirmed the osmium is real, I think we can do business. Enjoy the rest of your evening.'

When they heard the front door close and Aranda's SUV start up, Volkov sighed. 'I thought that asshole would never leave.'

Streng chuckled, taking another pull from his cigar. 'You think he enjoys these visits? Pretending to care while running back to tattle to the boss?' He shook his head. 'He's a snake. Always watching, always calculating.'

Volkov swirled his drink. 'He pretends and we pretend. That's business.'

Nyström laughed, lining up his next shot. 'Now that he's gone, maybe we can actually enjoy ourselves at last?'

They chuckled, the tension bleeding out of the room. A new game began. The clink of billiard balls filled the air once more.

'I'm hungry,' Volkov announced.

Outside, the wind picked up.

The two sentries stood at their posts, the other guard circled the swimming pool, all oblivious to a shadow by the wall that did not belong.

SIXTY-SEVEN

Three minutes later, Victor's burner phone buzzed. Which meant only one thing: Scragg, who had changed positions after dropping Victor off, had watched Aranda leave.

Because the swimming pool was illuminated with lights under the water, the guard patrolling around it could be seen by the two standing sentry next to the house. They could be seen by him in return when he was facing the house.

So, Victor waited until he was walking away from the house before beginning his attack.

The .22 LR round lacked stopping power outside of precision shots.

The head was the only viable target for a one-shot drop.

Paying attention to the slow rhythm of his pulse, Victor held his breath and squeezed the trigger between heartbeats.

A gentle kick of recoil in his shoulder and a hiss of muzzle report followed.

The first sentry collapsed straight down, a neat hole in the centre of his forehead.

The small-calibre bullet and low velocity meant no exit wound so no blood and brain left glistening on the brick-work behind him.

Working the bolt action, Victor ejected the empty shell and loaded the next into the chamber with a swift, smooth motion.

Adjusting his aim, the second sentry – the smoker – followed the first.

The guy on patrol was a harder target given he was in motion, plus the wind had picked up to a fierce bluster threatening to push a slow, tiny bullet from its path.

Victor waited until the man had changed direction after circling the far end of the pool from the house.

The guard began heading back towards the building, at a casual, relaxed pace.

Then he slowed, noting something was wrong.

Seeing the two corpses, he stopped, giving Victor the perfect opportunity to—

Shoot him in the side of the skull, just above the ear.

He collapsed sideways into the pool.

As the water bloomed red, Victor hurried across the lawn.

Because there were so many guards and no one was expecting any trouble, the door leading to the kitchen was unlocked and so the lockpicks Victor had brought along went unused.

The kitchen was spacious and modern, with stainless-steel countertops and an oversized island at its centre. The smell of cooked meat and spices lingered, remnants of the evening meal. The tall refrigerator door was open, Artur Volkov standing in front of it, perusing the contents.

Victor shot him in the back of the head then—

Dashed forward to catch the corpse and lower it with care so it made no noise against the hard floor tiles.

Victor continued through the kitchen without pause, keeping to the walls, his footsteps careful and controlled.

He stopped at the entrance to a narrow hallway, listening.

The house was quiet. The rumble of the refrigerator behind him and the clink of billiard balls from the entertaining room were the only sounds.

Then, footsteps.

Coming from his right, growing louder, nearer.

Switching the weapon to his left hand, Victor pivoted out, rifle up and aimed about his chest height because he could not know the height of whoever was approaching.

A guard no more than a metre away. As tall as Victor.

Who squeezed the trigger as he adjusted the aim.

The bullet went straight through the man's throat.

Victor worked the bolt action as the guard staggered, hands snapping to the hole in his neck, the SMG on a sling forgotten in the pain and panic.

His larynx in pieces, his screams were a thin whistle of air.

Victor swapped the gun back to his dominant hand before his next bullet relieved the guard of his pain.

Again, Victor slowed the fall of the corpse to avoid alerting anyone nearby.

The entertaining room had polished stone floors and walls lined with modern art. The expensive billiard table dominated the room, its green felt glowing under the lights.

Johan Nyström stood at the table, alone, lining up a shot. No sign of Atti Streng so he must have left the room at the same time Volkov had done to find food.

Nyström's back wasn't to him, but his focus was fixed on the ball so he failed to notice the intruder.

Victor moved closer, his rifle steady. Nyström struck the cue ball with a sharp crack, his focus then on the black that sank into a corner pocket.

'*Yes*,' he hissed in a pleased whisper.

He straightened just in time to see Victor.

His eyes widened. The cue slipped from his fingers.

'Where is it?' Victor whispered.

Nyström was frozen in place, confused, scared.

'The osmium,' Victor explained.

'Upstairs,' was the only word Nyström could manage.

The suppressed shot made no more sound than a breath.

Nyström's tipped forward, and his body collapsed onto the table. Blood pooled across the green felt, spreading fast, the cue ball rolling through the crimson trail.

Victor kept his rifle raised, gaze sweeping, ears tuned for any sign the shot had been heard. Nothing stirred. The house remained still.

He stepped forward, scanning the room again in case Nyström had had the wherewithal to lie, but Victor saw no sign of the osmium.

He left the room, his heartbeat remained even, his breathing controlled.

Leila Farahani's osmium was upstairs, and with it, Victor's ticket out of Malmö.

Two targets down.

One to go.

SIXTY-EIGHT

Victor moved back through the hallway, rifle raised, each step absorbed by the thick carpet beneath him. A purr of electronic music drifted from upstairs and blended with the occasional creak of old wood settling into the night. Every few paces, he paused to listen, his senses primed for the smallest disturbance – a footstep, a muffled voice, or the clink of glass.

He reached the first floor without incident – the rest of the guards on the ground floor he had expected having left with Aranda – pressing his back against the wall as he scanned ahead.

Light spilled from an open doorway, the blue flicker of a television casting shifting shadows onto the hallway walls. Victor advanced, his movements fluid, rifle steady in his hands.

He stopped at the doorway and listened.

Two voices drifted from inside, punctuated by the rapid

clicking of plastic. He leaned in, peering around the doorframe.

One man lounged on a leather sofa, engrossed in a video game. The sounds of exaggerated gunfire and explosions filled the room from the oversized television. Another man stood nearby, leaning against a dresser, eyes locked on his phone.

Neither noticed Victor as he stepped inside.

The shot made no more sound than a soft click of air, and the man on his phone collapsed, the phone slipping from his hand and clattering to the floor.

The man on the sofa tutted in reaction to the noise behind him.

'Jesus, man, keep it down,' he groaned, his focus still on the screen. 'I'm on a roll.'

Victor worked the bolt, ejecting the spent cartridge with calm precision. On the television, the screen went black for a second during a cutscene.

Without colourful pixels competing for his attention, the man saw Victor's reflection, standing behind him, rifle raised.

Realisation dawned too late.

He started to turn.

Victor fired again.

The bullet struck the man in the back of the skull, and he slumped forwards, the controller slipping from his hands. The flickering television illuminated his lifeless face, shadows dancing across his still features.

Victor moved back into the hallway, pausing at the next door, light seeping from the gap beneath it. Pressing his ear to the wood, he listened.

Inside, a man spoke with calm irritation. 'I told you to bring the other bottle from downstairs.'

Victor opened the door just enough to see inside.

A bedroom spread out before him – large, with high ceilings and a blend of modern and traditional decor. A short man stood near the bed, pulling off his shirt. His back was to Victor at first, but he turned when the door opened, his expression darkening in confusion and anger.

'What the hell—'

The rifle exhaled, the bullet striking him between the eyes.

His head snapped back and he collapsed onto the bed.

Blood soaked the white sheets, spreading in a widening stain. His body slid off the smooth bedding and folded onto the floor.

Victor worked the bolt again, ejecting another cartridge.

An en suite bathroom door opened.

A woman stepped out – her whole body freezing as she saw the corpse at the foot of the bed.

She was little more than a child. Far too young for the dead man, for any of the men present. She did not strike him as an escort but someone who had a habit of making bad decisions.

'Please,' she whispered, her voice trembling, hands rising.

Victor kept the rifle pointing her way and yet did not fire. He studied her with calm detachment. Dark hair. Simple dress. Fearful but controlled. No immediate threat.

She remained frozen, hands raised, waiting for him to decide her fate.

Victor considered the consequences of his decision. If she screamed, moved for a weapon, or tried to run, it would end here. She did none of those things.

'Go back into the bathroom. Lock the door. Stay there for five minutes.'

She hesitated, then nodded and stepped back into the bathroom.

The lock clicked into place.

Victor lowered the rifle, listening for any sound beyond the door. The house remained quiet.

He turned back to the hallway, scanning for movement before stepping out.

Leaving a witness was always a risk, he knew. Witnesses became problems, whether through unintended consequences or deliberate betrayal. But Farahani had been explicit: kill the three targets and anyone protecting them if he had to, recover the osmium, but do not touch anyone else – whether Aranda, his men, or any civilians who happened to be in the wrong place at the wrong time.

Victor moved on, his steps absorbed by the hallway carpet. His focus sharpened as he pressed forward.

Only the master bedroom remained.

Inside would be Antti Streng and the osmium.

So far, Victor thought, so good.

SIXTY-NINE

Luis Aranda lounged in the back of his black Lexus SUV, his fingers drumming on the armrest as the headlights carved through the winding coastal road. The leather seats absorbed every bump and sway, leaving the cabin wrapped in a comfortable stillness. His three associates sat in silence, waiting for him to speak.

He glanced at the driver. 'Any chance this thing can pick up some speed?'

The driver's eyes flicked to the rear-view mirror. 'I thought you wanted a smooth ride, to enjoy the scenery.'

'I've seen enough cliffs for one lifetime.'

The driver chuckled and pressed the accelerator. The Lexus responded with a low whine, eating up the road faster now.

'You know what I hate about nights like this?' Aranda said after a pause, his voice quiet, almost to himself. 'They never stay clean.'

The man in the front passenger seat turned. 'Messy, was it?'

Aranda's lips curled into a faint smile. 'Ever spent an evening cleaning up after a pack of stray dogs?'

The man chuckled. 'I thought you liked dogs.'

'I like quiet ones.' Aranda leaned forward, rubbing his temple with two fingers. 'Ones that don't think they run the house.'

'That bad?'

'Just too much noise. Like trying to think while a pack of hounds barks at your feet for your attention.'

The men in the front laughed, amused by their boss's ire, but Aranda didn't join in.

He slipped a silver-plated cigarillo box from his jacket, thumbing it open with one hand while patting his pockets for his gold lighter with the other.

His fingers slowed, and his expression darkened.

'Unbelievable.'

'Something wrong?'

'Let's just say I've been reminded why generosity is the worst of human afflictions.'

The passenger raised an eyebrow. 'Since when are you *ever* generous?'

'I haven't had you killed, have I?'

'*Ouch.*' The passenger laughed.

Aranda snapped the box shut and tapped it against his knee. He reached up and nudged the back of the driver's seat. 'Turn around.'

The driver hesitated, his eyes glancing towards the rear-view again. 'I thought you were in a rush.'

'I still am. But I forgot my lighter and I'd rather leave behind my left nut.'

The driver's knuckles tightened around the wheel as he slowed, pulling onto the shoulder before performing a

U-turn, the headlights sweeping across the cliffs before locking onto the road back towards the house.

A minute later, the building's outline came into view far down the road, a faint glow against the gathering storm clouds. Aranda watched it grow closer, his fingers drumming again on the armrest as the need for nicotine intensified with every passing second.

The house loomed larger as they approached, golden light spilling out from within.

The SUV rolled up the gravel drive, headlights sweeping over the house's façade before settling on the wide glass entrance. The three guards shifted in place, adjusting their stances as the vehicle came to a stop. They hadn't expected anyone to return.

Luis Aranda glanced at his watch, tapping its face with his finger. 'Stay here. Sixty seconds.'

The driver gave a slight nod. The man in the front passenger seat cracked his door, one foot on the ground, maintaining a casual but watchful posture.

Aranda stepped out and closed the door with unhurried annoyance. The guards acknowledged him with brief nods, but he didn't return them. He wasn't in the mood for small talk.

Get the lighter. Go.

The glass doors opened. He paused on the threshold, his eyes adjusting to the soft interior light. The house seemed untouched – warm, quiet, pristine.

'I'm back,' he called, his voice carrying through the open space. 'Forgot my lighter.'

No answer. No matter.

He made his way past the clean lines of expensive furniture and curated art, towards the billiard room.

'Just grabbing it and going,' he said as he entered. 'Won't be long.'

He took two steps inside and stopped.

Nyström lay on the table, his head twisted at an unnatural angle, his eyes wide and lifeless. Blood saturated the felt beneath him, pooling in a dark mass that dripped onto the floor with soft, rhythmic plinks.

Aranda blinked, his brain stalling on the image, refusing to make sense of it.

The metallic scent of blood filled his nostrils, overpowering the lingering scent of cigar smoke. His pulse quickened, and his eyes darted towards the shadows in the far corners of the room, searching for movement.

'*Get ... in here ...*' His voice broke before turning into a sharp command. '*NOW.*'

SEVENTY

Victor heard Aranda's first shout as he moved through the upper floor, swift and steady. The words didn't matter; the urgency did. His pulse remained level, his breathing controlled. He released the Ruger rifle, letting it hang from the sling attached to his harness, and drew up the Brügger & Thomet APC9K.

The time for silence had passed.

Footsteps entering the house below him – fast and growing louder. Multiple pairs.

They were coming.

Victor took cover in an open doorway as the master bedroom door slammed open ahead of him. Two guards rushed out, reacting to Aranda's voice, their rifles raised, eyes sweeping the hallway for threats.

They moved well, but not fast enough.

Victor fired.

The APC9K spat three rounds in a tight burst, the first guard jerking as blood sprayed across the wall.

He collapsed onto the floor as the second guard pivoted towards the gunfire, shock flashing across his face. His rifle began to rise before Victor adjusted his aim and shot again.

Another three-round burst.

The guard crumpled next to his partner, his weapon clattering to the floor.

The hallway fell silent.

Victor advanced without hesitation, his gaze searching through the open doorway.

Beyond it, the bedroom lay still – silent and waiting. He pressed his back against the wall to the side of the door, shoulder against the doorframe, then popped out, angling his weapon into the room.

His gaze swept left, then right, his instincts hunting for movement.

The statue in the far corner gave the guard just enough cover to save him from Victor's bullets, which struck the marble, stone chips flying as the guard ducked behind it, firing blindly in return.

Bullets punched holes into the wall and ceiling, the blind firing ineffective.

Victor dropped into a crouch and slipped across the open doorway, coming up fast on the other side.

The guard, cowering behind the statue and using its dense stone as a shield, saw nothing.

Downstairs, Aranda's men had poured into the house.

They would be upstairs and coming up behind Victor in mere moments.

Victor leaned out just enough to extend the APC9K's suppressor into the room and squeezed the trigger, spraying a wide arc of gunfire.

Picture frames shattered, furniture splintered, and shards of glass rained onto the floor.

The shots weren't intended to hit – they were designed to suppress – but if one bullet found flesh Victor wasn't going to complain.

The guard stayed kneeling behind the heavy marble statue, unwilling to expose himself. Which was what Victor wanted.

He kept firing until the magazine ran dry with a distinctive *click*.

Victor waited, still and silent, knowing the cowering guard was thinking one thing:

He's out of ammo.

Ejecting the spent magazine so it clattered on the floor, he released the APC9K to hang from his harness and drew his Five-seveN pistol in a seamless motion. The grip a perfect fit for his palm, the weapon as familiar as his own breath.

He counted to two, then stepped into the doorway and fired.

The guard, emboldened, had emerged from behind the statue and was hurrying across the room.

Victor's shots hit him twice in the chest, the third round following to the head an instant later.

Footsteps hurrying up the stairs behind him ensured Victor had no time in which to hesitate. He dashed into the bedroom – slamming the door shut behind him – gaze finding Streng pressed into the far corner, hands held high, his mouth opening in panic, to beg, to offer Victor a better deal.

He shot him twice in the head.

Streng tipped over sideways into a mahogany desk, papers

and glass scattering around him as he crumpled onto the floor.

Victor scanned the room, his eyes tracking every shadow, every corner where a threat might remain. He moved with purpose, quick steps on the polished floor. The bodies lay where they fell – motionless, their weapons scattered beside them. Blood dripped from where it had spattered on the statue, on the desk.

He saw a metal case, identical to the one Järnberg had brought to Scragg, sitting on the cushion of an armchair and opened it up to check the contents. It was filled with vials of dark metallic powder. Leila Farahani's osmium.

He holstered the Five-seveN, reloaded the APC9K, and scooped the case up into his left hand.

Holding the APC9K with only one hand was not ideal, but at close range, recoil and accuracy could be sacrificed for firepower.

Multiple sets of footsteps stamped the floor outside the bedroom.

Victor unleashed a long burst through the closed door, knowing the lack of cover in the hallway on the other side would make the new arrivals drop or retreat even if the spray of rounds failed to hit any of them.

They weren't professionals. They didn't know how to breach a room. And now, knowing a hail of bullets awaited whoever went in first, they wouldn't rush in.

They would hesitate, each urging someone else to be the first.

No one wanted to be the first to die.

While they dithered, Victor opened the bay window and climbed out onto the sloping roof of russet shingles.

Bursts of return fire shredded holes through the door.

Even better than burning time arguing over who would lead the charge, they were instead going to waste even more time hoping he had decided to stand still directly in the line of their blind shooting.

Amateurs.

He kept low and made his way along the roof, the automatic fire a perfect cover for the unavoidable noise the soles of his boots made against the shingles.

When he reached the back of the house, he edged to the lowest part of the roof and then dropped down onto the roof of the orangery a couple of metres below.

The impact sent a bolt of pain through his side that took a split-second to absorb before he followed the length of the orangery roof until he reached its furthest point from the main house.

From there, he released the APC9K, turned around, lay on his stomach and lowered himself to the ground. A process that was much kinder to his wounded flank but still awkward and painful.

The night air was cool, heavy with the scent of the storm and the rain. The distant rumble of thunder dampened the rustle of his hastened footsteps to gentle whispers.

Shouting from the house followed him as he dashed across the lawn, retracing his route, sticking to the perimeter, invisible in the darkness.

Not quite.

Noise behind him – a man running out of the back of the building – not having charged up the stairs like the others.

Smart, and yet dumb because—

He shot while he ran, the spray of bullets wild and in-accurate, churning up the lawn in hazes of grass and soil.

Victor snapped out the Five-seveN, dropping to one knee as he pivoted around, reducing his profile as he stabilised his shooting stance.

A double-tap to the head took his pursuer's legs out from under him and he collapsed straight down to the lawn.

With no pause to his momentum Victor twisted himself back around as he stood back up, holstering the pistol to scale the perimeter wall. The pain in his side, not yet sub-sided from the earlier drop, offering a protest that he ignored as he dropped to the other side and made his way to where Scragg waited.

Seeing the case in Victor's hand, the Kashmiri Scottish Viking said, 'Good job, Princess.'

SEVENTY-ONE

The storm had been intense, yet brief. Still, as Nikola Petrović emerged from the forest, his boots sank into the sodden ground left behind. He was smiling because it had been a good hunt. Two deer, both clean kills, their bodies slung across the back of an all-terrain vehicle idling near the trailhead. The blood on his coat was still fresh.

Petrović had always enjoyed a night-time hunt. There was something about creeping through a pitch-black forest in search of prey that made a man feel alive. And night-vision scopes these days were incredible at turning that darkness into wonderful shades of bright green. He drew the line at thermal scopes at night, however. That was cheating.

Radovan Leka wiped a gloved hand across his beard, smearing traces of blood across his cheek as he turned to Petrović with an amused smirk.

'You're getting slow,' Leka teased. 'Took you an extra second to pull the trigger.'

Petrović scoffed, slinging his rifle over his shoulder. 'I was letting you have your moment, you swine. Thought you might like to feel like the better shot for once.'

Leka barked out a laugh, clapping Petrović on the back. 'You always talk shit when you're outclassed.'

One of Petrović's entourage of Serbians, Nemanja, smoked a cigarette while the ATV idled, exhaust fumes bright under the moonlight as the storm clouds passed. The rest of his men were already inside the lodge with Leka's Montenegrins. Some had hunted too and returned earlier. Others had preferred to remain in the warmth and relax. Petrović could not understand how any red-blooded man would prefer comfort to a hunt, but he let his people unwind however they chose.

This trip was a break from business, but business was never far from their thoughts.

They walked towards the warm glow of the lodge, leaving Nemanja to finish his cigarette before using the ATV to take their kills to the game larder.

'You'll be heading back to Montenegro in a few days?' Petrović asked.

'Soon as we're done here. Once the shipment schedules are set, I need to make sure my end is ready.'

'We're almost there. Håkansson is finally letting go of his part of the business. Slowly, but it's happening. His people are being shuffled out of key positions. The contracts, the shipments, the money – it's all being realigned. He's getting weaker. Gustavus is dead. The fight in the old man has died with his son.'

'Then I'll make sure our partners are ready to move when the time comes.' Leka nodded, satisfied. Then he asked, 'But who is that outsider I've heard about that Håkansson has brought in? Is he going to be a problem?'

'He's some hitman who was a big deal in the Russian mafia until their head guy was killed. Håkansson calls him the Boatman.'

'The Boatman? That's his name? I don't get it.'

'Neither do I.' Petrović shuddered a little. 'I don't want to talk about him. He makes me . . . Let's just say the next time my kids won't go to bed on time I'm going to tell them the Boatman is coming to get them.'

As they neared the lodge, the scent of woodsmoke and slow-cooked venison carried on the wind, mixing with the briny sea air blowing in from the rocky shoreline. Inside, their men were drinking, laughing, relaxed.

The Vargön Lodge sat nestled at the edge of a dense pine forest, its timbered silhouette overlooking the cold, restless waters of the Baltic Sea. Located an hour's drive from Malmö near the Trelleborg coastline, it was a secluded retreat designed for those who valued privacy, luxury and discretion. The kind of place where deals were made behind closed doors, where men of power and means could step away from the city and indulge in controlled wilderness.

The main building was constructed from dark-stained timber, its architecture traditional yet subtly modernised with floor-to-ceiling glass windows that provided sweeping views of the nearby shoreline. A long wooden jetty stretched out over the water, where Petrović's speedboat, a Scorpion Serket 88, bobbed with the movement of the waves.

Petrović's way of doing business had always been from the position of being a friend first. That was how he liked it. He had built his network not on fear, not through brute force, but through relationships. It made things more pleasant, more stable.

When he was dealing with Håkansson, Malmgren and Farahani, there was always tension, always a hidden agenda, everyone watching for the knife at their back. That was politics. But when he was operating within his own network, when he was among his people, things were different.

He knew all of his men personally. He knew their names, their families, their birthdays. He had been to their weddings, drunk with them after funerals. He knew which of them were good with money, which of them were reckless. He treated them like people, not tools. Because in the long run, that was the better way to do business.

Which is why he noticed straight away when Milos Popović and Danijel Stanić were absent from the lodge's great room. Including Leka's Montenegrins there were thirty men in total, spread out drinking, laughing, enjoying themselves.

But not them.

He turned to one of his lieutenants, Nikša Radojević, who was leaning against the bar, sipping from a glass of dark Serbian rakija.

'Have you seen Milos and Danijel?'

Nikša frowned, shaking his head. 'Not since the hunt. I figured they were with you.'

Petrović narrowed his eyes. 'No, they left ahead of us. They bagged their own deer very fast, so they would have brought it back by now.'

Nikša exchanged a glance with another man nearby, Bojan Delić, who sat by the fire sharpening a hunting knife.

'No vehicles have come back before you,' Bojan said, not looking up from his blade.

Nikša shrugged. 'Maybe they stopped for something. Took a piss, had a smoke.'

Petrović waved a hand. 'Milos? Maybe. But Danijel? He hates the cold. He wouldn't be standing around outside for no reason.'

Leka, who was settling into a seat near the fireplace, smirked and took a sip of whisky one of his men had ready for him. 'Maybe they wanted some privacy,' he joked. 'Could be they're far closer friends than you realised.'

Leka laughed but Petrović frowned.

Because his men didn't just disappear.

SEVENTY-TWO

Leka leaned back in his chair, swirling the amber liquid in his glass. 'Maybe they came back, dropped off the deer, and left again,' he suggested. 'And simply didn't come into the lodge.'

Petrović considered this, nodding. It was possible. The lodge had a game larder – a dedicated outbuilding near the kitchen where hunters hung their kills to cool and mature before processing. Perhaps Milos and Danijel had returned, deposited their deer in the larder, and then headed back out for some reason.

There was an easy way to check.

He huffed, pushed himself up from the chair, and gestured towards one of his men. 'Nikša, call them. Try Milos first. See if he picks up.'

Nikša nodded, fishing his phone out of his pocket.

Petrović turned towards the back of the lodge. 'I'll check the larder. Maybe Nemanja has seen them.'

Leka raised an eyebrow but said nothing further, only watching as Petrović moved away.

Petrović headed down the hallway, past the dark wood-panelled walls, the polished oak floors creaking underfoot. The mounted trophies – heads of stags and wild boars – watched him with glass eyes, their lifeless gazes reflecting the dim glow of the wall sconces.

The kitchen was silent, save for the soft hum of the industrial refrigerator. The countertops were clean, copper pots hanging in neat rows above the stove. Through the back window, the larder was visible under the dull glow of a single motion-sensitive floodlight.

Petrović pushed open the heavy wooden door, stepping outside into the cold. He heard gravel crunching under his boots and the sound of the nearby waves lapping against the shoreline.

The all-terrain vehicle Nemanja had been riding was parked next to the larder as expected. One of the two deer lay across the back, the other already having been taken inside.

'Nemanja,' Petrović began as he stepped into the cool darkness of the larder, 'have you seen Milos or Danijel?'

The scent of blood was thick in the confined space. Hooks lined the walls, the wooden beams overhead darkened from years of use.

A single deer was strung up, its body still swaying – just hung.

But no Nemanja.

Petrović's brow furrowed. He had already opened his mouth to call out—

Then he stopped himself.

Something was wrong.

He turned back outside, stepping towards the all-terrain vehicle. His eyes scanned the area. No Nemanja.

Then something caught Petrović's attention.

A rifle, lying flat on the ground near the side of the larder.

No one – *no one* – in his crew would leave a weapon like that. Not Milos. Not Danijel. Not Nemanja.

Slowly, cautiously, he walked towards the rifle, bending down to lift it upright – the weight familiar in his hands. It was Nemanja's gun.

As he stood up again, he noticed something else.

A shadow peeking out from behind the far wall of the game larder.

He took slow, careful steps forward, his fingers tightening around the rifle as he rounded the corner and saw –

The body lay sprawled on the frozen earth, throat cut wide, the head lolling unnaturally to one side.

Nemanja.

His skin was pale, his blood soaked into his clothes, colouring the wall behind him and dirt around him. The cut had been done with a brutal, sawing motion, not only severing the arteries but the windpipe, cutting all the way to the spine.

Recent, he saw, because the blood was still glistening and wisps of steam curled up from Nemanja's almost-severed neck.

The rifle slipped from Petrović's fingers, clattering against the ground.

He turned, scanning the treeline of the darkened expanse of the forest a short walk away.

He sprinted back to the lodge.

He reached the kitchen door, wrenched it open, stumbled inside.

The heat hit him first, the fire-warmed air rushing over his skin, the scents of smoke and whisky and cooked venison thick in his nostrils. He staggered to the great room to see his men and Leka's lounging, talking, drinking, laughing, the weight of the world beyond the lodge forgotten for the night.

Nikša still had his phone in hand, his brow furrowed. He glanced up, shaking his head. 'They're not picking up.'

Then he saw Petrović. His face changed.

Petrović stood there, chest heaving, shoulders shaking. He forced his lips apart, fought to make the words come out, his body betraying him, fighting against itself.

'*Nemanja . . .*'

His voice came hoarse, barely more than a breath. He swallowed, felt his pulse hammering in his throat.

'Nemanja is dead.'

The laughter stopped.

Disbelief at first. Confusion following.

Nikša pushed himself upright, setting his drink aside. 'What?'

'The two missing men,' Petrović managed. His body still felt tight, his breath still caught just short of what he needed. 'They'll be dead too.' He forced a swallow, forced himself to say it. 'We're under attack.'

The men reacted at different speeds. Some froze, absorbing the words, letting the meaning settle. Others moved into action – pushing away from tables, reaching for weapons, knocking over glasses in their urgency. Chairs scraped against the wood floor. Hands gripped pistol grips, rifle stocks, shotgun barrels.

Scattered around the room, Leka's Montenegrins were slower to process the news because they were waiting to see how their boss responded, waiting for him to decide how seriously they should take Petrović's words.

Leka reached for his glass, took a slow sip. His voice came low, measured.

'What do you mean under attack?'

'Nemanja was murdered,' Petrović snapped, his voice finally breaking through the tightness in his throat. 'Not shot. Not an accident. His throat was cut to the spine. What else do you think that could mean?'

'Who is attacking us?'

Somewhere outside, the wind shifted, the trees creaked, the night felt denser than before.

'I don't know.' Petrović gestured for his men to move. 'We need to get out of here.'

Leka didn't stand. He didn't panic. He let his gaze move across the room, over the many men with weapons. Tough men, experienced. Some former military. Then his gaze settled on the lodge itself – the thick walls, the limited entry points.

'If we're under attack,' he said, 'then this is the safest place to be.'

A moment later, the massacre began.

SEVENTY-THREE

Victor and Scragg navigated the quiet streets of night-time Malmö, heading towards the western coastline. Their destination: a parking area that served the beach, empty at this hour, not a single other vehicle in any of the bays. Split into three sections, each was bordered by manicured hedges and mature trees, providing useful privacy and isolation. Victor could see why Farahani wanted to meet here. The dense foliage cast elongated shadows under the glow of nearby streetlights.

Across the road, modest residential buildings stood in a perfect row, their windows dark, occupants long retired for the evening. To the east, the silhouette of a mini-golf course stood silent, its whimsical obstacles casting peculiar shapes in the moonlight. To the west, the darkened façade of a hockey rink loomed, its vast expanse adding to the area's deserted ambience.

Victor noted the potential vantage points and escape routes, ever vigilant for signs of an ambush.

Scragg parked his car in the furthest corner from the entrance and the street. Victor buzzed down his window before the engine was killed.

'What did you do that for?' Scragg asked. 'We'll bloody freeze.'

Victor gave no justification.

To his left, a footpath led towards the beach, the scent of saltwater permeating the chill night air, still saturated with moisture from the recent storm. He listened to the gentle lapping of waves against the shore, mingling with the distant call of nocturnal seabirds, the occasional rustle of leaves, and the tick of the engine as it cooled.

Scragg's knee bounced with impatience. The osmium rested on the backseat along with the Ruger. The APC9K was in the footwell between Victor's knees.

Scragg checked his watch. 'She should be here by now.'

Victor reached for the door handle and began climbing out. Scragg turned to him, frowning. 'What are you doing?'

Victor, leaving the passenger door open, kept his gaze on the parking area, its shadows. 'Out here are options.'

'And in here is a little thing I like to call a comfortable seat.'

'If you prefer to trap yourself, be my guest.'

Scragg scoffed, but then thought hard, grunted, and climbed out too.

Shivering against the cold, he said, 'Happy now?'

'Overjoyed.'

Scragg sighed. 'Look, I get it. You don't trust her.'

'Anyone who uses my services is untrustworthy by default.'

'Aye, but I trust she wants the osmium as much as we

want to give it to her. We made a deal. We've done the hard part.'

' "We"?'

'I drove, didn't I?' Scragg shook his head. 'We've come this far, haven't we? You want to get out of this city and I want to get back in her good books. She wants to get her arrangement with that arms dealer back on the table. Now we just hand the osmium over and walk away.'

Victor moved the APCK9 from the footwell to the passenger seat, positioning it with the suppressor on the seat itself and the stock against the backrest, grip and trigger within quick reach. 'That's the part I'm most interested in.'

Scragg frowned. 'What part?'

'The walking away.'

The wind picked up again. Two sets of headlights swept across the parking area, their high beams blinding in the dark. The vehicles split up after they entered, approaching from different angles, moving slow but steady. Victor's gaze flicked back and forth between the two, but the glare made it impossible to see who was driving.

No way to tell if it was Leila Farahani, representatives of her, or someone else entirely.

Victor adjusted his position behind the open passenger door, the APC9K nearby, ready to be snatched up within a split second. The car door was no armoured shield but it could cause incoming bullets to ricochet if they came in from the right angle and it would slow and distort the trajectory of others.

He thumbed the SMG's selector to fully automatic.

The two vehicles came to a stop, one to Victor's ten

o'clock and the other to his two o'clock. Which was smart. Keeping their headlights on was even smarter. He could barely see whichever way he looked, and if the lights went out, he would have no night vision.

Doors opened on both vehicles. Figures climbed out.

Two from the one to Victor's left. Four from the right.

Scragg had one palm acting as a visor in an attempt to see better.

The four from the right approached first. They were Middle Eastern guys in sharp, dark suits. Iranians like Farahani and Mehran, Victor presumed. All four stood in the space between their car and Scragg's. The two figures from the other vehicle stepped forward too.

Leila Farahani and Darius Mehran.

Farahani wore a long cashmere coat and matching hat in emerald green. Her gloves were supple calfskin.

No one had any weapons drawn but every single suit jacket was open in readiness. Victor kept his hands visible, but still close to the APC9K.

'Pleasant evening,' Farahani said as she neared.

No surprise that Darius Mehran's attention was solely on Victor, and he said to her, '*Aamaadeh.*'

'Leila,' Scragg said in greeting.

'I'm only Leila when I have my osmium,' she told him. 'Until then, I'm Ms Farahani.'

He shrugged an apology. 'Good thing we have it with us.'

'Splendid. You may hand it over.'

Victor asked, 'What guarantees do I have?'

'You have my word, of course,' she answered with a warm smile that did not reach her eyes. 'No one will hinder you when you leave through my port.'

They held each other's gaze for a moment.

Then Victor glanced to Scragg. 'Give it to her.'

Scragg replied with a look that said, *Why don't you hand it over?* and yet he made no protestation.

Victor watched the four Middle Eastern guys in suits, but especially he watched Darius Mehran, as Scragg took the case from the backseat of his car and approached Farahani. All four men had unreadable expressions and postures.

'So,' Scragg said as he stopped in front of Farahani, 'I give you this and we're friends again?'

'Best friends in the whole wide world.'

He smirked and held out the case. She gestured for Mehran to take it. After Scragg handed it over, Mehran took it back to the bonnet of his vehicle and opened it up to check the contents.

After a moment, he said, '*Khoobeh.*'

Scragg was confused, almost worried, but Victor knew it meant 'it's good' in Farsi.

She said, 'I believe that concludes our business for the night.'

'Not quite,' Victor replied.

'Of course.' She showed him a small smile. 'There's a product tanker leaving for Philadelphia at five a.m. if you want to be on it. If you don't, you can find your own way out.'

'That doesn't leave me a lot of choice.'

'Indeed,' she said, then to Scragg, she added, 'I look forward to our next venture.'

'Aye, Leila, me too.'

To Victor she said, 'I may have work for a man of your talents in the future.'

'I won't be returning to Malmö for a very long time.'

'I suspected as much,' she replied. 'But I have many

ventures overseas. Mr Scragg knows how to contact me, so, once you're far away and settled, feel free to reach out.'

He nodded.

Accompanied by her men, she returned to her vehicle. The other four guys waited until she was inside before they returned to their own. Darius Mehran was the last one to climb inside.

Victor remained standing until both cars had left the parking area and he could no longer hear their exhausts.

Scragg reached for his cigarettes. 'See?' he said as he lit up. 'I told you it'd be fine. You worry too much.'

'*Aamaadeh*,' Victor said.

'I didn't know you spoke Iranian.'

'Farsi,' he corrected. 'Informal speech, meaning "he's ready".'

'So?' Scragg said, exhaling smoke.

'Mehran said it. He was warning her that I was prepared.'

'So?' Scragg said again. 'Darius noticed you're paranoid, which is hardly a trade secret, is it?'

'She hadn't decided,' Victor explained, 'whether to simply take the osmium or have us killed as well. That's why Mehran was warning her that I was prepared, so she knew if she did decide to give the order, it would get messy.'

Scragg coughed on his cigarette smoke as he absorbed the enormity of what might have been. '*You could've fecking warned me.*'

'I did tell you she was untrustworthy by default, but I wanted her to make the decision while she believed us ignorant,' Victor said. 'Now we know for sure that, regardless of her trustworthiness, she will honour her word as long as doing so keeps benefitting her.'

Scragg, throat still raw, tossed his cigarette away and climbed back behind the wheel. 'Then what now, Princess?'

'We have a few hours to kill until that tanker leaves,' Victor said, 'After that, I'm gone.'

SEVENTY-FOUR

The lodge's great room was a testament to rustic opulence, designed to impress and comfort in equal measure. The space soared to a triple-height ceiling, with exposed timber beams stretching across the expanse. A massive stone fireplace dominated one wall, its hearth wide enough to accommodate a roaring fire that warmed the entire room on even the coldest of winter nights.

Plush leather sofas and oversized armchairs were arranged in intimate clusters atop handwoven rugs, inviting guests to sink in and relax. The upholstery, in deep hues of burgundy and forest green, complemented the natural wood tones of the walls and ceiling. Heavy drapes framed large floor-to-ceiling windows that offered panoramic views of the coast to the front of the building and to the forest behind, the dense canopy creating a living tapestry that changed with the seasons.

A mezzanine level encircled the great room on three sides, accessible by a discreet staircase tucked away in a corner.

On one side, the upper gallery was lined with bookshelves filled with leather-bound volumes, hunting trophies and antique artifacts that spoke of the lodge's storied past. It connected to the upper floors of the lodge through two separate hallways, each leading off towards different wings of the building to the guest rooms and private quarters. The mezzanine's balustrade was crafted from wrought iron with intricate scrollwork.

Soft, warm light emanated from chandeliers suspended from the ceiling. Wall sconces, fashioned to resemble medieval torches, enhanced this glow with lights above armchairs that created little reading nooks along the room's periphery.

This great room was more than just a communal space; it was the heart of the lodge, a place where stories were shared, alliances forged and memories created, all under the watchful gaze of nature just beyond the glass.

In one corner of the room, a curved bar of richly polished wood provided spirits, wine and beers for guests to enjoy as and when they pleased.

It was the kind of space designed for relaxation, and refinement.

Not mass murder.

Petrović didn't hear the first shot so much as feel it – a violent, percussive rip through the air, faster than his brain could process, faster than anything he had ever experienced before.

A controlled burst of automatic fire – high cyclic rate, a thousand rounds per minute of inhuman relentlessness.

Nikša convulsed as three rounds punched through his sternum in a tight cluster, blood arcing as he collapsed backwards into a leather armchair. His hand was still gripping his pistol, the trigger half-pulled, but he had never got the chance to fire.

Next to him, Bojan had no time to turn his head.

The second burst ripped through his throat in a messy explosion of skin, sinew and arterial spray. He dropped his shotgun, hands clawing at his neck, blood fountaining between his fingers. He fell to his knees, his face frozen in the shock of a man unable to understand why he was seconds away from death.

The firing didn't stop.

Petrović's men reacted first – already primed by his warning moments beforehand – lunging for their weapons, dropping to the floor, diving under tables, sliding behind the bar.

Petrović threw himself backwards as the room hissed with destruction, diving towards the nearest doorway a fraction of a second before bullets shredded the floor where he had been standing.

The vibrations rattled through the wood, a brutal thumping staccato as high-velocity rounds tore through wood, upholstery, the very foundation of the room itself.

Petrović hit the floor hard, pain thumping through his ribs.

He turned, gasping, peering back into the chaos.

He looked up to the mezzanine level.

The shadows moved, and he saw him.

A single figure, almost unremarkable – just a shape in the gloom. Black tactical gear. The sleek, deadly form of an MP7 in both hands and angled downwards to track targets below with rapid, lethal efficiency.

Not a whole team of gunmen.

A lone shooter.

An expressionless face.

The Boatman.

The next burst of fire tore through the couch cushions, cotton and feathers flying out and coloured red.

One of Petrović's men had almost made it behind cover before his knee was blown apart, exploding in a flare of bone fragments and blood. He fell forward, screaming, trying to crawl, but another burst caught him in the back of the head, and he went still.

On the far side of the room, one of the Montenegrins swung his shotgun up, aiming towards the spectre of death above. He got as far as bracing the stock before rounds hit him high in the chest, the impact sending him reeling backwards towards the stone fireplace, blood splashing across the mounted stag's head above the hearth.

He fell into the flames, not yet dead, twitching and screaming as the stench of burning flesh mixed with the cocktail of death in the air.

The silver tray on the bar rattled as bullets struck the counter, shattering the bottle of rakija that Nikša had barely finished drinking from moments ago, sending a cloud of glass shrapnel sparkling into the air along with a mist of liquor that glimmered in the firelight.

A man cowering behind the bar took bullets to the throat, jaw, and then the back of his skull as he jerked several times – an awful, horrifying dance – then collapsed sideways into a nearby table.

Bloody ice cubes slid and rattled across the wooden floor.

Two of Leka's men made a break for it at the same time, one sprinting for a doorway leading to one of the connecting hallways while the other aimed his pistol up to shoot as he ran.

He never fired even a single shot.

High-velocity rounds stitched him from hip to clavicle in a vertical red line. He slammed against the stone fireplace, the force of impact knocking one of the mounted stag heads loose, the heavy skull and antlers clattering onto the floor beside his twitching body and the other corpse still smouldering away in the flames.

The second had almost made it to the side hallway when he jerked to a stop, his spine severed by a burst that caught him between the shoulder blades. He hit the floor still twitching, hands clawing at the wood for a few fruitless moments, as if he could drag himself to safety and away from his fate.

For a moment – a single, magical, blissful moment – Petrović thought it was over.

The air was thick with the stench of burnt cordite, of spilled blood, of shattered wood and upholstery torn apart. The room was wrecked, nothing untouched by the devastation. Bodies lay motionless across the floor, slumped over furniture, twisted into unnatural contortions.

The echoes of screams, of gunfire, of death still rang in his ears, but the actual sound – the tearing, unrelenting violence – had stopped.

It had gone on for minutes.

No. That wasn't right.

Seconds.

It had felt like forever. An eternity of horror. But it had only been seconds.

And now – silence.

Had the Boatman killed enough to satiate his demon's appetite for souls?

So many men in the great room were dead. The survivors

were hiding, scattered across the space, ducked down out of sight from above.

Had he been killed?

Petrović almost let himself believe it. Maybe one of his men – or Leka's – had blind-fired a lucky round into the shadows above.

As with the massacre that had seemed to last for ever, the hope inside Petrović's heart lasted mere seconds.

He heard it.

Click.

Metal sliding against metal.

The unmistakable, sickening sound of a fresh magazine slamming home.

A two-second pause. A brief, fleeting interval of worthless mercy.

Then—

The killing began once more.

SEVENTY-FIVE

The MP7 roared, controlled bursts – surgical, methodical, relentless. The Boatman was now moving, repositioning to change his line of sight to hunt the survivors, the shooting coming from many different angles along the mezzanine, never lingering in one spot for more than a second.

The Boatman was systematic, eliminating threats from greatest to smallest. The ones with rifles in their hands died first, then those with shotguns, then pistols. Then the ones who went to draw their weapons or reach for guns nearby.

Bullets once again chewed through the remains of the bar, shattering bottles, sending liquor cascading down in waterfalls, mixing into rivers of spilled blood pooling across the floorboards.

Someone hiding behind the bar screamed.

Another man sprang up amid the screaming, clutching his shredded throat, a garbled, choking sound spilling from his mouth before he collapsed into the broken glass.

More shots hammered the walls, sending wooden splinters

stabbing through the air, embedding themselves into furniture, into flesh as some made a desperate sprint for the safety of doorways leading anywhere else.

One of Petrović's Serbians managed to bring his AK halfway up, gaze locked on the mezzanine, finger ready on the trigger.

The MP7 caught him first, the first shot blowing his jaw apart, teeth spraying across the floor, the next rounds completing the annihilation of his face, leaving a bright smear of red on the wall as he slid to the ground.

Another pause.

Two seconds of reprieve.

A few who had escaped into the safety of adjoining hallways took up positions in doorways to return fire.

When the MP7 opened up again, they were the first to die.

Another man, hidden behind an overturned armchair, peeked out to aim his automatic pistol and caught a trio of rounds to the temple, his body snapping back, his lifeless fingers still gripping his pistol, dead finger compressing the trigger to empty bullets in every direction except the intended target.

One of the remaining Montenegrins, who had hit the floor at the start of the second volley, now tried to crawl out from under a table towards a downed rifle. His hand was millimetres from the grip when shots from above found him, punching through his ribs. He didn't writhe or spasm – he just went from motion to motionless.

Leka saw the opening first when the Boatman reloaded once more.

The Serbian moved, grabbing the shoulder of one of his men, barking, 'Let's go – Let's go.'

The remaining survivors – four of Petrović's men, three

of Leka's and Leka himself – all sprang into action at once, sprinting towards the hallway in which Petrović cowered in a desperate break for the exit.

'*Come on, come on,*' he urged them.

The only thing that mattered was speed. Speed and numbers. Numbers meant less chance of getting hit.

The first burst cut through the group, scything down the two men closest to Petrović. They jerked as bullets pierced their backs, their forward momentum sending them crashing into the nearest wall, limbs twitching as they slid to the floor in heaps, blood smearing the wood on their way down.

Another short burst took out two more men mid-stride, rounds punching through leather jackets, ribs, organs, and out the other side, spattering red across the doorframe, across Petrović's face.

Leka made it to the hallway, as did two of Petrović's Serbians and one of Leka's Montenegrins.

The shooting stopped.

This time there was no click of a reload because everyone inside the great room was now dead.

This time it was the sound of footsteps descending stairs.

The Boatman was coming.

Petrović didn't look back. He didn't count the bodies. He just kept running.

'*Who's got keys?*' Petrović shouted as they ran.

His legs felt numb, he was shaking, his pulse hammering so fast he couldn't separate one beat from the next.

One of his men replied, '*For the Rover.*' He held up the fob in his hand, gripping it like it was their only lifeline – because they had no other. 'Let's go, go – GO.'

They dashed through the kitchen doors and out into the freezing night, just five of them still alive out of so many.

The cold hit hard, the sudden shift from gunpowder and blood-soaked heat to the open air like a slap to the lungs.

The ATV was parked just ahead, its headlights still on, the single deer carcass still strapped to the back. Nearby were several parked cars they had arrived in, and with them, a Range Rover parked with black paint gleaming under the moonlight.

They sprinted for it.

Gunfire snapped from the shadows behind them, hammering into the trees, the gravel, the walls of the game larder, the sharp, disciplined shooting of the Boatman's MP7 tracking them as they ran.

Leka's man grunted, staggered, his leg buckling as a round tore through his thigh. He collapsed forward, tried to drag himself up, but another shot hit the back of his head, and his body pitched sideways into the dirt.

Petrović and Leka threw themselves down on the other side of the ATV. Bullets slammed into its seat and pinged off the curved engine block.

The two remaining men reached the Range Rover.

The first hit the unlock button, diving for the driver's seat. The passenger door flung open, the other survivor scrambling inside.

Petrović watched in horror – because he knew what was about to happen.

They weren't going to wait.

They weren't going to stop.

Everything he had built with his men, the friendships, the loyalty, the generosity, none of it mattered now.

Survival was all that mattered.

Neither man so much as looked back. They just slammed the doors shut.

Jammed the key into the ignition.

The blast was an orange-red inferno punching through the Range Rover's windows, turning the inside of the car into a furnace of shredded steel and vaporised flesh.

The roof split open, the shockwave shattering the side mirrors, sending fragments of glass and metal flying in a cloud of shrapnel.

The windscreen burst as a rolling wave of fire and pressure rushed through the open doors, sending Petrović and Leka, halfway back up, reeling over, their coats whipping against the force of the detonation.

They hit the gravel hard, ears ringing, the force of the explosion slamming into their backs by the weight of the shockwave. Petrović rolled, hands clamping over his ears, his body jolted with adrenalin, panic and raw survival instinct.

A fireball mushroomed into the sky, the smell of burning rubber and gasoline overpowering the night air, black smoke curling upwards, thick and choking.

He blinked against the brightness, his vision flaring white, and when it cleared, he saw the wreckage of the Range Rover engulfed in flames, the heat radiating outwards, warping the air around it.

There was nothing left inside.

Just blackened metal, melting seats, and the faint outline of two bodies reduced to charred ruin.

Petrović breathed hard, his lungs fighting for air. His hands trembled, the image of the explosion seared into his mind, into his body, into the marrow of his bones.

He had hated his men in that moment, when they had abandoned him to save themselves.

But he also understood.

Because if their roles had been reversed, he wouldn't have stopped either.

Leka groaned beside him, pushing himself up onto his elbows, coughing, wiping soot and sweat from his face. He looked at the wreckage, at the smouldering husks of the men who had almost escaped.

The lodge was a death trap.

The Range Rover was a funeral pyre.

Leka's hand latched on to Petrović's arm, fingers digging in hard, his breath coming in ragged, panicked heaves. His words spilled out too fast, barely coherent, barely sentences.

'The Scorpion – your *speedboat* – let's move – let's go – come on – we have to move – *now*—'

Petrović stumbled as Leka yanked him sideways, dragging him away from the wreckage of the Range Rover, away from the burning, twisted metal that was still spitting flames and black smoke into the night sky. He had no time to process it, to think, to breathe – he just ran because Leka was running, and that was all that mattered.

They turned, changing direction, feet pounding against cold, uneven earth, moving downhill now, the ground wet from the storm and sloping away beneath them, leading towards the shoreline.

The sea opened up ahead, vast and black under the moonlight, waves lapping against the rocky shore. The wind carried the briny tang of saltwater, mixed now with the thick, acrid stink of fire and burning fuel from the vehicle behind them.

Ahead, the jetty waited – a long, narrow walkway of weathered planks, its wooden surface slick from mist and sea spray. The support beams were thick, old, bolted deep into the coarse wet sand. Lanterns lined its length, their dull yellow light flickering in the wind, casting long, shifting shadows across the boards.

At the far end, the speedboat rocked and bobbed in the tide.

It was sleek, low to the water, a V-hull craft built for performance – an adult toy – its white fibreglass body glinting under the moon. The cabin windscreen was tinted, a Swedish flag fluttered in the breeze, the outboard motors sitting motionless, waiting, ready.

It was so close.

They ran for it, for their lives.

SEVENTY-SIX

Not with the speed of men in their prime, but with pure desperation, legs pumping, breath tearing through their chests, driven by fear, not endurance.

The slope worked against them – not steep, but just enough to throw them forward, making them pick up more speed than they could control on the slick, stony ground, their balance more and more compromised.

Petrović could feel it before it happened – the inevitability of it, the creeping certainty that his own body was going to betray him. The toe of his shoe caught on something uneven, maybe a root, maybe a rock, maybe nothing at all but his own failing sense of control, and then—

He fell.

His legs went, and gravity claimed him, wrenching him face down onto the cold earth.

The air rushed out of his lungs in a single, panicked exhale.

Fear screamed at him to get up, and, to his surprise, his

body obeyed. Until it didn't. The pain flared from his right leg, something deep and intense near his knee that refused to cooperate. He fell back down before he had even stood. His hands scrambled against the wet ground, trying to find purchase, leverage, anything—

But Leka did what Petrović alone could not, grabbing him under the arm, hauling him up, his grip strong and made stronger by urgency.

Petrović grunted, pain stabbing through his leg, his breath ragged. 'Thank you – thank you—'

Leka wasn't listening.

His grip tensed around Petrović's arm, and then, as though his thoughts were made loud—

'*Oh God.*'

Petrović turned his head, looked back over his shoulder—

The burning wreck of the Range Rover dominated the crest of the incline, flames roaring skyward, the metal warped and blackened, heatwaves rippling through the night air. The glow of the fire was blinding, its brightness washing out the surrounding darkness, casting twisting, flickering halos of light that made everything seem surreal, dreamlike.

Everything except the silhouette in front of it.

A single figure, walking forward.

Closer.

Not rushing. Not striding with urgency. Just walking.

Deliberate. Methodical.

The glow of the inferno wrapped around him, turning him into a shadow of impending doom. The light masked details, but not enough. Not enough to hide the way the Boatman moved, the economy of motion, the effortless, inevitable approach.

His footsteps unhurried, methodical.

He didn't rush because he didn't need to rush.

Together they pushed on with slow, agonising shuffles.

As Leka still yanked him on, Petrović reached for his side-arm with shaking hands, the metal feeling slick, unfamiliar, too light, his fingers barely able to find the grip. He raised it, not aiming, not thinking, just squeezing the trigger and praying that any bullet would find its mark.

They didn't.

The muzzle flashed, the shots roaring through the night, expended shell cases pinging off the stony ground as the bullets ripped into the darkness.

The Boatman kept coming.

Petrović continued firing, his knuckles white around the pistol's grip, his breath hitching with every shot.

The gun clicked empty.

The Boatman still walked, unrushed, unbothered, as if the bullets had never existed at all.

Unhit. Unstoppable.

Petrović was too slow. His right leg lame, every step a fight, every movement a losing battle against pain and gravity and the certainty of death.

Petrović knew. Leka knew.

Together, they weren't going to make it.

'I'm sorry,' Leka said.

He let go of Petrović's arm.

Then he ran.

Petrović shuffled forward using his left leg only, the right dragging behind him, every metre of distance an agony to endure, but he kept moving, trying to follow, trying not to stop.

Don't give up, don't give up.

Leka reached the jetty, his footsteps hammering against the wooden planks with the repetitive rhythm of desperation.

Petrović followed, hobbling, dragging himself forward, praying that his friend could not start the boat, could not leave him to die.

Behind him, he heard it.

The roar of fresh gunfire.

The burst tore through the night, loud – too loud, too near – the bullets slicing through the air past his head.

Leka staggered mid-stride, his body jerking and flailing, the impacts punching through his back one after the other many times over. His feet tangled beneath him, his arms flopping as he fell sideways off the jetty.

The splash was silent, swallowed by the crash of the waves.

Petrović didn't stop.

Couldn't stop.

The jetty – ahead, the boat so close now, bobbing in the water, waiting, waiting, waiting—

He shuffled forward, fighting through the pain, through the burning in his lungs, through the terror that had wrapped itself around his ribs in an inescapable vice.

His breath came in ragged, desperate gasps, but he pushed forward – limping, dragging himself onto the jetty, then along it, reaching his boat but expecting bullets in the back like Leka at any moment.

The Scorpion Serket 88 was low and sleek, designed for speed and control, its hull gleaming in the moonlight. The outboard engines sat motionless, waiting.

Petrović, wincing – crying out in pain – clambered aboard.

Somehow, he had made it.

And then – he looked back.

Petrović saw the Boatman reach the jetty, the lanterns up-lighting his blank, expressionless features. Nothing in the eyes, no flicker of exertion or anger or urgency or even satisfaction. His pale, nondescript features were set in something beyond calm – beyond human.

The MP7 hung at his side, the barrel hot and smoking, but his fingers weren't on the trigger any more.

Then Petrović's gaze moved lower, locking on to the front of the Boatman's tactical harness – and he saw the empty straps.

The magazines that had been secured in them were all gone, used up. Five magazines. Forty rounds each. Two hundred bullets.

All used up in a matter of minutes.

And now—

He's out.

This was Petrović's chance.

The Boatman wasn't running after him.

He could have. He should have. But he didn't.

Petrović felt his stomach twist because he understood – the bastard was dragging it out, savouring the slow collapse of everything, watching as panic consumed him, as exhaustion strangled him, as hope strained thinner and thinner.

But that was a mistake because Petrović had made it to the speedboat. His fingers shook as they reached for the ignition.

And then – a thought hit him.

What if it was rigged? Like the Range Rover.

What if the moment he turned the key, it all went up in flames?

His mind raced – would the Boatman have had time to rig

every vehicle? Would he have expected Petrović to run here? Was this all planned?

It was improbable. Unlikely. And besides, the Boatman was too close. He would be caught in any such explosion.

But he was still scared as hell as his fingers flicked the battery switch, then stabbed the ignition button.

No explosion.

A wave of relief washed over him – a single, blessed second of relief.

Then the dread came crashing back.

Because there was no sound.

No hum of the engine, no rumble of power coming to life. He tried again. Nothing.

His breath caught, his heart hammered, his fingers pressed the ignition over and over, hammering it, holding it down, tapping it furiously, anything – anything—

Nothing.

Pulling open the cabinet beneath the console, he saw the wires connecting the battery to the ignition had been cut.

Sabotaged.

Then he heard it.

Tap. Tap. Tap.

Soft, measured, rhythmic.

The footsteps on the jetty, growing louder, getting closer, deliberate and unrushed.

He was out of time.

He grabbed the first thing he could find – something, anything to defend himself with – his hands wrapping around a metal deck cleat, then a heavy mooring hook.

He was a big man. Strong. The Boatman was not.

If Petrović could just land one good hit – one solid swing—

Maybe. Just maybe.

The Boatman stepped onto the speedboat, his footsteps light against the deck, his body moving with the same terrifying ease as before.

For a second, he just stood there, looking down at the Scorpion upon which he was standing.

Then, in a flat, empty voice, he said, 'Fitting.'

The Boatman's gaze shifted to his victim.

He took a step forward, drawing a slim, curved combat knife from its sheath. The same weapon with which he had butchered Nemanja.

Petrović's pulse was as loud as the sea, his fingers tightening around the mooring hook, braced.

Desperate.

Ready.

When the Boatman spoke again, his voice was monotone, devoid of any emotion or temperament, just a quiet statement of inevitable fact:

'If you resist, it only means it will need to hurt for longer.'

SEVENTY-SEVEN

The port of Malmö sprawled across the coastline as a living, breathing beast of industry and commerce. It was a vast complex of interconnected facilities and many docks that stretched for miles along the rugged shoreline, a patchwork of modern terminals and older, weathered piers that bore witness to decades of trade. Large container cranes towered over the quay, swinging enormous loads of cargo with mechanical precision, while narrow lanes wound between warehouses where goods were sorted and distributed with relentless efficiency.

'I love it here,' Scragg said as he drove.

At one end lay the dry dock, a cavernous space where ships of all sizes were brought in for repairs and maintenance. The sound of metal striking metal echoed across the concrete basin, mingling with the hissing of steam and the low rumble of heavy machinery. There, massive vessels were lifted from the water on hydraulic jacks, their hulls exposed and vulnerable under the bright glare of floodlights.

Victor listened as Scragg provided a running commentary

on what they could see outside of the car. He had a passion in his voice, an awe.

Not far from the dry dock, the passenger terminal buzzed with a different energy altogether. Modern glass and steel structures, with smooth curves and reflective surfaces, housed busy check-in desks and waiting areas. In that part of the port, every minute was a countdown to departure, and the sense of organised chaos pervaded every polished surface and gleaming digital display.

Further along, the refinery and the liquid bay terminal formed the industrial heart of the complex. There, massive storage tanks, pumps and pipelines formed a network of arteries, transporting crude oil and refined products to and from the ships anchored in the deep water.

'Doesn't it make you feel small?' he asked Victor. 'Like an ant.'

In quieter corners of the port, smaller yards and ancillary docks served niche roles. One such area was the container terminal, where stacks of colourful containers were arranged in enormous, precise grids. Automated vehicles and engines moved among them with a calculated pace, guided by computer systems that tracked every single unit as though it were a piece of a giant industrial puzzle.

Ships from across the world came and went, each one a testament to the power of globalisation and the relentless drive for economic progress. At night, the facility was a tableau of lights and shadows. Although a twenty-four-hour operation, in the early hours of the morning, the port was at its quietest.

They drove towards the Liquid Bulk Terminal, where the tanker waited.

'Crazy idea,' Scragg began as they neared. 'Why don't you stay in Malmö? Keep your head down until all this drama has blown over. A couple of weeks and everyone will have forgotten about you.'

'Even if that were true,' Victor replied. 'Why would I ever want to stay here a second longer than I needed to?'

'*Ouch*,' Scragg breathed. 'I didn't expect you to go straight for the jugular.'

'Carotid,' Victor explained. 'You want to cut off the blood supply to the brain, not cut off the blood that leaves it.'

'That's ... not what I ... meant. I'm saying: we're a good team so why not exploit that?'

'Surely we don't qualify as a team. We're a partnership or a double act.'

'*Feck sake, Princess*,' Scragg grunted. 'Fine, we're not the Beatles, we're Simon and Garfunkel. Why is the terminology so important to you?'

'It's not,' Victor told him. 'But I'm not staying. And once I'm gone, you need to be a lot more careful because there is a professional known as the Boatman out there ... he is hunting me on behalf of Jorund Håkansson. He is exceptionally dangerous – I cannot overemphasise this point. If he finds out we are associated, it can only be very bad for you.'

'Professional? Please,' Scragg hissed. 'Let him try, yeah? We dance in different circles, Princess, but you're forgetting my circle is lined with barbed wire. If this lad wants to make moves, he has no idea of the whirlwind of pain that I will lay upon him. And when I say *lay*, what I really mean is open my breeches and bury him with the resulting avalanche of stinking Scottish shite.'

Despite the profanity, Victor could not help but smile.

'Anyway, the tanker's chief mate is a guy called Havel,' Scragg explained. 'You'll like him. He probably won't like you because you're the very definition of unlikeable, but after I've vouched for you, you're all set. Once he's seen your ugly mug we wait out the rest of the time until departure at the dry dock with Leila Farahani. And then this time tomorrow you'll be floating on the Atlantic. Easy peasy.'

Victor remembered the last time the Kashmiri Scottish Viking had said those last two words.

A bloodbath had followed.

SEVENTY-EIGHT

The fireplace crackled, the embers glowing deep red, shadows flickering across the stone walls of the drawing room. The only light came from the flames, casting the space in a shifting orange glow, illuminating the high wooden beams, the mounted stag's head above the hearth, the dark oak furniture worn smooth with age.

Jorund Håkansson sat in his heavy leather chair, a glass of *brännvin* in one hand, his fingers tight around the crystal tumbler, swirling the clear spirit while his gaze was fixed on the fire, his expression motionless, unreadable. The light reflected in his eyes, dancing in the deep-set creases of his face. The warmth of the flames reached his skin, but he barely felt it. His body was warm. His thoughts were cold.

He had been sitting like this for hours. Contemplating. Not thinking about what had already been done – there was no use in that – but about what came next.

Behind him, the sharp click of heels against the hardwood floor broke the silence.

A presence. Expected, yet still unwelcome.

Police Director Elise Wallin.

She stepped closer, stopping just behind his chair, but he didn't turn to look at her.

'The Boatman has confirmed that Malmgren and Petrović are dead. Only Farahani remains.' A pause. The fire popped. 'He is now making his way to the port since the assassin is attempting to leave the city.'

Håkansson nodded once. Slow. 'It's a moot point who hired the man to kill my son.'

Wallin exhaled. 'Do you still want to continue with this?'

He said nothing.

She stepped closer, the faint scent of her perfume reaching him.

'It's not too late to stop,' she continued. 'Farahani controls the port. She needs to be alive for the business to survive. If you spare her, then others can fill in the void left by Malmgren and Petrović.'

The flames danced, shifting across the logs, burning lower now, the light casting longer, darker shadows.

Håkansson took a long, slow sip of his drink, swallowing the spirit, feeling the heat spread through his chest.

Then, finally, he spoke.

'Gustavus will inherit a mansion,' he said, finding even speaking to be burdensome with his increasing weakness. He set the glass down on the small wooden table beside him, the sound muted, final. 'And a fortune.' He leaned forward, resting his skeletal hands on his knees, staring deeper into the fire. 'And he will be alive to enjoy them.' Another pause. Then, quieter, as if speaking only to himself – 'That is enough.' He turned his head a little, just enough to catch

Wallin's silhouette in the firelight. 'I will not have a legacy. But my son will have a future.'

She said, 'As you wish.'

Magnar Kaale entered the room, his heavy footfalls preceding him so that Håkansson had no need to turn around to know who was behind him.

'Mr Håkansson,' Kaale said. 'I've just finished on the phone with Ms Farahani and she agrees to the meeting. I did as you asked and hinted that you had come to a decision regarding what will become of your business interests after your passing. She requests you join her at the port to discuss things further.'

Smiling into the fire, Håkansson said, 'She believes her beak will be the first to have a bite from my corpse, of course. Thus, she wishes that peck to be from the tenderest of flesh.'

He stood.

An act that weeks ago he would do without thought, now he had to consider and manoeuvre to ensure he could even rise at all.

To Wallin, he said, 'Instruct the Boatman to wait for my arrival. The assassin is not the priority tonight.'

She nodded.

'And thanks to Farahani's greed,' Håkansson said as he headed for the door. 'I will now have the pleasure of watching her die.'

SEVENTY-NINE

The dry dock was a yawning chasm at the far end of the port, a colossal industrial pit carved into the ground, flanked by walls of reinforced concrete streaked with rust and salt decay. Empty of personnel, but never lifeless, it breathed with the weight of its purpose, the remnants of work left hanging in the air. Floodlights perched high on steel gantries cast stark, angular shadows, stretching the framework of cranes, scaffolding, and catwalks across the basin below.

Around the dry dock itself were several buildings: warehouses and machine sheds, workshops, pump and compressor rooms, the massive hall wherein the huge engines that powered tankers and cargo ships were installed into their hulls, and the testing facility to make sure such monstrous machines would work as intended. A network of towering cranes and gantries linked the various sections so the engines and other parts could be ferried between them.

Scragg pulled the car to a stop near a low stack of storage

containers, his fingers still loose on the wheel as he let his eyes scan the environment.

'I think Havel might have not even hated you.'

'Reassuring,' Victor replied.

'You might have to clean the latrines the whole trip to earn your keep, but I no longer think he'll sell you to organ harvesters when you arrive.'

Again, Victor said, 'Reassuring.'

'Come on,' Scragg said. 'Let's not keep her ladyship waiting.'

The engine test facility was built to contain the raw power of ship engines roaring to life in confined space. Thick, fire-resistant panels lined the walls, their surfaces darkened with years of heat exposure and oil vapour. The air inside was dense with the smell of diesel and chemical coolant, an atmosphere that clung to the skin and filled the lungs with every breath.

A series of test bays ran along the length of the chamber, each one designed to house the engines stripped from vessels for maintenance and calibration. Overhead, ceiling-mounted gantries supported heavy-duty hoists, their chains slick with grease, used to manoeuvre the massive engines into position.

At the far end of the room, a control station sat behind a blast-proof window, the glass thick and smudged with fingerprints from the countless engineers who had monitored stress tests from behind its barrier.

The door was a reinforced steel bulkhead, its surface dulled with years of wear, smeared with oil and the occasional scuff from heavy boots. A large circular locking wheel was mounted at the centre, thick-rimmed and ridged for grip, its metal worn smooth in places from countless hands turning it. A red emergency switch was mounted beside the door, its CO₂ FIRE SUPPRESSION label faded but still legible beneath a yellowed plastic cover.

The fire suppression system itself was built for rapid, total atmospheric displacement – the kind that left no chance for a fire, or anything else, to survive. CO_2 canisters were mounted across the ceiling, their nozzles pointed downwards, ready to flood the space in an instant. The piping network was re-inforced, designed to expel the gas under extreme pressure, ensuring that any flame was smothered in seconds. Mounted below the switch was a safety release bar. A final safeguard against suffocation, it was connected to the fire suppression system's emergency venting mechanism, designed to flush the room of carbon dioxide and restore breathable air before disengaging the locks.

Farahani's five men stood spread out, giving themselves room to move. Sharp suits, polished shoes, watchful eyes. The same ones from the osmium exchange, the ones who'd been with her in the car park.

One of whom was Darius Mehran.

He stood apart from the others, positioned where he could see everything, control everything. No wasted movement, no distraction. His posture was perfect, his attention split between Victor and Scragg, but mostly on Victor.

'Gentleman,' Leila Farahani said. 'Before we say or do anything else, I'm going to need your weapons.'

Victor didn't move.

The weight of the pistol inside his jacket had never felt heavier.

Farahani's men weren't nervous. But they weren't com-fortable either. Tension clung to them like humidity in the air. They weren't twitching, they weren't shifting on their feet, but they were ready.

They had to expect him to hesitate, expected him to resist – no one willingly gave up their weapon in a room full of potential enemies. That was enough to explain the tension.

Victor's hand stayed by his side, a few inches from the grip of his weapon, but not moving towards it yet.

Farahani watched him watch them, a faint trace of amusement on her lips, but her eyes were sharp, calculating.

'I can't let you take a ride on a tanker with a firearm,' she said, voice even, calm.

Not an order. Just a fact.

'Don't be like this, Leila,' Scragg said. 'My boy is wound tight enough as it is. And, *believe me*, you don't want to see what he's like when he finally snaps. I'm still getting nightmares.'

'If you want to leave the city without anyone noticing,' she continued, 'this is the only way to do so. And my terms are not for negotiation. You are free to turn around and depart the way you came if they are not acceptable to you.'

Scragg said, 'How about we hand them over when we're on board, yeah? That way, we know there's no funny business and you know there's no chance of the tanker going kaboom midway across the Atlantic?'

'This is not a discussion. This is the way we do it or we don't do it at all. I have my osmium so I'm very happy to go home and get into bed.'

Victor looked at her men again, reading them, trying to see past what they wanted him to see.

Mehran was the only one who wasn't tense. He stood as he had before, calm, disciplined, patient.

Victor thought back to what he had said to Scragg: Farahani would keep her word so long as it benefitted her.

Besides, since arriving in Malmö he was getting used to having no choice.

He reached inside his jacket, keeping his motions controlled. No one flinched, but they were all watching.

He withdrew the pistol, holding it by the grip, barrel pointed to the floor, and extended it towards Farahani.

She didn't take it. One of her men stepped forward instead, grasping the weapon without a word, before stepping back.

Victor's empty hand remained extended for a moment, fingers flexing, before he lowered his arm to his side. He turned his head towards Scragg, giving the barest inclination of his chin.

Scragg exhaled, shaking his head. He didn't like this any more than Victor did.

Still, he reached inside his own jacket, removed his weapon, and tossed it towards the man who had taken Victor's.

The gun hit the man's palm with a soft, dull slap of metal against flesh. He tucked the weapon into his waistband.

Farahani nodded once, like the matter was settled.

'Good,' she said.

She smiled, but Victor wasn't looking at her any more.

He was still watching her men.

And none of them had relaxed.

'I have to say,' she began, looking at Victor, 'I had high hopes for this arrangement. Not just for your benefit, of course – I'm not so sentimental – but for my own. You're a resource. You have value. And I had every intention of using that value to our mutual benefit. The problem, you see, is that circumstances have changed.'

Scragg grunted, '*Feck sake, Leila,*' because Darius Mehran and the four other guys all drew their guns.

EIGHTY

The Boatman drove without hurry.

Malmö slid past in the glow of sodium lamps and LED signage, the roads slick with rain that had stopped falling but still lingered in the sheen of the asphalt. He followed the route the GPS fed him, though he didn't need it. The map was already in his head, each turn, each deviation taken into account. There were faster ways, but none with the same level of operational control. The route he chose balanced efficiency with predictability – avoiding erratic movements, minimising the chance of external disruption.

The car had been bought for cash. Mid-range, unremarkable, pre-selected for reliability and anonymity. No trackers, no forensic liabilities. He'd swapped plates outside the hunting lodge, a precaution even though no one was left alive to report anything.

The massacre had been procedural. To get to Petrović the Boatman had needed to first eliminate any chance of interference. Their numbers hadn't mattered because he had method. Now the job continued.

Petrović was dead. Malmgren was dead. Farahani was next.

The city moved around him – people on pavements, light spilling from clubs, taxis slowing for late-night fares. He saw none of it. Only vectors, movement patterns, obstacles, opportunities. The way the streets were constructed, the flow of traffic, the positioning of surveillance cameras.

The Boatman drove at a precise speed – 53 km/h, not 50, not 55. The difference mattered.

Malmö's traffic system operated on a fixed-cycle control pattern, designed for smooth flow at an average speed of 50 km/h. But the sequencing had a fractional delay – he'd noted it within the first three intersections. A 0.6-second discrepancy in cycle transitions.

That was enough.

He adjusted in accordance. Not by speeding up or slowing down in reaction, but by calibrating his own pace to match the flaw in the system.

No wasted movement. No unnecessary stops. No interaction with the chaotic inefficiencies of the city.

Seventeen minutes and twenty-six seconds later, the Boatman arrived at the port.

He drove through the security checkpoint without issue. Routine traffic at this hour – freight haulers, late-shift dock workers, maintenance crews. He moved through it like any other vehicle, unnoticed, unremarkable.

The port unfolded in a sprawl of steel, concrete and sodium light, the air thick with the blend of brine, diesel and damp rust. Cargo cranes loomed above as giant sentries, their arms frozen mid-motion. Shipping containers stood in perfect stacks, their faded exteriors tagged with codes and company insignias, their contents unknown and irrelevant.

The Boatman drove through the network of roads and loading zones without hesitation, never needing to second-guess a turn. The dry dock lay ahead, past the stack yards and refuelling stations, past the corridors where engines manoeuvred pallets and tugboats idled against the quay.

As he drove, he noted key vantage points, exits, the positioning of overhead cranes, cargo lifts, blind spots in CCTV coverage. Harsh white halogen floodlights illuminated the dry dock – maintenance sheds, a huge engine assembly hall, and the skeletal form of a ship in partial repair, exposed hull plating gleaming under the light.

He parked as planned – close enough for efficiency, far enough for tactical movement. The engine cut. The door opened. He moved to the boot.

Lifted it.

Inside, his equipment bag lay beneath a folded tarp, meticulously packed, nothing out of place. His hand found the MP7 first, still warm from the last engagement. The compact submachine gun sat neatly in its custom-cut foam lining, the suppressor still attached. Highly effective. Now useless. Two hundred rounds expended. It stayed in the case.

He reached for the pistol.

The Laugo Alien was not a standard-issue sidearm. It wasn't carried by soldiers or mass-produced for law enforcement contracts. It was a specialist's weapon, built for precision, engineered for control.

The Boatman checked the chamber, feeling the smooth action of the slide, the deliberate weight in his hand. The barrel sat unnaturally low, almost aligned with his grip – an anomaly in pistol design. But that was what made it superior.

Most pistols had a high bore axis, meaning the barrel sat well above the shooter's grip. That created leverage, a fulcrum point that caused the muzzle to rise with every shot, throwing off accuracy, forcing constant readjustment.

The Alien had none of that. Its bore axis was lower than anything else in its class, the barrel sitting nearly flush with the shooter's hand. The effect was profound. Less felt recoil. No wasted movement. No muzzle flip. The sights stayed on target, even under rapid fire. Follow-up shots were faster, smoother, automatic in their precision. Like him.

The barrel itself was fixed, unlike the majority of semi-automatic pistols that relied on a tilting-barrel design. Most guns shifted during cycling, requiring the shooter to reacquire their aim with each shot. The Alien's barrel didn't move. That meant one less variable. One more factor eliminated.

The slide functioned on a gas-delayed blowback system, venting excess pressure to slow its rearward motion. That further reduced recoil and further stabilised the weapon.

He pressed the trigger once. Dry fire. The pull was crisp, the break clean.

The Boatman holstered it and reached for the rifle case, flipped it open, and pulled out the Knight's Armament SR-25 APC with integrated suppressor.

It was neither a sniper rifle nor an assault rifle, but something between the two – a semi-automatic precision rifle, adaptable to both urban and long-range engagements.

A bolt-action sniper rifle was too slow for manoeuvring engagements. An assault rifle lacked the range and accuracy for controlled eliminations. The SR-25 was the balance – powerful enough for extended reach, compact enough for mobility. A sniper rifle required the shooter to find a position, set up, commit to a single vantage point. The SR-25 allowed for movement, adaptation, the ability to transition between targets without sacrificing control.

He slotted in the 7.62mm magazine, feeling the weight distribution shift. The heavier rounds gave it an immediate advantage over standard 5.56mm ammunition. More stopping power. More penetration. More reliability when shooting through barriers – glass, metal and body armour.

He slung it over his shoulder, closed the boot and—

The Boatman went to work.

EIGHTY-ONE

Victor remained silent.

He watched, listened.

She continued, 'When I gave you my word, I did so under the assumption that my obligations had been fulfilled. The osmium was recovered, our exchange was made, and I could move forward. But it appears that in the process of completing your side of the deal, you made a mistake.'

She said it without malice, without accusation – like a teacher explaining an error to a bright student who should have known better.

Victor held her gaze. 'A mistake.'

Farahani's lips curved, like she'd expected him to say more. When he didn't, she continued.

'One of Luis Aranda's men was killed. Not just any man – one he was particularly close to. That complicates things given I was inflexible that Aranda must not be present when you made your move.'

'Aranda came back.'

'That is …' She leaned back against the console, stretching her legs out, taking her time. 'Bad luck.'

'I don't believe in luck.'

'Nevertheless, bad luck believes in you.'

Victor remained silent once more.

'For my deal with Vladimir Kasakov to move forward, I need to be a good team player,' she said. 'Kasakov does not care from where the osmium comes, but Aranda is the conduit to him and Aranda wants blood for blood. That's non-negotiable. And Kasakov won't back me unless Aranda is satisfied. You see how these things connect.'

She let it sit there for a moment, as if allowing Victor the opportunity to refute it.

He didn't.

Instead, he asked, 'What does it have to do with Scragg? It was my mistake, not his.'

Farahani exhaled, almost fondly, as if he had asked a question she had already considered answering.

'Oh, Scragg,' she said, turning her attention to him. 'You, I like. I've always enjoyed working with you. I appreciate your Scottish eccentricities, which is why I found it in my heart to forgive you for not supplying the osmium you promised. But unfortunately, you are simply collateral damage in all of this. I can't have you walking around feeling aggrieved, and you are, aren't you? I can see it all over your ruggedly handsome face. You hate me right now because of what I'm doing to your business partner. Or, given the intensity of the hatred, I think he's more than that, isn't he? You consider him a friend.'

Scragg stared at her, his features tight with rage and his body tensed and ready to explode.

'This isn't how I wanted it to go,' she said. 'If I had my way, we wouldn't be standing here like this. I would have honoured my word, and you would have been on a ship by morning, slipping away from Malmö like a ghost.' A slight sheen to her eyes matched the sadness in her smile. 'But this isn't about what I want. It's about what must be done.'

Victor could tell she meant it. She wasn't lying. There was no glee in her voice, no malice in her tone, no power play in her words.

She had weighed the options, calculated the benefits, and chosen the path that served her best. That was all.

Victor nodded once, slow. 'I see.'

Farahani tilted her head, intrigued. 'I knew you would understand.'

'What are you waiting for?' Scragg asked. 'Because I'm tired of listening to you talk.'

'I'm waiting for Jorund Håkansson to arrive.'

There was no gloating in her eyes, no pleasure in what she was about to say. If anything, there was a soft detachment – as though she were a physician preparing to deliver an unpleasant diagnosis.

'This is not about you. It's about opportunity.'

She watched Victor, weighing his silence, then continued, as if explaining a matter that required clarity but not cruelty.

'Håkansson is dying,' she said, as if it were common knowledge. 'His empire will fracture the moment he's gone, and everyone with a stake in it will start carving out their share.' She paused, not for dramatic effect, but to allow the truth to settle, that same physician now letting the weight of the prognosis take hold before moving to treatment options.

'Håkansson will never trust any of us. Not fully. Not while he still breathes. So the game is not about trust. It's about leverage. That's where you come in. He's sentimental. More than he wants people to believe. He mourns his son, though he won't show it. He resents that no one will suffer for it. That's why he's dangerous. A dying man with no future has no reason to be measured.' She let the words linger, as though ensuring he followed. 'But if I give him you,' she said, her tone the same as if she were offering a business proposal, 'then I give him something real. Something he can touch. Something to hurt. That makes me valuable to him in a way none of the others can be.' Another pause. Still no pleasure in her voice, just a calm certainty. 'He'll be generous to me. More than to the others. And when he's gone, when the empire is divided, I will already have my hands on the biggest share.'

'I tip my hat,' Scragg said. 'You get to satisfy Aranda's bloodlust for your osmium deal and at the same time you get to buy a bigger slice of the Håkansson pie. Very fecking efficient.'

She smiled. 'Like I said: I'll miss you.' She gestured to one of her men. 'Take our Scottish friend to the maintenance shed and hold him there until Håkansson arrives.' To Darius Mehran, she said. 'Meanwhile, I think it's best if you personally look after this one in here.'

This one being Victor.

Mehran nodded.

Scragg was taken out of the room by the man assigned to watch him, Farahani and her remaining men following, leaving Mehran alone with Victor.

Farahani had given Mehran the job of guarding Victor

for a reason. Mehran wasn't like the others. Not like the competent but ordinary security Farahani employed to enforce her will. He was on another level. Victor had seen him at Farahani's penthouse, standing just behind her, silent but present, his weight balanced, his attention shifting not with curiosity, but calculated awareness. He had seen him again at the osmium exchange in the parking garage, not speaking much then either, but always watching, always adjusting, always placing himself where he needed to be. Not just a bodyguard, not just a hired gun – something more than that.

A professional, in the same way Victor was a professional.

Not an assassin. That wasn't his trade. His skillset was something else – but he had the same cold precision, the same ingrained discipline, the same instinct for threat assessment that Victor had seen in the best of his kind.

And now, locked in the engine test room together, Mehran's actions only reinforced what Victor already knew.

Mehran wouldn't underestimate him. He would keep his distance. He wouldn't allow an inch of sloppiness, wouldn't give Victor a single easy opening. He wouldn't pace about, wouldn't lower his weapon, wouldn't fall into routine gestures or unguarded moments.

He was composed, focused, rigid in his control.

Victor had distracted and outplayed countless guards before. Mehran wasn't one of them.

There would be no sudden burst forward, no clever wordplay that made him glance away, no quick disarm manoeuvre that turned the tide in a heartbeat.

Mehran wasn't going to fall for any of the usual tricks.

Victor met Mehran's gaze, the dark, unyielding stare of a professional. No fear. No hesitation. That was fine.

Mehran said, 'Don't even think about trying anything.'

Victor raised an eyebrow. 'Wouldn't dream of it.'

EIGHTY-TWO

'But you don't understand,' Victor said, his voice even, his tone almost conversational. 'You think I'm the one trapped in here with you.'

Mehran's expression tightened, but he didn't take the bait. His stance didn't shift.

Victor took a step forward.

Mehran mirrored it backwards, keeping the exact same distance.

'You're wrong,' Victor continued. 'We're both prisoners.'

He watched Mehran as he moved, slow, careful steps, always keeping the same precise three-metre gap between them. A dance with a predictable rhythm. Victor stepped forward, Mehran stepped back. The gun never wavered, the muzzle locked onto Victor's chest, the finger resting steady on the trigger guard – not inside, not twitching, just there.

Ready. Disciplined.

'The difference is, you haven't figured it out yet.'

'Forget the mind games,' Mehran said, his voice calm and quiet. 'You're not getting in my head. I know who you are. I know what you are. You're not going to catch me lowering my guard. You're not going to trick me. I have the gun. I'm in charge.'

Victor gave a small nod. Like he was agreeing. Like he understood. Then he took another step forward. Mehran stepped back.

'That's where you're wrong,' Victor said. 'You think the gun gives you power. That it puts you in control. But it doesn't. The gun is the shackle that's keeping you here.'

Mehran's expression didn't change. But something shifted behind his eyes.

Victor saw it. That tiny moment where Mehran's brain paused on the words. A flicker of thought, a moment of processing, but not understanding.

Mehran kept moving in time with Victor, his steps deliberate. His grip on the pistol didn't change. Not yet.

But he was thinking.

Victor could see the thoughts turning over in his mind, trying to deconstruct what he had just said, trying to work out the angle. He wouldn't ask. Not yet. He wouldn't give Victor the satisfaction of knowing he didn't understand.

He couldn't see the narrative of the moment unfolding around him. Not the laws of the universe, but the laws of situations like this one. Rules that could not be broken.

The unspoken, immutable laws of inevitable conflict.

Victor understood them. Because there was always a structure, always an arc, a conclusion.

Silence lingered between them, the ambient whir and rumble of pumps fading away. Mehran's breathing was even, his trigger finger still disciplined, but Victor could see it in his eyes now. The struggle.

And then, inevitably, the words came.

'What are you talking about?'

Victor kept moving, slow, deliberate, precise. Mehran moved with him, always maintaining the three-metre gap, always adjusting, never allowing the distance to shrink. The gun tracked Victor's chest with unwavering control, the steel as steady as the man holding it.

A professional through and through.

'The gun only gives you power,' Victor said, 'if you're prepared to use it.'

Mehran didn't react. There was a beat of calm before a flicker of calculation behind his eyes, a thought forming but never quite reaching the surface. His stance didn't change, his trigger finger didn't flex.

But now he understood.

Victor continued. 'You're not going to use it, are you?'

A breath. A hesitation.

'Because Farahani needs me alive,' Victor said. 'She's handing me over to Håkansson. If you shoot me, that plan goes out the window. That's why you're backing away from me. Because you don't want me close enough that it forces your hand. You move away from me because you aren't prepared to shoot me.'

Another step forward.

Another step back.

'If you had stood your ground when I moved, if you let the distance between me and that pistol shrink from three metres to two, I would have known another step put me in danger. If that gap was reduced from two metres to one, I would have known for sure another step would kill me. But Farahani needs me alive so you keep your distance. That's why I said the gun is a shackle. Because you are shackling yourself.'

Mehran said nothing. But Victor could feel it happening, the realisation settling into the man's mind, the quiet struggle to dismiss it, to reject it, to pretend it wasn't true.

Victor took another step forward.

Mehran stepped back.

A phone chimed. Mehran was expecting it because he didn't need to check it. He said, 'Håkansson's early. Time to go.'

'I agree,' Victor said, and pointed at the door.

The door that was now closer to Victor than it was to Darius Mehran.

The moment he saw it, his stance stiffened. He had been so focused on keeping Victor at a distance that he had overlooked this.

Victor could see the thought process play out, the rapid-fire assessments running through Mehran's mind: What happens if his captive escapes? What happens if he kills the captive? Which one would enrage Farahani the most?

The inability to decide was a struggle visible in Mehran's stance, the way he was trying to stay in control but knew he had already lost something.

'If you open that door,' Mehran said, voice low, even, final, 'I will kill you.'

'Finally, you lose the shackles,' Victor said. 'Doesn't freedom taste sweet?'

Mehran smiled, thinking he had broken those immutable rules of inevitable conflict.

Victor held the pause, let it stretch, let Mehran feel the absence of movement and in that absence the rush of winning.

Then Victor said, 'But you're forgetting one thing.'

Mehran's brow creased, the smallest shift, his mind working fast, trying to see the angle, trying to stay ahead of whatever was coming next.

Victor winked at him, then elbowed the emergency fire suppression panel – positioned on the wall next to the door – the sharp crack of breaking plastic slicing through the hum of the machinery.

He slammed the button—

Taking a sharp breath—

Before the room flooded with carbon dioxide gas.

He filled his lungs to capacity in the fraction of a second before the system engaged. He held it, locking his jaw, pinching his nostrils.

Mehran was still catching up, his mind so focused on keeping his distance, then the door, then his decision to shoot Victor if he went for it, that he was slow to process the reality unfolding in front of him.

The nozzles hissed.

Not a mechanical whirr, not a slow release, not some safety-checked, controlled emission. It was a violent expulsion, a pressurised burst of thick, freezing gas spewing from the ceiling-mounted cylinders. It blasted downward in a powerful avalanche of white vapour, churning in dense, roiling clouds.

The sound was low and guttural, a heavy, gaseous roar as the air itself seemed to tighten, the temperature plummeting as the CO_2 displaced the oxygen, pushing it out, pushing it away, drowning it under an ocean of suffocating cold.

Mehran's eyes widened, a delay of less than a second, but that was enough.

His body did what it was programmed to do – breathe.

He inhaled.

And the freezing gas was sucked up into his lungs.

His throat seized, his body rejecting the foreign air, his lungs spasming in an effort to expel the poison he had just inhaled. His knees buckled, a shudder rippling through his frame. His free hand jerked up, fingers splayed, instinctively clawing at the nothingness in front of him, at the air he expected to be there and yet was not.

He coughed once. A sharp, brutal choke as he staggered.

The gas kept flooding, thickening, curling through the space; obscuring the ground, the walls, everything but the harsh glow of overhead lights, which were now just ghostly orbs swimming in an ocean of white.

Mehran coughed again, harder, his body doubling forward, the pistol wavering in his grip.

His brain was suffocating. Not just from the lack of oxygen, but from the sheer physiological shock of inhaling pure CO_2. His body thought it was drowning, his nervous system misfiring in every direction.

His limbs twitched, a series of jerky, disorganised spasms, his body trying to find equilibrium where none existed. He took a half-step sideways, the movement unsteady, clumsy. His vision was going, his peripheral field collapsing inward, the edges of his sight greying out as his blood became acidic, his muscles screaming for oxygen that would never come.

The gun in his hand lowered, his grip weakening, his knuckles loosening without his permission. His legs trembled, his balance failing.

His body folded, knees hitting the floor hard, the pistol clattering against the concrete.

His breath stuttered once – a single, final, disjointed gasp – before his head lolled forward, his arms going limp at his sides.

Beneath the cracked plastic glass was the manual shutdown lever.

Victor pushed it down and vents whirred into life, sucking out the carbon dioxide gas. The door could not be opened while the fire extinguishing system was in process. After a few seconds, the sensor detected safe levels of carbon dioxide and the door made a *clunk* sound as the lock disengaged.

Victor turned the wheel and pulled it open, casting a look back at Mehran's prostrate form. The gun was out of Victor's eyeline, having been dropped and maybe kicked away beneath machinery. He couldn't risk burning time searching for it when more of Farahani's men might be heading this way to see why Mehran had not already brought Victor to their mistress.

Mehran's hand twitched.

Not quite dead, after all. Maybe he would wake up in a few minutes, maybe an hour.

Either way, it wouldn't matter because—

Victor was gone.

EIGHTY-THREE

Victor moved through the dry dock compound, keeping low, stepping with care. The dock was vast, mostly silent except for the rumble of machinery and the occasional clang of metal on metal. The salt-stained air carried the scent of oil and rust, a cold wind shifting through gaps in the towering stacks of shipping containers. Puddles had formed in the depressions of the cracked tarmac, rainwater mixed with fuel, spreading in thin, iridescent sheets beneath the glow of high-mounted floodlights.

Victor moved past a row of heavy equipment, dark shapes against the sodium glare. He paused in the deep shadow of a cargo loader, exhaling slowly, keeping still as the sound of an approaching engine cut through the night.

A limousine rolled into view, gliding across the uneven ground, slow and deliberate. The armoured plating made it heavy, the suspension adjusting as it came to a stop outside the entrance to the engine assembly hall. The windows were tinted, thick enough to stop bullets, the body reinforced against explosives. Not invulnerable, but built to withstand more than most.

The back door opened. A giant stepped out first.

Victor had seen men like him before. Large, but not just in height – wide, powerful, built like a man accustomed to absorbing force and returning it with greater violence. His suit fit, but only because it had been tailored to accommodate the sheer bulk of him. He moved in a way that suggested restraint, his motions slow, controlled, as if he knew his own strength too well to waste it.

Then Håkansson stepped out.

He was not the same man Victor had seen in photographs. The years had hollowed him, thinned his face, sapped some of the vitality from his movements. His coat was draped over his shoulders rather than worn, his hand resting on a cane more for show than necessity. But he still carried himself with authority, still had the weight of a man who expected obedience. His eyes swept the area as he adjusted his coat, speaking to no one, his bodyguards moving into position around him.

Two more vehicles pulled in behind the limousine. More men stepped out. Not low-level security – professionals, moving with the ease of experience, their coats cut to conceal weapons.

Victor stayed where he was, motionless in the darkness, watching as Håkansson and his security detail moved inside.

The engine assembly hall.

He had known Scragg was going to be taken there, but now it was certain.

Victor should have turned away then. He should have

been thinking about the tanker. About escape. About getting out while he still could. But he was not moving.

Something else caught his eye.

Another car. Further back. Unremarkable. A vehicle that had not been there when he and Scragg had arrived.

Dark paint, but not glossy. No chrome, no distinctive markings. The kind of car that blended into the background, not because it was designed to, but because it had been chosen for that exact purpose.

He had used cars like that before. Stolen them. Driven them across borders. Chosen for efficiency and anonymity.

It could only mean one thing.

The Boatman was here.

Victor breathed in, held it, then exhaled through his nose. His pulse had not changed, his mind already accounting for the new variable.

Scragg was not just being handed over. This was an execution.

Victor turned the thought over, examined the angles, found the flaws.

Scragg was not his responsibility. They had helped each other because it had been mutually beneficial. That was all. There was no debt between them. No obligation.

It was over.

Yet he did not move.

He turned it over again.

Scragg had helped him. Not because it served him. Not because there was something to be gained. He had done it because he had decided to.

There were not many men left like that.

Victor pressed a hand against his side, feeling the wound

that was still healing. No risk of it reopening at this point and yet he was still not at his best.

If he had a weapon, he could do something.

If he was uninjured – maybe ...

Victor headed to the tanker.

EIGHTY-FOUR

The engine assembly hall was a massive industrial cavern, heavy with the scent of old oil, scorched metal and machine lubricant. The air was thick with particulates that had settled into every crack, stirred only when someone moved, hanging in the beams of flickering fluorescent lights. The concrete floor, once smooth, was scarred by years of heavy machinery grinding across its surface, deep grooves filled with grime, oil stains spreading in uneven patches. Some were fresh, dark and wet, pooling in shallow depressions where the ground had cracked.

Along the ceiling, steel girders ran the length of the hall, supporting a system of cranes and hoists used for lowering ship engines into their housings. The tracks along the ceiling were dulled from heavy use, thick chains dangling from reinforced pulleys, clanking if they swayed. Some had hooks the size of a man's head. Others ended in winches, cables coiled and smeared with grease.

Catwalks and maintenance platforms criss-crossed the upper levels, their steel grates covered in dust and welding slag. Some had missing sections of railing, others sagged where the bolts had loosened over time. A few emergency ladders led down to the floor, their paint chipped away, revealing bare metal corroded by salt air.

The workstations along the side of the hall were a mix of old and new, benches stacked with tools, thick power cables snaking across the floor towards generator units humming in the distance. A hydraulic press sat idle, its pistons streaked with oil, a wrench resting on the platform, forgotten when the shift ended. A row of industrial lockers stood against the far wall, some of the doors scratched and dented, some hanging open, revealing old boiler suits and protective gloves stiff with age.

Further along, the hall widened into a secondary workspace, separated by thick support pillars that bore the weight of the overhead walkways. Welding tanks stood in a loose cluster, some still connected to hoses, their regulators covered in a fine layer of dust. Scorch marks marred the floor where repairs had once been made, the residue of molten steel hardened into uneven lumps.

Light pooled in some areas, stark and clinical, while other corners remained in shadow, deep recesses where the overhead illumination didn't reach and local fixtures had been shut off when the last shift had left.

Leila Farahani walked forward, the sound of her own footsteps lost beneath the low hum of industrial ambience. She glanced around at the huge space that was built for work, for precision, for the construction and fitting of machines as large as a car or a house. Now it was something else. A waiting ground. A place where unfinished business would be settled at last.

Three of her men walked with her. A fourth would soon arrive with Scragg, and Mehran would accompany the killer.

Jorund Håkansson stood waiting for her, watching with that unreadable expression he wore. He looked at ease, comfortable in the damp chill of the assembly hall despite his obvious frailty. Each time she saw him he looked worse than the previous occasion. She hoped this would be the final time she was ever forced to endure him.

With Håkansson was Magnar Kaale, towering and still, a statue of silent power. Four of Håkansson's security personnel were nearby.

Farahani smiled as she approached, adjusting the cuff of her coat, her movements deliberate, controlled. This was a moment to be handled with care. She reminded herself to act with reverence and humility, to appear grateful to the old, dying man for the gifts he was about to bestow upon her – gifts that she deserved before all others.

She noted Petrović or Malmgren were not present. They should have been here by now. They needed to be here to witness the transfer of power otherwise they would never accept Farahani taking what they wanted for themselves.

'Where are the others?' she asked.

Håkansson exhaled, slow and deliberate, as if savouring something private. 'Oh, I wouldn't worry about them. This concerns only you and I.'

She studied him, looking for the tell, the sign that he was holding something back. But all she saw was a man enjoying the moment. Stretching it out. Playing with his food.

Movement caught her eye as one of her men approached,

leading a figure forward with hands bound in front of him. Scragg.

He looked at her with an irritated expression, as if this were some minor inconvenience, rather than a situation that could very well end with him dead in a few minutes. He didn't look afraid. If anything, he looked bored.

Håkansson's gaze drifted to him, his brow rising. 'And who is this?'

'A local fixer by the name of Scragg. He was involved in the conspiracy to have Gustavus killed.' She gestured, as if presenting a lesser gift, something to whet the appetite. 'I thought you might like to have him as a gesture of good faith. A gift if you will'.

Håkansson's eyes flickered with something she couldn't quite read. Interest.

Amusement.

'How thoughtful of you.'

Farahani let her smile widen, playing her part. 'But he's not the real prize.' She glanced towards the entrance of the hall. 'He should be arriving any moment now.'

Håkansson shifted his weight, leaning into the cane he had not needed before now. The amusement in his gaze hadn't faded, but there was something else now – something more settled.

'You and I, Leila, we are not so different,' he said, his tone light, conversational. 'We are both builders, architects of things greater than ourselves. We took what was small, what was fragile, and we shaped it into something lasting. Something powerful. For years, I thought the measure of a man was what he could construct in his lifetime. The businesses. The networks. The wealth. The empire.' He exhaled, tilting his head as if reconsidering his own words. 'I used to think that was all that mattered.' His gaze lowered, unfocused for a moment, then sharpened again. 'Lately, though, I've been thinking about legacy. Not in the way people like us usually think about it. Not as property, or influence, or territory. But as something deeper. More absolute.'

Farahani nodded, offering just enough engagement to keep him talking. He was building to something.

'When I was younger, I saw succession as a simple thing. A transition of power, like passing the crown from one king to the next. I believed Gustavus would step into my place, take what I had built, and strengthen it. Expand it. Transform it into something even greater. That was the way of things. That was how it was meant to be.' He paused. 'I was mistaken.'

Farahani kept her expression neutral.

Håkansson smiled, the kind of smile that didn't belong to a man who had just admitted failure. 'Legacy is still everything to me, Leila. But I didn't understand it before. I thought my empire was my legacy. I thought the business I built, the wealth I accumulated, the power I wielded – that was the thing I would leave behind. That was my great achievement.' His fingers tightened around the head of his cane. His voice, though quiet, carried an unsettling certainty. 'I was wrong. My legacy is not the things I built. It's not the businesses, not power, not wealth.'

He held her gaze, and for the first time, she felt the stirrings of something uncertain, something out of place.

'My legacy is my son.'

The present tense had to be a slip. A symptom of age, of illness, of a mind coming apart. A man like Håkansson didn't just let go of control – not unless it was being taken from him. Maybe this was what happened when men like him reached the end. The weight of mortality creeping in, the slow unravelling of reality.

Still, something about the way he said it – calm, deliberate – set her on edge.

She kept her voice steady. 'That's why we're here.'

'Yes,' he said, a cruel iciness in his tone. 'That's exactly why we're here.'

EIGHTY-FIVE

'Gustavus is my legacy,' Håkansson said. 'Nothing else matters.'

Farahani nodded, still trying to place his meaning, to anticipate where he was leading her. She glanced towards the entrance of the engine hall, expecting movement. Where was Darius? Where was the assassin? They should be here by now.

'When I learned that someone wanted him dead, I did what any father would do and tried to protect him,' Håkansson continued. 'I set a trap. Not just to protect him, but to capture the man sent to kill him. Because then, of course, I could find out who gave the order. And once I knew that, I could take steps to ensure it never happened again. The trap failed. The assassin escaped. So I never got my answer.' There was no frustration in his voice, no anger. Just a kind of certainty. 'That left me with a problem,' he said. 'A quandary, if you will.'

Farahani could do nothing except listen.

'Because if I couldn't ask the assassin who sent him,' Håkansson said, 'I had to look at the facts myself. And the facts were simple. Who had the most to gain from Gustavus dying?'

Farahani knew what was coming.

'Petrović,' Håkansson continued. 'Malmgren. You.'

'Jorund,' she started, her voice carefully measured, 'I don't—'

But he kept speaking, unhurried, unbothered by her interruption.

'My time is running out, Leila. And I couldn't allow myself to leave this world without ensuring Gustavus was safe. He was never at the gallery, let alone killed there. He's been safe at home this whole time while I discovered who wanted him dead. But since I could not be certain which of you was guilty . . .' He let the silence settle for a moment, then smiled. '. . . I have removed all doubt.'

'They're dead,' she found herself whispering.

The conversation had twisted inside out, every expectation flipped. Her mind raced to reassemble the pieces, to find the path back to where she had thought this was going. But there was no route back.

She glanced around, keeping it subtle, a slow scan of the hall as if only to absorb the weight of his words. Technically, he had one more man. But that didn't matter. When Darius Mehran arrived, the odds would switch. He was worth three of any of Håkansson's own, even Kaale.

She turned her attention back to Håkansson, her confidence settling. 'You believe this will go smoothly for you?' she asked, keeping her tone level. 'You think this won't be a massacre?'

Håkansson smiled, amused. She felt as though this was exactly what he had wanted her to say.

'That's the least important question you should be asking, Leila,' he said.

She held his gaze, feeling something shift beneath the surface of the conversation, something slipping just beyond her reach. She didn't speak. She waited.

Håkansson watched her for a moment longer, then said, 'How.'

She blinked, processing. 'How?'

'How did Petrović and Malmgren die?' His voice was quiet now, almost casual. 'How have you not heard about it?'

Farahani should have heard, she realised. Men like Malmgren, like Petrović, didn't die in silence. Word spread fast. And yet – nothing. No calls. No messages. Not even a rumour.

Håkansson smiled. Not wide, not cruel, just the satisfied expression of a man watching the inevitable unfold.

'And after *how* is answered,' he explained to her. 'The next question should be ... who.'

For a long moment, Farahani was just as confused.

But then the first rifle shot split the air in two.

EIGHTY-SIX

The sound wasn't just loud. It was a force, a hammer blow to her chest, slamming through the cavernous space, bouncing off concrete and steel, multiplying until it became something unbearable.

A muzzle flash from the catwalk above – blinding, searing into her vision for a fraction of a second.

Brighter than the sun.

Farahani flinched hard, body jerking, but she didn't move, didn't run, didn't drop. Her mind refused to process what had just happened.

Then the impact. Not sound this time. Something worse.

To her left, the man who had been standing there a moment ago was no longer standing. The top of his head was gone – a spray of red and something pink and pulpy hitting the floor with a wet splatter. He was still upright for a fraction of a second, but it wasn't real, it wasn't conscious – his body just hadn't caught up to the fact that he was dead.

Then gravity took hold and he dropped, hitting the floor with a dull, wet sound, limbs folding beneath him.

Another muzzle flash.

The second shot hit before she could even register the first.

The man in front of her was already twisting, his body rigid as the bullet ripped through him, tearing through his ribcage – his chest imploding, a burst of red spraying out behind him.

He staggered backwards two steps, gun halfway to his hand, eyes still alive, still seeing, and then he was gone. His body crumpled.

She could feel the gunfire – the percussive force of each shot rattling her bones, tearing the air from her lungs, making her legs weak.

Her vision blurred.

Another muzzle flash.

A third shot.

A third man obliterated.

The bullet hit the side of his head and ripped half of it away, spurting blood, brain and skull fragments in a violent arc. His body followed the momentum, snapping sideways before he even knew he was dead. He hit the concrete hard, convulsed once, then stopped.

Farahani inhaled but made no sound.

This isn't real. This isn't real.

A final muzzle flash.

The fourth man was the only one fast enough to react. His hand shot to his holster, fingers closing around the grip, pulling the weapon free—

His chest exploded open, the exit wound tearing through his back in a fist-sized hole, blood splattering across the concrete behind him. He made a sound – something wet, something fragile – and stumbled forward before his knees buckled and he collapsed onto his face, the pistol clattering beside him.

Four shots.

Four dead.

Farahani's ears roared with a piercing, high-pitched whine, drowning out all other sound. It was all she could hear, all she could feel – her body had gone numb from the sheer horror of the moment. She stared, eyes wide, vision shaking with her pulse, trying to process what had just happened.

The assembly hall was still.

Håkansson hadn't moved.

He was watching her. Enjoying it.

Magnar Kaale hadn't moved either. The giant stood impassive, unbothered, indifferent, as if this were nothing more than a conversation that had gone exactly as planned.

Farahani stared at the bodies.

She had been around killers before. Had ordered men dead. Had given nods that had sent people to shallow graves. But she had never been this close. Never had the sound of someone's skull breaking apart rung in her ears, never had their blood flecked against her shoes.

This was why she had Darius Mehran in her world.

But Darius wasn't here.

She was alone.

And she was next.

'He's known as the Boatman,' Håkansson explained, looking up to the catwalks above.

Farahani, her ears ringing and the stench of viscera flooding her nostrils, could say nothing. She followed his gaze and saw a dark silhouette rising from a kneeling position, a rifle in his hands.

'I recruited his services to track down the assassin but it turns out that was a criminal waste of his talents.' He set his gaze on her once more. 'You were always the one who had the most to gain from Gustavus's death, Leila. And, after myself, you were always the most cunning. Malmgren never liked to get his hands dirty and Petrović did not have the imagination. Admit it, and I'll be merciful. I will have you killed – nothing can change that now – but it shall be quicker and less painful than you deserve. Because you failed to kill my son, Leila. That is the only reason I am not torturing you to death at this very moment.'

Farahani found her voice. 'I did not order any assassin to kill Gustavus. Why would I? I wanted no disruptions to our arrangement. They're not good for business.'

'*LIAR*,' he screamed, then, to Magnar Kaale, he ordered, 'Bring her to me.'

'Think about it,' she pleaded. 'None of us thought Gustavus was ready to take over – you included – which is why we wanted restructuring to keep things together. Why throw it all away?'

Kaale approached and took her by the arm in a grip from which she knew she could never escape. He led her over to where Håkansson waited.

'Admit it or I will watch you die.'

'Jorund, please—'

To Kaale, he said, 'Strangle her.'

Before she could protest, two huge hands wrapped around her throat and squeezed.

'But take your time,' Håkansson instructed Kaale.

EIGHTY-SEVEN

Scragg stood still, hands loose at his sides, surprised to be alive. He wasn't tied up. No one had even tried. He supposed that meant something, though he wasn't sure what. Maybe they thought he wouldn't run. Maybe they thought he wouldn't be stupid enough to try. Maybe they were right.

He'd watched the killing unfold without so much as a twitch. He'd learned, a long time ago, that sudden movements around men with guns tended to lead to unpleasant outcomes – the incident in the cold storage unit had been recent proof. So he'd just stood there, relaxed but not limp while Håkansson's pet assassin had cut down Farahani's men like they were paper targets at a shooting range.

Four shots, four bodies. Clean, efficient.

One of Håkansson's guys had a gun pointed at Scragg but so far he was unharmed.

Now the old man had moved on to other things. His new hobby: choking the life out of a woman. Magnar Kaale's massive hands were wrapped around Farahani's throat, squeezing with steady, unhurried pressure. Scragg had seen a lot of bad ways to go, but this was a particularly nasty one.

Scragg resisted the urge to shift his weight. The guard next to him wasn't watching him any more, not really, but the gun was still there, and Scragg didn't like guns that weren't in his own hands.

Håkansson was talking, saying something low and purposeful. Scragg didn't care what. The old man was enjoying himself, stretching it out, savouring the moment.

Scragg wondered if he was next.

It gnawed at him, the not-knowing.

If they'd shot him when they took him, that would have made sense. If they'd tied him to a chair and started peeling off his fingernails, that would have made sense.

But this? Standing here like a forgotten parcel, waiting for someone to remember he existed? That wasn't Scragg's style.

He swallowed, forced himself to breathe slow and steady. Where was Darius Mehran? Where was Roman?

That they hadn't appeared told Scragg that Roman had escaped and was gone by now. *Good for him*, Scragg thought. No point hanging around when you can slip away unnoticed. The thing Scragg would have done, in his place.

The ship, the tanker.

Get out, disappear, live to see another day.

Nothing Roman could do here. Not against these odds. Not against Håkansson's men, against Magnar Kaale, against—

A flicker of movement caught Scragg's eye.

He turned his head just enough to see. A figure, descending

a ladder from the scaffolding above. Moving like a shadow made real.

Not in a hurry. Not slow, either. Just deliberate.

Scragg knew what that meant.

The professional Roman had warned him about, the man Scragg was supposed to stay on guard for, in case he came a-knocking. The Boatman.

Scragg swallowed, licking dry lips.

Håkansson kept talking, kept enjoying himself, and Scragg kept standing there, waiting to find out whether he'd be next.

Farahani was making horrible sounds, choked gasps squeezed into smaller and smaller spaces. Magnar Kaale had his hands wrapped around her throat, applying the kind of pressure that didn't leave bruises because it didn't leave survivors.

Scragg turned his head, looking at anything else.

The engine hall stretched around them, vast and cavernous, filled with monstrous, lifeless machinery. The overhead lights were dim, flickering in places, casting long, shifting shadows across the oil-streaked concrete. The air was thick with the stale scent of fuel, rust and old sweat. Tools lay scattered across workbenches, some abandoned mid-use, left behind by men who hadn't known they wouldn't be coming back.

He saw a fire axe fixed to a nearby wall. Thought about making a dash for it.

Don't be a fecking idiot.

He clenched his jaw, looking back towards Farahani, then regretted it.

He couldn't watch this.

'Don't be a sadistic bastard,' Scragg muttered. His voice came out too loud in the heavy silence. 'If you're gonna kill her, just shoot her in the head. This is not just cruel, it's sick.'

Håkansson heard – glanced his way – but the response came from the nearby guard who drove his pistol into Scragg's guts.

Scragg folded over and dropped to his knees, one hand bracing against the cold floor, the other clutching his stomach as he sucked in a ragged breath.

Maybe his plea had reached Håkansson's black heart because the old man gestured for Kaale to ease his grip on Farahani's throat.

'Admit it,' Håkansson said, 'and I will put you out of your misery.'

She wheezed and spluttered, gasping and hyperventilating until she was able to speak again.

Desperate, defeated, she said, 'I swear ... I swear it wasn't me. But ... Gustavus – he was never going to be ready ... you know that ...'

Håkansson nodded, then to Kaale said, 'Continue.'

Farahani had no time to protest before Kaale's huge hands were strangling her once more.

Scragg, on his knees and wincing from the blow to his guts, could not watch. He turned his eyes away to see the Boatman was standing next to him.

Scragg hadn't heard him approach. Hadn't seen him move. But he was there now, looking down at him.

The man was tall but not towering, lean but not thin, built like a blade – something designed for precision, not brute force. A little like Roman, although at least Roman was still

436

human. This man's posture was eerily still, no wasted movement, no excess tension. Just waiting. Just watching.

Scragg raised his chin, meeting the man's gaze.

There was nothing there.

No anger. No satisfaction. No irritation. Just empty space where expressions were supposed to exist.

Then the Boatman's posture changed.

Just a flicker of life in an otherwise motionless form. He'd seen something. Or sensed it.

In a blur of hand movement too fast for Scragg to register, a strange-looking pistol was in the Boatman's grip, but even that speed was too slow to prevent the bullet finding the head of Magnar Kaale.

EIGHTY-EIGHT

Blood splashed down over Leila Farahani's face. At first, she did not understand. Kaale's powerful hands choking the life out of her had demanded all of her attention so she had not registered the gunshot that had killed Håkansson's huge bodyguard.

The strength of Kaale's grip evaporated and she sank to the floor, gasping, wheezing, sucking in precious air that she had never expected to feel in her lungs again.

Chaos was erupting around her, she knew, and yet she could do nothing to stop it.

Gunshots.

Yelling.

Multiple voices overlapping and fighting to be heard over the din of the firefight taking place.

Her vision was blurry, shapes indistinct around her. People. Machinery. Blending together beyond her tears and her oxygen-deprived brain.

The only thing she recognised for sure was Kaale's

towering form toppling over next to her, hitting the ground so hard the reverberations rattled all the way through her.

She knew she had to move, had to do something, and yet she was too weak, in too much pain, too overwhelmed to act.

Amid the sharp cracks of gunfire and the shouts and screams, she heard a name. Her name.

Someone calling for her.

'LEILA.'

Still dazed, her head swivelled towards the sound to see a shape, a form. Someone. She blinked tears from her eyes as her brain received the oxygen it needed at last and she saw a man. Tall. Dark suit. Dark hair slicked back, curling at his neck.

Darius Mehran.

Something was wrong with him, she saw. His skin looked paler. His eyes redder. Whatever it was that was wrong, it was not stopping him.

Her saviour.

EIGHTY-NINE

Victor had been midway through determining the perfect time to make his move when Mehran made the entire thought process pointless by killing the giant bodyguard. Victor could not have asked for a better distraction to cover his own attack.

He had been approaching the product tanker when the first of the four gunshots had reached his ears.

The first made him pause.

The second made him think.

The third made him turn.

He was already moving by the time the fourth rang out.

Whatever their partnership of convenience, he could not leave Scragg behind to his fate after all the Kashmiri Scottish Viking had done for him.

That Darius Mehran had regained consciousness so fast was a testament to the man's physical endurance and powers of recovery. Victor had been able to tell the Iranian was a skilful, dangerous enemy just by the way he acted but he had not known Mehran's physical capabilities. Victor was glad he had not had to find that out the hard way.

A good combatant too, he saw.

The instant the huge bodyguard fell and Farahani was safe, Mehran ducked back into cover before either Håkansson's men or the Boatman could respond. Aside from the one guarding Scragg, every other enemy's attention was now elsewhere.

Victor moved with purpose, shadow to shadow, calculating angles, timing and routes of attack. The interior of the engine hall was vast and brutal. The floor was stained with old oil and coolant, the concrete slick in places, cracked in others. Nearby, industrial lights hung from beams, their flicker casting deep shadows along the walls.

Off to Victor's left, one of Håkansson's men was by himself, his attention focused forward. He fired the occasional shot at Darius Mehran as he ducked behind an idle forklift on the far side of the hall.

Ignored by everyone was Leila Farahani, who climbed to her feet and staggered towards the exit.

Elsewhere, Scragg was on his hands and knees, winded but alive.

Four guards.

One near Scragg, alert, with his weapon up, and yet his attention was divided between his prisoner and the new threat that was Darius Mehran. The other two were close to Håkansson himself. They thought they were securing their boss from Mehran.

Instead, they were ensuring their own deaths.

*

The Boatman adjusted his stance, shoulders relaxed, weight balanced, the pistol steady in his grip. The first shot had already been fired. Not his. Darius Mehran had opened the engagement, killing Magnar Kaale, and now the rules of the fight were set. The sharp crack of gunfire had left an after-image in sound, a lingering pulse that echoed off steel and concrete.

The next shot from Mehran was an assessment. His weapon – a Glock 17 – barked its challenge, a single shot from cover, probing. Not aimed to kill. A test. A way to gauge distance, reaction time and return fire.

The Boatman had given him nothing.

No wasted movement, no return shot into empty space. He had pivoted behind the nearest cover, a heavy-duty steel support column, its base thick with accumulated grime. He listened. Tracked. Mehran was moving. Fast. The rhythm of his footsteps over the concrete was crisp, controlled. Two strides, a pivot, a brief pause – reading the room – then moving again. Predictable, but not enough.

The Boatman's mind worked through the equation. Stride length: approximately 0.8 metres. Rate of movement: 4.5 metres per second. The gap between machines – the distance Mehran had to cover – was 24 metres. He would emerge in 3.6 seconds.

The Boatman's aim moved first, hand snapping to where Mehran would appear. The second the calculation closed, he fired.

The shot hit nothing.

Mehran hadn't followed the pattern. He had feinted left, then cut hard back into cover, using an engine hoist to shield his movement. A smart adjustment. The Boatman filed it away. Mehran was fast, but more importantly, he was wily. He wasn't moving for the sake of movement – he was using every piece of cover to full effect.

Fine. The Boatman adjusted.

He moved deliberately, efficiently, never exposing more than necessary. No sudden shifts, no wasted speed. Speed killed precision. The faster a man moved, the harder it was to maintain tight control over aim.

The Boatman never rushed.

Victor stalked along the perimeter, sticking to the deep shadows beneath the elevated walkways. His approach was slow, measured. He wasn't ready to announce his presence. Not yet.

But time was not on his side. Darius Mehran, however proficient, would not be alive for long. Three gunmen were waiting for him to reappear. And, already, Victor had lost track of the Boatman, the man disappearing into the shadows as though they were but an extension of him.

The security guy guarding Scragg, however, was out in the open.

Victor could not make a move on him without one of the other three seeing him coming.

A length of chain dangled from an overhead crane. It reached the floor where it brushed the concrete with a quiet, hollow creak.

Victor stepped alongside it, fingers wrapping around the cold steel. The closest guard was now just in front of it, back half-turned, pistol up. His gaze was elsewhere – searching for Mehran at the far side of the hall.

Victor looped the chain around his wrist and dropped his

weight. He swung it low, fast, hitting the guard in the back of the knees, dropping him downwards.

Before the man could cry out, Victor yanked the chain tight around his throat and pulled. Hard.

The man kicked and writhed, gun falling out of his hands – hands that clawed at the metal, scraping skin, but it didn't matter. Victor looped the chain around the protruding arm of a hoist, tightening it so it pulled the guard up to his tiptoes, hanging him by his neck.

If this thing was over before the man suffocated – which was going to take a while given the imperfect noose and the relief from pressure the tiptoes provided – Victor would put him out of his misery, but he had more pressing matters to take care of first.

He collected the hanging man's dropped pistol from the floor, and a spare magazine from a pocket. SIG Sauer P320. Not his preference, but serviceable. None of Håkansson's other men were aware that their numbers had been reduced.

Scragg hadn't noticed either.

Gunshots elsewhere in the hall ensured no one was paying attention to the flailing guard with the chain around his neck.

Whether the Boatman was firing at Mehran, or the other way around – or both at the other – Victor could not tell.

It would solve two significant problems for him and make his life a whole lot easier if they shot and killed one another.

But, given the run of events that had led up to this moment, Victor felt like this would be a little too much to ask.

NINETY

Mehran was repositioning, using the density of the machinery inside the hall as his ally – hydraulic presses, stacks of disassembled engine parts, generators. He was keeping the engagement at range, knowing Håkansson's security would not leave their VIP and so the Boatman was his only enemy for now.

The Boatman tracked his progress. The line of machinery was eighteen metres long. Mehran was cutting across it at an angle, changing his speed in unpredictable increments.

Another bullet from Mehran's Glock came his way.

A probing shot, then another. Not aimed – the bullets snapped off nearby steel piping, deflecting low.

The Boatman did not return fire. No wasted ammunition.

Instead, he moved in.

Mehran was not revealing himself. Either determined to remain defensive or luring the Boatman closer.

Bait or not, he advanced, following the path of inevitability – not where Mehran was, but where he would be next.

He didn't sprint, didn't chase. He moved as a noose tightening, step by step, the pressure constant.

Mehran appeared for a split second – three shots in rapid succession.

Closer now, he was finding his range.

The Boatman's body was already turning, his mind running the numbers. Muzzle flash angle. Arm position. The moment the shot fired, he had already mapped the Glock's recoil path.

The Boatman fired in response this time – not at Mehran, but at the machine beside him. The round struck steel, shattering a glass gauge, sending a spray of shards into the air. Mehran ducked down, an instinctual dodge, moving fast but backwards this time – retreating now the Boatman had disrupted his plan.

The Boatman listened. Heard no footsteps.

Mehran was holding. Waiting out of sight behind a generator.

The Boatman fired twice. Not to kill. To force a reaction.

Mehran didn't shoot back.

The Boatman could picture Mehran now, crouched low, his finger still half-pressed against the trigger, a split-second of hesitation running through his brain.

His next choice would determine how this ended.

Keeping low, Victor ghosted behind the guy guarding Scragg. The man never heard Victor over the din of gunshots. In one smooth motion, Victor's arm looped around his throat and dragged him back into the shadows.

Scragg noticed and looked on, surprised and almost amused.

A swift twist and jerk – a sickening *crack* – and the guard crumpled, lifeless, to the oil-stained floor.

The two remaining guys were escorting Håkansson away from the nearby firefight. Either they had forgotten about Scragg or were under the assumption he was still being guarded.

'Are you okay?' Victor whispered to Scragg a moment later, gaze still tracking the corners of the hall for any sign of the Boatman.

Scragg coughed and nodded, wincing. 'Aye ... I'll live. Thanks to you, Princess.'

He managed a crooked grin despite the situation.

'Least I could do,' Victor said.

Scragg said, 'You shouldn't have come back for me, but I'm glad you did.'

'You would have done the same for me.'

'*Would I feck.* I'd have gone for the tanker and left you to your well-deserved fate, Princess, and don't you forget it.' Scragg reached out and gripped Victor's shoulder in a firm hand. 'I owe you one. Again.'

In his voice was a sincerity and gratefulness that was almost alien to Victor. People never thanked him. Not really.

'Go,' Victor told him. 'I'll cover your escape.'

'Don't be soft,' Scragg growled. 'We leave together or not at all.'

'I can't do this if I have one eye on making sure you don't take a bullet to the face,' Victor told him.

'I don't need a babysitter.'

'You're too old, you're too slow, and you're just not good enough. If you stay, you'll get us both killed.'

Scragg took it on the chin without taking offence. He even

smiled as he said, 'Which would kind of defeat the purpose of you rescuing me, would it not?'

'Something like that.'

'Fine,' Scragg said. 'It's been quite the ride, Princess.'

'I think it's about time we retired that nickname.'

The Kashmiri Scottish Viking grinned and held out his hand.

Victor shook it.

Darius Mehran only had so many choices. He could stay hidden, but not for ever, and wait for the Boatman to round the generator, or he could—

Attack.

Mehran exploded from cover.

Fast.

No pistol. No hesitation. A knife in his hand.

Maybe his Glock had jammed or he had lost it when he was forced to retreat from the exploding gauge, either way—

The Boatman moved, adjusting. His pistol snapping to target, but Mehran was already too close.

The first swipe of the knife came with impressive speed – almost at the Boatman's level – the edge slicing through empty space where his neck had been. He had already pivoted, already angling to counter, releasing his grip on his pistol to free up his hands now Mehran was too close to make use of it.

The Boatman's left hand snapped up, catching Mehran's knife wrist, fingers locking tight.

Mehran used the momentum. A body-check, hard and sharp. The Boatman absorbed it, turning with the impact, keeping his balance.

The next attack came sharp and sudden, a lunging thrust with the knife, the blade angling in for the ribs. The Boatman shifted a fraction, letting the steel pass within an inch of his body.

Mehran adjusted mid-strike, twisting his grip, redirecting the blade towards the Boatman's throat. The response was immediate. A deflection, a counter, the Boatman's hand snapping up to catch Mehran's wrist, angling it outwards just enough to kill the momentum. A sharp strike followed, knuckles hammering into the side of Mehran's jaw. The force sent him back a step.

Mehran rolled with it, using the movement to reset, to shift his stance, to come again.

Mehran feinted left. The Boatman didn't fall for it. He stayed patient, waiting for the tell. Mehran adjusted his weight, shifting to the opposite angle, and the Boatman did not stop him. He let him come.

The Boatman wanted him close.

Across the hall, a panicked shout rose above the noise – one of the remaining guards had spotted one of his comrades hanging from a chain by his neck.

The barrel of an assault rifle swung towards Victor's position, spitting bullets.

Victor fired blind and dived behind a workbench as rounds punched through rusted metal and old toolkits. Sparks flew and a stray chain overhead rattled wildly. The guard advanced, urging Håkansson to run.

Victor popped up from cover for a split second and shot four times.

His first shot shattered a hanging work lamp, plunging

that corner into sputtering semi-darkness – the second punched into the guard's shoulder, spinning him around with a cry before a third and fourth shot found his face.

Only one of Håkansson's security remained now, and he was across the hall near the main doors – a burly blond man fumbling to reload a shotgun. Beyond him, through the gaping doorway, Victor glimpsed movement in the glare of the floodlights – Jorund Håkansson hustling towards his armoured limousine idling outside.

Victor's shots forced the blond man into cover.

Finished reloading, he fired in Victor's direction as Victor fired in return, buckshot peppering a steel pillar next to him. Using the cover of a massive engine block, Victor flanked to the right, shoes splashing through puddles of leaked oil.

When he emerged from cover again – shooting as he moved to catch the blond man unawares – the man was gone, having followed his boss from the hall.

Outside, an engine roared to life. The Mercedes limousine revved, its headlights cutting twin beams through the early morning mist.

Mehran dropped lower, quick and aggressive, the knife slicing towards the soft tissue beneath the ribs. The Boatman waited until the last possible split-second before angling his body away so the blade missed by millimetres, providing him with the opening to snap a lock around Mehran's wrist.

A brutal twist.

The blade clattered to the floor.

The Boatman didn't hesitate. He took the motion of the wrist lock and redirected it, pulling Mehran off balance, using the man's own weight against him. His free hand came up fast, hammering into Mehran's sternum.

Air shot from his lungs.

Mehran staggered, struggling to breathe.

The Boatman released him to pick up the fallen knife, and—

In one smooth, continuous motion—

Sank the blade into Mehran's chest, slipping it between ribs to impale the heart.

Turning, the Boatman caught movement in his peripheral vision – the killer darting behind a huge engine block.

For an instant, their eyes met.

Retrieving his dropped pistol, the Boatman readied himself to ferry one final soul across the river.

NINETY-ONE

Victor pressed his back against a massive engine block, pistol in hand and eyes scanning the gloom. The engine assembly hall was a maze of metal: hulking turbine housings, engines, generators and massive piston assemblies gleamed in the dim light. Overhead, a grid of metal catwalks and maintenance staircases criss-crossed the space. The air throbbed with the deafening hum of machinery – active generators that set the floor trembling underfoot. Flickering fluorescent tubes cast sporadic flashes across oil-slick concrete, creating stuttering shadows that danced with each tremor. In the cacophony and half-light, every shape was uncertain, every reflection a threat.

He checked his pistol, tightening his grip around the textured handle.

He crouched low and moved off to the right. The shadows thickened near a line of pipes with chipped and scratched paintwork. He paused by a console dotted with levers and dials.

A quiet metallic clatter echoed to Victor's left – impossible to pinpoint in the din of the machinery, but distinct enough to catch his attention.

He pivoted towards the sound, leading with his pistol.

A shape darted in the periphery of his vision behind a tangle of pipes.

Victor responded with two controlled squeezes of the trigger. The shots cracked, audible over the engine roar, the muzzle flashes lit up nearby machinery into stark relief, shadows jumping, the 9mm rounds striking the faraway pipes with a burst of sparks. A ricochet whined off into the darkness.

The movement had been too abrupt, too obvious – bait.

And Victor had fallen for it.

He saw it now – a length of chain dangling from an overhang of turbine housing. It creaked as it swayed.

Not just bait, a decoy.

He darted away before the Boatman could counter now he knew Victor's position.

From his right, a muzzle flash blossomed – brief, blinding.

The Boatman's pistol barked twice in rapid succession, the reports absorbed into the engine hall's din but the supersonic cracks unmistakable.

Bullets slammed into the engine block behind the console Victor had been using as cover, punching deep dents into the housing. One round deflected with an ear-splitting *ping*, slashing a line of sparks over Victor's ducked head.

He felt a hot spray of pulverised rust pepper the back of his neck from the impact.

Close. Too close.

No point trying to shoot back – the Boatman would have already melted back into the darkness.

Keeping low, Victor crept to a different location. He pressed into the shadow of a tall turbine casing. So far, the Boatman had measured him well. Anticipated cover, forced him to shift positions, baited him into giving himself away.

No sign of a miscalculation yet.

Victor tossed a small nut he found on the floor. It rattled against the concrete and skidded beneath a tangle of pipes in the distance.

He waited, prepared to catch any muzzle flash.

Nothing.

Not even a shift in the gloom.

The Boatman refused to react. He wasn't going to fall for the same trick he had used on Victor.

Whose next cover was a steel worktable, ten steps away.

He pressed close to the turbine casing and sprinted low. The moment he moved, two shots cracked from somewhere unseen, angled to catch him in mid-run. He dived behind the table as one round struck the corner of the turbine casing, spraying shrapnel that bit his cheek. Another bullet tore into the concrete near his foot.

He exhaled. This time, the Boatman had guessed the exact route. Victor felt warm blood on his cheekbone. A superficial cut. He ignored it, refusing to be distracted by anything except death.

The Boatman was forcing him to second-guess every step.

Victor rose partway and returned fire in the direction of those muzzle flashes. Two bullets, a short gap between each. The steel of an engine assembly screamed as the rounds glanced off an impenetrable panel.

He steadied his breath, considering his next move.

He eyed the safety of the bulky engine the size of a truck.

Ten or twelve metres away. Another set of steps angled around the console to the engine's left side. If he dashed for it, the Boatman might predict his route. If he tried a feint, the Boatman might punish that too.

Victor allowed himself three slow breaths.

He went for it.

His feet pounded across slick concrete. The engine's outline loomed.

Bullets sliced the space around him.

One struck an overhead chain with a sharp clang, sending it swaying. Another punched through a metal cabinet.

He fired blind as he slid behind the protective shield of the engine block, chest rising and falling as he pressed himself to the dense steel. The hall echoed with the Boatman's footsteps shifting to maintain a line of sight.

Victor ejected the spent magazine and loaded in his last one.

Seventeen rounds.

Already, it felt like far too few.

NINETY-TWO

Victor closed his eyes for a beat, breathing to control the surge of stress hormones his body was so eager to feed him. The next exchange would be decisive, he could tell. The Boatman's pattern was always half a beat off from standard logic, which meant every sequence of moves had to be reversed in Victor's mind. The usual rules of geometry and misdirection no longer guaranteed an edge against an enemy who had not only mastered those same rules but knew how to break them.

He holstered the pistol in his waistband for a moment and gripped a loose chain spool lying at the engine's base. He flung it hard towards an open corridor of space. It clattered and banged, the clamour echoing around the hall.

Victor used the noise to change position and heard the shots as the Boatman sent two bullets at the chain.

He would not have mistaken the noise for Victor moving so the shots at the chain were for another reason. The Boatman wanted Victor to use the gunshots to pinpoint his location.

Why?

Because he was intending to be somewhere else.

A single bullet struck the engine block, the impact a high-pitched whine of metal.

Victor rolled to his left, ignoring a sudden flare of pain in his ribs. He drew the pistol once more, keeping low and catching his breath.

He had to think two steps ahead.

Nothing the Boatman did existed in isolation.

Victor froze, eyes tracking a reflection in a steel panel. A silhouette glided behind a row of ductwork, avoiding any direct approach. He recognised a methodical infiltration, spaced footfalls, something he might have done himself to corner a target pinned down.

He eased around the engine block, steps quiet, throwing a second length of chain to clatter and distract the Boatman's sense of distance so Victor could move again.

His enemy must have heard him anyway, because sparks crackled off steel, and a shard nicked Victor's sleeve. He pressed harder against the engine's side.

He needed a new plan. The usual logic would see him create a flanking angle, but the Boatman anticipated that. Victor darted straight forwards instead, hugging the engine's outline. A bullet hissed past, close enough that the pressure wave brushed his ear. He saw the Boatman's silhouette in a gap between two smaller engine blocks.

They fired almost at once.

Victor's bullet struck a control panel with a harsh clang. The Boatman's shot smashed the ground at Victor's feet, concrete dust rising in a cloud.

They both dived behind cover, knowing to stay in one place for a single second too long was to die in the next.

The hall's flickering lights cast shifting shadows over snaking pipes and the shattered panel.

He listened for any further sign – breathing, a footstep, a shell casing knocked aside.

Nothing but dripping water and a buzz from ancient wiring amid the ambient din of heavy machinery. The Boatman had gone still, waiting for Victor to make the next mistake.

He kept the pistol raised, fourteen rounds now remaining in the magazine, muzzle tracking the edges of the gloom.

Victor crouched behind the engine, eyes scanning each scrap of cover in the gloom of overhead lights. The Boatman was still out there, hidden behind engines or ductwork, waiting for the next move.

A pipe creaked.

Water dripped into a puddle.

Victor rose partway, keeping his profile small. The engine's metal guard creaked at his slight movement. His gaze found an old control station near the far wall, thinking it might offer him an angle to flank. Three metres of open floor led to it, another two metres around a cluster of stacked crates. If he could get there without the Boatman placing a bullet in his back, he would have a vantage into the corridor of machinery where he figured his foe waited.

Victor took a breath, then sprang forward.

He took two quick steps. A single shot cracked the air.

Sparks flew from the engine, the round angled for a target crossing that open gap. Victor slid back into cover, chest heaving once. The Boatman had not moved. No footsteps, no scuff of shoes. Just a shot placed to clamp Victor down.

He glanced around for any alternative. On his right was a narrow aisle between generators leading deeper into the hall. The rest of that aisle vanished into darkness. He suspected the Boatman would string it with bullets if Victor tried to slip through. Still, it was a route that broke the line of sight.

He moved fast, keeping low. Step by step, he navigated behind a row of steel drums. His side ached each time he ducked now, the constant movement a strain despite the previous week of healing. He reminded himself it was only pain, not the wound reopening and hampering the muscle enough to slow him.

Halfway along the row of drums, he paused.

Metal scraped across concrete. The sound was distant, near the south-western corner of the hall. It could be the Boatman circling wide, or it might be another false lead. Victor listened, breath shallow. He heard nothing else.

He moved again.

Another step, then a flicker in his peripheral vision. A muzzle flash tore the darkness from the top of a generator behind him. A bullet ricocheted off the drum, the clang so loud it left a tinnitus whine behind inside his ear.

Victor dropped, pressing flat to the floor. Oil smeared across his sleeves. The next round hit the drum's rim, a dull punching thud.

He lay prone, scanning for the Boatman through a gap between the drums. The generator sat high, nearly three metres tall, with catwalk scaffolding beside it. The Boatman's vantage was elevated, maybe perched on some piping that intersected the catwalk. Victor eased himself backwards, little by little, until he reached the massive engine again.

No further shots came.

He drifted behind the engine, scanning upwards.

Another tangle of pipes angled above the catwalk, leading to an overhead crane. If the Boatman was on that generator, he would have a partial view of the engine's immediate vicinity, but probably not the far side. Victor decided that was his best route forward: slip around the engine and keep out of line of sight behind a wide stack of crates near the hall's centre.

He glimpsed a flicker of motion on the generator. The Boatman's silhouette, blending into the metal. The man was preparing to shift positions.

Victor raised his pistol and squeezed off rounds at the figure. Sparks pinged off steel. The silhouette vanished behind the piping, leaving no sign of a hit. Victor dropped again. If the Boatman returned fire from some unexpected angle, he needed to be out of sight.

Seconds crawled by. No shots.

Victor hesitated, balancing caution against the knowledge that waiting too long would only let the Boatman seize momentum.

High above, a metal catwalk rattled – just audible through the ambient rumble of machinery. Victor risked a glance up. Any movement up there was hard to track amid the strobing lights and gyrating shadows cast by overhead pipes. If the Boatman was relocating, even if he was directly overhead, the sound of his footfalls was masked by the constant vibration and the periodic hiss of steam from pressure release valves. Victor knew better than to chase a phantom upwards without a plan. Instead, he stayed low and crept along the row of engines, keeping his profile tight against them.

He glimpsed movement and dived behind a hoist station

just in time as another gunshot cracked out, hitting the concrete floor near Victor's foot and sending chips of aggregate skittering away.

The angle was steep – the Boatman was shooting from high above, maybe from the catwalk running parallel to Victor's position. A second shot followed almost from the same location – the Boatman hadn't shifted yet.

The bullet sparked off a metal railing close by, showering Victor with a burst of orange sparks that flickered out as they fell to the ground.

Quick and controlled, Victor leaned out from behind the hoist station, eyes tracking the catwalk where he'd seen the movement, and opened fire.

His bullet pinged off a catwalk rail – above a silhouetted figure prone beneath it – and he ducked back down behind the hoist station as the Boatman's third shot barked amid the rafters, blending into an echo that seemed to come from everywhere at once.

Thirteen rounds left in the SIG.

Victor felt a bead of sweat trace down his temple. The Boatman was predicting his predictions, countering his counters. It was all Victor could do to remain a step ahead – or at least not fall a step behind. He allowed himself no frustration, only focus.

He had to change the equation. Staying pinned down would only encourage the Boatman to encircle him from his superior vantage point.

During the brief lull that followed the third shot, Victor decided to move.

He spotted a maintenance ladder bolted to the side of a support column about ten metres ahead, leading up to the network of catwalks that criss-crossed the hall over which the Boatman now loomed.

If Victor could climb up and flank the Boatman from an unexpected angle, he might seize the initiative.

If the Boatman caught him mid-climb, he was dead.

Victor, never one to defend when he could instead attack, went for the ladder.

NINETY-THREE

He fired blind in the direction of where he had seen the Boatman prone on the catwalks. No chance of hitting, he knew, because his enemy would have already moved, but a stray round might land close enough to force him down again or into cover. Victor just needed a moment's distraction so he could—

Shoot out the lights near the maintenance ladder.

Then, crouching low, Victor darted from behind cover, feet light on the oily concrete. He kept his silhouette low, moving between the hulking bulk of two adjacent engines. Their rhythmic chugging masked what little noise he made. In near synchrony with his dash, another bank of lights overhead flickered and went dark – whether from some automated process or a stray bullet's damage, he didn't know, but it was a good sign.

The darkness – always an ally of his – deepened in this area of the hall.

Reaching the ladder, Victor glanced upwards for signs of the Boatman and saw nothing in the gloom above.

The ladder was a big risk and yet so was staying on the ground floor with a deadly enemy above him.

Pistol in one hand, he ascended, slow and controlled, trying to limit the inevitable noise and trusting the darkness and ambient rumble of machinery would hide him.

The metal rungs felt slick with condensation and grease; he wrapped his hand tight to avoid slipping. Halfway up, a tiny clink above was all the warning he received.

A shot rang out and sparks exploded centimetres from Victor's hand as a round struck the ladder. The impact shuddered through the frame and he pressed himself against the ladder's side to reduce his profile.

Another shot pinged off the rung just below his feet.

The Boatman could not have seen or heard him so he must have anticipated the change in tactics.

Each muzzle flash lit the grated floor of the catwalk with harsh light, framing the Boatman's dark outline.

Victor froze in place, hugging the ladder. In this position, returning fire was a gamble he could not take – his one-handed aim upward would be unsteady, and the Boatman would see his muzzle flash and adjust his own aim. An easy shot at a static target.

Instead, Victor forced himself to wait, pressing stillness into his muscles despite the instinct to act. The next muzzle flash came, the bullet way too high and then higher again with the following one, the Boatman making a rare bad call and assuming Victor was ascending.

When the firing stopped, he made his move, knowing the Boatman was reloading.

The top of the ladder led onto the narrow catwalk platform. Victor rolled onto it, feeling the steel grating flex under his weight. Without pause, he positioned himself behind the nearest support strut, making himself small. He scanned for the Boatman in the darkness. The catwalk extended in two directions: to his left, it ran above the central aisle of the engine hall; to his right, it intersected a series of pipes and a suspended crane. Nearby, another flicker of failing fluorescents played tricks with the shadows.

Without the benefit of muzzle flashes to guide Victor, the Boatman was invisible to him.

Should he risk a shot at where the Boatman had been?

He decided against it.

A decision he regretted when he rose into a crouch and the grate beneath his feet flexed and creaked in response.

He was up and sprinting as the Boatman's pistol barked in response, incoming rounds whistling past him, sparking off the railings and ricocheting from steel beams.

He threw himself down behind the protection of the dense rail that ran the perimeter of the room, and across it at several points, so a crane could run to lift up engines and huge components.

A hint of movement flashed at the edge of Victor's vision on the right. He turned, gun ready, but held fire. Just a sway of cables hanging from the ceiling. Nothing. Or perhaps something – another attempt to bait him.

The catwalk vibrated beneath him.

The Boatman moving, steps aligned with the timing of the heavy engine pistons firing below, masking his footfalls.

Victor tried, and failed, to determine distance and direction through the vibrations alone. The Boatman could be anywhere on the catwalks, hidden by the gloom and the many pipes, barriers, pillars, crane rails and rafters.

Then, nothing.

The vibrations ceased. The Boatman was in his new position. Like Victor, waiting.

Peering beneath the rail, he saw a dark shoe in the darkness.

Hopping up, Victor opened fire and—

Almost hit the Boatman before he disappeared behind the crane itself, maybe ten metres away over the centre of the hall.

The catwalk that led to it extended in two directions only.

At last, Victor had the Boatman trapped.

Action always beat reaction, so the Boatman fired first when he popped out of cover from the crane's cabin side.

Accurate for a snapshot but Victor had the protection of the rail. The bullet pinged off the solid steel in front of his chest.

His return shot gouged a streak in the crane's shell centimetres from where the Boatman had appeared.

A pause.

Victor shifted stance, tried to anticipate the Boatman's inevitable next shot and squeezed the trigger the moment he expected the Boatman to appear.

Too soon.

Another gouge in the crane.

Victor ducked and the Boatman's bullet sliced through the air where Victor's head had been a split-second beforehand.

Two shots, both from the end of the crane where the cabin was located.

Now, Victor understood.

The Boatman was building a narrative, as Victor had done many times with other enemies who could not think more

than one move ahead. He adjusted his position, rising out of
the cover of the rail and aiming his pistol at the far end of the
crane, knowing the Boatman would break the pattern for his
third shot, expecting Victor to have fallen for the narrative
the Boatman had been building.

With eight bullets left, Victor applied five pounds of pressure on the six-pound trigger.

One shot.

One hit.

And it would be over.

The Boatman reappeared from the cabin side.

The first bullet clipped Victor on the right shoulder, causing him to stumble backwards.

The second bullet smacked into a pipe a foot from Victor's
head, rupturing it.

Superheated steam screamed out in a scalding jet.

Victor backed away as the burst of white steam filled the
catwalk area with a roiling cloud. The pipe's contents, under
immense pressure, created a ferocious hiss that rivalled the
engines' roar.

Bullets cut through the steam, the Boatman firing blind
and yet considered. He wasn't wasting rounds, each one
aimed at where Victor might have headed in response to the
blast from the damaged pipe.

He felt the catwalk vibrate beneath his feet as the Boatman
moved away from the crane, no doubt crossing from the
middle of the hall to the periphery to reduce the distance and
get closer to Victor.

He could wait in response and try to ambush.

Instead, using the steam as cover, he dropped low and
slipped off the catwalk and down a set of steps to where a

maintenance platform led both down towards the floor and to a second catwalk system that ran the periphery of the hall and yet did not cross it like the one above.

Metal stairs clanged under his soles as he descended two steps at a time, trying to put distance and variety of terrain between him and the Boatman's last known position. He winced as his left forearm throbbed from where the scalding steam had caught it. The burn was superficial but searing, The graze to his right shoulder painless in comparison.

Above, the high-pitched shriek of the ruptured steam pipe continued, filling that quadrant of the hall with a dense fog. It was a double-edged sword; the Boatman had obscured Victor's sight, but he too would be blind if he remained near the billowing steam that was not relenting. More and more of the upper section of the hall was blanketed by it.

Not enough to smother the entirety of the catwalks, but it gave Victor an idea.

As well as the pipes circumventing the hall to ferry steam away from the colossal engines, fuel lines did the same to keep those same machines in motion. They were thick pipes with bright yellow warning labels.

From the maintenance platform, he was above them.

Victor angled his gun and opened fire, shooting down on those pipes to open a tiny hole along the upwards facing curvature.

An intense jet of misty fluid blasted outward, atomised by the pressure that sent an aerosol cloud of fuel swelling high into the air beneath the catwalks where the Boatman had been heading.

Victor fired again – the billowing steam above him shielding him from view – this time aiming for the steel pillars that supported the catwalks.

The pillars were bullet proof, so dense that Victor's rounds ricocheted away with pings and twangs until—

One sparked.

NINETY-FOUR

In the same instant, a ferocious flash of light and fire roared to life – the spark from Victor's bullet igniting the atomised fuel and blossoming into a massive fireball.

A rolling wave of flames whooshed upward, engulfing the catwalks above in a sudden blast of yellow-orange light that illuminated the entire hall in hellish brightness – every engine, every machine, pipe and gear stark against the glare.

The heat was immediate and intense, washing over Victor, stealing away his breath.

The fireball dispersed throughout the upper section of the hall, a billowing cloud of flames and smoke.

The fuel line continued to feed the inferno with the pressurised expulsion of more and more flammable liquid becoming jets of roaring flames.

They licked along the catwalk.

Dense black smoke formed a choking cloud.

The heat forced Victor away and the powerful glare of

the blaze blinded him so that, at first, he did not understand what he was seeing when a dark shape fell from the catwalk through swirling smoke and steam.

Then he knew.

The Boatman, saving himself from the fire, dropping down to where tall generators broke the distance to the floor.

This was Victor's chance.

He leaped from the maintenance platform, landing in a controlled roll, coming up into a dash.

A mistake, because—

Agony exploded in his side from the wound he had ignored.

His vision darkened. He stumbled, whole body shaking, unable to maintain his pace, balance wavering as he fought to stay vertical. He thrust out a hand to a pillar as he passed by, pushing himself back upright.

He shoved away the pain.

He could not let anything stop him.

The Boatman was vulnerable – maybe burned by the fire, maybe blinded by the smoke; perhaps disabled by the fall – but that vulnerability was temporary.

Now or never.

Victor hurried to where he had seen the figure drop, gaze sweeping back and forth for signs of organic shapes among all the hard edges of machinery, and finding those edges soft and blurring into one another in his faltering vision.

No, no ...

He fought through the disorientation, refusing to let his injury cheat him of this singular opportunity.

Close to the ruptured fuel line, Victor could feel the heat

inside his lungs, his throat burning with every breath. His skin prickled. Sweat poured from every pore, soaking his hair, slickening his face.

He didn't care.

He would gladly set himself ablaze to end this duel.

Heated steel nearby creaked and groaned, expanding beyond its design, stressing welds, testing joints.

Where? *Where?*

On the far side of a tangle of pipes – a crouching shape with tendrils of smoke rising from it.

Victor opened fire.

Too fast, too eager. His vision still unclear. His hand shaking.

Bullets slashed through the air.

His first pinged off a pipe.

The second buried into concrete.

Victor, almost out of ammunition, kept shooting regardless, willing the pain and disorientation to cease robbing him of the kill because when the Boatman reached full height and raised his own weapon to shoot back, it was over.

The Boatman, unhit, stood tall, black smoke caping around him.

Click.

The magazine was spent.

Heat haze rippling the air between them, the Boatman's gaze turned Victor's way.

The Boatman's face was streaked by soot, the whites of his eyes stark in contrast and still unreadable, still nothing in them.

Victor would never give up, never accept defeat, and yet there was nothing he could do now to prevent his own death. A single shot to the head was inevitable because the Boatman would not miss.

As Victor recognised the futility of his situation, he realised his pain had lessened, and with it his vision sharpened again and his hand was steady once more.

Patience, the most fundamental of the many skills he had mastered, had failed him.

All he had needed to do was to wait, because—

There was no gun in the Boatman's hand.

Lost in the sudden fireball Victor had fashioned or in the Boatman's leap to save himself from the resulting inferno, it was irrelevant.

Victor, so eager – so *desperate* – to finish the foe before him, had not noticed until this moment that the Boatman was unarmed.

In turn, he was not rash enough to fail to recognise the slide was back on Victor's pistol, that he was out of bullets.

Without hesitation, the Boatman reached to his belt and drew forth a slim, curved knife.

As he edged closer, the nearby flames danced along the blade.

NINETY-FIVE

'You're by far the best I've ever faced,' the Boatman said in his dry monotone. 'And yet this was only ever going to end one way. But know that it will … affect me … to kill you.'

Genuine sentiment, Victor knew.

Nothing had mattered to the Boatman before, and yet this did. He could not feel grief or loss or envy or anything else … except respect.

Victor had earned that.

He had given the Boatman his first taste of sincere emotion.

For an instant, Victor remembered a brief nod – a subtle bow – long ago on a riverbank in Tanzania, a mere inclination of the head – a note of respect from a deadly enemy who had come so close to killing Victor it had only been that man's singular indulgence in hubris that had been his undoing.

The best plastic surgeons in the world had failed to cleanse Victor of the scars he had gained that day.

The Boatman was beyond such hubris.

He would not make the same kind of mistake and provide Victor with an opportunity he had not earned.

However, there was a telling difference here there had not been back then: the fire.

Up close, Victor could see the burnt clothing, the scorch marks. Blackened, peeling skin.

The Boatman's eyes, unreadable still.

And yet ... a flicker of eyelids, a tautness in his jaw.

The Boatman was in pain.

From the fall, from the fire, from both.

A new sensation for him, Victor saw.

A peerless professional, the Boatman was unprepared for such a development.

He had no experience on which to draw.

Victor, in comparison, had been in constant pain for days, and he had taught himself long ago that pain was just a message that could be put to one side, that could be ignored.

The Boatman did not understand this because he had never needed to before. Pain had only been a theory until this moment – not a lesson for him to learn from, and therefore one impossible to master.

Still, it was not going to stop him.

He said, 'Please, let me grant you a quick death.'

In answer, Victor spun the empty pistol around in his hand and closed his fist around the barrel housing, the grip extending out in front of his knuckles as a short but solid club.

Not much against a blade and yet anything was better than nothing. No short lengths of pipes or chain within reach to use in the pistol's place otherwise Victor would have already scooped one up.

Smoke and steam swirled between them as Victor and the Boatman circled each other. The broken fuel line nearby continued to spew fire across the wall, heat rippling the air. Overhead, a ruptured valve howled, spitting out clouds of scalding steam that mingled with the smoke. The atmosphere was a stifling, distorted haze – blurred shapes and flickering light.

The Boatman struck first.

He darted forward – almost too fast to be believed – and slashed in a sweeping arc.

Victor jerked back a half-step. The knife missed his ribs by a centimetre.

Before the Boatman could retract, Victor countered with a swing of the pistol now they were close.

Metal whistled through empty air; the Boatman had already slid aside.

Victor adjusted his footing, careful not to stumble on the trembling metal floor. He jabbed forward with the pistol to force distance. The Boatman faded just out of reach, controlling the space with minimal steps.

He was patient, testing.

Victor feinted high then swung low, trying to catch the Boatman's lead knee. He skipped back with almost no effort.

His timing was perfect – he moved a fraction before Victor committed to each attack, always one step ahead and—

Victor felt the sting of impact on his attacking arm.

A minor cut only and yet telling. He had not even seen the counter, let alone begun defending against it.

Victor needed an equaliser.

He needed more reach.

He glanced around, searching through the smoky gloom

for anything usable. A heavy wrench lay on the floor seven paces to his right. Too far. He'd never reach it before the Boatman pounced.

A length of iron pipe rested against the wall near the sheet of flame. Reaching for it would mean stepping into an inferno – suicide.

A red-handled fire axe hung in a bracket on the bulkhead behind the Boatman.

Victor's pulse beat faster at the sight of it. The perfect weapon to outrange the Boatman's knife, but he read Victor's glance and edged sideways, positioning himself between Victor and the axe.

The Boatman then came in low, knife probing.

Victor knocked the thrust aside with the pistol's muzzle and countered with a downward smash aimed at the Boatman's collarbone. The Boatman twisted and the improvised club whooshed past him and clanged as it struck a steel pipe behind, ringing out.

In the same breath the Boatman slashed at Victor's extended arm.

He yanked back and the blade sliced only the empty air where the underside of Victor's wrist had been a split second before.

A near miss. Arteries spared.

They clashed again in a flurry of strikes and parries.

A burst of steam roared from a valve rupturing nearby, and the Boatman moved in response. He sidestepped into the edge of the billowing cloud, disappearing as the fog of vapour swallowed his outline.

Victor's eyes narrowed.

He kept the pistol raised and pivoted in a slow circle, every sense straining through the noise and dim light. The fire's glow flickered off shifting curtains of smoke.

Heat pressed on Victor's right side from the burning fuel line; the steam mixed with smoke to create a dense smog that smothered all.

Victor eased back one step, then another, careful not to lose balance or expose his back. He squinted, searching for any sign – movement, a shadow, a noise out of place.

A whisper of motion stirred the smoke to Victor's flank.

Instinct saved him.

He spun, bringing up the pistol just as the Boatman burst from the haze.

A flash of steel swept towards Victor's throat.

He yanked the pistol to intercept the knife, hitting himself in the neck to save his carotid from the blade's edge.

The Boatman's weapon skittered off the pistol's frame and Victor felt a sudden hot sting in his shoulder.

Now they were close, he threw a headbutt that missed by a fraction; an elbow that missed by more.

Then the Boatman was gone, disappearing back into the smog.

Victor coughed, his throat raw from the pistol's bludgeoning; irritated from the poisonous air he breathed in.

Blood dampened his jacket where the knife had sliced across his left anterior deltoid.

He turned on the spot, knowing another attack was imminent, and saw the bracketed fire axe nearby.

Victor went for it, trusting to speed—

Realising the opportunity was too good to be true too late—

A moment before the knife sliced the back of his right

leg across the hamstrings, the Boatman crouched low and hidden in the smog – knowing Victor would go for the axe – herding him into another trap.

His leg buckled, the ruptured muscle losing strength, and with that loss, Victor's stability went.

His momentum stalled and he dropped to one knee, pivoting around with the gun raised to ward against any follow-ups.

The Boatman rose a short distance away, flames flickering through the smog behind him.

Another valve burst. More steam blasted into the air.

Victor waited, assessing the cut to his leg. Painful and yet not deep. The initial shock had seized the muscle and made him fall, but he could fight through the pain to stand back up.

Instead, he stayed on one knee as the Boatman approached.

Smoke burned in Victor's lungs; sweat dripped into his eyes.

Appear weak, he urged himself.

Be beaten.

Over and over again, he tensed and relaxed the muscles of his right arm in rapid succession to make it tremble – to make it seem like he was too weak to keep the pistol raised.

The Boatman drew nearer.

In no rush, patient.

Inevitable.

To finish Victor, he had to be close. Close enough for Victor to grab him. He outweighed the man by around ten kilos. Maybe enough difference in strength to overcome the Boatman's skills.

Victor let his head hang a fraction and his eyelids droop as if he were fighting to stay conscious.

The Boatman stopped just out of arm's reach, seeing through the deception as Victor overplayed his hand.

This enemy was not going to give a larger foe the opportunity to grapple him by getting too close.

Only that was not Victor's plan.

He hurled the gun.

With so little distance for it to travel, even the Boatman's unparalleled reflexes were insufficient.

All he could do was jerk his head backwards out of the projectile's path – in doing so throwing himself off balance and taking his gaze from Victor who—

Sprang to his feet, ignoring the many sources of pain to power forward and barrel right into the Boatman.

Victor could not outmanoeuvre this opponent; he could not out-time him or beat the man's speed.

But, bigger, stronger, he could out-brawl him.

Before the Boatman could recover his balance, Victor's accelerating mass collided with him, followed by elbows and knees, punches and headbutts.

A frenzied, relentless series of blows that overwhelmed the Boatman's defences – too many to dodge, too savage to ignore.

Victor seized the moment.

He grabbed the Boatman's hand and twisted as he wrenched – no skill, no technique – pure strength, pure fury.

The knife clattered from the Boatman's grip onto the concrete.

Victor ceased his assault to snatch it up, the Boatman reacting with his extraordinary reflexes to sweep Victor's legs out from under him in that brief respite.

Content with the exchange, Victor rolled backwards over his head to come to his feet with the blade soaked with his own blood now grasped in hand and ready to redress that balance.

The Boatman, wasting not even a single second – already dashing past Victor as he was rolling – tore the fire axe from its wall mounting.

When he turned to face Victor, blood glistened at one corner of the Boatman's mouth. Around his left eye, the tissues had swollen and were beginning to darken. His cheekbones and jaw were marked.

Not only in pain, but now weakened.

Slowed.

At last, Victor thought as he stepped closer, *it's a fair fight*.

NINETY-SIX

For a long moment, both men were still. Each looked at the other. Assessing. Evaluating as flames raged nearby and steam bellowed.

Victor saw the Boatman analysing him as he analysed him in return. Neither professional was going to rush now. No one would act in haste when they both knew a single mistake would be fatal.

There was no trepidation or uncertainty in the Boatman's eyes, but he was aware. He knew the danger that Victor posed, especially now the Boatman was in pain and weakened – new experiences for which he needed to compensate. That adaptation was itself another new experience. The Boatman had never before had to change the way he operated.

He raised the axe, holding it high in both hands, the head close to his face. A defensive posture, ready to counter because the axe was designed for function, not combat. It was a top-heavy, impractical weapon.

Devastating if it connected – designed to break through doors, skin and bone meant nothing in comparison – only it had to hit first.

The knife in Victor's hand was a fine weapon. A curved, sharp blade perfect for slicing. Light, fast, it could attack from any angle. Unlike the heavy axe, the path of the knife could be adjusted with a mere flick of the wrist. And yet that blade was small. The reach disadvantage was huge.

Victor had to be close, had to get beyond the axe's head, to draw blood.

With his speed, he knew he could slip past the long, slow weapon. Given the Boatman needed both hands to wield the axe, he would be defenceless with Victor inside his reach.

Then, a slash to the throat to sever a carotid, or inside of the thigh for the femoral artery. Maybe enough time for both.

However, if Victor struck first, he would then be too close to avoid the Boatman's own counterattack, whether he withdrew or his enemy backtracked to create optimal distance. The edge geometry of a fire axe meant it was no good at cutting skin, but the force alone would be deadly even delivered by the Boatman's reduced strength. No wound Victor could cause with the knife could shut down the Boatman's central nervous system fast enough to stop the axe then landing.

Victor thought through angles and variables, and came to only one conclusion.

He had to bait the Boatman into attacking first.

If the Boatman swung the axe, Victor would dodge out of its sluggish arc and exploit the fact the Boatman – weakened, slowed – was vulnerable with all that inertia, to close the range and stab and slash vital areas with the knife.

Again, those attacks would sever arteries, ensuring the kill.

Again, it would not be an instantaneous death.

The Boatman would live on. Maybe for minutes. Maybe mere seconds.

In either case, more than enough time to land that deadly counter with the axe.

Attacking first or baiting the Boatman into attacking first ended the same way.

Victor stared at the Boatman, wondering what he was thinking in return.

The Boatman, expressionless as always, revealed nothing.

No reflection of himself, and yet Victor realised now he had spent his entire adult life trying to become something close to what stood facing him.

From the moment he had first taken a life – that first confirmed kill – he had understood emotion was a weakness. The past was a weight. Memories, attachments, the echoes of another him – all distractions. He had worked for years, ruthlessly training to suppress his emotions. He had drilled himself to erase regret, to bury every flicker of sentiment before it could form into something tangible. It had been a gradual process, a stripping away of everything unnecessary, every impulse that might cloud his judgement or slow his reaction time.

He had mastered it as he had any other skill – one as vital as marksmanship, hand-to-hand combat or the ability to read a room before anyone inside even knew he was there. He had been taught early in his professional career that his past, his memories, were only liabilities, things that would detract from the odds of him surviving.

Victor had squashed down his humanity, pushed it into something so small and insignificant that it could be hidden away in his mind, locked behind a door that could never be breached. And then, when he was certain it was contained, he had discarded the key.

For a time, he had believed that he had reached the end of it – that final point where emotion no longer existed, where instinct replaced thought, where decisions were made without the interference of anything human.

But despite his best efforts, that lock sometimes loosened.

And yet as he readied himself to kill and be killed, Victor saw the difference between himself and the Boatman, who had never had to train himself.

The absence of emotion was not learned. It was natural.

The Boatman was not dead inside, because he had never been alive in the first place.

And now, knife versus axe, Victor realised something he hadn't expected. Something else he shouldn't have been capable of feeling.

He was envious.

That after all these years, after all the training, all the discipline, he still hadn't perfected the one skill that should have come above all others.

A skill that was as effortless to the Boatman as drawing breath.

It was not just a level of control. It was a level of removal.

Not a man.

Not a killer.

Just a function waiting to be executed.

Victor had spent years training to be something the Boatman had always been. And that realisation came with another: he had failed to achieve the perfection he had always sought.

A feeling the Boatman could never know.

To the Boatman, an action, an inaction, a result – they were all inevitable. The inarguable sum of an equation.

And because of that, the Boatman could never fail.

However, patient, waiting, he had come to the exact same conclusion as Victor.

Attacking first meant death.

Attacking second meant death.

A being of pure function, the Boatman understood the inevitability of this particular sum and so he changed the equation.

He lowered the fire axe.

He said no words.

His blank expression did not change.

The Boatman, fought to a stalemate for the very first time, backed away – the smog enveloping him until only the whites of his eyes remained in the gloom – and then he was gone.

NINETY-SEVEN

The coastline was quiet at this hour – a black expanse of sea to their right, cliffs rising on the left. In the soft glow of the limousine's interior, Jorund Håkansson studied his son's profile.

Gustavus looked exhausted – ripped from his bed and bundled into the limousine before he understood what was happening. Håkansson did not explain events at the port. Gustavus did not need to know of such horrors.

His father told him, 'It's only for a little while. Just until things have quietened down. Once I've passed, you'll return to Malmö alone. But you'll need to make some changes. Scale things down ... keep a lower profile than we are used to.' He managed a thin smile. 'It'll be tough at first but you'll find your feet. I know you will.'

They would disappear far away while Wallin handled the clean-up. The business would downsize naturally now he had no business partners.

He reached over and squeezed Gustavus's shoulder. 'You

won't get everything I've created, I'm afraid. But you'll have enough money to start new ventures, legitimate ones maybe. It'll be up to you, what you want to do with your life. With the time I have left, I'll teach you everything I can about—'

A white flash erased the world in front of them.

Håkansson's words never left his mouth as the SUV ahead – carrying his remaining security personnel – vanished in a fireball.

The blast rocked the limousine, shoving the heavy vehicle backwards half a metre and sending it skidding through the long pale vapour trail left by the rocket-propelled grenade.

Through the windscreen, Håkansson glimpsed a rolling cloud of flame and debris where the road ahead had been. The lead vehicle was gone, reduced to a rain of shrapnel and fire.

Debris pattered against the limo's exterior; one fist-sized chunk of metal smacked the bulletproof glass next to Gustavus, leaving a star-shaped crack. He flinched away with a startled curse, his exhaustion replaced by adrenalised shock.

'*Get down*,' the driver shouted, slamming the accelerator to the floor.

The limousine surged forward, Håkansson's body pressing into the seat as the tyres fought for traction.

A new thunderous noise filled the night: machine-gun fire.

Orange tracers streaked from the dark cliffs, carving into the limo's flank.

High-calibre, armour-piercing rounds hammered the armoured glass with a relentless patter of deadly hailstones.

Blossoming cracks exploded across the windows on the driver's side, each impact blooming opaque across the multi-layered polycarbonate. The front windscreen starred under the first hail of bullets but held.

They kept coming in an unyielding stream, chewing into the limo's exterior.

Håkansson heard the ping of rounds deflecting off steel plating, the thunk of others burying into the body panels. The vehicle swerved; the driver was jerking the wheel, trying to present a harder target even as he pushed for escape.

A second stream of machine-gun fire joined the first, both concentrated on the windscreen. The layered glass, already speared white, could not endure for ever. Dozens of bullets impacted in the same, small area until the glass succumbed.

A fist-sized hole erupted in front of the driver as multiple rounds punched through. The driver's voice turned into a wet gurgle as 7.62mm rounds tore through his skull, spraying the inside of the windscreen with blood.

His corpse lurched against the wheel.

Deprived of control, the limousine veered.

Håkansson felt a jolt as the front tyres left the asphalt.

The Mercedes ploughed off the road, momentum launching the five-ton vehicle over a strip of gravel shoulder. There was a sudden, stomach-lurching drop.

Håkansson's vision went black for an instant as he was thrown against his restraints.

The crunch of metal was deafening; his head snapped forward and back until the limo shuddered to a stop with a final metallic groan.

The world was tilted at an angle. Cold night air poured in through the ruptured windscreen. He tasted blood in his mouth and realised he'd bitten his tongue. He blinked, trying to clear the haze from his vision.

Silence, except for the ticking of the engine and the rumble of the sea. They had come to rest partway down an embankment, nose-first. The limo hadn't rolled, thanks to its low centre of gravity, but the front end was crumpled from the collision with the rocky ground. Håkansson's chest and shoulder throbbed where the seatbelt had wrenched tight.

His son was slumped against the opposite door, held in place by his seatbelt. Blood ran from a cut on Gustavus's forehead, trickling over his right eyebrow, but his eyes were open, wide with shock.

They needed to move – get out, escape – but he was slow with shock and disorientation, his mind still reeling from the ambush.

Who? How?

The attackers must have been lying in wait along the cliffs that led to his estate.

He heard the crump of secondary explosions – the remnants of the lead SUV burning itself out on the road above.

Through the smoke, figures approached. Four or five – it was hard to be sure. Tactical gear bristling with weapons and ammunition. Body armour. Masks. Night-vision goggles.

Håkansson heard a high-pitched hiss and sputter. He gasped, understanding the sound – a blowtorch.

Sparks sprayed through the gap between the door and frame on the right side, bright orange flecks spitting into the dark interior.

Håkansson fumbled under his jacket, drawing out the compact pistol he carried. His ears still rang, but he could make out the muffled thud of boots on earth and the terse, indecipherable shouts of men coordinating.

He did not understand what they were saying because they were speaking German.

The blowtorch's hiss stopped.

For a heartbeat, only the crackle of flames from the ruined SUV above filled the night. Then the limousine's rear door was wrenched open with a squeal of tortured metal. Cold air flooded in. Håkansson squinted against the sudden glare of a tactical flashlight as a dark-clad figure loomed in the doorway. He made out the silhouette of a rifle barrel trained on him, and behind it the outline of a man in full combat gear – helmet, night-vision goggles flipped up, face streaked black.

'Out. Now,' a hard German voice commanded from the darkness beyond the door.

The man with the rifle stepped aside, making room. Håkansson hesitated.

He could feel Gustavus trembling against him. He squeezed his pistol, concealed against his thigh – a futile comfort. He raised his free hand and pushed Gustavus upright.

Together, father and son scooted towards the open door. Håkansson kept his movements slow and deliberate, cradling the pistol out of sight as long as he could. If there was even a sliver of a chance ...

Strong hands yanked Gustavus out first. He cried out in surprise as he was dragged into the open. Håkansson's grip on his pistol tightened. He slid across the seat, trying to follow, but a rifle barrel jabbed into his chest, stopping him cold.

'Drop it,' another voice said.

The torch angled down, catching the glint of Håkansson's

pistol. They knew. Of course they knew. Håkansson's shoulders sagged and he let the gun slip from his fingers onto the floor mat. In the same instant, rough hands seized the front of his coat and hauled him out of the wreck.

One of the Germans kicked his legs out from under him, forcing him to his knees. Another frisked him with brutal efficiency, patting for any additional weapons. Finding nothing, the figure stepped back. Håkansson lifted his head, breathing hard, and saw Erik Stahler.

Stahler stood a few paces away on the uneven ground, silhouetted by the glow of the burning vehicle above. He wasn't wearing a helmet – Håkansson recognised that close-cropped blond hair, the angular face now drawn tight with grim purpose. In Stahler's grip was a handgun with a suppressor attached. The German was rigid with strength and icy intent.

Behind Stahler, two more of the former KSK operators held Gustavus. They had forced the young man to his knees as well. Gustavus's clothes were smeared with dust and blood, his face ashen.

Gustavus caught his father's gaze across the few metres between them, and in his eyes Håkansson saw the plea and the terror: *Do something.*

Stahler's voice was calm. 'Lukas's head was full of .45 calibre ammunition and yet the assassin shot out the gallery's window with 9mm bullets. We retrieved them from the brickwork of the building opposite that window.' He paused, then asked, 'Why? Why did you kill our colleague ... our *friend*?'

Håkansson's composure cracked. Lying here would serve no goal, he knew.

'I – I had no choice,' he stammered, voice hoarse. 'Lukas ... he failed. He let the assassin escape. I had to protect my boy—'

A sharp gesture from Stahler silenced him.

The suppressed pistol swung away from Håkansson's face.

And pointed instead at Gustavus.

Håkansson reached out a hand towards his son, as if he could somehow stretch across the distance and pull Gustavus out of harm's way. But there was nowhere to go. Gustavus squeezed his eyes shut, a single tear carving through the grime on his cheek.

'Then in trying to protect him,' Stahler said, 'you've killed him.'

The pistol clacked and a splash of crimson erupted from the side of Gustavus's head as the bullet struck just above his ear.

An animal howl clawed up from Håkansson's lungs and tore out of his throat – raw, broken, bereft.

Blood was pooling beneath Gustavus's shattered skull, dark and shiny in the faint light.

Stahler allowed Håkansson a few seconds to grapple with the reality, to drown in it. Håkansson's breath came in ragged gulps. A keening sound, low and guttural, kept spilling from him.

All his power, all his wealth – none of it meant a thing now. He blinked, trying to focus through the tears, and mouthed his son's name once more, soundlessly. Gustavus. The boy he had raised and protected, the boy who was supposed to outlive him, carry on the legacy – gone.

'For Lukas,' Stahler told him.

Håkansson didn't hear the shot.

He didn't feel the impact.

But he glimpsed the stars above before his eyes closed for the final time.

ONE WEEK LATER

NINETY-EIGHT

Scragg pulled at the collar of his new suit, the stiff fabric pressing against his throat in a way that made him want to claw it to pieces. He had never liked wearing them, never had much need to, but he was stepping into a larger world and he needed to look like he belonged. He adjusted the cuffs, rolling his shoulders, trying to make the expensive material sit right. It didn't. No amount of tailoring could hide the fact that he felt like a man wearing someone else's skin.

The pale winter sun cut across fresh-fallen snow outside, while inside the bubble-like dome, bright overhead lights illuminated two tennis courts. Heating units rumbled in the corners, maintaining an artificial warmth that kept the chill at bay.

'Let's do this,' he said to his companion.

Together, they approached.

Scragg kept a firm hold on the black case in his left hand, its weight a constant reminder of the stakes. He was used to feeling out of place, but the grounds of the huge dacha just outside Moscow made him feel not only out of place, but small, insignificant. A short corridor led to the largest enclosed court, where Vladimir Kasakov was coaching his young son under the watchful eye of a tall, poised woman, elf-like and beautiful – Kasakov's wife, Izolda. The boy, Illarion, perhaps seven years old, flicked the ball high but swung too early, sending the serve into the net.

Kasakov adjusted the boy's posture, guiding him with a patient hand. Towering in a sleek track jacket, his greying hair clipped short, he didn't match Scragg's mental image of what the world's most prolific and successful trafficker in arms should look like. Scragg's gaze lingered on that family tableau: father teaching, mother offering a gentle nod whenever the boy's stance improved. He felt an odd pang of envy, then banished it. He was here for business.

He corrected himself: *they* were here for business.

The boy attempted another serve, which clipped the line and spun out of bounds. Kasakov still offered a calm correction, placing a large hand on the boy's shoulder. At last, the father straightened, turning to acknowledge Scragg standing there, suited and yet ill-suited to the environment.

His companion, however, was perfectly at home.

She was poised and yet the air around her carried an unmistakable energy. She had always been a presence, even when standing silent. The way she held herself, the way her dark eyes moved without revealing too much, the way she dressed with precision rather than indulgence. The deep green of her blouse was expensive but understated, the fit of her coat sharp against the frame of her shoulders. Her hair, jet black and not a strand out of place, framed high cheekbones and a mouth set in something just shy of indifference.

She was no longer flanked by bodyguards, no longer held the quiet command of an empire at her fingertips.

Yet, Leila Farahani stood with the same air of control as if none of it had ever been taken from her.

With a word to his wife – some affectionate aside that made her smile – Kasakov left the court. He unzipped his track jacket and offered a cordial handshake, the fabric rustling. Scragg accepted it, trying not to adjust his collar again. Kasakov then kissed the back of Farahani's hand.

'Thank you,' the Ukrainian began, 'for coming all this way to see me.'

Wanted for illegal arms sales in dozens of countries, Kasakov never travelled outside of Russia's protective embrace. Given recent hostilities, Scragg could not help but wonder where Kasakov's loyalties truly lay and where the osmium would ultimately end up.

'Our pleasure,' Farahani said. 'And we can only apologise for the previous interruptions that delayed this deal.'

'Few things in this business happen without setbacks. All that matters is the osmium has ended up in the right place and our future interactions are more punctual.'

'They will be,' Scragg assured, offering up the case.

Kasakov looked at it and smiled. 'One of my men will take it from you in due course.'

Farahani rolled her eyes and Scragg tried to hide his embarrassment.

The boy on the court called for his father, tennis ball in hand, wanting guidance on his swing. Kasakov raised one hand in a patient gesture.

'Give me a moment, my son.' Then he looked back at Scragg and Farahani. 'You'll stay a while? There might be other ways in which we can work together, rare-earth metals aside. Feel free to have lunch, drinks. Just tell the staff you're with me.'

'Sounds wonderful,' Farahani said.

Kasakov turned, striding across the court with casual confidence, returning to Illarion, whose little face lit up as his father neared.

'This is going well,' Scragg voiced.

'For now,' Farahani cautioned. 'But you're playing a different game. The rewards are greater but the stakes are much higher.'

'Then it's a good thing I'm not doing it alone, isn't it?'

Farahani said nothing.

'Come on, Leila,' Scragg said. 'I know I'm not your dream partner but there's literally no one else left alive in Malmö who fits the bill.'

'You don't need to remind me.'

Scragg nudged her with a light elbow. 'Besides, considering how you were happy to throw me at the mercy of Håkansson's blood lust, I'd say we've made pretty big strides forward, you and I.'

A hint of a smile on her lips.

'See? I know you love me really. Let's go get smashed at Kasakov's expense, eh?'

'We have more business to discuss after he's finished with his family,' she reminded him. 'So it's two drinks each only, I'm afraid.'

'*Feck that*,' Scragg said as he headed towards the bar. 'You stay sober so you can sweet talk ole Vlad if you like. Meanwhile, I'll drink your two as well as mine.'

NINETY-NINE

Fog rolled low across the docks, swallowing the harsh glow of the halogen lights and muffling the groan of monstrous cranes. The sea was calm, black and flat, lapping against the stone breakwaters. Cargo containers loomed in neat rows, silent and numbered, each one a locked vault of commerce, contraband, or both.

Police Director Elise Wallin stood beneath the canopy of a decommissioned gantry crane, its rusting arms stretching overhead in an impotent reach. She wore no coat despite the chill. Her uniform was immaculate, her hands clasped behind her back. She faced the small crowd before her.

Six of them in total.

Some with entourages further back. Others on their own.

The engine assembly hall on the far side of the dry dock had been cleared out over the intervening week. What couldn't be scrubbed had been buried – bodies, reports, footage, careers. The port had continued to operate, but the Håkansson empire that had moved through it had fractured, its founders either dead or, as with Leila Farahani, stripped of power.

She had been forced to relinquish her dominion over the port in exchange for immunity and a surgical fix to her problems.

Now came the aftermath.

'This is not a negotiation,' Wallin told those standing before her. 'It's a bidding process.'

In the distance, a ship horn blared.

'The business is broken into distinct parts,' she continued. 'Imports. Exports. Green tech. E-waste. Logistical infrastructure. Deliveries. Sourcing. Each of you has been given access to the ledgers, shipment schedules and shell companies. By now you know which part you are interested in.'

A woman with sharp cheekbones and leather gloves raised her chin. 'And if we want more than one piece?'

Carina Hede was Swedish, and more dangerous than she looked. She wore an ankle-length navy wool coat that flared at the bottom like a tailored weapon. Her platinum blonde hair was slicked into a tight bun, her pale eyes the colour of steel left out in winter. Used to run private security for a petroleum logistics firm until two tankers went missing under her watch – then reappeared weeks later, repurposed for other ventures in West Africa. She hadn't been fired. She'd been promoted. Now she trafficked in permits, shipping manifests and ironclad silence. Her operation was thin on muscle but thick with influence.

'Then outbid the others.' Wallin was stone-faced. 'But keep your ambitions realistic. I'll be assigning based on more than just krona. Reliability. Efficiency. Discretion.'

'I still don't know what happened to Håkansson and his partners.'

'You don't need to know.'

Wallin had planned it with care.

She'd hired the killer herself – under a layer of intermediaries and false leads, through channels built to insulate her from fallout. No matter what Håkansson did to him had the ambush worked, the killer could never identify her. She hadn't needed Gustavus dead. Just targeted. Just enough to light a fuse.

Because she knew Jorund Håkansson. Knew how he thought. How paranoid he'd grown in the shadow of his own mortality. He would turn on the people closest to him – Farahani, Malmgren, Petrović. That was the design. Sow chaos from within. After the killer had escaped, Wallin had even paid him the second half of his fee to further direct blame their way should he then be captured.

She expected them to react. To retaliate. To align against Håkansson and ensure his son would not inherit the throne. With neither the old man or his son around to run that side of the business, Wallin would be able to step into the void, offering an impartial solution to the three partners who would otherwise then turn on one another.

What she didn't expect – what no one could have predicted – was that the old bastard would act with so much speed and decisiveness. That he'd burn the whole thing down rather than lose control of it. That he'd bring in an outsider whose lethal efficiency had been impossible to estimate.

Wallin had tried to stop Håkansson, of course. Tried to convince him to spare Farahani, at least. The port was too valuable to risk. But Wallin could only do so much without putting herself under scrutiny. Farahani had managed to survive, and had brokered a deal: giving up her hold on the port, and Wallin, in turn, cleaned the blood from the walls and ensured Farahani was spared from the fallout.

Wallin, who had never been in a position to run the entire operation alone, improvised.

She would sell it to the next generation of Malmö's underworld who could rebuild it, restructure, innovate and she would then continue as she had before. Albeit with a much larger cut this time around.

'You're handing over the keys to one of the most profitable criminal networks in Scandinavia,' a man said. 'You must want something besides the purchase price.'

Kasper Vestergaard lit a cigarette with one hand, the other shoved into the pocket of a military-style parka too clean to have seen service. He was Danish, but not old-school Copenhagen cartel – new money from the Øresund corridor, where smugglers in trainers now moved more value than gunmen in boots. Tall and narrow-shouldered, with a sharp, fox-like face and a silver incisor that caught the dock lights when he smiled, Vestergaard had started with pills on ferry routes and moved up fast. He now ran micro-ports along the Danish coast, but Malmö was the jewel he'd never managed to crack. In recent times, his crew had taken to robbing other mid-level criminals. His favourite tactic was to ambush them while they were trading with one another, when all their paranoia was focused on those they were dealing with and not external threats.

'I want stability,' she told him. 'Quiet operations. No more bloodbaths. No egos. Just a return to predictable patterns. That's good for everyone.'

There was a long pause.

'And what about him?'

The question came from Jobril El-Masri. He leaned on a cane – not because he needed to, but because he liked the performance of it. A second-generation Moroccan-Swede with gold-framed glasses and the voice of a talk-show host. Late thirties, dressed in a cashmere trench coat that was a perfect fit over his navy pinstripe suit, he looked like the owner of a successful consultancy firm – and he was. The consultancy just happened to advise on how to obscure supply chains, manufacture phony ESG credentials and sanitise crypto flows through shell companies in the Emirates. Jobril's hands were soft, but his methods were anything but. He'd never run a crew, never pulled a gun, and never needed to so far. Every warehouse that burned and every witness who vanished had been paid for twice over in plausible deniability. He wasn't a gangster. He was what came after gangsters evolved.

'What would you like to know?' Wallin asked in return.

El-Masri said, 'Is he bidding too, or just here to haunt the place?'

The man in question stood alone, maybe ten metres off, half-shadowed beneath the overhang of a cargo container. A black coat, collar turned up. Hands loose at his sides. Still. Unmoving. Watching everything. The fog clouded around him and yet somehow he seemed untouched, as though it dared not gather too close.

'He's here to ensure you all play nice,' Wallin said, 'with me now, naturally, but especially you all with one another going forward.'

Vestergaard blew out smoke. 'One guy? That's the total of your enforcement?'

Wallin nodded. 'Exactly.'

Another pause.

Wallin watched their expressions change one by one. Amusement gave way to puzzlement. Puzzlement turned to unease. Even the boldest of them – the ones who'd come armed, who'd brought backup parked in idling black SUVs beyond the fence – found themselves shifting on their feet, glancing sideways and now unsure of themselves.

'So, who is he?' Hede asked.

'You may call him the Boatman.'

El-Masri clutched his cane in both hands. 'Why do we call him that?'

Wallin's gaze turned to the figure in the fog as she said, 'Pray you never need to find out.'

ONE HUNDRED

Victor leaned against a sunlit railing on the Nordhavn *Skadi*, an MR product tanker over one hundred and eighty metres in length and with a width of thirty-two metres. With a capacity of fifty thousand deadweight tons, the *Skadi* was transporting ultra-low sulphur diesel from the refineries in Sweden to the Port of Philadelphia. With seven days already spent on open water, it would take another week to cross the Atlantic. After the chaos of Malmö, Victor found himself appreciating the quiet monotony of life on the open seas.

The sky overhead was clear, an unblemished wash of blue that merged with the ocean's lighter hue near the horizon. A faint smell of engine exhaust mingled with the salty wind. Solar glare off the deck made the metal plating warm underfoot despite the chill air.

He was seated on a folding stool, adjusting the position so the sun rested on his left side, leaving his right in partial shade of the canopy of tarpaulin that shielded a metal table and the collection of mismatched chairs around it. Sunbeams streamed through the open sides, and the breeze fluttered the edges of the canopy.

Four men were with him at the table: Chief Mate Havel, all wiry angles and sly grins; Second Engineer Boura, with grease under his nails and a ready laugh; Abel, an oiler who favoured a grimy baseball cap; and Salazar, one of the ordinary seamen who kept a short, neat beard and seldom spoke. A battered deck of cards lay on the table between them.

Texas hold 'em was the only version of poker they played despite Victor mentioning he preferred five-card stud. The pot was a scattering of small coins – pennies, a few nickels, a sprinkling of leftover foreign currency.

The cards snapped against each other as Havel dealt out the hole cards. Each man picked them up with casual interest as Victor checked his two cards. They were a mismatch that promised nothing. He maintained a neutral expression, gaze flicking to the others. Boura nodded to himself, perhaps seeing something in his own hand. Abel rubbed his nose once, gaze flicking from Havel to the pot. Salazar offered a slow blink, calm as ever.

After a round of checks, Havel dealt out the first round of community cards: the flop.

Victor had nothing. Still, he slid two pennies to the centre. In the past days, he had accumulated a little over three dollars in winnings. Salazar trailed with a dollar. The others were in the red but no one cared if they ended the journey having lost ten whole dollars in coins.

Abel raised, throwing in two pennies. Boura glanced at his hole cards, stroked them once, and did the same. Salazar pushed in coins. Havel, expression bright, followed.

Victor studied them. Abel used his cap's brim as a shield, but he tapped his foot under the table when he held a strong set of cards. This time, the foot was still. Boura often drummed his fingertips if he intended to bluff. Now, his hand stayed motionless on a half-empty soda can, suggesting he might hold something decent. Salazar remained impassive, but his eyes narrowed a fraction whenever he was uncertain. Havel's grin telegraphed little.

The turn card arrived, courtesy of Havel's steady dealing. Victor's hand did not improve, but he had no intention of folding. He watched for fleeting expressions. Boura swallowed once, set down the soda can. Abel scowled, then tried to mask it by exhaling. Salazar's left eyebrow twitched.

Victor checked, letting them make the first move. Abel placed two more pennies, less certain this time. Boura, though, raised a penny on top, hand unwavering. Salazar tossed his cards in, deciding not to continue. That left Havel, who matched, still smiling.

Smiling too much.

Victor slid his coin forward, ignoring the worthless cards he held. He had read enough signals.

The pot was a modest cluster – insignificant outside this game, but in the moment, it carried weight for each of them. They played to pass the time, but passing the time with a win was better than with a loss.

Havel flipped the river card onto the table. Victor's set remained abysmal, just a high card – a queen – that would lose outright if anyone else had paired up, which was all but guaranteed with three players still in. He displayed no tension. Instead, he pushed his coins forward, going all in.

Abel shook his head and folded without a second thought. Boura took a moment of hesitation to do the same.

Only Havel left. No longer smiling.

He stared hard at Victor, who met his gaze.

Neither man blinked.

Then Havel sighed and threw down his cards.

Victor used both hands to drag the pot closer to him.

The breeze ruffled the edges of the canopy. The sky remained bright, the horizon a deep line between blue water and paler sky.

They cleared the cards from the table, reshuffling for another round if time permitted. Boura wanted a chance to reclaim a few pennies. Abel tapped the brim of his cap, adjusting his seat. Havel tossed out a half-smile, rummaging in a tin for more coins.

The *Skadi* forged ahead, each passing hour bringing them closer to Philadelphia.

Victor leaned back, enjoying the sunlight on his face as he touched the fresh pink scar over his ribs. Healing well, there was little pain even under pressure. The flesh wounds the Boatman had given him hurt more.

As the cards were dealt, Havel told him, 'Your luck has gotta run out at some point.'

Victor almost replied that he didn't believe in luck, but after recent events in Malmö, maybe he needed to accept Leila Farahani's words that bad luck believed in him.

'There's no such thing as luck,' his mentor had told him back then.

Not opinion. Fact.

He acted unbothered as he arranged the piles of pennies into neat little stacks. He didn't smile because that was one of the first things she had taught him. He still had to fight to keep his enjoyment hidden all these years later.

With danger a week away in any direction, for once he allowed himself to remember. Not out of a desire to block pain so he could try and fail to remove a bullet from his flesh with tweezers, but because he wanted to think of those early days when he thought he knew so much and she had taught him so many classes about his ignorance.

He could imagine her disappointment if she knew he was reminiscing, because another lesson had been:

'Memory is distraction. Distractions will get you killed.'

Regardless, he thought about all those games of poker. All those lessons in how to hide what he thought while he read the minds of others on their faces. In their actions and inactions.

'If you become no one,' she told him while laying out playing cards on the stone floor that day. 'You will feel as no one.'

As she had instructed, he had chosen a name for himself back then so he could become whomever he needed to be and maintain his sanity in the process.

She had been right.

She had always been right.

He smiled as he laid down the four jacks.

As per her wishes, Victor had not told her the name he had decided upon, but in this moment he understood that young version of him – so raw and unrefined – could never have hidden it from her. Even so, he should have selected one that took her more than a minute to work out.

'You can't change it now but I already know the name you picked for yourself and why you chose it,' she

511

said, noting his triumphant grin as he dragged the huge pile of poker chips closer. 'You like to win a little too much.'

ACKNOWLEDGEMENTS

For this novel I worked alongside a new editor for the first time in over a decade. Change can be scary, but I'm relieved to say that Jack Butler proved to be a pleasure to collaborate with from the start. His comments and suggestions, advice and support were all invaluable. This novel is far better for his input. Likewise, my agent James Wills has continued to be a stalwart champion of Victor on every level. A huge thank you to both these fine gentlemen.

Further thanks are due to the tremendously talented people who have worked on this book in different capacities, including Nithya Rae, John Appleton and Edward Wall. Thank you to every friend, fellow author and family member who gave me their time and their patience. My heartfelt appreciation goes out to the many readers who have contacted me via email or through social media. Their kind messages and enthusiasm always make the process of writing a book go a little smoother.

Finally, thank you to Bodo Pfündl, who has been a reader,

contributor and friend for some years now. As with many of Victor's exploits, Bodo has assisted immensely with this novel at every stage. This work is rightly dedicated to him.